To my husband Sean

With love

Thank you for your support through the rough and the smooth, for the cups of coffee that always arrive at the right time, and for listening to my convoluted plots that are sharpened by your words of advice, caution and wisdom.

PROLOGUE

His wife collects mirrors. So many shapes and sizes on the walls: oval, round, square, star-shaped, bevelled, one studded with red stones and a tiny mirror sunk in crystal. The cold glitter of glass traps him when he enters her bedroom. Candles have guttered and gone cold. The uneven stalactites hanging from the holders suggest that they burned late into the night and the faint smell of wax still lingers in the air.

Voices chant softly from the CD player on her bedside locker. An obscure Russian recording of male choral singers she picked up on one of her trips abroad. The tenor's voice soars, as if lifted high on the stanchions of bass and baritone. He has always disliked the recording, too dirge-like, yet, in a chilling jolt of awareness, he understands why Sara listens to it with an almost trance-like rapture. These voices, unaccompanied by music, have the power to elevate the listener, each chant one step closer to heaven. He shivers, knowing that this harmonious chorus is playing on repeat but she can no longer hear their sacred song. The mosaic of mirrors glints as he drags his gaze away from his reflection and he is conscious of a shift in the air, as if something terrifying but as yet undefined is rushing towards him.

He approaches the bed where she rests. She appears to be sleeping, yet her stillness tells him everything he needs to know. Her slender fingers are bruised to a purple hue. Her skin is alabaster, frozen.

Sara… Sara. Does he call out her name? Or breathe it as a soft accusation? He has no memory of doing either as he lifts her in his arms and shudders into her hair.

She did not leave a note. No explanation. As in life, the death of Sara Wallace will remain a private business.

PART ONE

CHAPTER ONE
Anaskeagh – the early years

Her father was a magical musician. Mr Music Man.

'Dance, Beth, dance!' he shouted. 'Dance, my pretty girl.' He played for Beth, tapping his big black boots on the kitchen floor. It was dark outside and Beth wanted to keep dancing on her toes… on and on and on… until the sun came up again and chased the monster away.

The monster lived upstairs in the wardrobe with the moth-ball smell and the old clothes Mammy didn't wear any more, hiding small and mean until the light went out and Beth was left alone. He hid behind the red dress with the velvet buttons and made noise when he touched it, soft as trees whispering in her room. She knew he would carry her away in his arms as soon as she fell asleep.

'Your mother was the talk of the town when she wore that dress to the Emerald Ballroom.' Her father winked when he told her the story of the red dress. His words made pictures in Beth's mind. The spotlight spinning rainbow colours across the ballroom and the feet of the dancers crashing thunder as they spun up and down, in and out, round and round to his music. Her mother was a bright flame and the dancers whirled her away from the stage where Mr Music Man stood tall and handsome, playing magical tunes only for her.

'All the boys whistled at her, Beth. But I was the only one she heard.' He moved his fingers up and down the keyboard and the accordion sang sweet and high. 'I danced my pretty lady the whole way home and changed her name to Tyrell.'

'A pity I bothered listening.' Beth's mother tossed her hair and frowned. 'Will you stop filling the child's head with nonsense, Barry Tyrell? It's way past her bedtime.' She took out her knitting and clicked the needles. She wrapped pale pink wool around her fingers. Beside the fire Sara lay in her Moses basket, tiny under the pink blanket. She had little fingers and a bump where her belly button should be. Her mother powdered it and shouted if Beth touched the soft place on top of her head.

'Bold, *bold* girl! I told you to leave the baby alone. You'll hurt her.'

Beth's father put his accordion in the cubbyhole under the stairs and she felt herself growing smaller, curled up tight inside, when he lifted her onto his shoulders and carried her up the stairs. He blew kisses with his fingers and turned out the light. The darkness sighed around her.

In the Emerald Ballroom the dancers were waiting for Mr Music Man. The van with 'Anaskeagh Ceili Band' written on the side and shamrocks for dots above each 'I' stopped outside the house and off he went. Her mother climbed the stairs, making shushing noises when Sara cried. Their bedroom door closed and Beth could no longer hear the love noises. She wanted to be with them, snuggled warm and cosy under the eiderdown with only the clock ticking in the dark and the baby smells.

On the road outside she heard a van. Maybe her father was coming home to chase the monster away. He would chop the wardrobe into matchsticks. She waited for the squeaky sound he made when he whistled but the van went by the house… away… away… and the light went chasing along the wall and along the wardrobe and the monster was free.

She could see his devil face. His breath tickled her cheeks. Her hair lifted when he put his claws on her head. Even when she hid under the pillow she could see his bold eyes watching.

She cried, quietly at first. But the sound kept coming up her throat and bursting right out of her mouth. Her mother was sleepy-cross when she came into the room. She wore a night-dress to her toes and her hair hung over her face. 'How often must I tell you? There's no monster. Stop being such a silly girl. If I hear any more of your nonsense I'll have to bring up Charlie.' She pulled down Beth's pyjama bottoms and slapped her bummy. Stingy pains down her legs and the door closed hard.

Charlie hung on a hook behind the kitchen door. A bamboo cane that her father called 'an instrument of torture'. He threatened to break it in half. He never did. Nor did he chop the wardrobe into matchsticks. Charlie hurt more than her mother's hand so Beth did not make a sound when the monster sighed and growled and crept to the wall, watching her, ready to carry her away if she fell asleep.

CHAPTER TWO

The doorbell never stopped ringing throughout the week before Christmas. Beth, who was responsible for answering the door, wondered if it was possible for anyone in Anaskeagh to buy a coat, dress, trousers or skirt that would fit without being altered. Marjory Tyrell was a genius with a needle and pins, the women said as they marched down the hall to her sewing room. She knew where to place a tuck, release a seam, rest a hemline on the most flattering part of the knee. They crowded her small sewing room with their ill-fitting clothes until Beth wanted to scream with annoyance.

Her Christmas dress was still not ready. The sleeves had to be inserted and it lay forgotten on the shelf, alongside the material for her new coat. If she asked when it would be ready her mother got cross and said Christmas was not just about new dresses or presents from Santa Claus. It was the birthday of the baby Jesus and Beth should remember that *He* was born in a manger and wrapped only in swaddling clothes. He didn't go on and on about green velvet dresses or demand expensive presents because he understood the meaning of money and how difficult it was to earn it.

Sara's dress was finished. So was her navy coat with the silver buttons down the front and across the shoulders. At the children's Mass on Christmas Day, she would carry the baby Jesus in her arms up the aisle of the church. Beth fell into a sulk every time she thought about it. Usually the girl chosen to carry the baby Jesus was older than Sara, who was only four. Uncle Albi said she was a natural born angel and Father Breen agreed.

'That brother of yours is a right fixer,' Beth's father said when he heard the news. Beth could see he was really pleased but her mother's mouth tightened as if he had said something mean. Marjory told him he should be proud of his youngest daughter instead of making his usual smart remarks about Albert Grant, who was the most successful businessman in Anaskeagh. Sometimes she called him Albert Harrison-Grant in a posh voice but her father always called him a 'chancer'.

He winked at Beth. 'He may be able to pull the wool over the eyes of the world but Barry Tyrell can spot a chancer a mile away. Isn't that a fact, Beth?' He winked again, but she was afraid to smile at him in case her mother saw and took down Charlie.

On Christmas Eve Marjory was still snipping, hemming and speaking to her customers with her mouth full of pins. Barry carried the turkey from the garden shed into the kitchen. It had been hanging there since Uncle Albi had given it to them the previous Saturday. He won it playing golf. His third turkey since the competition began, he said, smiling at Beth with his big, strong teeth. What else would he do with it except give it to his favourite sweetheart?

'Right you are then, my fine girls,' her father said. 'We've got a turkey to pluck.'

He cut off the feet and pulled the sinews so that the turkey's claws wiggled. When it seemed as if they were dancing, he chased the girls around the kitchen. Beth didn't want to make any noise in case it disturbed their mother but Sara shrieked. She ran round the table with her father chasing her, pretending he couldn't catch her. Beth's heart thumped. She knew her mother would hear and say it was her fault for not setting a good example. She imagined Charlie on her legs, the pain running hot to her toes. When Marjory came out of the sewing room she was as angry as Beth expected, but she used her hand instead of Charlie.

Afterwards, she said: 'Let that be a warning to you, young madam. Next time I have to come out you'll feel the full weight of my cane on your fat backside.'

'Don't be so hard on her,' Barry shouted. 'It's Christmas, for Christ's sake. All we're doing is having a bit of fun.'

'I wish I had time for fun,' she shouted and slammed the sewing-room door behind her.

He put cold water on Beth's legs and said the magic chant that made pain go away. Only the pain wouldn't go away. She wanted him to go into the sewing room and tell her mother she had been quiet, as good as gold. Even when the horrible sharp claws scraped her cheek she had hugged the shout into herself. Sara was too excited about the baby Jesus to care, showing off with her doll in her arms and marching up and down the stairs, not helping to make the breadcrumbs for the stuffing or putting the feathers into the sack.

It was dark when Beth was called into the sewing room. The floor was covered with pieces of material and empty thread spools. Marjory pulled the dress over her head and stood behind her, staring into the long mirror. The dress was green and had a lace collar that could be taken off and washed separately. The dress was identical to the one she had made for Sara but it looked different on Beth, too tight at her waist where the wide white sash tied in a bow. Her ankles looked as thin as sticks peering from beneath the hem.

'That will do fine.' Marjory snipped a loose thread.

She sounded so relieved that Beth was afraid to say anything about her new coat. The material was still on the shelf. Her mother followed her gaze and frowned.

'You'll have to manage with your old coat, Beth. It'll be fine after a good brushing.' She grabbed Beth's hand and swung her arm up in the air. 'I've escaped from prison!' she said and laughed out loud, forgetting all about Charlie and the turkey claws until she entered the kitchen and saw the feathers and breadcrumbs all over the floor and the giblets leaking blood on the draining board, and Beth's father sitting in front of the fire with a glass of stout in his hand.

'You lazy, good-for-nothing slob,' she shouted and burst into tears.

'Oh for Christ's sake, you're not the only one who's tired around here,' he cried and banged the glass of stout on the arm of the chair so hard that foam shot out over his hand. 'Can't you get it through your head, woman, that I have to work at night?'

Beth wanted to hide from their anger and the sight of her mother's crumpled face. Her father noticed Beth and ordered her up to her bedroom. She ran upstairs, followed by Sara, running as fast as they could but still they could hear the voices rising and a chair crashing on the kitchen floor.

Sara kept talking about Santa. She put her hands over her ears and asked if Beth had ever heard sleigh bells or saw him flying with his reindeer across the sky. They peered out the window. At first, all they could see were the street lights on Fatima Parade and Christmas trees winking in windows. Then Beth saw a light streaking across the sky. It could have been a shooting star and stars always shone bright on Christmas Eve to guide the three wise men to the stable. The only other possible explanation was that a sleigh, guided by Santa and his reindeer, was on its way to Fatima Parade to bring joy and peace to everyone.

At the children's Mass on Christmas Day the choir sang 'Away in a Manger' as Sara walked up the aisle carrying the baby Jesus. Beth knew the baby was only a doll but it seemed so real when her sister walked past, her face not laughing or pulled into funny shapes but serious, as if she was doing the most important thing ever. She laid the baby in the centre of the crib with the snow and the straw and the silver star shining overhead, and Marjory sighed, as if she had been holding her breath all the time her daughter had been walking up the aisle.

When Christmas dinner was over and Barry had had a snooze, they visited Cherry Vale. Uncle Albi's house had big bay windows and steps up to the front door. The angel on the Christmas tree had golden wings and blonde hair like Sara, so small and dainty, her tiny feet in poms, ready for dancing.

'Don't you dare touch anything, Beth.' Marjory started fidgeting as soon as they entered the drawing room where all the precious ornaments were made of glass and china, and would break if Beth stood too close to them.

'Guess what Santa Claus put into my stocking?' Aunty May giggled and flashed her arm, showing off a charm bracelet. Tiny figures glinted every time they caught the light. Her lips looked bigger than they really were because she had drawn a bright red line over the top one. Uncle Albi had a pet name for May. She was his 'Blossom', he said, as fair as the fields of May. He kissed her on the lips when people were looking, which, Marjory said, puckering up her mouth as if she had seen something bold, was a very rude thing to do. A bad example to set in front of the children.

'And how's the accordion business, Mr Music Man?' Uncle Albi poured whiskey into a glass and handed it to Beth's father.

'Excellent!' Barry smacked his lips and stared into the sparkling glass as if he could see pictures swirling inside it.

'Wait until the new year is over and then there'll be a different story to tell,' said Marjory.

Beth's heart gave a little hurting kick. That was the sort of remark that made her father angry and she would hear them shouting in the night, even when she pulled the blankets over her head.

Her cousins sat beneath the Christmas tree, playing with a train set laid out on tracks. Conor was ten, big for his age. Kieran was eight, Beth's age but smaller, which he hated. He looked up as she approached and brought the engine to a halt.

'What did you get from Santa?' Kieran asked.

'A book and a tennis racquet,' she replied.

'You'll be able to make a racket then,' said Conor. He waited for everyone to laugh. When the adults did not turn around he repeated his remark in a louder voice. Beth stuck her tongue out at him, hating him because he was always making fun of her and doing Chinese burns on her arm worse than anyone she knew.

The previous summer, the back garden of Cherry Vale had been as smooth as a carpet, marked with white lines, with a net stretched across the centre.

'Lady Muck, showing off as usual,' said Marjory, sounding cross when Aunty May invited them over to see the new tennis court and have tea on the lawn. Her cousins, dressed in white shorts and tops, were hitting balls at each other across the net.

'You could play with Kieran and Conor if you had your own racquet,' Aunty May said.

Beth told her she was not allowed to make a racket and everyone except her mother laughed.

'Really, Marjory, does the poor child know anything?' Her aunt's thin brown eyebrows disappeared under her fringe and Uncle Albi lifted Beth high up in the air. He said she was a great one for making a racket wherever she went but she was still his favourite sweetheart.

When Christmas tea was over, Barry played his accordion. Sara danced a reel, her hair bobbing around her face, light on her toes, and when she bowed, everyone clapped as if they were never going to stop. She would have danced again only her father said it was Beth's turn. He squeezed the accordion and the notes seemed to dance with her. In her head she could hear his voice saying, 'Listen to the beat, Beth.' She felt herself rising, moving into the rhythm, her legs swinging high, her arms stiff beside her green velvet dress. Her mother frowned, saying something with her hand over her mouth to Aunty May. They laughed together, a silent sound buried under the music. The accordion raced away in front of Beth, her feet no longer able to find the notes. Her father slowed down and stopped. He told her to start again and not to be nervous — she was a terrific dancer. She felt hot and cross, her cheeks heavy as if she was going to cry.

'I've got the very thing to cheer her up,' said Uncle Albi. 'Come with me, Beth.'

The back garden was cold and dark. Beth could hardly see Anaskeagh Head, the big mountain behind Cherry Vale. Her father said it was higher than Mount Everest. Fairies lived under the rocks where they spun the magic gorse blossom and covered the mountain in a coat of gold. Uncle Albi switched on a torch. It shone on the tennis court and the high bushes that bent like crouching animals, reminding her of monsters in wardrobes, silly things she had imagined when she was only a kid.

He opened the door of the garden shed. 'Look at what we have here,' he said, shining the torch over Sadie. His voice made goosebumps on Beth's skin. The dog lifted her head and growled but did not move.

'Don't go too close,' he warned Beth. 'She'll snap if you touch her babies.'

The pups had golden coats and floppy ears. They tugged at Sadie's belly, making thin yelping noises and swiping at each other with their paws.

'We're not supposed to go near the puppies.' Uncle Albi looked cross, as if it was Beth's fault they were in the shed where it was cold and smelly from the dogs.

'Blossom will murder us if she finds out. So we must keep this our secret. Do you understand me, Beth?' He crouched down in front of her, trapping her between his knees. 'If you don't tell anyone I showed you the puppies I'll give you one when it's weaned from its mammy. What do you say, Beth? Our big secret, huh? Say it now. Come on now, our big secret.'

'Our big secret.' Her throat felt sore, as if it was closing over and she would never again be able to swallow. She wanted to go back to the drawing room with the log fire and the Christmas tree and Sara, sitting between her cousins, watching the train running fast and far away along the tracks. She made herself think about Jess O'Donovan, her very best friend in school, and she sang the song Sister Maria had taught them, singing it so loudly inside her head that she couldn't hear anything else except the words of 'Over the Sea to Skye'. *Speed bonnie boat like a bird on the wing… Carry me safe to Skye.*

He ran his finger inside the collar of her green Christmas dress, the material rustling soft as the crepe paper they used in school for the Christmas decorations. He untied the white sash at the back and she heard the silvery clink of the zip opening.

'I didn't think little girls wore woolly vests any more.' He was laughing softly, as if he had said something very funny. He pushed down the shoulders of her dress, lifting out her arms – first one and then the other. The vest her mother had knitted hurt her face when he pulled it over her head because he didn't know he was supposed to open the buttons at the top. But she was afraid to cry in case he told her mother, who would sigh and say, 'Honest to God, Beth, I can't take you anywhere.'

Sadie's eyes were closing. The pups were quiet, sleepy quiet. Their names were Goldie, Banjo, Lily and Pete. Uncle Albi asked her if he was her favourite uncle. She nodded her head and he said, 'Then give me a kiss to prove it.'

Her heart pounded as the hot red feeling opened up in her head and Uncle Albi kept whispering, 'Jesus… Jesus… Jesus,' as if he was in church, on his knees and saying his prayers.

CHAPTER THREE

Statues was a game of absolute stillness. The girl who was 'on' stood with her back to the other girls, trying to guess the exact moment to spin around and catch one of them moving. Sara was the best at the game, nimble on her feet or frozen as a statue. Beth was always caught, stumbling forward, swaying to the side, sometimes falling.

When her uncle called to Fatima Parade she stayed perfectly still and silent. Invisible until he looked at her and smiled. 'Little liar, Beth. Black spots on your soul. If your mother finds out you're a liar she'll take you to Sergeant O'Donnell and he'll put you where he puts all the bad girls… In jail forever.' In Cherry Vale, when no one was watching, he pointed to her reflection in the big mirror above the mantelpiece and said, 'God sees your soul, Beth Tyrell. He sees the dark stains upon it and his heart bleeds because he knows you're a naughty girl, a girl who tells wicked lies.'

Her eyes had been stolen from a witch, he said, his breath warm in her ear. Green eyes that cast a spell and bewitched him. She didn't want to be a witch with big bold eyes. She wanted baby-blue eyes like Sara and long blonde hair in ringlets. But her black hair never curled, no matter how tightly her mother twisted it in rags at night.

'Forked lightning,' sighed Marjory, trying to comb it in the mornings. She cut it short with her dressmaking scissors, traced a parting at the side and said, 'At least it's manageable now.'

Beth stared at her white witch's face in the mirror and saw what her uncle saw. Her soul was no longer small and pure as the Eucharistic Host but spotted like a sheet of blotting paper, inky sins that spread and spread until all the space was gone and she was ready to burn in everlasting flames. How to make it pure again? At night she prayed, her knees numb on the lino, and Sara shrieked, complaining about her sister's cold feet, when she finally climbed into bed.

In confession Father Breen was silent when she told him she had committed a grievous mortal sin. His face beyond the grille was lost in a dark holy place. He leaned towards her. She could see his eyes. He was searching beyond her body, staring deep into her black soul.

'Tell me this sin, child. Don't be afraid.' His stern voice commanded the truth. She tried to find the words to describe what had happened in those hidden moments. When she sobbed Father Breen sighed, as if he was very tired. 'Child, you must talk to your mother. Come back and see me next week when you have done so. Do you promise to talk to her?'

She nodded wordlessly, afraid to explain about Charlie and jail and how hell was waiting for her because of the disgrace she would bring on her family. Little liar Beth. Black spots on your sinful soul.

Her uncle was the most important man in Anaskeagh. He owned a factory with fields all around it and a fancy furniture shop in the centre of the town. He called his shop his 'showrooms' and put red notices in the window about 'Unbeatable Bargains'. When he called to Beth's house he did not knock on the front door.

'Anybody home?' he shouted and opened the door with his own key. He brought gifts, presents for Christmas and for the girls' birthdays, furniture from his factory and envelopes with money. When no one wanted new clothes and people no longer danced to the music of the Anaskeagh Ceili Band, he opened the kitchen press and placed the envelopes behind the milk jug.

'When are you going to get yourself a real job, Mr Music Man?' He would slap Beth's father on the back and jerk him forward. 'One that supports Marjory and the children? Just say the word and I'll fix you up tomorrow. A regular wage and the delivery van to take home with you in the evenings.'

'I'm well able to look after my own family, thank you very much.' Barry's face would turn red. 'When I want charity I'll ask for it. But you'll see me eat grass first.'

After he left, Marjory always sighed and said, 'Thank God for the goodness of Albert. I dread to think how we would manage without his kindness.'

Her father talked about moving to Dublin where he could get proper work with a proper band in proper dance halls. There was nothing 'proper' about Anaskeagh, he said. It suffocated him, its small-town gossip, with people interfering in other people's business and running to the confession box every time they put a little finger out of place. He would rather die than drive a delivery van for Albert Grant. The sooner they all moved the better. He told Beth about the wide streets in Dublin and the lights that shone in shop windows, and how the women in their clicking high heels and red lipstick always met their boyfriends under Clerys' clock. Marjory said her roots were in Anaskeagh and it would take more than the word of Barry Tyrell to persuade her to pull them up.

Sometimes she allowed Beth to stay overnight at Jess O'Donovan's farm, where yellow cats dozed under the tractor and geese marched up and down the cobbled yard, flapping their wings when they were shooed away from the open kitchen door.

Jess's mother, Catherine O'Donovan, wore wellingtons and jeans and drove a tractor. When she wasn't herding cows down the lane to be milked or digging up turnips in the fields, she read books about the stars. She kept a telescope under her bed and on clear nights she went up to the hill field to study the sky. Sometimes she took Jess and Beth with her. She pointed to Venus, traced the Milky Way, the Plough and the Great Bear. When they returned to the kitchen they toasted bread in front of the range and drank hot milk with sugar sprinkled on top. In the evening Frank O'Donovan and his sons milked the cows in the byre and sang cowboy songs. They asked Beth to sing 'Papa Oom Mow Mow', which her father had taught her, and Frank swore her singing turned the milk into pure cream.

On the farm no one told Beth she was wicked. When she accidentally broke the cut-glass bowl used only for the Christmas sherry trifle Catherine said it was one less dust gatherer to worry about. She handed Beth a blouse from the laundry pile and ordered her to dry her eyes. Tears should only be shed for reasons of the heart. Beth wasn't sure what she meant. Maybe it was supposed to stop her heart pounding, and it did, but she knew deep down, no matter what Catherine or anyone else said, that she was a very bad little girl.

The friends were separated in fourth class when they were discovered playing dot games on the back pages of Beth's copybook. Sheila O'Neill was moved to the bench beside Beth. She had chilblains on her ears and her pale blue eyes reminded Beth of a frightened rabbit. Not that Beth had ever seen a frightened rabbit. Only dead ones that the O'Donovan brothers had shot. Or a fleeting glimpse of their bobbing tails disappearing into burrows on the slopes of Anaskeagh Head. When the rabbits were dead their eyes were as pale as glass stones. Sheila's eyes moved all the time, darting around as if she believed people were watching her behind her back and she would catch them staring. Her three sisters in America sent her parcels of jeans and candy bars and dresses with flounces and sequins. She talked about them all the time, whispering behind her hand in case their teacher, Mrs Keane, heard.

Another sister called Nuala lived in London. Mrs O'Neill told everyone she worked in a fancy department store. Beth's mother smiled and said that was a lie. Even the dogs in the streets knew that Nuala O'Neill had shamed her family's good name forever.

One day, Sheila brought photographs into school. Before she showed them to Beth, she made her cross her heart and hope to die screaming if she broke her promise not to tell.

'Nuala made the baby inside her tummy. Swear to God you won't tell *anyone?*' She leaned closer, her hand cupped close to her mouth, breathless with the need to share the secret that had caused her sister to disappear one day and her mother to cry whenever Sheila asked when Nuala was coming home.

Beth studied the photographs, holding them on her knees in case Mrs Keane saw. A baby with plump cheeks in a lace christening cap and gown sat on his mother's knee. Nuala O'Neill used to play camogie for the Anaskeagh Juniors and had danced every Saturday night in the Emerald Ballroom.

'How did she make her baby?' Beth whispered.

'Derry Mulhall put a seed from his willie inside her tummy and the baby grew from it,' Sheila whispered. 'That's how grown-ups do it but it's a mortal sin if you don't wait until you're married. That's why Nuala had to go away.'

Beth felt hot and sick, as if the air had suddenly been sucked from the classroom. Sheila's whispering hurt her head. The photographs merged into dots, black and dancing, causing her to sway forward as they fell to the floor.

'Oh God, we're done for!' hissed Sheila, scrabbling frantically to retrieve them. When she straightened up Mrs Keane was standing at the desk with her hand outstretched. The teacher studied the photographs, frowning when she recognised Nuala.

'You two! Come with me,' she ordered.

Their footsteps echoed along the corridor as she escorted them to Sister Rosa's office. The photographs were spread out on the head nun's desk. Her long black habit reminded Beth of crows flapping on the schoolyard wall. Sheila twisted her fingers together as if she was playing cat's cradle without the twine. She began to cry. Tears splashed the toes of her heavy black shoes. Sister Rosa said she would be expelled if she ever dared bring such sinful photographs into school again. The rosary beads hanging from her waist rattled as she raised her arm and slapped their hands with her leather strap. The floor tilted in a see-saw sway when Beth walked from her office and back into the classroom of curious, staring girls.

That evening she tried to drown Goldie in the zinc bath that hung on a nail in the backyard. Sadie's pup, as her uncle had promised. Beth hadn't looked at Goldie when her uncle had carried him into the house. She refused to feed him or clean up after he peed on the floor. Goldie became Sara's dog, trotting behind her wherever she went and sitting on his hind legs when she said, 'Beg!'

Beth's head felt like a red-hot fire as she pushed the cocker spaniel under the water, ignoring his terrified, wriggling movements until Sara came running into the yard, fists pummelling wildly, and pushed Beth against the wall. She lifted the dripping animal in her arms and ran weeping into the kitchen to tell her mother. Beth welcomed the stinging pain that followed. It was the only way to let the badness out.

CHAPTER FOUR

Barry Tyrell was driving a van now. 'Grant's Fine Furniture' was engraved on the side. His accordion was silent in the cubbyhole under the stairs. When Sara begged him to play music so that she could practise her Irish dancing he refused and shouted at her to stop being a nuisance.

When he played in the band he used to bring chips from Hatty's Chipper home with him. The sisters would tiptoe downstairs to eat them, giggling and huddling around the kitchen table, nervous in case Marjory woke, their fingers digging into the vinegary chips, which tasted so different late at night. Now they no longer smelled chips and the only sounds they heard were the loud slamming of the hall door and Barry's footsteps on the landing as he passed their bedroom door without stopping.

Beth would waken instantly, as if an alarm had gone off inside her head, knowing he had been drinking in The Anaskeagh Arms. She would wait for the voices on the other side of the wall to rise. Smothery and hot from her sister's closeness, she wondered how Sara could sleep so peacefully when even the walls seemed to blister with her parents' anger. Her father still talked about moving to Dublin. Beth no longer believed him and suspected he didn't believe it himself. The father who had made these promises no longer existed. In his place was a small, grumpy man who told too many stories and drove a van for the person she hated most in the world.

Beth woke one night and heard his footsteps thudding down the stairs, his suitcase bumping against the banister rails. From the cubbyhole in the hall he took his accordion and slung it across his chest.

'You needn't think you'll get back into this house again,' Marjory shouted, leaning over the top rail. In her long night-dress, her hair tousled, she reminded Beth of a figurehead on the bow of a ship, riding furiously through a storm. 'Not in a million years will you ever set foot in here again!'

'That'll be too soon for me.' The crash of the front door was followed by a stark silence. Beth's mother stared at her then looked away again, her hand moving over her stomach as if she was brushing crumbs from a tablecloth. 'He's gone for good. Your precious father has dumped us.'

'Where's he gone?' Beth couldn't grasp what her mother was saying. 'Has he joined the band again?'

'I haven't a notion where he's gone. I only hope it's to hell and that he stays there forever.'

Sara woke and ran to the landing, her eyes glazed with sleep.

'Your cruel father has left us,' Marjory said, soothing her plaintive wailing. 'He doesn't want us any more, but that doesn't matter. Don't cry, my pet… don't cry. I'll always be here to love you. We don't need him. We never have.'

Sara's tears dried as her mother comforted her, speaking soft, insistent words of hate. She brought the girls into her bedroom where they slept for the rest of the night. The door on one side of the wardrobe was open. The space inside was empty except for a few coat hangers. Empty space was all her father had left behind.

Soon the empty spaces were filled with other things. He became a memory that only took shape when the girls heard ceili music on the radio or found an old photograph that had escaped Marjory's ruthless efforts to remove his presence from the house. Once a week he sent a registered letter from Dublin. It contained money, she said. Money that would be sufficient to manage on if she were feeding a family of mice. The girls should thank their lucky stars they had an uncle who cared about their welfare or they would be sleeping on the streets.

Occasionally, Barry sent letters to his daughters. He lived near a church on a hill. Christ Church Cathedral, a very old and famous place, he wrote. The cobblestones would make a man's bones rattle. The smell of hops and yeast from the Guinness brewery was as sweet as the nectar of the gods. He missed his girls every ticking minute on the clock. They must visit him one of these fine days.

CHAPTER FIVE

'Beth Tyrell – thirteen years of age. Well, fancy that now!' In Hearn's grocery shop, Maggie Hearn's eyes beamed behind her glasses. She leaned her elbows on the counter. 'It only seems like yesterday your mammy was wheeling you out in your big fancy pram.'

Behind her, high wooden shelves stretched to the ceiling, stacked with everything from fishing tackle to flypaper, sides of smoked bacon, bags of sugar and golden mounds of butter that Maggie sliced and wrapped in greaseproof paper.

'So? What's the plan for the big day?' she asked. 'I've heard terrible stories about them teenage parties.'

'I'm not having a party,' said Beth. 'Me and Sara are going to visit Daddy in Dublin.'

'Are you now? Tell the old rogue I was asking for him. Many's a tune I danced to his accordion.'

Beth almost laughed out loud at the idea of Maggie Hearn dancing in her wrap-around apron and cardigan, the rainbow-coloured lights twirling on her bottle-top glasses. When she was leaving, Maggie gave her a packet of Rolos to celebrate her birthday. 'You'll be running from them boyos before much longer,' she said, chuckling. 'Take Maggie's advice and make sure you pick the right one before you let him catch you.'

On the morning of their departure Sara woke, sulky and hot. She puckered her forehead and refused to get out of bed.

'I don't want to see him... You can't make me,' she cried, twisting the sheet around her neck and turning her back on

Beth. 'He's a horrible, cruel man. Mammy says he hates me. And you're horrible too… A big bully… I'm not going and that's that!'

She sobbed and cowered under the blankets.

'Poor baby. What's the matter? Let Mammy make you better,' Marjory crooned and Beth knew her sister would stay in bed all day, eating ice cream and drinking lemonade, even though she was only pretending to be sick.

'Make sure you behave yourself,' Marjory warned when Beth was ready to leave. 'There are very few girls in Anaskeagh who will ever have the opportunity of staying overnight in an expensive hotel, isn't that right, Albert?'

'It is indeed.' Beth's uncle smiled at her. 'But then there's very few girls in Anaskeagh as beautiful as my Beth. And it's not every day that one of them gets to be a teenager.'

Barry Tyrell had grown a beard, and his face was fatter, not flushed and tense any more. At first he seemed like a stranger with her father's voice and the familiar way his eyes crinkled when he smiled. Her uncle did not stay and talk to him. He had people to meet in the city and would call back later for Beth.

'Well, well, well! This is good, isn't it?' Barry rubbed his hands together. He made sandwiches and cut slices of sponge cake, insisting that Beth eat every crumb on her plate. The house where he lived was on a terrace similar to Fatima Parade but he only had one room and a sofa bed. The lace curtains had holes and blue mould stains. Dead leaves were trapped under the weatherboard. He wanted to know about school and if Beth had a boyfriend yet. On the mantelpiece a black china horse reared up on its hind legs. A gas fire steamed the windows. He told her about his job, delivering planks of wood to building sites, and how at night he played in pubs. Not dance music any more but whistle tunes with a ballad group called Celtic Reign who, he said, were going places very fast.

'How much do you miss me?' Beth demanded.

'You pull my heart to pieces every single day,' he replied.

'Then why can't I live here with you?'

'Don't be daft, Beth.' He glanced quickly at his watch, pretending he was pushing up the sleeve of his jumper. 'You don't want to live in a slum like this.'

'I don't care. I'll be with you. I can get a job and we'll move somewhere bigger.'

'You're still only a child.'

'I'm thirteen now.'

'That's still far too young to leave home. Your mother would have my guts for garters.'

'I don't care… I hate living with her. I hate – I hate…' She sobbed, unable to continue.

At the side of the sofa squashed against the wall she saw a cardigan. A woman's cardigan, pale yellow angora with pearl buttons. Maybe, said Barry, his eyes skittering away from the cardigan when Beth pulled it free, when she was older, they would talk about it again.

He would never change his mind and even when he offered to teach her to play the tin whistle she knew he was watching the time, waiting for her uncle to collect her.

'Still chasing rainbows, Mr Music Man?' Albert asked when he returned.

How tall he seemed, standing strong in the little room, rain glistening on his oiled hair, which he'd combed back so neatly from his forehead. Her father's hair was a mess, long on the back of his neck and as frizzy as his beard.

'Get your coat, Beth.' Barry nodded brusquely towards the door, his good humour disappearing. In the hall she heard him tell her uncle that what he chased was his own business.

'Ah, but it's also my concern, Tyrell. Rainbows don't help when it comes to feeding your children. That pittance you send to Marjory every week is a joke.'

'It's as much as I can afford. She makes enough from the dressmaking to manage.'

'If you believe that you're more of a fool than I thought. She's gone to skin and bone with the work she's forced to take on to keep her family together. My sister was always too good for you but you married her and it was your duty to take care of her.'

'So what's the penance, Father? Three Hail Marys and a hair shirt... With slight alternations?' He raised his voice. 'Are you ready, Beth? Don't keep your uncle waiting. He's a very busy man.'

Beth wondered how it was possible to love and hate her father at the same time. Such mixed feelings confused her, so different to her feelings for the man standing beside her. Those feelings oozed from some slimy part of her stomach, knotting it so hard it was impossible to think of anything else. He stopped at the hall door and studied his reflection in a grimy mirror, flicked a dark hair from his shoulder and lifted the collar of his coat around his ears. He took Beth's hand and held it against his side, pulling her forward when she turned to wave to her father. Surely he would change his mind and call her back. Was she the only person in the world to see the monster's face? The front door was closed by the time her uncle turned his car and drove away.

The button beside the hotel lift glowed orange when he pressed it. Far below she heard a low murmur, as if a mighty beast had been disturbed and was coming to carry her away. It grew louder, shuddering movements that stopped when it reached their feet. The gates clanged when he pushed them apart. Her stomach swooped in a ticklish thrill as the lift began to ascend.

Their footsteps were silent on the corridor leading to her room. Outside, buses were still running. She could hear them braking, the engines idling as late-night passengers crowded the platforms, hurrying to a place where they could shelter and be safe.

Speed bonnie boat… She closed her eyes and thought about the ocean. Such a tiny boat to be tossed about on the turbulent waves and how the wind screamed… Unlike Beth, who never made a sound, and even after he left, closing her door so softly she didn't even hear a click, she kept her eyes closed until the boat was safely brought to shore.

In the next room she heard him clearing his throat. Such thin walls between them, no stronger than a sheet of paper. After a while a snoring sound rose and fell away in a whistling sigh, as if he was blowing air through his nose and she, behind the thin walls, was comatose… the same as the Statues game. What would he do if she lived for the rest of her life in a death-like trance? Or if she died? She imagined her family weeping around her grave as her white coffin was lowered deep into the earth. Inside, she would be pale and dead. As still as she was now. Only she would be at peace and her father would be there with the mourners, ashamed of himself because he would not let her live in his mean little room with the grimy wallpaper and the yellow woman's cardigan stuck between the sofa and the wall.

She swayed when she sat up, afraid she was going to fall from the bed. She stayed in that position, her head bent forward, until it felt safe to move again. She would tell her father. The decision came suddenly, as if it had been waiting to find space in her fear. Slowly she curled her toes, bending the soles of her feet, tensing her legs. She searched for the light switch and gathered her scattered clothes, dressing silently, terrified the snoring sounds from next door would cease.

Along the hotel corridor fan-shaped lights threw a dim glow against the walls. She pressed the lift button, seeing it light up, hearing the murmuring noise from down below rushing towards her.

'What in God's name are you doing, Beth?' His red dressing gown gaped open, reaching only to his knees, showing off his hairy chest as he hurried towards her. It made him look silly, no longer important, but as he reached her the horror pushed up into her mouth and she was terrified she would throw up on the spot.

'I'm going to my daddy,' she cried. 'I'm going to tell on you.'

'Poor child, you've had a bad dream. Come back inside now and stop making such a fuss.' As the lift clattered to a halt he lifted her in his arms. Easily, as if she was only the weight of a feather, he carried her back to her bedroom. He sat her on the bed and wagged his finger in her face. 'Now! You stop this hysterical nonsense at once. Do you hear me?'

He told her about her father and the woman who owned the cardigan. How she had a family, children who had become his children. Barry Tyrell no longer cared about the girls he had left behind in Anaskeagh. When Beth put her hands over her ears he pulled them away. She must listen to the truth. Then, perhaps, she would stop being a selfish, ungrateful child who was breaking her mother's heart with her tantrums.

In the Church of the Sacred Heart Beth stared at the crucifix above the altar. She felt the nails being thudded into the Christ figure one by one. She examined her own hands, hoping to see blood pouring forth. A stigmata. A whore of Babylon, old Sam Burns shouted at young women when they walked through the town. The words seared her mind, even though Jess's mother said Sam was shell-shocked from the war, when he'd been a soldier in France, and harmless behind all his ranting.

On Jess's thirteenth birthday, they climbed to the summit of Anaskeagh Head. Jess liked rituals, solemnity, the grand gesture and, on this significant occasion, she intended burying the symbols of her childhood. In a tin biscuit box she had placed her diaries, a copy book, her favourite glass necklace, a rag doll, her First Communion prayer book, her confirmation medal, a *Bunty* annual and her favourite sweets. The headland, with the crashing Atlantic Ocean on one side and the town of Anaskeagh sloping away into the distance on the other, offered her the perfect ceremonial altar to move into adulthood.

When the burial was over, the friends pricked the middle fingers of their right hands with a needle. They vowed to be blood sisters for as long as they lived, sharing secrets, even the smallest, most trivial secret. This meant never lying to each other, said Jess, telling Beth she sometimes heard God's voice talking to her in the wind.

How could she share her secrets with Jess, signed in blood? How could she whisper such ugly words to her best friend, a Child of Mary who made an altar in her bedroom every May with lilac and bluebells and heard God's voice in the wind? Far below her she could see Cherry Vale and the houses beside it. How tiny they looked. So neat and orderly, the front road winding like a skein of fine grey thread into Anaskeagh. She imagined her uncle, a scurrying insect, small enough to be crushed under her foot, the sole of her shoe stamping him into a smear of blood that would be washed away forever when the rain fell.

CHAPTER SIX

Everything was simple once Beth decided to run away. No rush, no panic. The right moment would present itself and she would be gone, dust on her heels, churning up the road from Anaskeagh. She knew she must do it or else go mad, as loopy as old Sam Burns or Mrs McIntyre, who once ran down Fatima Parade in her nightdress waving a carving knife.

One Sunday afternoon on Anaskeagh Strand she confided her plan to Jess. 'I can't stick it a moment longer,' she said. 'I'll go nuts if I don't escape from this dump.'

'Did you have another row with your mother?' Jess asked. The rows between mother and daughter were a source of fascination to her.

'Does the Pope say the rosary?'

'What was it about this time?'

'Oh, the usual.' Beth was dismissive. 'She wants me to do a secretarial course after my Inter and work for my uncle.'

'I'd hate to work in an office.'

'Well, there's not much danger of that, is there?'

'Thank God!'

'You'll have plenty of time to do that.' Beth still couldn't believe her friend was serious about entering a convent. At the spring retreat, Father Ford, the mission priest who was home on holiday from Africa, had talked to the pupils of the Star of the Sea Convent about the joy of becoming a beloved bride of Christ. Jess had absorbed every word. Afterwards, her face glowing with conviction, she said she finally understood The Voice. An insistent voice, no longer blowing uncertainly through the wind as it told her that the way to salvation lay in loving God above all earthly things.

'Even Wham!?' Beth demanded.

Jess grinned. 'Especially Wham!'

If Jess was a 'holy Mary' like Breda Gilligan, who had a crush on Sister Clare and wore a Miraculous Medal pinned to the front of her school blazer, Beth could have understood. But Jess adored Michael Jackson, hated *The Sound of Music* and had shown *The Joy of Sex*, which she'd found at the back of her parents' wardrobe, to Beth – but only after she'd read it twice.

'It's so sexy, isn't it?' Giggling, she demanded her friend's opinion.

Beth gave a wooden smile and nodded. It seemed childish to admit that she had found it disgusting, so sickening that she wanted to throw up all over the pages. The future they had planned together seemed childish now. Jobs as fashion models or air hostesses, all-night parties and strange men with beards and guitars sleeping on the floor of their flat. Only when she finally accepted that Jess was serious about her vocation did Beth realise how much she had depended on the escape route provided by such daydreams.

'What will you do in Dublin?' Jess asked.

'I'll get a flat and a job.'

'It's a big city.'

'I'll find my way around easily enough. I'll stay with my father until I get my own place.'

'What about – you know – The Cardigan?'

'What about her? He's my father. I come first.'

Jess glanced sideways at her. 'Are you going to tell Sara?'

'I don't know. If I do she'll kick up an awful fuss.'

'She'll go nuts if she finds out afterwards.'

'Why should she? It's different for her. She gets away with bloody murder.'

'I don't know what I'll do when you go.' Jess put her arm around her friend's shoulders.

'Talk to God. He'll tell you.' Beth was brusque, shrugging away her friend's arm because Jess cried easily and the last thing she needed was to dent the armour she had built around herself.

Jess was struck by a sudden thought. 'Do you think your mother's going through the change? My mother says women get awfully crotchety at that time.'

'Change! What change?' demanded Beth. 'She's always been the same. Anyway, she's too young.'

'It can happen at any age from thirty-five,' said Jess. 'Mammy's got a book about it. Madness and depression and hot flushes. Remember Mrs McIntyre?'

'Jesus!' Beth was horrified. 'I hope I die first.'

Hatty Beckett, who owned Hatty's Chipper on the corner of River Mall, needed someone to work from six to midnight, five evenings a week. Marjory was furious when she heard that Beth had accepted the job. Hatty had gone out with Barry Tyrell in his single days and Marjory had often accused him of going into her chip shop for more than a portion of chips.

'I'm not having my daughter serving every drunk in Anaskeagh,' she declared. 'If you insist on doing part-time work instead of studying for your Inter your uncle will be more than happy to let you work on Saturdays in his showrooms. It'll be good training for you. He's kind enough to pay for your education so the least you can do is show him some appreciation.'

'I wouldn't work for that creep if he paid me a million pounds.' Beth's voice was low and taunting.

'How dare you use that kind of language in my house.' Marjory flushed angrily. 'Apologise at once!'

'Make me. Why don't you take down Charlie and make me?'

'I'll break that cane across your back if you give me any more of your lip. I don't know what's come over you lately. Cheek! That's all I get from you. Apologise at once.'

'He's a creep and he can stuff his stupid job up his arse for all I care.'

For an instant Marjory was too shocked to move. Then she reached for the cane and struck Beth across her legs, lifting her arm to strike again.

Beth laughed. She was no longer afraid. Charlie was a piece of bamboo, a thin cane with a hook that only came to life in her mother's hand. It was important to scream, to shout insults, to fling plates against the wall in sudden outbursts of fury so that Marjory would hurt her, hurt her so much that she would no longer feel trapped beneath her sins.

Neither of them noticed Sara entering the kitchen. The younger girl pushed between them, crying at them to stop. Too panicked to avoid the cane she took the force of the blow on her face. Her hair spilled over her hands as she clutched her cheek. Outside in the yard Goldie barked furiously.

'This is all your fault,' Marjory panted. She avoided looking at Beth as she ran a dishcloth under the cold tap and bent over Sara, gently dabbing at the blotch that was deepening into an angry red weal. 'You're nothing but trouble.'

'It's not my fault!' Beth screamed. 'You're the one holding the cane yet all you ever do is blame me for everything. Everything. I hate you so much it makes me sick.' She spat out the words as if they were pebbles in her mouth. 'I'm taking that job in Hatty's, and you'd better not try and stop me, or…' Her voice shook, unable to utter the words, knowing she would never be able to empty herself of them. Not that it mattered. Marjory had stopped listening. She helped Sara to her feet and tried to bring down the swelling that had already closed one of her eyes, smoothing back her blonde hair, crooning her love.

Beth battered cod and haddock and ladled chips into white pa-per parcels. The smell of fish clung to her, a pervasive scent on her clothes and her skin, no matter how often she washed herself and doused her body in Apple Blossom talcum powder. Mar-jory demanded half the money she earned. The rest was hidden in the dressing-table drawer beneath her underwear. When her uncle visited Fatima Parade she willed herself to think of other things. His suit had tiny, fine hairs that tickled her face when he greeted her, enveloping her in his bear-hug embrace, jovial and kind, as Marjory rushed to plump the cushions on his fa-vourite armchair and make him tea. Beth imagined his fingers grubbing about in her mind, searching out her thoughts, the knowledge they shared visible only to each other. The bicycle he gave her for her fourteenth birthday sat shining and unused in the coal shed, waiting. Soon she would cycle it for the first time. It would carry her far away from Anaskeagh. Such plans, counting her money, studying the map of Dublin, checking that her bike was oiled and the tyres remained firm, gave meaning to her days. Everything else, the normal things she always did, was performed in a dream state, as if her mind had already fled and only her body waited to follow.

Sara never stirred as her sister eased from the dip in the horsehair mattress and opened the bedroom door. It was four o'clock in the morning when Beth stepped into the kitchen. With her hand she felt along the kitchen door, lifting Char-lie from the hook. In the coal shed she wheeled the bicycle through the yard where the bath still hung, gleaming palely in the gathering dawn. Goldie stayed in the shadows as Beth leaned the bicycle against the wall and hunkered beside him, feeling his withdrawal, growling low in his throat when she touched him.

'You'll never be able to forgive me, will you, you old mutt?' Her throat tightened in a spasm as the dog continued to strain away from her. She thought of Sara snuggling deeper into the mattress and then, deliberately, allowed the image to fade. Sara was not going to be her cross. She refused to carry her into her new life.

At Cherry Vale she dismounted. She lifted a large stone from the rockery and flung it towards the bay window. Glass shattered. A light was switched on upstairs. She cycled out through the gates, head down, her feet pumping to the same frantic rhythm as her heart, and headed towards Clasheen, which was twenty miles away and led to the Dublin Road. She did not glance back as the distance between herself and Anaskeagh lengthened. When she reached Clasheen she flung the bicycle and the cane into a ditch.

'Bye bye, Charlie!' she shouted, hearing it strike the leaves and sink out of sight. Beyond the hedgerows the sky began to glow. A new day was beginning, caught in the stillness between dawn and morning. A truck lumbered towards her, heading for Dublin. She lifted her hand and it slowed.

'You look like someone in search of adventure,' said the driver when she climbed aboard.

'How did you guess?' She slung her duffel bag, packed tightly with her clothes, onto the seat between them. Clouds trailed across the rising sun, mountain squiggles on a blood-red painting.

CHAPTER SEVEN

The small terraced house with the yellow door was in darkness. Beth knocked twice, relieved when a light flashed on at an upstairs window. The wind blew the rain into the wooden porch where she was trying to shelter. She heard footsteps on the stairs and a boy in his late teens opened the front door. He had pulled on a pair of jeans and was still struggling with the zip. When he saw her standing outside with the rain in her hair, her clothes sculpted to her body, his hands paused, as if frozen with embarrassment, then he gave a quick jerk and the zip slid into place.

'Does Barry Tyrell live here?' She tried to speak calmly but her teeth chattered as she swayed forward, exhausted from the effort of hitching lifts to Dublin and walking long distances between them.

He nodded, the sleep still in his eyes and the warmth of four safe walls behind him. 'You're Beth,' he said, opening the door wider and beckoning her forward without hesitation. 'I've seen your photograph.'

'Is he here?' she repeated. 'I've been looking everywhere for him.' Rain ran from her coat and formed a puddle on the hall floor. She heard footsteps crossing the landing and her father's voice on the stairs. He was wearing a pair of rumpled pyjamas. His beard was bushier than she remembered, a balladeer's beard, which he chewed in mortification when he saw her. 'Beth! Jesus, Mary and holy Saint Joseph! What the hell are you doing here?' he demanded.

'Don't blaspheme in my house, Barry Tyrell.' The Cardigan's voice was soft but it was also firm enough to demand attention. Her hair was dyed so black it shone with a hard blue sheen under the hall light. She clutched the lapels of her dressing gown across her chest and surveyed Beth. 'Can't you see the poor child is half dead from exhaustion? Come into the kitchen, love, and get them wet clothes off you.'

'How did you know where to find me?' her father demanded.

No one interrupted Beth as she described how she had searched for the house where her father used to live only to discover it had been replaced by a building site with a hoarding around it. An old man with string on his coat waved his hands towards the hoarding and shouted insults at an invisible army of speculators who were tearing the soul out of his city. He'd taken her to a nearby pub where Celtic Reign played every Wednesday. The bar manager, seeing her distress, had rung the singer in Celtic Reign, who had given him her father's new address.

'He's gone to live in the sticks,' said the manager, scribbling down the address. 'There's not too many buses go to Oldport but let's have a look and see.' He took a timetable from behind the counter and ran his finger over a page. 'If you rush you'll just catch the last one.'

Beth didn't mention the tears and the despair that had swept through her as she'd tried to follow his directions to the bus stop or how the city had swamped her with its indifference. Nor did she describe her terror when the bus had headed northwards, racing through grey housing estates and out into the country, brushing against overhanging branches and swerving around corners until her stomach had heaved and she'd been afraid she was going to throw up over the seat.

'If you'd had the decency to write Beth a letter and tell her where you'd moved she wouldn't be tramping the little legs off herself searching the city for you.' The Cardigan spoke sharply to Barry then turned to the young man who had answered the door. 'Stewart, you get up them stairs as fast as your legs can carry you and wake your sister. Take no nonsense from her. She's to bring down that flannelette nightdress from the hot press and make room for Beth in her bed.'

Beth listened to the raised voices above her. An argument was taking place between Stewart and his sister, who was obviously furious over being woken in the middle of the night and told to share her bed with a stranger. A door banged and he reappeared with a tall, sulky girl in tow. She was older than Beth and flashed a hard look at her before sighing loudly in Barry's direction.

'You want my bed and my clothes for your daughter. What next?' Dramatically, she held her wrists forward. 'My blood? Go on, take it. You've taken everything else.'

'Be quiet, Marina, and sit down.' The Cardigan placed a towel over Beth's head and began to dry her hair. 'No one wants your blood but some manners would be appreciated around here. Barry, bring that pot of tea over to the table and get some heat into the poor child.'

Barry pushed at the sleeves of his pyjamas and glanced at The Cardigan. 'Well, we'd better let her stay the night,' he said, pretending he was glad to see Beth when it was obvious that he wanted her to vanish from his life as suddenly as she had appeared.

Marina did not believe in pretence. 'Your father's to blame for everything,' she stated when they were alone in her bedroom. She forced a bolster down the centre of the bed to separate them. 'Parasite! All we need now is his other daughter – and his wife – then we'll all have the perfect happy family.'

The Cardigan's name was Connie McKeever. She was a supervisor in a local clothes factory where her son also worked. Over the following days she did her utmost to make Beth feel welcome, advising her to ignore Marina, who, she sighed, had a tongue sharp enough to cut through steel.

'I'll talk to Mrs Wallace about getting you a job in Della Designs,' she said. 'I'm sure we'll be able to fit you in somewhere on the production line.'

High green railings surrounded Della Designs and the bars across the windows reminded Beth of a squat, ugly prison. The factory was silent on the outside until the doors opened and she was swept into the clack of machinery, music booming over the loudspeaker, the smack of irons and the steaming smell of freshly pressed fabrics. Female voices rose and fell like water over her head. She was petrified by the noise and the rows of women in blue overalls who ignored her, their hands moving with such speed at their machines that she wanted to turn and run weeping back along the road she had taken. Connie escorted her up wooden steps and into her employer's office. Mrs Wallace laid down the rules in a rasping voice. Beth would go on a month's trial and train as a machinist. There would be no smoking in the Ladies. Flirting with the boys in Dispatch was strictly for after hours. Punctuality was next to godliness, she said, and as for slacking off at the machines or absenteeism, she shook her head threateningly. No words of warning were necessary. She simply jerked her finger towards the exit door.

'I'll leave her in your capable hands, Connie.' She waved Beth from her office as if she were swatting a fly from her sight and picked up the telephone.

The glass front wall of her office overlooked the production floor. Nothing, Beth was to discover, escaped the hawkish gaze of Della Wallace. Stewart was an assistant to the production manager. He attended night classes in electronics and read technical manuals, propping them against milk bottles on the kitchen table and staring with fierce concentration at the pages whenever Beth sat down beside him. He blushed when he caught her eye, as if he, like Marina, hated having to speak to her. She soon realised this was shyness rather than hostility and a slow friendship began to grow between them.

'Is Marina giving you a hard time?' he demanded one day when he discovered her in tears at her machine.

Beth shook her head. 'I'm just homesick,' she admitted, not mentioning the letter that had arrived the previous day from her mother. Bitter and short, the words had jumped from the page, shocking her with their venom. 'Since you have refused my request to return home and insist on living with your adulterous father in his whore's house I no longer recognise you as my daughter.'

She had burned the letter, watching the notepaper blacken and curl the words into ash.

At night, when she tried to sleep, the bolster firmly established as a no-man's-land between herself and Marina, she heard creaking noises from the bedroom next door. A rhythmical, boisterous sound that forced her head deeper into the pillow. She suspected that Marina was also awake, restlessly turning away from the evidence of her mother's lovemaking.

'If my father was alive he'd break every bone in your father's pathetic body,' she muttered one night after the sounds from next door had ceased. Beth pretended to be asleep. She knew the story of Marina's father. How he'd drowned at sea, his body swept ashore many miles from where his fishing trawler had sunk. When Marina called her a culchie parasite it no longer hurt so much. She realised she was simply a target for Marina's anger, nothing more.

Oldport was different to Anaskeagh yet many things reminded Beth of home. On sunny mornings the sea had the same fierce glitter but it flowed into a calm estuary. The land around it was flat, miles of fields filled with straight rows of vegetables and flowers for the markets in the city. It had once been a fishing village, but the old harbour beyond the estuary was no longer in use, and the remains of sunken fishing boats could be seen at low tide, arching from the water, smooth and sleek as seals. The biggest difference was the sense of space. Beth could look in all directions, unlike in Anaskeagh where the headland loomed over everything.

In the evenings, Connie's house was filled with noise and music. Barry practised his tin whistle, Stewart played his records and Marina giggled in a high trilling solo whenever Peter Wallace entered the house. He was Stewart's best friend, the son of Mrs Wallace, and Connie had known him since he was a baby. She called him her 'almost son' and treated him the same as the rest of her family, scolding him when he teased Beth or flirted with Marina.

'Keep your eyes to yourself if you don't want them scratched out,' warned Marina one night after he left. 'Peter Wallace is madly in love with me. He's going to immortalise me in oils.'

'Oh! So that's what it's called nowadays?' said Connie, overhearing. 'In my day it was called 'getting a girl into trouble'. You concentrate on your studies, Marina McKeever and you'll be far better off.'

'You should know all about trouble.' Marina cast a belligerent look towards Barry, who was watching television. 'When's he leaving? I'm sick of putting up with strangers in my dead father's house.'

'Stop your nonsense, Marina. I won't have it.' Despite the firmness in her voice, Connie looked distressed.

'And I'm sick of all this.' Marina's chin jutted. 'You're the talk of Oldport… Living with a married man when my father's hardly cold in his grave. Don't give me any lectures about morality unless you understand what it means.'

From the frying pan into the fire, Beth thought. Trouble and strife, no matter where her father laid his head. She wanted to return to Anaskeagh and climb to the top of the headland with Jess. She longed to see Sara, to snuggle against her in the dip of the mattress, to hold her warm and cosy as they drifted off to sleep. But Anaskeagh was also her dark shadow and she knew she would never return to its shade.

CHAPTER EIGHT

Beth had spent six months on her machine when she discovered that a typist had been sacked for arriving late. She approached Mrs Wallace and told her she had studied shorthand and typing for a year before leaving the Star of the Sea Convent.

'If you give me a chance to show you what I can do you won't regret it.' She tried to sound confident under the astute gaze of her employer and succeeded.

'A week's trial,' agreed Della Wallace. 'One mistake and you're out on your ear. Start on Monday.'

The office staff ignored Beth. It was the first time anyone from the factory floor had become part of the clerical section and her sudden promotion upset the insular pecking order that existed in the company. The machinists were also suspicious of her.

'Stuck-up cow,' said Marina. 'She thinks she's too good for us since she moved up with the la-di-das.'

Marina had been expelled from school for smoking. She did it openly during her commerce and bookkeeping class and blew smoke rings at her teacher. Shortly afterwards, she joined Della Designs, sulking as she sewed collars onto coats, only brightening up when Peter came to the factory to tease the older women and whisper in her ear. She ignored Beth, making jokes about culchies and bog accents when she walked past. Sandwiched between the factions in the factory and the office, Beth kept her head down. The sales manager's secretary had become engaged. She flaunted a large solitaire and confided to her friends that she intended conceiving a baby on her honeymoon. When her job fell vacant, Beth would be ready to take it over.

At the weekly disco, called the Sweat Pit by those who packed the small parish hall, Marina danced with her friends until the music slowed and she could twine her arms around Peter's neck. She confided intimate secrets to Beth across the bolster. She 'did it' regularly with him on bales of blue velvet material in the stockroom. She posed nude for him in his artist's studio when his mother was out. She was his Mona Lisa. She laughed at Beth's shocked expression and tossed her long dark hair. 'When he finishes art college he's going to become a famous artist and we're getting married. I'm going to live in Havenstone – then we'll see who's the la-di-da around here.'

Havenstone, where Mrs Wallace and her son lived, was a large house set in its own grounds with a back view over the estuary. Beth imagined Marina in her high boots and leather trousers strutting through the rooms and smiled to herself. She suspected that Marina's escapades mostly happened in her head. But untangling the lies from the truth was a tedious task so she stayed silent and listened to fantastic stories that ended abruptly in the Sweat Pit when Peter danced the slow numbers with Sharon from quality control. Later, reported Marina's best friend, they were seen outside, kissing each other against the wall.

'She's a bike,' Marina sneered. 'Cheap peroxide slut.' She was going to move to London and become a proper model on a catwalk instead of a canvas. Oldport was the tomb of the living dead.

'I have my eyes set on higher things,' she said when Beth found her in the bedroom wiping mascara from her eyes. 'Peter Wallace can stay down on his bended knees forever but he won't make me change my mind.' She blew her nose and applied a heavy layer of panstick make-up, demanding to know why Beth was staring. Peter Wallace was nothing but a swollen ego and a tiny prick. She hated his guts. Beth left her weeping into the bolster.

A week later Marina left for London, armed with her portfolio of photographs and a letter of introduction to a modelling agency from Della Wallace.

The sales manager's secretary duly became pregnant on her honeymoon and Beth moved smoothly into her place. Andy O'Toole, the sales manager, filled the office with cigar smoke and refused to allow windows to be opened because he suffered from draughts. She discovered a bottle of vodka in the filing cabinet and understood why his wife rang in so often with excuses about his ill health. His bullying became a ritual part of every day. She quickly realised that no matter how hard she worked she would never please him.

'What a diligent young lady you are,' said Mrs Wallace, coming upon her one night when everyone had gone home. 'It's the third time this week you've stayed on. Don't you have time to do those invoices during the day?'

'I didn't get them until late,' replied Beth. 'And Mr O'Toole wants them on his desk first thing in the morning.'

'Does your boyfriend mind you working such long hours?'

'I don't have a boyfriend so there's no problem.'

'At your age I would see that as quite a problem.'

Beth was surprised at the personal direction the conversation had taken, especially when Mrs Wallace smiled, a rare occurrence that softened the tough lines around her mouth. Not knowing how to reply, she stayed silent, knowing that her employer understood this need to work compulsively, even if she pretended otherwise.

The Wallace money came from spinning – three generations of tweeds and worsteds making the family fortunes. But Mrs Wallace's childhood had been far removed from the graciousness of Havenstone. Connie, her childhood friend and neighbour, liked to remember those humble beginnings: one room on the top floor of a tenement; a dismal block of flats in the centre of the city where the walls wept in winter and rats froze to death in the outside toilets.

'Such hard times, Beth,' she would sigh, remembering, a hint of nostalgia in her voice. 'But Della always vowed that one day she would wear pearls and live in a mansion higher than the highest tenement.'

Mrs Wallace was fourteen when she set up her first factory, making overalls for a local businessman in a cramped back room of the same tenement block. Her second factory, a ramshackle building that was always damp- and rat-infested, burned mysteriously to the ground. Beth asked if Mrs Wallace had organised the fire to collect the insurance money. This question made Connie shake her head so vehemently that Beth knew it was true. By the time they moved to a custom-built factory in Oldport, Della Wallace had her pearls, many strings of them, and Connie was still by her side, still supervising.

Bradley Wallace was sixty years old when he married the young Della. She was in debt to his textile company and wrote it off by signing her name on their marriage certificate. He gave her security and she gave him a son whom she never had time to love. Connie shook her head sadly.

'She could have married many times before Bradley waved his chequebook in her direction but a man was only of use to Della if he could balance her books or run an efficient production line. Poor Peter – he has everything and nothing.'

One evening, shortly after their late-night chat, Beth's employer brought her to the stockroom where rolls of fabric were stacked on shelves. Mrs Wallace unrolled a thick bale of tweed that had been delivered that afternoon and asked her opinion.

'There's nothing different about it.' Beth rubbed her hand over the rough texture, imagining the heathery flecked coats being assembled piece by piece along the production line and, finally, draped on the shoulders of mannequins in department stores. 'It'll make up into the same coat style we've been manufacturing since I started working here.'

'What's wrong with that, may I ask?' her employer demanded. 'It's proved to be a very successful design for this company.'

'But it's so old-fashioned. People want modern styles, not something their grannies wear to Mass on Sunday.'

Della Wallace seemed startled by her blunt reply. 'How old are you?' she asked.

'Sixteen.'

'Aren't you rather young to be so opinionated?'

'You asked my opinion so I assumed you wanted the truth.'

'That's not Mr O'Toole's opinion and he's the one who brings in the orders. I haven't noticed any decline in our customer base – have you?'

'But there's no growth either. Young people don't even know the label exists.'

'We're not in the business of pleasing young people. Perhaps that's just as well if they're all as outspoken as you. Are you as honest when my son asks your opinions on his paintings?'

'Yes,' Beth replied. 'But Peter only pays attention to his own opinions.'

She wondered if she would be fired for her outspoken views. If so, she would emigrate to London and live with Marina, who wrote occasionally, boasting about her success on the catwalks and offering Beth a bed if she ever decided to leave the tomb of the living dead. She could do worse, Beth supposed. Like lying down on a bed of nails. She could endure Andy O'Toole and his small-minded meanness. When he finally took the bottle of vodka from the filing cabinet she would be ready to take over his job.

At first she had refused to visit Havenstone. The thought of entering her employer's home intimidated her. It looked so big and grand with its tree-shaded walls and high wrought-iron gates but Stewart had finally persuaded her to come with him.

'You never go anywhere,' he argued. 'Come on. Peter's a big mouth but he won't bite you. All we ever do is listen to music.'

To her surprise she had enjoyed the evening, which turned out to be the first of many. Peter led them up a curving wooden staircase into his studio, a large L-shaped room, south-facing and filled with natural light. He was in his third year at art college and planned to study in Italy when he graduated. The studio was filled with what looked like rubbish: pieces of driftwood, broken glass, jagged bits of steel, all marked with 'Hands Off – Artist at Work' warnings in case his mother threw anything out. The only nude Beth saw was a self-portrait of Peter hanging from the moon in chains of barbed wire. He looked mortified when he realised it was among the canvases she was examining.

'It's a protest against the Apollo moon landings,' he explained, quickly turning the painting to face the wall. He believed that man had desecrated the moon by trespassing on its surface. She did not agree. Neil Armstrong was right: the moon landing had been a giant leap for mankind.

Stewart joined in the argument, insisting that technology was the new religion. One day the world would be ruled by robots with human brains. This suggestion then triggered another discussion about the integrity of the human psyche. They listened to Michael Jackson and David Bowie, lolling on bean bags as the music pounded around them.

'That was good, wasn't it?' Stewart said on the way home. 'Aren't you glad you came?'

'Very glad.' A full moon reflected on the estuary. A melon moon pitted with craters, desert landscapes, a vast empty space – but all she could see was the long slim body of Peter Wallace filling it.

On Saturday afternoons they drank mugs of coffee and listened to music. Peter talked about artists who had influenced him, Cézanne and Picasso, and his favourite artist, Paul Klee, who had painted a famous golden fish with a flower instead of an eye. He said Beth had incredible eyes. He wanted to paint them. Cats' eyes. The mirrors of the soul. She was the perfect Muse for his Cat-astrophic Collection.

'Cat-astrophic,' he would chant. 'Cat-apult, Cat-aclysmic, Cat-walk, Cat-atonic, Cat-erpillar, Cat-holic, Cat-hedral.'

She sometimes wondered if he was mad. Mad in a harmless way that translated itself into crazy paintings of cats, destructive, dangerous cats, sometimes so distorted that they resembled nothing she could recognise, apart from their eyes – familiar eyes that she saw every time she stared in the mirror.

In his first completed painting – which he called 'Cat-apult' – a cat figure with a grotesquely large head and elongated body hurtled through stars; a flaming comet hell-bent on destruction. In his Cater-pillar painting, he painted the bank in Oldport, recognisable by the ornate pillars at the entrance. A cat with blazing eyes arched against one of the pillars, an almost playful pose until it became obvious that the building was buckling beneath the force of the animal's fury.

'Have you ever wanted to destroy something and obliterate it from the face of the earth?' he asked when he was doing 'Cat-walk'.

'Yes,' she said and, just for an instant, the past rushed back and threatened to overwhelm her. She focused on the painting he was holding up for her inspection. A monstrous misshapen cat that looked more like a bulldozer, it crouched in the centre of a green shady space that would soon become a building site. Beth's eyes were the headlights, glowing vengefully.

Afterwards, away from the studio, she was uneasy, aware that she was being manipulated. He painted such emotion into her eyes, as if they were indeed the mirrors of her soul. She felt like a vessel, his voice pouring into her, opening her up with words that touched her fears, the anger she tried to suppress. The loneliness that swept over her when she allowed herself to remember. Yet she went back each Saturday, drawn by the growing intimacy between them, the sense of being part of something they were both creating. There were layers to his paintings that were not always apparent. She suspected the completed collection would contain a lot more of herself than she, or even he, realised.

At the end of each session he drove her home in a red low-slung two-seater that always attracted attention when he drove too fast through Oldport. Flared denims sat low on his hips, his sallow skin showing between the hip band and his paint-streaked T-shirt. His hair hung to his shoulders, scraggy, un-combed. A true artist at work.

'Artist, my arse!' hooted Connie, soon after the painting sessions began. 'That brat couldn't whitewash a wall if I stood over him with a whip. If he touches one hair on your pretty head I'll tear his heart out. There's no need to look so shocked, Beth Tyrell. All that painting nonsense and the two of you alone up there in his bedroom for hours on end – it'll come to no good.'

'It's his studio, Connie.'

'Oh, so that's what he's calling it now?'

'Yes, Connie. I've never been inside his bedroom.'

'Well, there's many a girl in Della Designs can't say the same thing,' warned Connie. 'Not to mention my poor Marina with her broken heart. Drinking, dancing and double-dating – that's all that fellow wants from life.'

She wondered what Connie would say if she knew about the hash. Peter said it was a winding-down smoke and Beth wouldn't be so uptight all the time if she shared an occasional joint with him. It annoyed her that he saw her like that, especially when he painted her in so many different images, none of them human, some not even animate.

'You mind what I'm saying, Beth Tyrell,' Connie warned. 'Peter Wallace has a tongue that would charm snakes from a basket. But easy words are soon forgotten.'

Forgotten by whom, Beth wondered. She never forgot anything he said to her. Every casual compliment was branded on her mind. Words as airy as thistledown, blown carelessly in her direction, floating light, without substance.

Della Wallace also disapproved of their Saturday sessions. She usually found some excuse to enter the studio, cold with Beth for encouraging her son, sarcastic when she looked at his work. Her attempts to undermine his confidence infuriated Peter. Her presence was a constant reminder of the future she planned for him. The thought of working in the factory filled him with dread.

Beth was unsympathetic when he complained. 'It's your own fault. This studio, the way you live. It's all laid on for you. Maybe you should move out and let your mother know you're serious – that's if you are serious.'

'Of course I'm serious. It's all I've ever wanted to do.' She had annoyed him and it pleased her that she could reach beyond the charm and confidence he displayed so effortlessly.

Every Saturday afternoon Beth wrote to Jess and Sara. Only Jess replied.

Dear Jess,

I was sorry to hear you only achieved three honours in your Leaving Cert, especially as you made three novenas to St Jude. An honour per novena is an extremely poor return on your investment. If God intends on making you his bride he should do a better job of looking after your interests.

Dad's been unwell. Something to do with his breathing. He's not playing his tin whistle so much now. Connie bossed him into going to the doctor and he ended up in hospital for tests. He's fine again but my mother didn't want to know when I phoned. She wouldn't even let Sara come to Dublin to visit him. He's home again and back at work. Says he's as fit as a fiddle but he misses Sara something awful. If you see her, tell her she's to write back to me.

And now for my confession. Will you still be my friend if I tell you I've lost my faith? When you hear God's voice in the wind (how those words haunt me) I hear silence. But that's all right. It doesn't make me sad or anything. I'm an atheist now. I debated between becoming atheist or agnostic but I chose the former because I don't want any uncertainties in my life. It's strange, not believing in anything, but it makes me feel free.

However, I still believe that our friendship is stronger than faith.

Write soon with all the news.

Beth, your very best friend

Dear Beth,

Your loss of faith saddens me but I agree - our friendship is indeed stronger than faith or, as in your case, the lack of it. With your permission I will pray for your conversion back to the one true religion. My novitiate begins in September. I'm coming to Dublin with Mammy to buy everything. You should see the list of things I need! Glamour personified.

Latest news flash from Anaskeagh.

1. Your mother has opened a boutique on River Mall. It's called First Fashion; a most appropriate name since it's the first time fashion ever got its nose inside Anaskeagh.

2. Your uncle has become a county councillor. Big party in Cherry Vale. All the nobs went.

3. His creepy son Conor, he of The Thousand Chinese Burns, is studying law in University College Dublin. God help the criminals, that's all I have to say on that subject.

4. Saw Sara on Anaskeagh Head last week taking photographs with the camera you sent her for her birthday. I asked her to reply to your letters but she told me to mind my own business. Sorry, Beth.

5. Best news last - I've persuaded Mammy to book us into the Oldport Grand when we come to Dublin on our shopping spree. I want you to spend every spare minute with me. Imagine - four years since we've seen each other. A lifetime ago.

Counting the minutes until I see you.

Love you forever xxxxx

Jess

CHAPTER NINE

Catherine O'Donovan no longer had time to read books or study stars. The farm was losing money and when she took off her wellingtons in the evenings it was to change into the flat white shoes she wore on her night shift at the Anaskeagh Regional Hospital. She looked tired when she arrived in Oldport. Beth wondered if she ever felt lonely. Jess was her second child to leave home. Her oldest daughter sold second-hand clothes from a market stall in London. In Beth's opinion, bartering from a second-hand junk stall was a far more civilised existence than getting up in the small hours of the morning to chant at a non-existent God.

'Will you miss Jess when she goes into the convent?' she asked Catherine.

'Of course I will,' Catherine replied. 'But I'd have more chance of stopping a tornado in its tracks then making that young lady change her mind.'

She enjoyed being back in the hospital where she had originally trained but she had to keep on her toes to understand the changes that had taken place, particularly the drugs. She shivered just looking at the labels.

'I did my training with your Aunty May,' she said. 'The pair of us were great pals in those days.'

'I didn't know you were friends with May.' Beth was surprised.

'Not any more.' Catherine smiled ruefully. 'May's been cutting a lot of old ties since she became a councillor's wife.'

Beth's mouth clenched. Her pleasure in hearing about Anaskeagh was always marred by the mention of *him*. Even after four years, his name still had the power to terrify her.

Catherine lifted the heavy fringe from Beth's eyes.

'Don't cover them up, honeybun. They're beautiful. Are you happy since you left Anaskeagh?'

'Very happy.'

'The truth, Beth.'

'It is the truth. Honest.'

'Then why do you have the saddest pair of eyes I've ever seen on a young girl's face?' She took out her photographs of Anaskeagh and handed them to Beth. The familiar farm, the O'Donovan children with their big bones and cheeky grins. Sara was included in some of the photographs. How tall and leggy she looked, playing Hamlet in the school play. She was dressed as the Blessed Virgin in a Lourdes tableaux, which was performed in the Star of the Sea assembly hall. Her eyes stared past the adoring crowd at her feet. Another photograph showed her dancing at the Anaskeagh Feis, ringlets bobbing as she did her reels and jigs. Beth handed the photographs back without a word. The older woman held her close when she began to sob.

'Come home, honeybun. Your mother misses you.' She sighed when Beth shook her head. 'Young people... Why do they always hurt the ones who love them most?'

'Mum doesn't love me so I can't hurt her.'

'Of course she loves–'

'No, she doesn't. Not the way you love Jess. Anyway, I don't want to leave Dad. He pretends he's all right but he keeps losing weight and he doesn't have the breath to play his tin whistle any more.'

Catherine frowned when Beth told her about the hospital tests. The questions she asked added to Beth's uneasiness but it was difficult to think dark thoughts when Jess was around.

She laid out her new clothes on the bed and giggled, holding up a thick pair of knickers with elasticated legs. Beth snatched them from her and waved them over her head.

'Black knickers! This looks like a serious mortal sin, Sister Mary Wham! Shame on you.'

'Black everything,' sighed Jess. She fitted on one of her dresses and admired herself in the mirror.

'You look more like the bride of Dracula than the bride of Christ,' declared Beth. 'And your boobs have disappeared.' She prodded her friend's chest. 'Is this a miracle of the flesh – or just bad tailoring?'

'Oh shut up and be serious for a minute.' Jess's eyes were solemn, accusing Beth of making fun of her. 'You think this is all one big joke, don't you?'

'Of course I don't, Jess.' But it was difficult to understand this all-embracing need her friend described. It transcended the loneliness she must feel at leaving her family, of never falling in love or having babies of her own. A life that had become so alien to Beth she was afraid it would separate them. They would no longer be able to talk and laugh and simply be happy being together. 'It's just... Oh, I don't know... Do you still hear His voice calling you?'

'Just my own voice,' Jess replied quietly. 'That was all I ever heard. And it always told me the same thing. My life belongs to Christ. I can't see myself living any other way.'

Beth felt like crying because her friend spoke and looked like a stranger, pale and stalky under the voluminous black folds. This was actually going to happen. She was going to become a bride of Christ. Even the words sounded crazy. What would it be like to experience the kind of love Jess described? Consuming, adoring, safe.

On their final night in Oldport they went to a local pub called The Fiddler's Nest to hear Celtic Reign playing. Peter

Wallace joined them, pulling his chair close to Jess and flirting with her. Her vocation was a crime against mankind, he declared. She was too earthy, too vibrant to be incarcerated behind high walls. Saints were all mystery and soul. Jess was all heart and curves. She enjoyed him, giggling into a gin and orange and getting quite tipsy.

All heads turned when Marina McKeever entered. She had returned to the tomb of the living dead for a short visit. She wore a flouncy skirt and a cropped top that showed off her tanned midriff. She no longer wore falsies in her bra or any bra at all, for that matter.

The photographs she showed Jess and Beth had been cut from a trade magazine for medical aids. She had modelled an acne face wash, a surgical shoe for fallen arches and tablets for indigestion. Her ambition was to do an advertisement for chocolate.

'Subliminal sexual desire,' she said. 'It's what everything's about these days, darlings.'

She giggled in disbelief and tossed her shaggy hair at Peter when she heard about the cat paintings. 'Oh – you're such a pseud, darling. But you can show me your silly etching any time you're in London.'

Beth envied Marina. She envied the way she clicked her fingers at sex, laughing and batting her false eyelashes at all the men in the pub. Beth wondered how it would feel to do it on a bale of blue velvet material – or on a sighing bed in the darkness of a London flat. Her stomach heaved at the image that came into her mind. She pressed her hand against her mouth and slowly the choking feeling went away. Love was red dresses and swirling music. A rainbow of dreams.

She wanted to tell Jess about the terror of those moments when the atmosphere in the Sweat Pit changed, grew quiet, expectant. The deepening breath of the young man beside her, knowing he was going to put his hands on her skin and how the horror would swoop through her chest. It didn't matter where it happened – the back seat of a cinema, the shelter of the sand dunes, the dark shadows in the back of a car.

'You're a raving lunatic,' Billy Brennan from dispatch had yelled after his one and only date with her. When he parked his car on Pier's Point, the sloping estuary jetty, and forced his hand inside her blouse Beth had released the handbrake. His frantic efforts to stop the car entering the water had been successful, but only just.

'You could have fucking drowned me.' He was unable to stop shaking as he drove her back to Main Strand Street.

'So I could.' Beth laughed her terror away. 'Imagine what a loss that would be to humanity.'

In the office the young women knotted scarves around their necks to cover love bites, slyly showing them off to their closest friends. Over coffee breaks and lulls in typing, Beth listened to their conversations, hoping to find a clue, something to reassure her that her fears were normal.

There had been others besides Billy Brennan. Men from Della Designs or those who danced with her in the Sweat Pit. But when Stewart took her for a ride on his new motorbike it should have been different.

Stewart had changed from the painfully shy boy she had known when she first came to Oldport. His slouching, lanky frame had filled out and his powerful hands no longer looked too big and awkward for his body. He was not handsome in an obvious way like Peter Wallace, with his honey skin and luminous eyes, but she liked how his strong square face came to life when he laughed.

'Since when did you join the Hell's Angels?' she asked when he arrived home one Saturday in leather and parked a motorbike outside the house.

'I've been saving for this for years.' His excitement was palpable as he stood beside the gleaming bike. 'What do you think?'

'A Harley Davidson – it's fantastic.'

'Want a ride?'

'What are we waiting for?'

He placed the helmet over her head and steadied her on the pillion.

She allowed herself to feel the speed, the roar of the engine throbbing beneath her, his body shielding her from the wind that rushed past, singing in her ears. She held tightly to his waist as they left Oldport and headed towards Skerries. Black suited him, she decided, unsure whether it was the novelty of the motorbike or the image of him, dark and vaguely threatening in his biker boots and jacket, that lifted her spirits. Impulsively, she tightened her grip, hugging him closer.

'Like it?' he shouted.

'Love it,' she shouted back.

He pressed her hands briefly and she felt a sudden shiver along her arms, as if his touch triggered some dormant emotion, rushing it free in the exhilaration of the moment.

The house was empty when they returned. Connie and Barry had gone to the cinema and would not be home until late.

She sat on the sofa with Stewart, mugs steaming on the coffee table, sharing a plate of biscuits and reminiscing about the first night they met.

'I can still picture you when you came into the house. As if you wanted to cut us in half with your eyes.' He smiled, speaking so low she could hardly hear him. 'God, you were terrifying, standing there in that skimpy coat with the rain running out of your hair. I think that was when I fell in love with you. Or maybe it was five minutes later when you smiled and I realised you were the most beautiful girl I'd ever seen… You must know how I feel, Beth. You *must*.'

She glanced down at her hands as they began to tremble, a faint vibration that she tried to control, tightening them into fists as he leaned towards her. He held her shoulders, his eyes warming her, drawing her to him. A waiting space opened between them, questions asked and answered in the silence. He slid his arms around her waist. She felt the hard contour of the sofa underneath her, the ridge at the edge pressing into the back of her knees.

'I'm crazy about you.' He muttered the words into her neck, his breath warm on her skin. She heard again the shyness in his voice. The effort it took to say what he needed to say. He kissed her, softly at first, then pressing more firmly, moving, searching for some response and she heard a moan deep in his throat, terrifying her with its force. Her breath shortened, catching dry.

'No! Leave me alone – leave me alone.' She pushed him away and sprang to her feet. Only when she saw the scratches on his face did she realise she had torn his skin.

'I'm sorry, Stewart… I'm terribly sorry… I can't stand it… You mustn't… Mustn't…' She gripped the arm of the sofa, willing the horror away.

For an instant he seemed dazed by her reaction. He tried to speak but couldn't get the words out. Abruptly, he stood up. 'I thought – ah, forget it. I've been a fool.' He grabbed his jacket and slung it over his shoulders. She could smell the new leather, hear the faint creak it made when he walked up the hall and out the front door.

Stewart should have been different. He was not Billy Brennan or the other faceless young men with whom she sought oblivion from the haunting past. Stewart was her friend. His passion should not threaten her. But his hard cold strength overwhelmed her, crushing her into nothing.

CHAPTER TEN

At first Celtic Reign played quietly, afraid their music would intrude too harshly into the world the sick man had created within himself. Crowded together in Connie's sitting room, the musicians filled their glasses with whiskey or snapped the tops off Guinness bottles. This small room with its glass ornaments and dried flowers in the window was the 'showing-off room', used only when visitors arrived. Cigarettes were lit, smoke spiralling upwards. Barry coughed and muffled the sound into his fist. The session was Connie's idea. At first he was irritable when she suggested it. He feared the musicians were humouring him. He didn't want them to see him like this – a sickly, dried-up shadow. She assured him they needed this time with him. They wanted to participate. She did not say 'in your dying', but the words hung there and Beth felt this understanding flow swift as a current between the two of them.

Before the musicians arrived, Connie eased him from their bed, exchanging his crumpled pyjamas for a pair of jeans and a shirt with neon flowers, a gaudy pattern that only succeeded in emphasising his wasted body. She seated him in the armchair so that his friends wouldn't notice how slowly he moved. Beth trimmed his beard. Like his hair it had grown sparse over the past few months and was cut into shape with a few snips.

As the glasses emptied the tempo of the music quickened, carrying its own momentum. Soon the musicians were lost in the notes and Barry became one with them, his eyes bright as he jigged his foot. For a short while he played the spoons. His hands were skeletal, the spoons rapping off his skinny knees. The sound reminded Beth of rattling bones. He called on her to dance. She was seized by a familiar embarrassment, reverting to the panic of a small child asked to perform in front of adults. She had not danced since that Christmas at Cherry Vale. Something painful caught in her memory and was released in the same instant. A sensation so familiar she hardly noticed it.

The fiddle player, Annie Loughrey, ran the bow over her fiddle, shouting, 'How about a reel, Beth? We'll go easy on you.'

Beth took off her shoes, but her feet still felt heavy, clumsy because she hadn't danced for so long. When the musicians yelled and stamped she was carried away by their enthusiasm. She was aware of Stewart watching her, his shoulder propped against the wall, a glass of beer in his hand. She moved to the increasing tempo, arms stiff by her sides, hair flying. Her legs kicked out, her shirt swirled. His eyes told her he liked what he saw before he looked away. Peter did not look away. When she finished dancing he swung her around and kissed her cheek.

Soon afterwards her father's shoulders slumped. The animation left his face. Connie moved swiftly towards him but he insisted on one more tune.

'Play "Carrickfergus", Annie. No one can stroke that tune the way you can.'

'It would draw tears from a stone,' agreed Blake Dolan, bending his head dolefully over his bodhrán.

Annie began to play. The young girl had long delicate fingers. The notes rose, a thin quavering lament. The thoughts of each person in the room seemed to fuse, achingly aware of the wasted man sitting so still in their midst.

Soon afterwards, the musicians left to play in The Fiddler's Nest, hearty in their farewells, not admitting that this was the last goodbye. Barry, equally anxious to keep up the pretence, joked them from the room.

'Cheer up, me darlin'. I've seen him looking worse on many a morning after a hard session in the Nest,' the bodhrán player joked with Beth at the front door. He patted the back of her head, as if he was already offering his condolences. Peter also said goodbye. He had a painting to finish before morning.

When Connie came downstairs after settling Barry for the night she poured a glass of whiskey and drank it neat, tilting her head back. Under the light Beth noticed grey roots fading into her black hair.

'You're going to collapse before this is over if you don't watch yourself,' Beth warned. 'Daddy should be back in hospital.'

'You know how he feels about hospitals,' replied Connie. 'Anyway, what can they do for him except prolong his agony? He wants to die here and as long as I can look after him I'll be with him.'

'Connie… does he realise… does he talk to you about it?'

'We've talked about it, yes.' Connie's voice was slightly slurred. Lipstick stained the glass, a bruised kiss clouding the rim.

'Then why won't he talk to me?' demanded Beth. Her eyes scalded with unshed tears but her father had not given her permission to cry. He always spoke to her about cheerful things and what he would do as soon as he recovered, meaningless plans that made her ashamed when their time together was so short. 'He keeps pretending he's going to get better.'

'He hasn't the words to tell you what he's feeling. It's different with me. We have no history, no regrets.'

Beth reached forward and squeezed her hand. 'Celtic Reign coming here was a terrific idea. I hope he's carried away on a stream of music.'

The older woman poured another drink, sipping it slowly this time. 'Sara should be here. I can't understand why your mother's being so stubborn. She's breaking his heart.'

Stewart came into the room. He took the empty glass from her and placed it on the table. 'You should try and get some sleep, Ma, while you have the chance.'

Connie's footsteps dragged wearily as she mounted the stairs and entered the bedroom where Barry dozed uneasily. It seemed so unfair, Beth thought – all that wasted time with Marjory and only a few short years with the woman he loved. An unforgivable love in the eyes of so many people, selfish in the demands it had made on their families, yet Beth didn't resent the brief happiness they'd known.

'I'm going for a walk.' Stewart took his leather jacket from a hook on the door. He glanced at the empty bottles, the overflowing ashtrays and stale sandwiches. 'I need some fresh air before I tackle this lot. Want to come?'

Beth's head throbbed from the stuffy heat in the room. She linked her arm in his as they turned without hesitation towards the estuary road. A light burned from one window in Havenstone. Peter's studio. He sometimes slept on the floor when he was working and everything was flowing in the right direction. An animal in his lair, she thought, comfortable where he dropped, stretched out on an old mattress he kept propped against the wall. Moonlight touching the half-finished canvases as he drifted off to sleep.

At Pier's Point a heron, caught in the glow of moonlight, lifted its wings and glided into the darkness.

'I had a dream about flying last night,' she said. 'I woke up thinking that that's the way it must be when you die – flying into the sky and everything down below becoming dimmer and dimmer until you're all alone in the dark.'

'Maybe you're flying through the dark to get to the light,' said Stewart.

'That sounds like something Jess would say.'

'How is she?'

'On her knees chanting litanies, I should imagine.'

Jess still wrote every week. Serene letters brimming with descriptions of silent meals, needlecraft, woodwork sessions, basketball practice, prayer vigils, meditation and contemplation. Sometimes, in the early hours when she was in the church praying, she felt herself lifted high on a wave of bliss so powerful it made her tremble in case it was ever taken away from her.

'I touch the core of my being,' she wrote. 'And God is there waiting for me to arrive.'

Beth believed this was magic-mushroom stuff. Smoke some grass and see the Lord. Or a state of mind brought about by overwork. Jess's daily work schedule read like the itinerary of a Siberian gulag.

In her last letter Beth wrote back: 'It must be wonderful to know yourself so well that when you feel the touch of happiness you can claim it as your right.'

Reading over what she had written she was puzzled by the meaning in her own words. She left them there, knowing Jess would understand.

'I don't know what to do.' She touched Stewart's arm as they stood on the pier.

'About Sara?' he asked.

'Yes. She won't come to the phone when I ring. I can't believe she'll let Daddy die without saying goodbye to him.'

'I'm sure she'll change her mind. Come on – let's go back. Standing here in the cold won't solve anything and we have a war zone to tidy up.'

Reluctantly, she left the pier and turned in the direction of Main Strand Street. As they approached the house she noticed the long car parked outside.

'A Mercedes!' Stewart stopped to examine the registration plate. 'Very flash.' He sounded impressed. 'Wonder who that belongs to?'

'I know the owner.' Beth was surprised at the calmness in her voice. She turned the key in the front door and entered.

Albert Grant had put on weight. She could see it on his face, under his chin. He stood in front of the fireplace, smiling. He had grown a moustache. It tickled her cheek when he hugged her. She was swamped in his warmth, the familiar scent of Old Spice and soap.

She forced herself to stand still until he released her.

'What the hell are you doing here?' she demanded.

'What a way to greet your uncle, love. I'm surprised at you,' Connie said reproachfully. She made an attempt to tidy bottles out of the way then stopped, embarrassed by the debris of the party.

'Well, I'm surprised too. He only comes to Dublin when he has something nasty to do. I'm just wondering what it is this time.'

'I came when Marjory told me the sad news. Poor Barry. A fragile grip on reality at the best of times.' He stared at Stewart, then back at Connie. 'I presume this young man is your son, Mrs McKeever?'

'He is indeed.' Beth saw her mouth tremble as Albert ignored Stewart's outstretched hand. A whistle shrilled from the kitchen: the kettle was boiling. She rose to her feet. 'Tea or coffee, Councillor?'

'Tea will be fine, Mrs McKeever.'

When she left the room he took off his jacket, easing his shoulders in circular movements. 'That's better. I've had a long drive. It's good to see you again, Beth, although I hoped we could have met under happier circumstances… Like a visit to your unfortunate mother.'

'I asked you a question and you still haven't answered it,' she replied. 'What are you doing here?'

'I think it's fairly obvious. I've booked into the Oldport Grand for the night. In the morning I've organised an ambulance to collect your father and take him home to Anaskeagh.'

Beth froze. 'No fucking way!'

'Beth!' Connie, horrified, stood in the doorway, a tray in her hands. 'I can't believe my ears. Shame on you.'

'I'm sorry, Connie. But he can't just suddenly appear and start taking over. He wants to take Daddy away.'

Connie placed the tray on the coffee table. She glanced fearfully towards the councillor and shook her head. 'I'm afraid there's some mistake, Councillor. Barry has no intention of going back to Anaskeagh.'

'Please, Mrs McKeever, don't make a scene,' he interrupted her smoothly. 'I'm only doing what is right and proper under the circumstances. This is not exactly the ideal environment for a sick man.' A smile touched his lips as he surveyed the room, raising his eyebrows at the sight of the empty whiskey bottle lying on the floor.

'Daddy isn't going anywhere,' Beth shouted. She was aware of Stewart holding her hand, trying to calm her down.

'Mr Grant, you can't just ignore what my mother is saying. Barry wants to stay here with us.'

'Young man, I mean no disrespect to your mother.' Albert gave a slight bow in Connie's direction and swept his gaze back to Stewart. 'But I need hardly remind you that she is not Barry Tyrell's wife. As the law stands she has absolutely no rights, no say, no decision.' His tone changed, became placating as he turned his attention back to Connie. 'Let's look at it this way, Mrs McKeever – you must be worn out looking after a sick man. I'm relieving you of the burden of responsibility—'

'She's worn out all right but that's the way she wants it,' Beth interrupted. 'He made her promise to be beside him when he… goes.'

Her uncle shook his head firmly. 'I'm afraid it's not that simple. Your father is coming home to Anaskeagh where he belongs. To be with the people to whom he belongs. With his wife's permission I've booked him into a private ward in the Anaskeagh Regional. He'll have the best of care and the chance to die peacefully, with dignity and surrounded by his own family.'

'Appearances!' Beth yelled. 'That's all you care about. Just because you're a county councillor – you don't give a tinker's curse about my father. Neither does she! She wouldn't even let Sara visit him.'

'Beth – calm down. I'm not having any arguments in my house when Barry is so ill. Tomorrow when he's stronger we'll let him decide what he wants to do.'

'I'm afraid not, Mrs McKeever. It is as I've stated. There will be no further arguments.' Albert Grant did not try to disguise his anger. 'In the morning you will come with me, Beth. You will do what a good daughter should do and look after your father instead of allowing outsiders to do it for you. As for you, Mrs McKeever, an ambulance will be at your house at nine in the morning. You can't deprive a dying man of his last opportunity to see his wife and daughter. If there are farewells to be made let them be made before then. I don't want to see you or your family near Anaskeagh at any stage. Is that clearly understood?'

CHAPTER ELEVEN

Barry Tyrell took a month to die. Once he was admitted to hospital the stoicism he had shown in Oldport deserted him. He snarled and spat and suffered his way through his final weeks until even Beth dreaded spending time with him in the small ward he called 'Death Row'. When his lips dried into cracked sores she swabbed them with wet cotton wool. She spooned cold drinks into his mouth and wrote the letters he dictated to Connie until his mind wandered, unable to concentrate. Then she composed them herself, escaping into the fresh air for a few minutes to post them. She read Connie's replies to him, taking the letters with her when she left the hospital in case Marjory found them. Twice his family were called to his bedside in the middle of the night and twice the doctors brought him back again. Lonely, resentful, frightened, he lingered on.

'Meddling bastards,' he raged. 'Why can't they let me die in peace? I'm spent, washed up. What good will it do to give me a few more days?'

Catherine O'Donovan said he was the most bad-tempered patient she had ever nursed. 'I've had some lulus in my time but he takes the biscuit. Poor devil.'

Every time the postman called, Beth expected a letter from Mrs Wallace informing her that she was fired. Twice a week she rang Stewart from the public phone at the hospital. She looked forward to hearing his voice, reassuring her that there was another world outside Death Row and its cocooned, glasshouse atmosphere.

Sara had grown tall and leggy. Why should this surprise Beth? Time hadn't stood still for her sister either, though Sara's face still held the same childlike contours, a little too much puppy fat on her cheeks and around her chin. A fringe almost covered her eyes and her long, blonde hair hung limply over her cheeks. Beth longed to gather it in her hands and twist it into a ponytail. Then, perhaps, she would know what Sara was thinking and how she felt about Beth's return.

Marjory's visits to the hospital were brief and businesslike. She talked to the ward sister and the doctor on duty. The nurses brought her cups of tea and biscuits. They wanted to know what new styles were in the boutique and were thrilled when she promised them a discount of ten per cent. Father Breen, doing his hospital rounds, blessed her and called her a saint in the truest sense of the word. Beth always left the ward as soon as her mother entered, ignoring the pleading look Barry gave her, the tight, dry grip of his fingers. He wanted her with him all the time. She resented the responsibility his dependence placed on her, longing to be back in Oldport, feeling guilty at the intensity of this need, knowing she would only be released when he was laid to rest.

So many changes to be absorbed. The First Fashion boutique added to the prosperous air of the town. Even Marina would be impressed, Beth decided, staring in the windows at mannequins with tousled curls dressed in glittery jumpsuits and wide-shouldered suits. A Chinese restaurant and a launderette had opened on River Mall. The old cinema, known as The Flea Circus, had been turned into a bingo hall. Maggie Hearn had sold her grocery store and a modern supermarket with chrome shelves and pale strips of fluorescent lighting stood in its place. Fresh pebbledash livened up the grey walls of the council houses on Fatima Estate. But Marjory had been determined to move and had bought one of the new houses being built on the site of the Emerald Ballroom.

'The next time you decide to honour us with your presence I'll have moved as far as possible from this slum your father forced me to live in,' she informed Beth soon after her arrival.

'I'm glad things worked out so well for you.' Beth attempted to soothe old wounds.

'Oh no, things didn't work out,' Marjory interrupted, her voice quickening. 'I made them happen. Despite everything!' She too had changed. The weight she had lost was emphasised by the ruffled curls framing her face and the width of her shoulder pads. Her sewing room was now a spare bedroom where Beth slept for the duration of her visit. The wardrobe, the den where monsters once crouched and waited in the darkness of child-hood fears, had been moved into the room. Standing on carved claws, in need of a good polishing, it looked curiously alien in its new surroundings but the smell of mothballs was instantly familiar. There had been no monster. Only the shadow of her uncle, vague and threatening. She had been four years old when she'd opened her eyes one night and seen him standing beside her bed, the wardrobe door open behind him. For an instant she thought he had been hiding inside and had jumped out to scare her. Four years of age... Maybe he'd come to her room before then. She had no memory. Only when she'd reached four did she understand the meaning of fear and she had carried it in front of her as a shield ever since.

No matter how often she tried to change the subject, his name ran like a magnetic thread through her mother's conversation. Since becoming a councillor he had galvanised the county council with his energy and dedication. A new primary school was being built. He had plans for attracting tourists into the town. He was the driving force behind the GAA. He was lobbying for funding to improve the town's sewage system.

'At least that should give him enough space to take a shite,' sneered Beth.

This remark was the end of the uneasy truce mother and daughter had tried to maintain since her return home. She was relieved they did not have to pretend any longer.

'How dare you use that kind of filthy language in my house.' Marjory glared at her. 'You're disgusting! Working in a factory certainly hasn't improved your manners. Your uncle may be a busy man but he never forgets his family. We wouldn't have anything if it wasn't for him.'

'Can we occasionally change the tune?' Beth tried to control her temper. 'I'm sick of hearing about St Albert, patron saint of the needy.'

'Then you can hear it again,' insisted Marjory. 'While your father was swanning around Dublin with his whore my brother took the time to sit down and help me draw up my business plan. He's financed my boutique, lock, stock and barrel. When Sara finishes her Leaving she's going to university, thanks to him. At least one of my daughters will be able to rise above the level of working in a factory.'

'What about me? What favours did he ever do for me?' Beth leaned towards her mother. 'Fuck all – that's what!'

'Stop it! Stop it… both of you.' Sara, who had been sitting between them, jumped to her feet. 'I'm sick of listening to the two of you going on at each other.' She turned furiously to Beth. 'At least we have peace when you're not here. If you can't stop fighting with Mammy I don't want you to come home ever again.' She ran from the room, slamming the door behind her.

'Satisfied?' demanded Marjory.

'It's strange,' said Beth. 'Daddy's dying and all we can do is say hurtful things to each other. I hoped it would be different when I came home but it's still exactly the same.'

'And who's to blame for that, may I ask?' Marjory lit a cigarette, inhaling deeply. 'It's too late for apologies, madam. Over four years too late. The only reason you're here is because your uncle insisted you do your duty.' She removed a flake of ash from her lip, appraising her daughter behind a haze of smoke. 'How do you think I felt? My daughter disappearing without a word and not even one visit the whole time. Not even for Christmas. You certainly gave the gossips plenty of ammunition—'

'So what did I have?' Beth interrupted. 'A boy or a girl – or was it twins?'

'You think it's so funny? Well, let me tell you something, miss. If it wasn't for Sara I wouldn't let you set foot in this house again. Any more smart remarks or language and you're out on your ear so fast you won't know what hit you. Do I make myself clear?'

'Crystal clear,' replied Beth. 'It's great to be home.'

Sara never stayed for long at the hospital. Her father's laboured breathing made her fidget and stare out of the window. His presence placed a burden upon her young shoulders that she was ill-prepared to carry. She made no effort to talk to Beth and spent most of her time in her bedroom.

Anaskeagh Head was still a forbidding challenge. One afternoon the sisters climbed to the summit. Goldie moved stiffly, limping slightly. Arthritis, Beth guessed. She rubbed his back, noticing grey hairs in his coat, pleased when he didn't pull away. Time had obviously healed his fear or brought him to terms with it. His breath grew quieter as he rolled over and offered his belly to be stroked. They followed a passage Sara had discovered on the slopes of the headland, almost overgrown with ferns and briars that clung to their jeans. It might have been used by sheep or maybe it had been created by the way the wind blew into the scrub, forcing it to grow naturally apart. It led them to Aislin's Roof, one of the biggest rocks Beth had ever seen, almost cavernous in its width and overhanging slant. Sara was unable to keep still. The camera Beth had sent to her for her twelfth birthday hung from her neck. She photographed birds in flight and a dead tree, twisted stunted limbs outlined against the sky.

The wind blew stronger as they climbed upwards and the sun, clearing the clouds for a few moments, struck against the granite rock, surrounding the girls in flickering walls of mica.

'This is what I miss most,' said Beth. She sat down and waved her hand at the peaks. 'Oldport is so flat. Just fields of vegetables and flowers – although Peter says I should enjoy it while I can. Soon it will be covered in houses.'

'Tell me about him. Is he a good painter?' Sara asked.

'How should I know?' She was taken aback at the suddenness of the question. 'Personally I don't like what he does. I can never figure it out.'

'Even when he paints you?'

'Especially when he paints me.' She laughed abruptly.

'Are you in love with him?'

'I certainly am not!' She was glad her sister wasn't looking at her. 'He's the most self-opinionated person I've ever met.'

'What about the whore who was living with my father? Tell me about her.' She turned and stared down at Beth, challenging her.

'You sound just like Marjory.' Beth was furious. 'Connie McKeever is not a whore and you'd better stop calling her one.'

Her sister shrugged and aimed her camera, moving closer to Beth, focusing on different angles of her face.

'Why did you run away and leave me?' she asked abruptly.

'Stop it, will you?' Beth shielded herself with her hands.

'Why? Why? Why?' Sara clicked on each word then ceased as suddenly as she had started. The camera dangled from one hand. A bemused expression settled over her face, as if she was trying to remember the question.

'You know why! All that shit with Charlie. Imagine calling a cane Charlie. When I think how terrified I used to be of it.'

Sara sat down beside her and flung her hair back in a sudden jerk. 'Did you break Uncle Albert's window?' she asked.

'No.' Beth's heart leapt. 'Which window?'

'The big bay one in the front. Someone broke it the night you went away.'

'Why would I want to do a daft thing like that?'

'I don't know. I'm just asking. You're always saying horrible things about him so I thought…'

'Well you thought wrong. It wasn't me.'

'If you say so.' She giggled suddenly, nervously fisting a hand in front of her mouth. 'Tell me about the whore's son. Do you fancy him too? Stewart. That's his name, isn't it?'

'Sara! Why are you behaving like this?' Beth's anger snapped. 'What's wrong with you?'

The young girl drew her knees to her chin and encircled them with her arms. Her hands were hidden under the loose sleeves of her jumper. The slate-grey shade drained her face of colour. Shapeless over her jeans, it was the most unattractive thing Beth had ever seen her wear. Sara was a circle within herself, projecting neither thought nor emotion until suddenly, without any change in her posture, she began to cry.

'Don't go back to Oldport,' she sobbed. 'There's no reason to go back to those people. You don't belong to them.'

'Why should I stay here? I'd smother if I had to live an extra minute in this one-horse town.'

'It's not so bad. We're somebody here. Mammy has her shop and we're moving to the new house soon. It'll be great, Beth. She wants you to work with her. She's afraid if she asks you'll say no.'

'Are you away with the fairies or what?' Beth was glad to have something to rebuff. 'Why don't we bring Charlie as well? Then we could all have a jolly old reunion.'

'It doesn't have to be that way, Beth, it doesn't. It was easier when you lived here – she didn't expect so much from me.' Sara's voice was husky. She coughed, trying to clear mucus from her throat. 'Please stay here… Please, Beth.'

'No!' She felt trapped by Sara's closeness, the guilt her sister aroused in her. 'I won't stay here and that's the end of it. Stop going on at me.'

'I should have known you wouldn't listen. You don't care about anyone but yourself – and that Peter Wallace. Cats' eyes, cats' fucking stupid eyes! I've never heard of anything so stupid in all my life.'

'Sara... what are you saying? I can't believe you're using such language.'

'Look who's talking. Anyway, I'm just telling the truth. I don't want you here – or him either. Why can't he just die and get it over with?' She began to shout, banging her fists off the grass.

'Don't worry,' Beth replied coldly. 'I'm sure he'll oblige us before long. Then we'll all be out of your precious way again – only he'll be gone for good. Your precious Uncle Albert hijacked him from the people who loved him and he allowed it to happen so that he could be with you.'

'So? Am I supposed to fall on my knees and thank him? He was the one who left in the first place. Just the same as you did, and you're leaving me again so you can be with your precious artist. You needn't write any more of your stupid letters. I never bother reading them.'

'Sara, please stop.' When Beth stroked her sister's shoulder she felt the slightest of tremors, almost a reflex, a nerve impulse. 'As soon as you want you can come to Oldport and live with me. You'll love it.'

'Lay off, will you?' Sara whipped back from her touch. 'I'm not a fucking dog. Perhaps that's just as well – you'd probably drown me if I was.'

For an instant Beth was too shocked to speak. Then she realised that there was nothing she could say, or wanted to say, that could erase the cruelty of her sister's remark. They did not speak as they descended the headland. As soon as they arrived home Sara entered her bedroom and slammed the door behind her.

One day, when Sara was at school, Beth looked inside the room they had once shared. Sara had painted the walls white. She had filled it with white veneer furniture, white curtains and a pale blue carpet. A large white bear was propped on a wicker chair, the only childish thing in this cold clinical room. Enlarged photographs hung on the walls. Shots of Fatima Parade, doorways, alleyways, open gates, starkly empty. The river running through the centre of the town had a sinister fury. It reflected the high octagonal tower with the clock face on River Mall. Sara had written 'Time Flows By' at the bottom of each photograph. Beth felt uneasy as she closed the door quietly behind her. She felt as if her presence had left a smudge on the pristine surroundings, like the twiggy footprints of a bird running over a surface of snow.

Barry Tyrell died in the middle of the night, suddenly and alone. By the time his family reached the hospital it was over. Sara did not want to see him. She sat outside the ward, a mug of tea untouched by her feet.

'I'll have nightmares,' she said. 'He's only a shell anyway.' She had knotted a bright red scarf at the neck of her jumper and nervously pulled at it, twisting it tighter. Her feet tapped rapidly against the floor, sending tremors through her legs. She seemed unaware of her skittish movements until Beth put her hand on her knees to calm her down. The younger girl's face was white, glistening with a sheen of perspiration. She swayed and slumped forward. Beth tried to press her head between her knees but Sara fended her off, struggling to remain conscious.

'I have to get away from this place.' She walked down the corridor, almost running as she neared the lifts. On the tiled corridor her boots clacked loudly, red, the same shade as her scarf. She stopped briefly to speak to Catherine O'Donovan, then hurried on again.

'Poor little Sara. She's very upset.' Catherine sat down beside Beth and handed her a mug of hot tea. 'No matter how well prepared you think you are it's always a shock when someone you love dies. God bless him, he's at peace at last. Have a good cry if you feel the need.'

Beth leaned into the crisp white uniform to be hugged. The hospital was silent. The small hours when death comes quietly. She didn't feel like crying but the solid feel of the nurse's arms comforted her.

'I'll phone Jess first thing in the morning and tell her the sad news,' said Catherine.

'I miss her something awful. I wish she could be here now.'

'We all do.' Catherine sighed. 'But as long as she's happy that's what counts.'

Her mother and uncle were still inside the ward, making decisions. Beth wondered if she should try to find her sister. The effort of moving was too great. She stared dully at the opposite wall. She must feel something. There had to be certain emotions suitable for the occasion.

Exhaustion. She was floating on a wave of exhaustion. Her father's death had given her permission to be tired.

His coffin gleamed on the altar steps. Voices murmured the responses. The silence of transubstantiation was disturbed by someone coughing at the back of the church. The Eucharist bell jingled. Everyone bowed their heads except Beth, who stared woodenly at the altar. At communion the congregation held back, making space for the Tyrell family to lead the procession to the altar rail. Father Breen stood waiting, the host upheld in his hand. Marjory walked slowly towards him, sharp and dramatic in high heels and a black suit with impeccable shoulder pads.

'Move,' whispered Sara, standing up to follow Beth.

'I'm not receiving.' Beth shifted her knees, allowing her sister to pass. Her uncle slid into the space vacated by Sara.

'Have you no respect for your father's memory?' he asked, his voice low but commanding. 'Stand up at once and go to the altar.'

'No.'

'Do as I say!'

'Why? God doesn't exist.' She hissed the words into his ear. 'He's a fake – just like you.'

She wondered if the tabernacle would shatter. If blood would flow from the Eucharist in a tidal wave of outrage. Would the flame from the sanctuary lamp gutter and die? Blasphemy was a sin that marked the soul of the sinner with an indelible brand – Sister Clare had warned them in First Year. Her uncle's mouth opened, shocked.

'May God in his mercy forgive you. You have disgraced the memory of your dead father.' He bowed his head and moved past her.

The congregation rose respectfully to its feet and followed him.

CHAPTER TWELVE

It was good to be back in Oldport, like coming home, thought Beth, not sure whether she should feel sad or happy at this realisation. Much to her surprise Mrs Wallace informed her that she would be working directly under her. Away from cigar smoke and the grumbles of the sales manager, life was good, provided she didn't think about Sara and the tears she had shed on Anaskeagh Head. Or the silent phone calls that had haunted her since her return. They came late at night when she was getting ready for bed, always around the same time. She dreaded the eerie silence as she waited for someone to speak. She confided in Stewart one evening when he returned from a motorbike rally in Skerries. He believed they were obscene phone calls and should be reported. She disagreed. Obscenity was heavy breathing. Fear and control. Ugly suggestions and demands. This was different. An invisible presence, wraithlike, holding on, trembling at the brink of words.

'I know it's Sara.'

'Why don't you go home and see her?'

'I can't... not yet.'

'You've more important things to do, I suppose.' He made no effort to hide his jealousy. 'Surprise me and tell me he's finally finished those paintings.'

'Almost.' She did not want to discuss the Saturday sessions with anyone, particularly Stewart, who always looked sceptical whenever Peter's name was mentioned. He seldom went to Havenstone any more.

'What exactly is he doing?' Stewart asked. 'Please educate me on the finer aspects of art.'

She tried to explain about the Cat-astrophic Collection and watched his eyebrows climb.

'I'll say this for him, he's feeding you a great line in bullshit,' he interrupted her angrily. 'And there's only one reason you're falling for it.'

'It's not like that,' she protested. 'You've got it all wrong.'

'Have I? What have I got wrong? The bullshit or the fact that you fancy him like mad.'

'Both!' she snapped. 'I'm too busy to fancy him – or anyone.'

'Busy doing what?' he asked. 'All you ever do is work. No one expects you to run Della Designs single-handedly.'

He lifted his arm as if he meant to put it around her shoulders, then let it drop to his side. 'Everyone falls in love sooner or later. For some of us it's sooner…' He paused and cleared his throat. When Beth stared stonily ahead, he left the sentence unfinished.

The final painting was called Cat-holic.

'Sacrifice,' said Peter, smiling in his know-it-all way as he stood in front of her. 'No more cats. This is about martyrdom. Washed in the blood of the Lord.'

'I'm an atheist,' she retorted. 'Shouldn't you be talking to Jess about this?'

'I'd have to carry her over the convent wall. She has a steely vocation, unlike my father, who jumped that wall the first chance he got.'

He occasionally spoke to her about Bradley Wallace, a frail, elderly man, who had entered a monastery in his youth but left when he'd realised he lacked the necessary discipline to live the life of a monk. He'd grown vines in the garden at the back of Havenstone and had collected art, specialising in painting of martyred saints. Peter had been twelve when he died. The vines perished in a frost soon after his death and wild ivy crawled across the vineyard. His paintings had also disappeared. Della needed new machinery for Della Designs and what was the sense in all those paintings gathering dust when she had a factory to run?

Peter raised Beth's arms above her head and linked her fingers together. Her body felt as if it was suspended by chains. Her heart began to pound when he moved closer. She sensed his excitement, felt his body pressing lightly but insistently against her. She was aware of his strength and also of her vulnerability as he drew her arms higher and her breasts tautened, her hips thrusting forward involuntarily. Her face tilted upwards, their lips almost touching, before he moved away and picked up a sketchpad.

'Try and hold the pose, Beth. Sublime ecstasy, that's what I want to capture. I want to lift your body into the celestial light.'

'Stewart's right. You do talk a load of bullshit.' Her eyes challenged him. Her arms ached with the effort of holding them aloft.

'What's the problem, Beth? I'm trying to paint you, not rape you.' Peter put down the sketchpad and walked towards her, lowering her arms, then resting them on his shoulders. When she tried to pull away his grip tightened. 'Who are you, Beth Tyrell? What's the big mystery behind those eyes? Beautiful girl, no boyfriend. No existence outside the walls of a boring factory. I can understand my mother being a workaholic, but you're too young – too gorgeous – and I want to kiss you. What have you got to say about that?'

She resisted for an instant, drawing back from the pressure of his mouth. Then, with a low sigh of surrender, she kissed him back. His hand touched her waist, sliding inside her blouse, confidently moving towards her breast. Her heart pounded, suffocating her with its fury. She felt him slipping away, vanishing in front of her eyes. The walls of the studio folded in and crushed her into darkness where nothing existed except the sound of heavy breathing and the touch of flesh stealing away her senses. She struggled, flailing wildly, dragging herself back from the edge of memory.

'Leave me alone! Don't you dare touch me… Don't you dare!' Ashen-faced, almost hysterical, she stared at him, his face swimming into view again, angry, puzzled, then frightened when she began to weep violently.

'I can't. I just can't!' She covered her eyes, no longer able to look at him. 'I have to go… You don't understand… No one does. Leave me alone!'

She understood now why she had never been jealous when he talked about his girlfriends. The women he loved briefly had helped her to play a waiting game. To deny her fear. To dream that when the right time came it would be different with him. She would experience the sensations that made the women in the office coy and giggly when they discussed their boyfriends. She knew the names they called her. Frigid Brigid. Arctic Knickers. She deserved them – her skin lifting in horror, her body clenched, rejecting even him.

The following weekend, four months after her father's death, she returned to Anaskeagh to visit Sara.

CHAPTER THIRTEEN

Since leaving Dublin the rain had been falling steadily. Beth shouldered her rucksack and left the fuggy heat of the bus, crossing Turnabout Bridge and heading towards the town. The river was swollen, swirling high under the bridge, carrying the sheen of bogs and the dead chill of underground caverns. In the early spring old Sam Burns had died in this river. Some said it was an accident. Too much red biddy and a belief that he could walk on water. Others believed it was suicide, an old man tired of ranting. The smell of chips made her mouth water. Through the steamy windows of the corner building on River Mall she saw Hatty, busy as ever on a Friday night. She opened the door and joined the queue.

'Would you take a look at what the cat dragged in!' Hatty waved a vinegar container at her. 'And a drowned one at that. I must say you picked a strange weekend to come home considering your mother only went away last night.'

Startled, Beth stared at her. 'What do you mean? Where's she gone?'

'Ah now – that's a good question. There's many around here would like an answer to it.' She worked fast at moving the queue along, talking non-stop over her shoulder. 'She's kicking up her heels with the rest of them chancers in the Anaskeagh Chamber of Commerce. They're supposed to be at a conference in Blackpool finding out about tourism but it could be Timbuktu for all we know.'

'Blackpool? Are you serious?'

'Taking that lot off on a "fact-finding mission" is enough to make a donkey stop laughing.' Hatty, as sturdy and round as a small barrel, was an insatiable gossip. Barry used to claim she could draw secrets from a corpse.

She lifted a pan of sizzling chips, expertly pinching one between her fingers, then plunged them back in for extra crispness. 'It's not that I'd begrudge your mother the break. It was time for the poor widow to kick up her heels after the terrible spell she's had – and who is Hatty Beckett to even mention the word "junket"?'

'Where's Sara?' Beth asked.

'You'll find her at Cherry Vale.'

'Did my uncle go on the trip?'

Hatty nodded emphatically. 'He organised it. He wants to bring the tourists here to the Western seaboard to enjoy our golden beaches and quaint little town. And why not? It's time to put Anaskeagh on the map and there's no better man knows how to organise a junket – sorry, fact-finding mission – than Albert Grant.'

Beth's aunt was watching television and eating chocolates when she arrived at Cherry Vale.

'Hatty Beckett would be wise not to go bandying words like "junket" around the place.' May was not amused when Beth repeated the conversation. 'How long are you staying this time, may I ask?'

'Only the weekend. I'm so busy.'

'Well, you're back in Anaskeagh so you can just ease your foot off the pedal. You can sleep in Conor's room but don't touch anything. He gets very upset when he comes home from university if his things aren't exactly the same as he left them.' May smiled her wafer-thin smile at Beth. 'Why didn't you come back for your sister's show?'

'What show?'

'The nuns, for reasons best known to themselves, decided to show off her photographs. Not that I'm one of Sara's fans. I told her so, straight out. She had the nerve to make Fatima Estate look like a slum after all the great work Albert did on the houses.'

Sara appeared to be asleep but she opened her eyes immediately when Beth entered the room.

'What are you doing here?' she asked, limply lifting her head before letting it fall back again on the pillow.

'I came to see you.' Beth sat gingerly on the edge of the bed. 'May told me about your exhibition. Congratulations. I'm really sorry I missed it.'

'It wasn't anything much. Just an old school thing…' Shadows smudged the skin under her eyes. She yawned and pulled the blankets over her chin. 'Go away, Beth. I'm too tired to talk to you.'

'Just tell me first – are you ringing me at night and then not speaking?'

'Don't be so stupid!' Sara muttered then turned her face to the wall. 'Why would I waste my time making phone calls to *you*? Let me go back to sleep.'

By the following morning the rain had eased to a light drizzle. May applied a slash of lipstick to her mouth before driving off to Anaskeagh to have her hair set. Her statuesque figure was encased in a purple suit. A blouse frothed lace at her neck. She intended dropping Sara off at First Fashion to help in the boutique. If Beth wanted a lift into town she could come with them. Beth shook her head. She planned to visit O'Donovan's farm.

Catherine was still in her nurse's uniform when Beth arrived. Night duty in the casualty ward always left her exhausted. Beth made her a mug of tea and persuaded her to go to bed. She promised to feed the fowl and fetch Frank from the hill field when the vet arrived to look at a sick horse.

The day passed swiftly. Frank and Jess's brother, Bernard, arrived in at noon for lunch. A pot of stew simmered on the range and Beth smiled, remembering how, when the O'Donovan children had complained of hunger, Catherine used to wave her hand towards the pot and say, 'You know where it is, honeybuns. God gave you your hands for a reason. Help yourselves.'

The men were joined briefly by Sheila O'Neill, who had cycled over from Anaskeagh. Sheila was engaged to Bernard. They planned to build a bungalow on the farm. She still had jittery eyes and the same compulsion to talk about her sisters, who were coming home for the wedding. She took off her engagement ring and showed it to Beth.

'Twist it towards your heart and make a wish,' she said.

Beth twisted the ring and pretended to wish before handing the ring back to Sheila.

'How's Nuala?' she asked. 'Is she coming home for the wedding as well?'

'I don't know.' Sheila looked away, embarrassed. 'I'd like her to come but you know my mother. Anyway, she's mad busy working in this craft place. It's some kind of co-operative that these women run in a basement. They make pots and candles, that sort of thing. Nuala sells the stuff for them.'

'Did she ever get married?'

'Married!' Bernard held up his hands as if warding off an evil word. 'The only man in her life is the kiddie she had after she was in the traces with Derry Mulhall. She's one of those feminists. A holy terror she is when it comes to us poor men.' He winked at Beth. 'What about you? Are you stepping out with one of them jackeens or saving yourself for the local lads?'

'That's for me to know and you to find out,' retorted Beth, slipping easily into the familiar banter of the O'Donovan household.

Sheila was working in the new supermarket. She listed the recent engagements, marriages and births that had taken place in Anaskeagh. When Beth mentioned Oldport, Sheila checked her watch and said she had to run, bored by events that had no relevance outside the circle of her own life.

By evening the rain had cleared and the countryside was bathed in sunshine. Goldie lay on the lawn in Cherry Vale, his head flopped between his paws, looking reproachfully at them through the open French doors. May fluttered anxiously around the table, her bare arms quivering as she ladled mashed potatoes, carrots and peas. Two slices of roast beef glistened on each plate. She talked throughout the meal. She had always been a talker but Beth was surprised at how aimless her conversation had become: rambling monologues that relayed the minutiae of her daily routine and the demands that were made on a busy councillor's wife. Her nieces were not expected to participate in the conversation, only to nod at appropriate intervals.

Sara moved her food around, chewing continuously on a piece of meat, as if the effort of swallowing was too great. Her aunt leaned across the table and coyly tapped her knuckles with a fork.

'I heard about your latest conquest, you sly puss.' The young girl looked up from her plate, puzzled. 'What do you mean, Aunty May?'

'Ben Layden!' She glanced over towards Beth. 'His family own the new supermarket. I was talking to his mother last week and she spilled the beans.'

'Baked were they?' asked Beth.

May ignored her. 'He fancies our little Sara but she gives him the cold shoulder, don't you, you heartless vixen? It won't do, my dear. It won't do at all. You can't dazzle the poor boy with your wiles and then pretend not to notice him.'

'I don't pretend—'

'Every boy needs a little push to get him moving in the right direction. And he's a shy one, God bless him.' May's eyebrows arched, coy slivers of brown pencil. 'I'll have to arrange a little tête-à-tête to get the two of you together. More carrots, Beth?'

'No thank you, May.'

'Eat up now and none of your nonsense.' She ignored Beth's protesting hand, ladling another helping of vegetables onto her plate. 'You're far too scrawny for your age. A man likes a girl he can cuddle and there's little to cuddle on a broomstick.'

'I saw Conor at a dance in Dublin a while back,' said Beth, staring at her aunt's flushed face. 'When did he start drinking so heavily?'

May's smile disappeared. 'What do you mean? Conor's never broken his Confirmation pledge.'

'Oh! Then maybe it was drugs. This fellow came up and asked me to dance. He vomited over my shoes. Suede. Such a waste. I had to throw them away. I was sure it was Conor – but under such circumstances it was hard to be certain.'

'I'm quite sure it wasn't my son,' May replied grimly. 'Conor is a student of law. I don't imagine he's in the habit of frequenting the same dance halls as common factory girls.'

'She's unbelievable. Yap, yap, yap,' Beth muttered when their aunt went into the hall to answer the phone. 'She never shuts up for a minute.'

'She's lonesome with the boys gone all the time,' said Sara. 'And Uncle Albert's so busy he's never here.' She swayed, slumping forward. Sweat broke out on her upper lip.

'What's wrong?' Beth half stood but Sara lifted her hand and pushed her back. An action that was surprisingly strong, considering her crumpled position. 'I've got a stomach cramp,' she gasped. 'I think I've picked up a bug.'

'Were you sick during the night?'

Sara nodded and rose unsteadily to her feet, holding the edge of the table for support. For an instant, as she bent forward, she was silhouetted against the evening sun. It shone through the fabric of her dress, pale blue chambray, soft creased pleats falling loose to her ankles. Her stomach, high and swollen, stretched tight. Her small full breasts rested on the curve.

It was so obvious. Beth wanted to fling the reality far back into the cold reaches of her mind. Her eyes, seeking relief, stared down at the linen tablecloth and almost immediately came back to Sara. Dust motes danced in the shaft of light, shimmering energy. It had to be her imagination. Sara had just turned fourteen, a schoolgirl who played with her dog and took strange photographs of empty lanes and time running away. The young girl moved from the light, oblivious of what she'd revealed, moving heavily, her hand reaching instinctively to touch the small of her back. She opened the door and disappeared from view. Beth tried to detain her but her throat was too raw for words. Her breath wheezed, carried on a wild sob.

The phone call ended and May was back, annoyed at people's lack of consideration, ringing at meal time when they knew her husband was away and wouldn't be able to deal with their problems.

'Sara's gone upstairs to lie down for a while,' Beth said.

'Poor child, it's probably her monthlies. I used to be cursed with them myself when I was her age. You really are a bold little brat, Beth, teasing me about Conor.'

'I'll go and check if she's all right.' Beth ran up the stairs, her heart pounding at the thought of confronting her sister.

The bedroom was empty. When she ran downstairs May was standing in the hall, her jacket slung over her shoulders. 'Is she all right? Does she want me to bring her up a hot-water bottle before I leave?'

'No, she's sleeping.'

'That'll do her good. I'm off to play bridge with the ladies. I should be back about midnight.'

As the puzzle pieces slotted into place one by one Beth realised she was not surprised. The signs had been obvious yet she had deliberately ignored them. No, surely not deliberately. How could she have guessed what was incomprehensible? Sara had put on weight, a fine layer of puppy fat softening her face. Her strange behaviour, sudden outbursts. Hormones. Moody teen blues. An explanation for everything except the truth. Sara crying on Anaskeagh Head because there was no one to tell. Sara on the phone, panicked, desperate, silent. She had dismissed her suspicions, refused to give them any credence because she wanted to be with Peter Wallace, playing word games, stupid, stupid word games with no meaning. Images on canvas – the mirror of the soul.

CHAPTER FOURTEEN

Goldie had disappeared from his position outside the French windows. The gate at the foot of the back garden had swung open. A narrow road ran along the back of Cherry Vale with hedgerows on either side. At one end it swept around to join the main road leading into Anaskeagh. The other route led to the headland. Beth followed the curve until it ended on the bottom slopes in a boundary of ash and willow. It was easy to find an opening through the thicket. Soon she was walking over clumps of stubby grass that squelched under her feet. Boggy moisture seeped into the thin soles of her trainers and the bottom of her jeans. This was a spent area that had been flattened and dug, leaving trenches of bog water and scaly steps hacked into the earth.

She strained her ears, hoping that Goldie would bark. The moon became visible, a pale disc that lit the trail, but once she moved from the path the dense shadows of rock and gorse were almost impossible to penetrate. She switched on the torch she'd grabbed from the garage before leaving Cherry Vale. Slate-grey clouds banked behind Anaskeagh Head. The peaks, the rocks, the black jagged trees rising above her were fleeting impressions, a nightmare glimpsed through a swirl of descending mist.

Sara crouched under Aislin's Roof. She was kneeling, her stomach thrust forward, the pale blue dress rucked around her waist. Goldie lay beside her. He whimpered, licking her ankles, shivering. This was the picture Beth absorbed when she finally stumbled upon them, illuminated in the glow of the torch. A tableau that was to imprint itself forever on her mind.

'I'm here, Sara.' Beth collapsed on the grass. Her heart hammered with panic and exertion.

Her sister did not look up. She seemed incapable of focusing on anything other than the pressure that fused her body into the downward contraction and tore a shuddering gasp from her. Her hands gripped the edge of the rock. When the moment passed and her body relaxed she began to sway backward and forward. The sound she made, a humming monotone, seemed to rise through the roof of her mouth, almost inaudible.

'Are you having the baby? Tell me what's happening to you.' Beth put her arms around Sara. She sobbed with terror because she didn't know what to do. She lifted Sara's hair, pushed it back from her face, wiped her hand across her sister's cold, damp forehead. The swaying movements ceased. Sara stared at her. No recognition flickered in her eyes as she pushed Beth away. She crawled into the shelter of the overhanging rock and crouched in the darkness.

'No one can see me.' She ground the words between her teeth. 'No one can see me... no one... no one can see me.'

'Are you having the baby now?' Beth repeated, trying to follow her. She shone the torch under the slant of rock. Framed in the glow, Sara hunkered against the sloping wall, cornered. Her body was in spasm, her breathing heavy and fast. Goldie barked, responding to her panic. Mindlessly she touched his head, shushing him. He pawed the earth, scattering damp muddy clay. Beth noticed he was digging in a hole that was already partly dug.

'Sara, I'm here with you... it's Beth. I've found you... everything's going to be all right... come out from there and let me help you—'

'Get away... get away! Don't come in here... get away,' Sara hissed. She pressed her face into her knees and waved her hands outwards as if she was pushing against an invading force.

As Beth came to terms with the unfolding tragedy she realised that Sara had not just fallen into the earth to give birth. Aislin's Roof had been carefully chosen. The rock, embedded on a flat shelf of earth, offered shelter and protection. But Sara was restricted by the low level of the ceiling and the tight space into which she had wedged herself. If Beth was to help her sister she must concentrate only on what was about to happen, not on what had happened. Softly she coaxed Sara forward.

'You should be out here. Sara… it's safe out here. no one can see you… it's the best place to be.' She reached out one hand, continuing to talk softly, concentrating the beam of the torch on the ground in front of her, using it to beckon the young girl forward.

Clouds parted. The moon shone on Sara's upturned face. She leaned back into the rough grass. Her elbows supported her weight. She drew her knees forward, tensed her feet, arched her body like a bow then sank again into the earth. Time had ceased to have any meaning. Beth had no idea how long she crouched there, comforting Sara when she screamed, waiting for each spasm to pass and bring her sister to that final, terrifying moment. When Sara screamed again, the sound was different, more primal, and Beth knelt in front of her, spontaneous actions, intuitive knowledge. She reached into the dark space between Sara's legs and her hands felt something moist, solid.

'Sara. I've touched the baby's head, push again, it's coming – coming – push, you have to push harder, Sara, push!'

The young girl looked outwards, unseeing, her eyes opaque with terror. Beth sensed her travelling beyond the moment, her mind moving away even as her body pulsed and prepared to give life. A sundering cry was forced from her – a hard cry of denial. Beth placed her hands over the emerging head and drew her sister's child into the moonlight. Still kneeling, she held the baby in her arms. She ran her hands over the tiny frame, hair slicked smooth with blood and mucus. She touched the smooth incision between the baby's thighs. A thin wriggling body that could slide so easily to the ground.

'It's a girl, Sara,' she whispered.

'Give it to me.' Sara's voice was hoarse. She lay still, her legs splayed, milky white in the angled glow of the torch. Blindly, refusing to look, she allowed Beth to lay the child on her stomach. She shuddered at the contact. Her movements were slow, trance-like.

'Cut the cord,' Sara cried. 'Cut it quick. In there – under the rock. The bag, get the bag.'

In the gap under the rock Beth discovered a white plastic bag. Inside it she found a towel, cotton wool, pieces of ribbon and sanitary towels. Her chest knotted when she saw Marjory's dressmaking scissors. They clanged against the handle of a small shovel from the bronze companion set her mother kept beside the fireplace. When she cut the cord, instinctively using the ribbons to clamp it at either end, her sister's head flopped sideways, as if someone had released her from the pull of an invisible string.

The placenta came away. A rippling, muscular tremor passed through Beth's hands when she placed them on Sara's abdomen. A fusion of smells rose around her: blood, excrement, perspiration – bodily emissions that had swept this tiny life into existence. She needed water. She had seen it in films, steaming cauldrons of boiling water. She needed to clean Sara and stem the flow of blood. She needed blankets. It was cold on Anaskeagh Head and the wind was rising. Sara appeared to be drifting in and out of consciousness. Her body was flat, as if it were being absorbed into the grass. The baby, now wrapped in the towel, lay in her arms. Each time she cried, Sara started awake and gazed with blank eyes at the tiny bundle. When her sister tried to take the baby, she kicked out with such ferocity that Beth froze, afraid a wrong word or movement would send her over the edge and out of reach.

'We have to leave here, Sara. Can you try and sit up?'

Dully, Sara pulled herself upright. The movement disturbed the child, whose mouth puckered as she turned her face inwards towards the young girl's chest.

'Monster… Monster!' Sara screamed suddenly. Her free hand scrabbled in the darkness.

'Stay easy.' Beth tried to hold her but Sara drew back from her and, in the instant before the blow was struck, Beth saw her upraised hand, the stone clenched in her fist.

'No! Sara, no, don't!' She flung herself across her sister's knees, knocking her hand sideways. The blow lost its force and scraped against the side of the child's forehead. The startled wail – a shrill, outraged cry – reminded Beth of Goldie, scrabbling frantically up the side of the bath.

'Leave me alone… I have to destroy the monster's baby,' Sara sobbed, flailing out.

'Listen to me.' She forced Sara's hand backwards until it was twisted behind her back. The stone fell with a soft thud. 'I'm here. I'll help you. It's your baby girl, Sara. You can't harm her. Calm down! I'll take care of the two of you.'

The baby continued to cry. Beth was terrified in case she fell from Sara's arm or was flung against the rock. 'Give her to me, Sara. You must rest… sleep.'

'Fucking monster!' Sara began the familiar rocking movements, still squeezing the child.

'She's a beautiful baby, Sara. They'll find her if you bury her here. Look at Goldie. Tomorrow the dogs will come and dig her up. Everyone will know you killed your baby. Mammy will know and Uncle Albert—'

'Oh, Jesus.' Sara rocked faster. Her face twisted in a grimace, distorted. 'You left me here… You left me all alone! Bitch! Get away from me.'

'Sara, listen! I'll hide the baby. I'll hide her in a place where no one will ever find it. Give her to me, Sara. This is our secret.'

Beth's voice lulled her, controlling Sara as she lifted the baby into her arms. She stood up, her legs cramping, pins and needles causing her to stumble when she tried to walk.

'I'll be back soon… stop crying, Sara. Everything's going to be all right.'

It was almost eleven o'clock, only an hour since she'd found Sara. She tried to imagine the terror that had sent her sister crawling like an animal under a rock to give birth and then try to get rid of the child she had been forced to carry. The baby made a snuffling noise as if she was having breathing difficulties. Beth pressed the corner of the towel against the wound. She shone the torch on the tiny face, the withered blue flesh. Panicking, she wondered if she should baptise her because she would surely be dead by the time she was discovered. It seemed hypocritical to chant words she didn't believe. If she was wrong and there was a merciful God waiting to receive this child then a meaningless ritual should not hinder her progress into the light.

If she had allowed Sara to kill her, a swift merciful blow that would have crushed the fragile skull, their secret would be resting under Aislin's Roof, slowly decomposing into the earth. How many babies born in the same secret desperation were mouldering in fields and ditches and rivers, alive only in the minds of those who had shared their brief existence? Yes, Sara would have suffered, remorse ebbing and flowing through her life. But there would have been an ending; a secret in the shade of Aislin's Roof. Instead, Beth was unleashing a story that was going to have so many consequences. The police could come to their house and arrest Sara, arrest them both. And if the baby died they would stand in the dock accused of murder, their lives over before they'd even got used to living them. Yet she also knew that this frail child had to live or they would never be able to move forward from this terrible night. Her legs juddered as she pushed her way through the narrow trail, treacherous with unseen briars and moss. The path reached a fork, dividing sharply to the left. This was a little-used trail, leading away from the boggy slopes and onto firmer ground. A trail she had travelled many times with Jess when they used to take a shortcut to the farm. She beamed the torch, keeping it low in case it was noticed. Not that she expected to see anyone. Anaskeagh Head was too rough and formidable to attract young couples seeking privacy.

At first, her concern had been to escape from Sara and her rage. The decision to go to O'Donovan's farm only crystallised when she reached the dividing fork. A light shone in the front porch. Early risers, the family usually went to bed around ten o'clock – except for Catherine, who was on night duty.

In the barn Beth pulled an empty sack loose from the bundle on the floor. Next door in the stable she heard the sick horse coughing. It seemed incredible that on this same day she had fed chickens and walked to the hill farm to call Frank O'Donovan when the vet arrived. She removed the towel and wrapped the baby loosely in the coarse sacking. She laid the bundle in the centre of the porch and knocked hard on the front door. When an upstairs light was switched on she slipped silently back down the lane.

She heard the door opening, voices raised. Her chest ached where the baby had rested. She blended into the night, murmuring. Goodbye... goodbye... goodbye.

CHAPTER FIFTEEN

Sara was slumped against the rock, her hands covered in clay, when Beth returned. She didn't speak as Beth coaxed and supported her to her feet. They descended slowly, Beth half-carrying her, their feet slipping, thorns tearing their clothes, not noticing until they reached the back garden of Cherry Vale. The knowledge that her aunt's car would soon be pulling into the driveway filled Beth with terror as she helped Sara into bed. She lifted her dress over her head, noticing with growing horror the seeping bloodstains. She sponged her, crooning words without meaning.

'Why are you always following me around?' Sara spoke for the first time since they'd left the headland. Her voice shook, gaining strength. She flung her head from side to side. 'Leave me alone – do you hear me? Leave me alone.'

Beth slumped on the edge of the bed. 'Sara, I have to tell you—'

'No!' The young girl began to tremble. Her eyes slanted upwards until only the whites were visible. 'I buried it… deep in the clay… dead in the clay.' She fell back against the pillow, holding Beth's arm in a vice-like grip.

'Sara, that's not true. Talk to me. We have to talk about this.'

'Our secret.' Her grip tightened. 'Promise. Don't tell. We'll forget… don't tell… don't! It's done. Swear to God you won't tell… ever. Swear it to me.'

'I swear.' Beth began to sob, her body swaying in terror. She stayed by her sister's side throughout the night. The hall door closed. She listened to May's heavy tread on the stairs. The luminous hands on the alarm clock moved into the small hours. Sara never stirred. Her breathing was so shallow that Beth held her own breath until she made out the faint rise and fall of her sister's chest.

Towards morning Sara's temperature began to rise. When she tossed the bedclothes from her shoulders the metallic smell of blood was so strong that Beth recoiled. She sponged her down again, horrified by the amount of blood she was losing. When May left for Mass, Beth washed the dress and put the sheets into the washing machine. The sound of footsteps crossing the landing alerted her. Towels lay on the floor of the bathroom, covered in bloodstains. Sara had returned to the bedroom and was on her knees, frantically rubbing the mattress with a facecloth.

'Leave it, Sara,' Beth pleaded. 'I'll turn the mattress. It's going to be all right.'

'No one must know.' Frantically Sara kept rubbing, beating Beth's hand away.

'Stop it!' Beth screamed. 'You're driving me crazy.'

Desperately she lifted her sister off her knees and half-dragged her back into bed. Sara moaned softly but did not move. Her arms felt rigid; skin, bone, sinew and muscle rejecting any form of comfort. They heard footsteps on the stairs, the bathroom door opening, the startled exclamation. May, finding the bedroom door locked, rapped loudly.

'Sara, open the door immediately. What's going on? What happened to my towels?'

'It's all right, May,' Beth shouted. 'She's trying to sleep. I'll be out in a minute.'

'Open the door immediately. Do you hear me?' She knocked a second time, louder, prolonged. 'This is my house, remember? I don't allow locked doors.'

Beth tried to ease herself from Sara's grip but her sister held her, entreating her to stay silent.

'We can't hide it any longer.' Beth prised her hands free and stood up, protecting Sara from her aunt's shocked gaze.

May still had her hat and jacket on. 'Sweet heart of Jesus!' She gasped, looking at the bed. 'What's going on here? Speak up will you? What's wrong with you, Sara?'

'She's sick… she's haemorrhaging… we have to call the doctor.'

Sara shook her head from side to side, whimpering. She stared dully at May. Her eyes glittered, the flush of fever on her cheeks.

'How long has this been going on?' May demanded.

'Since last night…' Beth bowed her head.

'Last night?' May pressed her hand against her chest, then pointed towards the door, shouting at Beth. 'You get out and wait downstairs. I'll deal with you later.'

An hour passed before she came downstairs. 'Who else knows about this?' she demanded.

Shakily, Beth got to her feet. 'No one.'

'Marjory? She must surely know?'

Beth shook her head. 'No one but us. Is Sara going to die?' she sobbed.

'It's a heavy bleed and an infection. She'll recover. I remember enough from my nursing days.' Hard-faced she stared at Beth. 'The whole town's talking about an abandoned baby left outside O'Donovan's. Jesus Christ! How could she have allowed this to happen in my house? And you – didn't you think about me? That I had a right to know?'

'I didn't know myself until last night.'

'I don't believe you. You were always a liar, Beth Tyrell. If it was you I wouldn't be surprised. But Sara—' Perspiration shone on her forehead. She dabbed her skin with a tissue, touching her lips, smudging lipstick, hardly aware of what she was doing. 'I don't want to know the whys and wherefores of what your sister's been getting up to but it's obvious she was doing more than taking photographs in her spare time.'

'What about the baby?'

'As dead as makes no difference.'

'Dead!'

'With a fractured skull it probably is by now. And just as well too. What luck would it have coming into the world the way it did?'

'Why are you blaming Sara?'

'Because it always takes two to tango and Sara has landed us in a fine mess. Any shame on your family reflects on mine. That baby is probably in the morgue by now and Albert's name could be dragged into this sorry mess. Dear Jesus! You Tyrells have bad blood in you and that's a fact. Between yourself and your father you've caused enough tongues to wag in Anaskeagh and now this—'

'He's to blame... Albert... ask him...' She was unaware that she had sobbed his name aloud until she saw the shock in her aunt's eyes.

May sat down suddenly. Her face sank, grew old. 'You disgusting little slut! How dare you use my husband's name in that vile way? Has your sister been making those accusations?'

Beth shook her head. 'She doesn't have to. I know.'

'You know nothing.' May's bosom heaved.

Beth stepped backward from her fury. 'I know everything.' She was unable to control her tears. 'That's why I ran away. He's to blame... he is... he is...'

'Get out of my house,' May's voice rasped with fury.

'I won't leave Sara.'

'I'll take care of your sister because, and only because, she's my niece. If you dare utter one word – one word – that could damage my husband's good name I'll drag you through every court in the land for slander. Do you hear me, Beth Tyrell?'

'I'm not leaving her with you... and him.'

'Get out! Get out! Get out!' Unable to restrain herself any longer, May ran from the room, her breath wheezing. She flung Beth's clothes into her rucksack then walked past her as if she didn't exist. Downstairs, she flung the hall door open with such force that it slammed back against the wall. A crack appeared in the frosted glass; a hairline fracture running through fragile bone.

'I have to see Sara before I go,' Beth gasped. 'Please let me say goodbye.'

'Get out... Get out.' May continued to chant the words. Saliva had dried on the corners of her lips. She flung the rucksack into the garden. Then Beth felt herself gripped by the shoulders and shoved forward. 'Get out of my sight and don't ever darken my door again.'

Rain whipped her face as she struggled towards Aislin's Roof. Last night when she returned from O'Donovan's farm she had been unaware of anything except the need to get Sara back to Cherry Vale. Now she saw that the hole had been filled in, the loose clay already flattened into mud. She picked up a twig and loosened the mound, finding what she had expected to find. Quickly she scrabbled the clay back over the placenta. She allowed the tears to flow down her cheeks. They rolled into the corners of her lips, hot, salty.

The rain continued to fall as she turned her back on the headland. It seeped into gorges and ancient fissures where streams murmured and roared, splashing white over rocks or free-falling into space, seeking hidden ravines to shape their journey through the centre of Anaskeagh. The earth was being cleansed, baptised.

PART TWO

CHAPTER SIXTEEN
Twenty-six years later

Birds sang from trees whose leaves had yet to fall and the swallows, preparing to migrate, congregated on the electrical cables stretching along Estuary View Heights. This was an ordinary day turned extraordinary but Beth McKeever was unaware of anything other than a quickening of her heartbeat – a reflex so familiar she hardly noticed it – when her mobile phone rang and she realised the caller was Peter Wallace. He was in Germany on a business trip with her husband and, unable to think of any reason why he would call her in the middle of the afternoon, she wondered if something had happened to Stewart.

'He's fine, can't wait to go home,' Peter reassured her. 'I'm ringing about Sara. Has she been in touch with you today?'

'No,' Beth replied. 'I haven't seen her since the day she came home from Africa. Why?'

'I'm anxious to contact her. I've left messages on her phone but she hasn't rung back.'

'You know Sara.' Beth shrugged, unsurprised. 'She probably headed off to photograph something or other that caught her fancy and has forgotten that time exists. She'll be in touch when she comes back down to earth again.'

'We'd an argument before I left. Nothing too serious… she went off the deep end over something…' He hesitated, as if reluctant to discuss his marital problems with her. 'We haven't spoken since Friday. I spent the weekend in the Oldport Grand before leaving for Germany. Did Lindsey tell you?'

'No, she never mentioned anything about the weekend. What did Sara do to annoy you this time?'

'Oh, it's not worth discussing.' He sounded offhand but she knew by the slight inflection in his voice that he was lying and it annoyed her that she was still so attuned to his emotions.

'Would you mind driving over to Havenstone to check if she's there?' he asked. 'She's deliberately avoiding me, but I need to speak to her. Tell her to call me.'

Instant action and no questions asked. Just like his late mother, Beth thought. She told him she was busy. Dinner to make, children to collect from school, homework to correct and she was leaving early to take Connie out for the night. It was her mother-in-law's birthday and Beth had booked two tickets for the Abbey Theatre. Busy, busy, boring him. She heard it in his sharp intake of breath. Not that she blamed him. She was boring herself and this awareness sharpened her tone.

'I haven't time to sort out your domestic squabbles, Peter. Buy Sara some flowers when you come home or book a restaurant.'

'I appreciate how busy you are.' He ignored her irritation. 'But it won't take long if you leave now. You know where to find the spare key. Please, Beth. There's no one else I can ask.'

'I'll call in on my way home from the school run and give you a ring. How's the trip going?'

'Good, so far. We're looking at a pretty impressive piece of machinery. We'll probably invest. Thanks, Beth. Talk to you later.'

She hurried from the house to her car and joined the queue of parents trying to find a parking spot close to the school. Paul and Gail were being escorted across the road by the lollipop lady when she arrived. As always, the traffic was frenetic for about twenty minutes when the school gates opened but it showed no sign of easing as it snaked through the village. A trench was being dug along Main Strand Street and a stop–go system was in place. It was easier for Beth to detour and take the shortcut along the estuary shore. She would call at Havenstone on her way to the theatre.

At four o'clock Robert, her eldest son, rang the doorbell in successive blasts in case his mother had developed chronic deafness since he left for school that morning. He treated Beth to an obligatory grunt when she enquired about his day. A routine question, a routine response. Since his fourteenth birthday, Robert's grunt was capable of expressing either joy or anguish and, after a year of communicating with him in this fashion, Beth interpreted this one to mean he was not in danger of imminent expulsion. He was followed soon afterwards by Lindsey, who headed straight for the kitchen, piling a plate high with crackers and peanut butter.

'I don't want any dinner,' she announced. 'I'm going to Melanie's house to work on my French project. Her mother is making coq au vin.'

'Forget about coq au vin,' Beth warned. 'You promised to babysit. I told you I was taking Granny Mac to the theatre for her birthday.'

'Babysit?' Lindsey sounded outraged. 'They're seven and ten – some babies! Anyway, I never promised. You just assumed I'd do it without even asking if I'd other plans. You *never* remember anything I tell you.'

Beth sighed. 'Despite your best efforts, Lindsey, I haven't started suffering from senile dementia yet. You made a promise. I expect you to keep it.'

'All I'm trying to do is get honours French in my Leaving. Is that a crime? Ring Melanie's mother if you don't believe me. There's six of us meeting there. Why can't Robert look after the *babies*?'

Robert's grunt expressed agreement and a phone call to Joanna Murray assured Beth that six young people were descending on her house in thirty minutes. She was up to her elbows in garlic, chicken and wine. She sounded surprised and politely amused by Beth's obvious anxiety.

'Okay. You can go,' Beth told her daughter when the call ended. 'I'll collect you from Melanie's on my way back from the theatre.'

'But we've arranged to walk home together,' Lindsey wailed. 'Why do I always have to be different to everyone else?'

'All right! All right! But I want you in here by ten thirty. Is that understood?'

'*Heil* Hitler.' Lindsey goose-stepped towards her bedroom, her right arm outstretched, her left bent in a salute. She returned shortly afterwards in leggings and a skirt that was, by Beth's estimation, shorter than a tutu. The front door slammed and peace of a certain kind settled over the house. Since she'd turned sixteen, Lindsey had developed a staying power that constantly challenged her mother. Such rows exhausted Beth but Lindsey seemed to gather energy from them, forcing her into roles she had no desire to play: prying, suspicious, nagging.

'Oh yuck!' moaned Paul, inspecting the dish of cannelloni Beth had removed from the oven. 'Dog's vomit for dinner again.'

The beginnings of a headache tightened across her forehead. Sixteen years since she'd last walked out of her front door without a thought or care. Was this motherhood? she often wondered. This obsessive anxiety that clung like a dank paw to her shoulder. Get a life, Mother. Get a life, Lindsey's familiar refrain mocked her. Sara had a life. A career as a photographer. A fine old house Beth had once coveted. A husband she had once cherished. Bad old days, Beth, she warned herself, checking her watch. Five minutes fast as usual. She ruffled Gail's hair when her youngest child entered the kitchen, her spelling book in hand, with an expression that demanded instant attention.

The house had been just as chaotic the last time her sister had called. Sara had taken a taxi from the airport, arriving unannounced just as Beth had been preparing the evening meal. She'd been exhausted and pale after her flight but anxious to tell Beth about her experience in Malawi. She'd sat at the kitchen table while Beth chopped vegetables and attended to constant demands from Gail. The little girl had been in a fretful mood, refusing to sit on her aunt's knee and tugging repeatedly at Beth's hand whenever the sisters tried to talk.

Sara, unable to endure the interruptions, had pressed her palms against her cheeks and asked, 'Why is it never possible to have a sane conversation in this madhouse?' She'd tried to smile but it had been a fleeting grimace that only emphasised her annoyance. 'Ask Lindsey to look after the younger ones and come back to Havenstone with me,' she'd added. 'We need to talk, Beth.'

A prolonged roar from upstairs had startled them. Paul did not believe in suffering in silence, especially when he'd accidently slammed the bathroom door on his fingers. By the time he'd been consoled and his bruised fingers soothed with arnica, Sara had left. Beth had promised herself she would call into Havenstone later that night but when the house was finally silent she'd been too tired to move. Sara's nervousness, her anxiety as she fought for Beth's attention had begun to blur – to become just another scene from a fraught and tiring day. Beth was startled to realise that a week had passed since then. Sara would be cool with her when they met. She had no idea what it was like to run a home with four tempestuous children and remain upright at the end of each day.

The traffic was even heavier in the evening, snarling in from the city and forming a bottleneck through Oldport. Beth became part of the slow-moving tailback until she reached the gates of Havenstone and turned into the driveway. The old house had once blended into its country landscape but now it sat arrogantly above the newer housing estates, an anachronism in a village gripped by suburban bliss and blight. The march of progress. But who was she to complain? Ten years previously, when she and Stewart had moved back from London, they'd set up house in that mushrooming belt: third right, first left after the tasteful granite slab carved with letters that spelt Estuary View Heights.

An evening mist hung over the grass as she drove up the avenue. Rooks, disturbed by the car, whirled above the trees, raucously calling down the night. The blinds were drawn on the windows and the chiming doorbell had an echo that belonged to empty spaces. Sara could be on a photographic commission, capturing the play of shadow and light on the slopes of a mountain. Maybe she was photographing winos huddling around a bottle in a dingy back alley, focusing her camera on their wizened hands, old shoulders drooping, the bleak urine stains on the wall behind them. Or perhaps not. Perhaps she was in a luxury hotel enjoying the attentions of a lover. Champagne in an ice bucket, fluted glasses, curtains closed against the intrusive twilight. Sara's lifestyle had always remained a mystery – vaguely exotic, filled with foreign travel and photographic exhibitions where sophisticated strangers shook Beth's hand and moved a step backward when she confessed to being a housewife and mother of four.

The spare key was hidden under a terracotta plant pot at the back of the house. She debated searching for it but Connie, a punctual woman, was waiting and Beth was already twenty minutes late. She rang Peter from her mobile and told him that Sara was not at home. She fought against old yearnings as she pictured him running his hand through his dark hair in frustration at the antics of his elusive wife, yearnings that seemed incapable of being erased by time. Familiarity didn't have to breed contempt but it should be capable of overlaying a memory and replacing it with newer ones. So many years had passed. Yet nothing in that passage of time seemed capable of eradicating the night when Beth Tyrell, twenty-seven years old and at the height of her career, finally laid her past aside and opened her heart to joy.

Did she glance in the rear-view mirror as she drove away? Afterwards, Beth tried to remember that final instant when she pressed the accelerator and drove out through the gates of Havenstone. There should have been an omen to alert her: a banshee wailing through long, wild hair, dogs howling, a murder of crows, mirrors falling, splintering. Such an ordinary day turned extraordinary. How could she not have noticed that the earth had shuddered and signalled the breaking of her heart?

CHAPTER SEVENTEEN

Peter was puzzled by time. How it could pass so relentlessly while he was still trapped in glass? Her face... Such stillness. A peaceful passing, the right concoction of pills. Nothing left to chance. No note. No clues. How could Sara do this to him? To leave without a sign that acknowledged their sixteen years of marriage.

A month had passed since he'd held her cold hands against his lips. Today, he would scatter her ashes from Pier's Point. His mother-in-law had refused to attend. Marjory had written a curt note to that effect. An unchristian ceremony was of no interest to her. She had wanted her daughter's body buried in consecrated grounds. How could she pray to a mound of ash, she demanded in the terrible days following Sara's death. She'd been supported by Albert Grant, who'd argued for her, softly persuasive, gently threatening, unsuccessful.

'Sara discussed this with me once.' Peter had remained firm. 'She was very specific about a cremation. She wanted her ashes scattered into the sea off Pier's Point and that's what I must do.'

'It's not right, Peter. It's barbaric.' The older man had shaken his head. 'Marjory needs a place where she can mourn her daughter in peace.' He'd pounded his fist on the table. For an instant the smooth mask of the politician had slipped, replaced by savage grief. 'For God's sake, man, is it too much to give the poor woman a grave in Anaskeagh that she can tend with flowers and pray over?'

'Pier's Point is where I first met Sara and that is where I will lay her to rest.' Peter's sympathy for Marjory had kept him calm but he'd remained adamant. 'I'm determined to honour her wishes.'

'Peter's right.' Beth was present during the argument. 'Sara wouldn't want to be buried in Anaskeagh.'

Anger had darkened the politician's face. 'Unlike you, Beth, your sister loved her hometown. How dare you presume to speak for her.'

'I'm not presuming… I know.' Flint in her eyes, those wonderful slanting eyes that had once captivated and charmed him. She'd tried to comfort her mother but Marjory had pulled away from her and bent to kiss Sara's face once more.

In the small cremation chapel she had sat stiffly beside her brother and fluttered her dead-leaf hands when her daughter's coffin had rolled out of sight behind red velvet curtains. Beth, on her other side, remained dry-eyed throughout the short ceremony, Peter's own desolation reflected on her face. She had apologised repeatedly to him for not entering Havenstone that night. She was rushing, late for Connie, worried about Lindsey, stressed. Her voice faltered as she realised the futility of what she was saying. Sara had been dead by then but it was the aloneness of her death that would forever haunt them.

He had resisted ringing Sara before he left for Germany, still furious with her but clear about his intentions. A clean break. This time he would see it through. She could have Havenstone. The house meant nothing to him. It was impregnated with her presence. Not with children, most definitely not with children. He had been down that road too many times to indulge the fantasy. The glossy hardwood floors, the cold marble fireplaces, a beautiful, treacherous staircase where he had fallen as a child, the scar still faintly visible on his right cheek – that was Havenstone, his inheritance. Child unfriendly. She was welcome to it.

His resolve remained firm throughout Monday as he'd inspected computerised systems with Stewart. Later that evening, he'd taken Beth's call in the hotel bar where he'd been having an after-dinner drink. Havenstone was empty, she'd said. His wife was not at home. A young woman had sat at a white piano and played a medley of love songs. Her voice had the late-night rasp of too many cigarettes, a husky decadence at odds with her long blonde hair and fresh complexion. When the music ended, she'd eased her body into the bar stool beside him and touched his hand, asked if he would like a particular tune. A tired cliché to which he'd responded in kind, glad he didn't have to play any new games.

'Emma from Essen,' she'd said, and so he remembered her name. She'd worn a low-cut glitter top and many rings on her fingers. If she was in the mood she chatted up tired businessmen and drank champagne from the minibars in their hotel rooms. She carried a packet of condoms in the back pocket of her leather trousers, a precaution she had taken since she was sixteen.

'The same packet?' Peter had asked, already bored with their conversation.

'What do you think, silly man?' She'd laughed deep in her throat.

Young women like Emma confused him: so much confidence, so little charm. Yet her laughter had reminded him of Sara, as seductive as the midnight music she'd played on the white piano, and he'd been tempted to kiss her glistening lips, to sate a momentary passion that had flared when she'd moved closer, willing him to breathe in the subtle promise of her youth.

Stewart had disapproved of Emma from Essen. The production manager disliked the challenge of strange cities, the edginess of new experiences, resenting the time he was forced to spend away from his family. When Peter insisted on another drink, he'd shaken his head and retreated to his bedroom. No doubt he'd expected to find Emma at the breakfast table the following morning but he'd made no comment when Peter came down alone. A moral victory against temptation but one that was based on lethargy rather than virtue. At least Peter could be thankful for small mercies. He was faithful to his wife in death, if not in life.

At night, unable to sleep, he joined the world of the insomniac. He opened a bottle of whiskey, watched old films and educational programmes on The Learning Zone. He read newspapers and remembered nothing, drew up business plans, which he shredded before morning. By the light of dawn he saw her wraithlike figure flitting by on the edge of sight. In the mirror above the mantelpiece he saw her phantom smile and cracked the glass with his fist. The following morning he stared at the crack. He had no memory of the previous night but the blood-stained bandage on his hand told its own story.

His visits to Della Designs were becoming more irregular. When he did make an appearance he found it difficult to concentrate on what people were saying to him. Jon Davern, the company accountant, treated him as carefully as a convalescing invalid, insisting that everything was under control. When Peter, suspicious of such forbearance, demanded to know exactly what was under control, he shied away from the spreadsheets the accountant placed on his desk. His life seemed suspended, unreal, as if he was waiting for a signal to awaken and take control of it again.

He removed Sara's clothes from her bedroom and took them to a charity shop in Oldport. He gave Beth a folder of photographs of Anaskeagh he had discovered in the studio. Her name was written on the front of the folder and also on the cover of an old chocolate box containing letters.

'Sara must have wanted you to have these,' he said. 'You'd better take them with you now. In fact, take whatever you want. I'm clearing everything up to the attic.'

'The only thing you should clear out is the whiskey,' Beth replied. 'It's not going to solve anything.'

'You'll have to allow me to be the judge of that,' he said and she agreed, unwilling to enter into an argument with him.

He checked the last emails Sara had received. Her London publisher acknowledged an attached file of African photographs. An email from Albert Grant reassured her that he was always there for her. She was not to worry about Marjory, whose health, thought frail, would remain stable as long as those she loved took care of her. Jess O'Donovan had also written, her email filled with witty anecdotes from the Malawian village where the nun worked. The villagers loved Sara's photographs and looked forward to the publication of *Silent Songs from an African Village*.

He had been away on an overnight trip to London when she'd got back from Malawi and she'd left Havenstone again before he'd returned. Another assignment, she'd said, vague on the phone as to when she would be back. Assignment or assignation? he had wondered, but his jealousy was a jaded emotion. He'd come home late from work two nights later and seen a light shining in her studio. Her pale, cold face when she'd greeted him, her frenzied gestures as she'd worked had told him she was in the grip of a manic energy that always excluded him. Weary of arguments, he'd left her alone and later, in the chilling aftermath of her death, he'd seen the last photographs she had taken. Moody shots of rocks and a configuration of slabs that reminded him of a dolmen. She'd taken the photographs at night and the moon, shining above the looming boulders, added a surreal, almost pagan appearance to the desolate landscape.

The McKeever family were waiting for him on Pier's Point. Beth huddled into the collar of her coat, her short dark hair fluttering around her face, her eyes dulled with grief. She stood beside her husband and gripped the rail of the jetty as Peter scattered Sara's ashes on the water. A pewter sky merged with the sea and eddies of fine grey dust were bathed in the early-morning stillness. Seagulls ran across the shallows, tracing twiggy prints in the estuary mud. It seemed appropriate to pray but no prayer seemed appropriate. Beth was an atheist who refused to contemplate a god, merciful or otherwise, and Peter was indifferent to religious dictates. Lindsey read a poem she had written, simple words that reduced her to tears before she finished. She tore the paper and flung the pieces into the water. Lapping rhythms soothed them as Connie McKeever fell back on old rituals, reciting tried and tested decades of the rosary, forcing them into long-forgotten responses.

He walked home alone, refusing Beth's invitation to join them for breakfast. On Estuary Road he took the shortcut through the field at the back of Havenstone. The outlines of a slip road that would eventually lead to the new motorway were visible in the distance, arching steel edifices and the arms of high yellow cranes bent over iron girders. A woman walking along the estuary shore caught his attention. The wind gusted suddenly. She lifted her hand to push back her hair and, in that gesture, Sara came to mind with such piercing clarity that he was forced to look away. Is this how it's going to be, Sara? he raged into the emptiness of the morning. Did you spare a thought for what I would find when I entered your crazy bedroom of mirrors? I won't have it. Do you hear me? Leave me alone, Sara. Can you hear me? Leave me alone.

CHAPTER EIGHTEEN

Three mornings a week, before the family woke, Beth drove to the Oldport leisure centre. Earlier in the summer, when she'd originally joined the swimming club, she'd hoped to tone up and lose some weight. It had also allowed her to steal precious time for herself before the day began. Her motives had changed since then. In the painful cramp of muscle, the shudder of breath in her lungs, she was able to snatch a short respite from the clamour of guilt and grief that filled her days.

Carrie Davern always set the pace during the early-morning sessions, her arms pumping energetically, focused on laps and time. She was a competitive swimmer, an ambitious, toned woman, whom Beth avoided whenever possible. Their husbands worked for Peter and this tenuous link was the only interest the two women had in common. Most of the early-morning swimmers had already left the pool and headed to the changing rooms as Beth completed her last lap. She debated swimming one more length but the energy that had fuelled her for the previous forty-five minutes suddenly seeped from her.

Carrie was already limbering up for a busy day in her estate agency when Beth entered the changing room. 'You've really increased your time, Beth.' She tilted her head towards the hairdryer, finger-combing her red hair into shape. 'I'm glad you came back to the club. It's good to exercise when you're trying to get your life back on track again. How are you coping, you poor thing?'

'I'm fine, thank you.' She winced away from Carrie's patronising tone. Her thinly disguised curiosity about Sara and the circumstances surrounding her death was a constant affront to Beth. Women, already dressed, slung sports bags over their shoulders and shouted goodbye to each other.

Carrie switched off the hairdryer and sat beside her on the slatted bench. 'It's such early days yet and you're obviously still in shock. We must invite you and Stewart to dinner soon. Maybe Peter too, if he's in a fit condition to come. I'm worried about him. He's drinking heavily—'

'Don't worry about Peter,' Beth quickly interrupted her. 'Everything is under control in the factory.'

'That's not what I hear from Jon. I sympathise with Peter, I really do, but there's far more than his own feelings at stake here. It's been over two months now, so it's time he was pulling himself together. Have you seen the state of Havenstone? So sad. I believe he's going to put it on the market. I've told him I'm interested. He's promised to notify me as soon as he makes up his mind. The sooner the better. Sara must be turning in her grave – oh dear, how insensitive of me. Forgive me, Beth – I forgot about the cremation.' She smiled apologetically and patted Beth's hand. 'Did Sara ever indicate why she was so troubled—'

'Stop it, Carrie!' Beth pushed herself to her feet. 'I've no intention of discussing my sister with you now, or ever. As regards dinner, forget it. Stewart and I are busy for the foreseeable future.' She walked into the shower stall and slid the glass door closed.

'Our husbands could be out of work if Peter Wallace doesn't pull himself together.' Carrie stood outside, a woman unable to leave without the last word. 'That's a fact, Beth. Ignoring it won't make it go away.'

Without replying, Beth turned on the shower. The urge to stand still, paralysed by the force of water, came over her. What if she never moved again, if she dissolved into the enveloping steam? No dragging backward, no reaching forward. A moment of nothingness absorbing her into an infinity where she would cease to exist. Was that how Sara felt? Was that the urge that had driven her into her bedroom of mirrors and the darkness beyond? There was no answer to this question and, knowing she would never be able to ask it, Beth raged quietly into the cascading water.

Even now – when women talked openly in the media about traumatic childhood experiences, and crimes of the past were exposed in unflinching documentaries – she found it impossible to confide in anyone. The blood and tears, the sighing terror, the smell of earth and the moon casting its light on the birthing stones of Aislin's Roof – and, later, back in Cherry Vale, the disgust on her aunt's face as she stared down at the young Sara – these were scenes Beth could only endure through silence. With Sara, it should have been possible to reach into the past. But the clumsy efforts she made were always met with resistance, defeated by the frozen stillness of her sister's face, her suspended breath whenever that lost night was mentioned. Then Beth too would fall silent, fearing Sara would collapse under the leaden atmosphere her words created.

Was that what Sara had tried to discuss with her on the last afternoon they'd been together? Was it the reason why she'd asked Beth to call to Havenstone? 'We need to talk, Beth… We need to talk…' Hindsight was a stick constantly beating at Beth's chest and, yet, within those all-consuming emotions, a treacherous thought sometimes slipped through her grief. The fleeting sense of release. Freedom from a weight she had carried for too many years. This shameful emotion added to her distress and was instantly banished as she turned her attention to the house or garden. No lack of choice there. She ran a tight ship, an organised housewife who could account for every minute of her day.

Oldport was beginning to stir as she drove home from the leisure centre. The newsagent was open and Woodstock, where Judith Hansen, back from the airport with boxes of fresh irises and chrysanthemums, was unloading flowers from her van. The younger children were awake and clamouring for attention, and the older two glowered their way downstairs after repeated calls.

When she returned from the school run, she opened the door to Lindsey's bedroom. This converted attic, with its slanting ceiling and posters of rap stars glowering from the walls, was her daughter's private domain. Lindsey demanded the right to live in squalor and pinned defiant 'Keep Out' notices on the door whenever Beth uttered fumigation threats. Since Sara's death she spent all her free time there, playing aggressive rap music – a rhythm with an incessant beat that vibrated inside Beth's head until she banged on the door and ordered her to lower the volume. This, at least, was familiar territory for both of them. Without replying Lindsey would lower the sound, gradually increasing it again when Beth had gone downstairs.

Clothes, towels, magazines, CDs and various hair products were strewn across the floor. Study plans for her Leaving Certificate were pinned to the wall above her desk. A neat, detailed plan, the corners already curling from neglect.

Beth searched methodically through the clutter for scraps of tinfoil, scorched spoons, burned matches, strawberry stamps, magic mushrooms, weed, opiates, anything that would help her to understand Lindsey's mood swings. They could be explained by the shock of Sara's death but Beth was certain they were caused by more than grief. Tearful outbursts followed by giddiness, thunderous rows with Robert over some imagined slight, her silences so deep that Beth could only stand on the outside and wait for them to pass. Resisting the urge to tidy up, Beth gave up. A warehouse of drugs could remain undetected beneath this clutter.

She was leaving the room when a row of books caught her attention, their precise arrangement on one bookshelf arousing her suspicions. After a quick search she discovered Lindsey's diary hidden behind her collection of Harry Potter books. She opened it without hesitation, her eyes scanning each entry, but all they contained were brief mentions of the weekends Lindsey used to spend in Havenstone. Shopping sprees with Sara, visits to the cinema and theatre, what Sara cooked for dinner, recipes Sara had shown her how to cook, advice Sara had given her about boys – always keep them guessing – the jokes they had shared. Beth came to the last entry, written two weeks before Sara's death. Nothing since then. No outpourings of grief, no fond memories or scribbled words of love. Beth closed the diary and eased it back into its hiding place.

She closed the door quietly behind her and entered her own bedroom. The pillow still bore the imprint of Stewart's head. She fluffed it up and shook the duvet. The radio played quietly in the background as she worked. She would vacuum the carpet, maybe give it a quick shampoo, clean the bathrooms, change the sheets... Stop... *Stop*... She sank to the edge of the bed and clutched her face in her hands. This feeling of running her life on autopilot was increasing. At night, when she finally sat down, she was unable to remember where the hours had gone, or what she had done with them.

She shuddered, her shoulders drawing inwards, her skin tingling. Her uncle was in the room with her. She could hear his voice. He would touch her if she moved. She must stay still, so still – a statue, stiff, unbreakable.

Her breath steadied. There had to be a trigger. There always was. Recognising it was the only way to control these panic attacks that came without warning since Sara's death. She lifted her head, aware for the first time that he was being interviewed on radio. Since his appointment to a junior ministry he was regularly in the media and the interviewer, polite but insistent, was demanding an answer to his question. As always, Albert Grant was as adroit as an eel at ignoring it. Calmer now, Beth recognised the interviewer – Greg Enright. Last night she'd watched him on television. Some investigative programme about the closure of a hospital… Or maybe it was about corrupt land deals. She couldn't remember and now, knowing Greg Enright's tenacity would be equally balanced by her uncle's evasiveness, she switched off the radio.

She shivered, remembering his words of condolence on that horrific morning in Havenstone. How he had clasped her firmly in his arms and said, 'A sad time for us all, Beth. Be kind to your poor mother. Her heart is broken.'

His hair was white, as thick as she remembered, and still brushed back in the same glossy sweep. Age had distinguished him, giving him a stately air of assurance – a man who understood power; how to acquire, how to use it. A scream had rammed in her throat as she'd pulled away from him and tried to comfort Marjory. But what comfort could she give? What words could she use to ease Marjory's grief? Both knew that the wrong daughter had died.

Beth opened a drawer in her dressing table and untied the faded ribbon on the chocolate box she'd taken from Havenstone. It was filled with the letters she had once written to Sara, the pages yellowed and much folded. She had forgotten how often she'd written to Sara, as if, in those far-off years when she'd first come to Oldport, she was making amends for leaving her sister behind. She wrote about the village, the raucous women in the factory, their jokes and turbulent love lives. The snobbish, gossiping women in the office. Through these letters Sara came to know the tough and bossy Della Wallace and the maternal Connie McKeever, who had loved their father in sickness and in health. She knew about the boys Beth had dated, the rows with

Marina, the heady rides on the back of Stewart's motorbike, and Peter with his paint-streaked jeans and honey skin – he filled the pages with his deeds. She wrote about Havenstone and the light-filled studio where he immortalised her eyes in oils. In these letters there was no mention of homesickness and loneliness – and how she cried at night, remembering. She created a fantasy world and Sara came to Oldport to claim it, armed with her fragile beauty and the memory of a bloodstained oath the two sisters had promised never to break.

CHAPTER NINETEEN

For weeks after Sara died, Lindsey had cried at night until her throat felt as scratchy as sandpaper. Somewhere, hidden behind a press, lost in the post and still to arrive, there had to be a note. Sara loved her. How many times had she told her? Millions. How could she go without a word, a sign, anything?

She had avoided Havenstone since then but Peter was so insistent on the phone this evening. He wanted to give her jewellery belonging to Sara. All Lindsey wanted was an explanation. Why… Why… Why?

The fastest way on foot to Havenstone was the shortcut through Bailey's Field. Estuary Road had been closed to traffic since work on the new slip road began. All the old cottages along the shore were deserted, waiting to be demolished, along with the garage where her father used to have his motorbike serviced in the old days. Her mother said it was a disgrace that a local amenity should be destroyed in the name of progress. Lots of people agreed. Last year, they mounted a campaign and carried banners with 'Swans or Road Rage – Your Choice' printed on them. Sara had held an exhibition of her estuary photographs. Brilliant images of birds skimming the water at dawn and swans swimming down the centre of the road when it flooded during the spring tides. It was impossible not to imagine them supplanted by cars and fumes and noise. It made no difference in the end but, for the moment, it was the perfect hideaway for the garage gang.

She stopped outside the old garage and tried to peer through the cardboard on the window. Impossible to see inside. On Friday nights her mother believed she was still involved with the study group. She never bothered checking any more, which was perfectly fine by Lindsey. The garage gang was her salvation. The one good part of a sick, mixed-up world.

In the garage no one worried about the Leaving. They were too busy dancing and having a good time. All that studying and trauma for what? Kev Collins had set up the sound system and got the electricity working. The black cardboard stopped the light shining across the estuary. It was cool dancing with the candles and the cobwebs. Kev knew how to get E and that was no big deal either. The double standards imposed by adults drove her crazy. By all means drink beer and throw up over the pavement. Multicoloured puke was learning about life. By all means buy drugs from a pharmacist in a white coat and over-dose without leaving a note – that was learning about death. Ecstasy was not addictive, unlike heroin or coke. It was a buzz drug, recreational – the happy drug. Everyone was entitled to happiness.

Lindsey found it hard to remember how much she'd once hated Oldport with the cold wind blowing off the estuary and screeching seagulls swooping over the garden. She'd been six years old when her parents had moved there from London. Her father had promised her new friends, a long garden with a swing and grass, not concrete, like the playground outside their flat. They would have a big house where she wouldn't hear the next-door neighbours shouting, even if they were the same as the Binghams, who had a row every Saturday night and smashed plates. But there was no grass in Estuary View Heights, no swing – only mountains of mud and men on scaffolding, who whistled at her mother. Then Sara came and scooped her away from the mud and the sickening smell of paint.

'You're such a beautiful little princess,' she'd said. It was the first time anyone had called Lindsey beautiful. Her aunt knew all about being beautiful. She had golden hair and silver spirals in her ears. She smelled of flowers. She took Lindsey to Havenstone where there were new dresses and toys waiting. They played pretend games and explored the garden at the back of the house, hiding in the crab-apple orchard and wild bushes. In bed, with the old trees bending creaky into the night, she'd told Lindsey the story about a princess with a secret. When the princess could no longer carry it inside her head or in her heart, she knelt on the edge of a bottomless well and screamed it into the black depths.

'Sometimes silence is more important than honesty,' she'd said, closing the book of fairy stories and smiling down at Lindsey sitting on the bed beside her, the fluffy pillows propped behind them. 'Sometimes it's necessary to carry secrets inside us so that those we love don't suffer our pain.'

Then Marjory had come to visit and everything had changed. Even at six, Lindsey had known her relationship with this grandmother was different. Loving Granny Mac was as effortless as breathing, but this tall thin woman had glittery eyes and long fingers that pinched Lindsey's shoulders. Every time she'd made noise Marjory had pressed her hands to her forehead. Lindsey was spoiled and demanding, she'd said. Even if her father came swanning back to Oldport as the production manager of Della Designs, it was only because of Peter's generosity and family links.

She'd been just as nasty to Beth, going on and on about bad blood and how she'd rubbed salt into her mother's wounds by marrying a McKeever. They were bred from generations of poor, ignorant fishermen and now she was carrying their seed and breed into another generation. Her voice had been so sharp it made Lindsey sink deep into the sofa, wishing she could disappear and not have to listen to grown-ups fighting like the Binghams.

Sara had begged them to stop. 'Let bygones be bygones,' she cried. 'Why drag up the past every time you meet each other?'

After they had returned to the new house her mother had said Marjory was just being jealous and to pay no attention. Lindsey understood jealousy. When Robert was born she'd been so jealous she'd hoped he would be carried up to heaven by an angel. But she also knew the difference between jealousy and cruelty. Marjory had said a cruel thing. Granny Mac's husband had drowned when his fishing trawler sank to the bottom of the sea. A year afterwards, she'd met Lindsey's other grandfather and fell in love with him. Lindsey had wanted to know about the old days but Granny Mac had said it was all a long time ago. A long foolish time ago. She was as bad as Lindsey's mother when it came to talking about the past.

She still found it impossible to like her Tyrell grandmother, who insisted on being called 'Marjory' because she did not want to be associated with grandmotherly labels. She never came to visit them now. Beth had to go to Anaskeagh if she wanted to see her. No chance of that. Lindsey had never been to Anaskeagh. Not once. Sara had said it was a wonderful place but Beth had hated living there so much she'd run away. How could two sisters carry such different memories of their childhood?

The old photographs her mother had taken from Havenstone had offered Lindsey her first glimpse of Anaskeagh. The river running through the centre of the town writhed like a snake and the small houses hunched together had dark narrow lanes running behind them. The shapes behind the houses could have been children playing. It was hard to be certain because they seemed different each time Lindsey saw them. In some photographs her mother looked really young and pretty with her flowing black hair, her Cleopatra eyes, and her legs in skintight jeans. She was sitting in long grass, her hand outstretched, as if she wanted to snatch the camera from Sara. Her face was angrier in each shot. Big leaning rocks surrounded her. Lindsey had asked where it was and her mother had said, 'Hell on earth.'

'Why was it "hell on earth"?' She'd been disturbed by the passion in Beth's voice.

'Places are not hell,' she'd replied. 'It's people who turn them into hell.'

No wonder she never wanted to talk about Anaskeagh. Lindsey figured her memories were horrible. She'd done cruel things to Sara and now she was riddled with guilt. She'd forced Goldie, a lovely little cocker spaniel, underwater and tried to drown him. Lindsey saw him in the photographs, curled up beside a high rock, the sun on his coat turning him into a blob of melting butter. When Sara had told her the story about her pet dog, Lindsey had cried. She couldn't believe that anyone, but especially her mother, could do such a cruel thing.

Two months had passed since Sara's death but Lindsey still saw her everywhere. A flick of blonde hair, a smile, a gesture, so many reminders. Passing Woodstock one day on her way to meet Melanie in the Coffee Stop, she glanced through the window and saw Sara's ghost standing beside the freesias, her arms filled with dried reeds. When she threw back her head, laughing at something Tork Hansen said, Lindsey's skin lifted in goosebumps. The sound of her laughter carried out through the open door. It was loud and free, unlike the laughter of a ghost, which would surely be a thin, terrifying sound.

Later, on her way home from the Coffee Stop, the woman was still in Woodstock. She carried a baby in a sling and Judith Hansen kept making coo-che-coo noises. 'Planting Thoughts' was printed on a van parked outside. The laughter was still on her face when she left the shop. Up close, she no longer resembled Sara. Younger, her shoulders were too broad, her hair wild and yellow, the colour of grapefruit, rippling down her back.

Her uncle looked haggard when he answered the door, the skin sagging under his eyes, his stare bloodshot. He took her into Sara's bedroom where her jewellery box lay open on the dressing table.

'Take whatever you like,' he said. She wondered if he was thinking about the row. How could he forget it? Had they made up before Sara died, apologised to each other over the phone? She wanted to ask but how could such a question be phrased? Did he feel guilty? Her mother did. So did Lindsey. He, too, had to cope with the *why*. But she was unable to feel sorry for him. That night… The row… A hand seemed to clamp on her brain whenever the memory slipped through Lindsey's defences.

She lifted a charm bracelet from the jewellery box. It looked so old-fashioned but all those little charms must have a story. Sara had never worn it, as far as Lindsey knew, and that made it easier to choose. Her uncle fastened it on her wrist and asked if she'd like tea. He had bought cupcakes. She shrank from having to make further conversation with him and muttered an excuse about the amount of studying she had to do. He stood in the doorway and watched as she walked down the driveway. The charm bracelet tinkled as Lindsey slowly released the breath she'd been holding and began to run.

CHAPTER TWENTY

Outside the factory Peter sat motionless. He had not bothered with breakfast and the iced water he'd drunk before leaving Havenstone sat heavily on his stomach.

'You're late.' Stewart was pacing the factory floor when he entered the stark, grey building. 'Everyone's waiting in the boardroom.' His eyes narrowed accusingly as he took in Peter's appearance. 'Jesus Christ, Peter. Are you too broke to buy a razor? In case it's escaped your attention, this is a crucial meeting.'

'Then why are we wasting time?' He walked rapidly up the stairs to the boardroom where Jon Davern waited with the two proxy board members, Ben Layden and Harry Moore. Peter ignored the frosty atmosphere and opened the meeting. The discussion was acrimonious from the beginning. Stewart wanted to move the factory forward with an investment in state-of-the-art technology. Jon Davern simply wanted to move the factory. He had established useful contacts in Asia, where governments were stretching out beckoning hands to manufacturers. Massive grants, low wages, high technology, no union problems. An unbeatable combination, especially as Della Designs' costs continued to spiral and the union was determined to negotiate a new pay deal.

'We'll postpone any decision on investment until after we've had talks with the union,' Peter said. 'If the workers are going to make unrealistic wage demands we have to look at any future decisions in that light.' He hoped he sounded authoritative but he noticed the dismissive tilt of Jon's head and Stewart's frown.

'I thought the purpose of our German trip was to buy new equipment.' Stewart stayed behind when the meeting ended and flung his report on the boardroom table. 'You know as well as I do that we need to modernise to stay in business. Davern's been insisting on too many cutbacks. We're not making a quality product any more and it's beginning to be noticed. One bad season and we're down, two and we're out.'

'So?' Peter shrugged. The need for a drink cramped his stomach. He wanted to return to Havenstone and sink into its silence once again. 'You're the production manager. You know that cost and quality have to be finely balanced. If that isn't working then it's time to do as Davern suggested and look at new strategies.'

He was detached from his own words, as if his opinion floated on a string that could be pulled in to argue an opposite point of view with equal conviction. 'You needn't worry about your job. Your position with the company is safe, no matter what changes we make.'

'A global sweatshop! Is that what you want me to run?' Stewart demanded. 'If you think I'm going to spend my time in some godforsaken hole on the edge of Asia then think again.' His voice was quiet but determined. 'I've no intention of being separated from my family now or in the future.'

Peter swallowed hard, fighting his way through nausea. This was proving to be the mother and father of a hangover. He longed to smash his fist into his production manager's angry face. A tight curling excitement tensed his stomach, as if he was already lunging across the desk and Stewart was reeling backwards in shock.

Abruptly he stood up and lifted his coat from the rack. 'I'm through for the day. As I said at the meeting, I can't make decisions until we negotiate with the union. You'll be fully informed if I decide to make any changes.'

Outside the factory, he braced his body against the wind and walked towards his car. The fury he had felt in the office astonished him. Stewart McKeever was his childhood companion. The brother he always wanted. His trusted friend. How could he know a man all his life and then discover he was a stranger? How could this quiet man be a keeper of secrets – a custodian of lost love and past mistakes?

Albert Grant called that evening. He rang the front doorbell three times in quick succession, a shrill summons that Peter was unable to ignore.

'I'm on the way home from the Dáil so I thought I'd drop in and see how you're faring.' His breath hazed in the hall light as he entered the house, his bulky frame wrapped in a voluminous overcoat. 'I thought you were never going to answer the door. It's brass-monkey weather out there.'

'How are you, Albert?' Peter moaned inwardly at the idea of having to entertain him.

'Glad to be out of that bear pit for the weekend, I can tell you that for nothing.'

'I hear there's talk of a cabinet reshuffle?' He led the politician into the drawing room and handed him a measure of whiskey. He refrained from pouring a drink for himself, hoping to shorten his visit.

'Ah, sure, even the walls gossip in that place. They're worse than a gaggle of ould ones outside the church on a Sunday.' The politician settled himself into an armchair and raised his glass. 'Cheers, man. How are you doing?'

'I'm coping.'

'Life's a rough road, God knows it is. It's nearly two years since my dear Blossom passed away. God rest her sweet soul. Never an hour passes without her being in my thoughts.'

What did the man want? A heart-to-heart on the widower experience? Peter decided he needed a drink after all.

He had attended May Grant's funeral, an impressive gathering that had filled the church in Anaskeagh. The politician had been the centrepiece of the occasion. His long eulogy delivered from the altar was an exercise in rhetoric and nostalgia. Peter's mind had wandered after the first few minutes. His memory of May Grant did not match the eloquent words pouring from the mouth of her husband. He remembered her as an overweight, flustered woman who worked throughout her married life as his unpaid secretary, receiving neither appreciation nor acknowledgement until she was safely encased in her coffin.

'Kieran has invited myself and Marjory to New York for Christmas,' Albert said. 'Obviously, Marjory won't come here and it would be impossible for her to spend the day with the McKeevers. It'll be difficult for us all, God knows it will, but New York will be a distraction for her.'

'That sounds like a good idea. How is she?'

'Distraught. You should visit her in the new year. You know you're always welcome in Anaskeagh.'

'Thanks, Albert. I'll think about it. But at the moment I'm too busy—'

'Busy?' Albert raised his eyebrows and glanced around the room.

Suddenly self-conscious, Peter saw the drawing room through the older man's eyes. The stale smell of neglected, airless space. The shabby tracksuit he had pulled on when he returned from the factory embarrassed him. He rubbed his chin, his hand scratching rough stubble.

'According to Jon Davern you're finding it... shall we say *difficult* to focus on the job in hand,' Albert continued. 'Understandable, of course, given your sad circumstances. But a lot of people are depending on you, including my niece, Beth.'

'I've never known Beth to be in need of anyone's help, especially yours.'

'She's an independent woman, that's for sure. But Sara's death was a hard cross for everyone. The last thing Beth needs is to have any uncertainties in her life. There's trouble with the union, I believe.'

'We do have negotiating skills, Albert. You needn't worry – your investment is quite safe.'

'These are tough times, man. Costs have to be our main consideration. Any talk of wage increases could force the closure of the factory.' He rose to leave. 'God give you strength at this testing time.' He grasped Peter's hand in a warm, comforting clasp. A well-used hand, skilled at pressing the flesh and the heads of babies.

Peter had never understood Sara's respect for the old fraud, who always treated her with a patronising tenderness when he came to visit. Her manner towards him had been deferential, as if she was still his indebted niece.

'When my father abandoned us we would have been destitute but for his kindness.' Her voice had risen defensively whenever Peter had criticised him. On such occasions she sounded like Marjory, unable to mention Barry Tyrell's name without biting deep into an old festering sore.

Peter understood what it was like to be indebted to Albert Grant. Ten years previously, when Della Designs had been on the brink of liquidation, the politician had invested heavily in the company.

'You're my family,' he said. 'I always look after my own.' But he never allowed Peter to forget that his money was responsible for Della Designs' increased profits, though his investment in the company remained a secret. Jon Davern, who would become Della Designs' accountant, and Conor Grant, the politician's son and solicitor, handled the paperwork. Ben Layden and Harry Moore, two businessmen from Anaskeagh, were officially listed as shareholders. With this major cash injection Peter had persuaded the McKeevers to return from London, and Stewart had taken over as production manager of Della Designs.

Peter had always regretted accepting the politician's money. Far better to have walked away and flung the keys into his mother's grave. Ghosts didn't have the power to rise from the dead and reproach him, or so he believed in rational moments. He wondered how Della would react if she knew he now only owned 51 per cent of the company she'd worked so hard to build.

'She'd turn somersaults in her grave.' Connie McKeever had still been the factory supervisor during that troubled period. 'It's not the first time you've had to make tough decisions.' She'd cast her experienced eyes over the figures he'd showed her and shaken her head. 'But on the last occasion you had Beth to help you. You lost a good business head when you let her go.'

'I never let her go,' he'd protested. 'She resigned without notice and married your son. She never even—'

'You let her go,' Connie had repeated in a voice that could instantly quell a factory of boisterous woman. 'And I'll say no more than that on the subject.'

The politician finished his drink and left. Unable to settle, Peter climbed the stairs and entered Sara's bedroom. The wardrobe doors hung open. He was about to close them when he noticed a dress he had missed when he cleared out her clothes. He pressed the material to his face and breathed in the scent of her… Or perhaps that was only his imagination. The stored memory of a subtle perfume she had always exuded when she entered a room.

He recognised the dress. She had worn it to Della Designs' fiftieth anniversary celebration. Under the chandeliers in the Oldport Grand, the material had gleamed with the richness of a fine burgundy wine. Her creamy shoulders had been bare, her upswept hair held in place by an elaborate bronze comb. She had mingled with the guests, moving from one group to the next, remembering names, personal details, making the right enquiries about families and careers. How long had it taken Peter to realise she was playing a role, the perfect response for all occasions?

The McKeevers had returned to Oldport some months previously and Beth, if she experienced any nostalgia for the past, showed no sign of it. She'd been a mother of two by then. The same commitment she had shown when working for his mother, and later for him, had been effortlessly transferred to her family.

'Why won't you come back and work for me?' he'd asked, sitting next to her during the meal. He'd gestured to the guests surrounding them: factory and office staff, suppliers and buyers; people she had known and befriended during her years with Della Designs.

'I've no interest in working outside my home,' she'd said. 'I came back for Sara's sake. You know, and I know, that that's the only reason I persuaded Stewart to accept your offer.'

She was so different to Sara and yet he had loved them both. With Beth his passion had been strengthened by years of friendship whereas Sara had overpowered his senses the instant he'd met her.

Love at first sight. He had never believed in the existence of such an all-consuming passion until she'd stood on Pier's Point and filled his eyes. She had remained beyond his reach until they married, teasing him with phone calls in the middle of the night, her laughter beckoning, her voice softly provocative. In his arms she was pliable, a promise waiting to be fulfilled. They were married in Rome. Two strangers had witnessed their union. She'd wanted a quiet wedding with no family involvement and he agreed, relieved that he wouldn't feel Beth's reproachful eyes on his back when he spoke his vows.

On their first night together, she'd come to him in a sheer white robe, the colour of chastity. Her eyes seemed enormous as she lay beneath him. Two bruises. There was nothing in her demeanour to suggest she did not welcome his mouth, his hands, his deep plunging need. Exquisite pleasure, staring down at her, devouring her with his eyes, ravishing her with his body.

Shame set in as pleasure died. He had given her so little. She'd smiled, sleepy satisfaction, as if the spasms that had racked him had also sated her. She'd stretched back against the pillows, her young firm breasts jutting beneath the sheet, her gaze already reaching beyond him.

'I will love you until the day I die,' he'd promised. 'And in whatever eternity comes afterwards.'

'You make me sound like an addiction.' She had laughed softly.

'If that's the case,' he'd warned. 'Don't ever try to rehabilitate me.'

They had returned from their honeymoon to Havenstone. Sunlight had spilled through the open doorway as he carried her over the threshold. She'd run her fingers along the embossed wallpaper, lightly touched the white roses on the hall table, stared upwards at the long, winding staircase.

'Havenstone is so beautiful, Peter,' she had whispered. 'It's just as I imagined.'

Later, in bed, she turned into his arms and murmured, 'Melt me into your love, Peter. Never let me go.'

Had he dreamt that moment? To melt was to be absorbed but Sara Wallace was ice, untouched by heat. He loved her. He hated her. How could two such strong emotions have coexisted without him losing his mind?

The chill of the white room seeped into his bones. His grief for all he didn't understand, and all he had lost, surfaced with such ferocity that he groaned aloud. He allowed the dress to slip from his hand and watched it coil like a question mark on the white bedspread.

How lightly she danced on the night of the anniversary celebration. She'd been the most beautiful woman present. His opinion was objective. He was used to the company of elegant women. The fashion industry prostituted itself on such elegance and made its profits from the wish fulfilment it created. She'd danced with Stewart, whose bulky figure looked surprisingly imposing in an evening suit, and with her uncle, his hand splayed across her back as he guided her around the floor. Steve Maguire, the owner of Fashion Lynx, had been captivated by her attention. Poor deluded fool. He'd probably rung her afterwards, convinced that her interest in his opinions must carry a hint of sexual intrigue. Sara would have treated him with an icy politeness that stayed his words before they were uttered. But what did Peter know about anything? Maybe they shared a brief affair, amusing and stimulating her while it lasted. She would have cut Steve adrift as soon as he began to demand more from her, and he would have demanded more, striving to reach the deeper promise lurking behind her laughter.

When she returned to Havenstone that night she'd demanded to know why he had never revealed his business partnership with her uncle. 'Albert assumed I knew everything about his loan,' she'd said. 'How dare you keep that information from me?'

'Why are you so upset?' He'd been surprised by her agitation. She seldom showed any interest in Della Designs and, as the politician had insisted on secrecy, Peter had never considered discussing his investment with her. 'It wasn't a loan,' he'd argued. 'It was an investment and he'll be well rewarded for it.'

'That's not the point,' she'd replied. 'I'm your wife. I've a right to know about your financial dealings when they involve my family.'

The row that had followed was bitter, her anger moving so far inwards that it seemed as if he had assumed another identity and it was easy for her to hate him. He'd never found a way to avoid such rows or the aftermath, when she would lie in bed without speaking, turning from him when he tried to comfort her, shaking her head vehemently if he suggested a psychologist, a psychiatrist, anyone who could help. Her tablets were hidden from him but he'd found a prescription once and realised she was on antidepressants. She'd refused to discuss the reasons with him. Then, somehow, drawing strength from deep within herself, she would grow strong again, absorbing herself in her work, trying to make amends to him in small ways that he had ceased to appreciate.

When he'd moved into his father's bedroom she accepted his decision, displaying neither regret nor relief. Alone in the room of a man who'd once collected paintings of saints with tortured expressions, their skin sculpted down to bare bone and illuminated from within, Peter had wondered if it was that same translucence that had drawn him to Sara, the hope that he could unveil her mystery and rouse her to the heights of his own passion.

There had been other women. Brief affairs that had given him fleeting satisfaction but also forced him to accept the abnormality of his relationship with his wife. For this reason such affairs ended cleanly, without regret. His marriage had nowhere to go yet he kept believing that his love for her would eventually triumph. How many times did he try? How many times did he fail? When did it cease to matter?

He hung her dress back in the wardrobe. Her mirrors glinted on the white walls. They looked mysterious, slightly decadent, promising much. He grimaced at the irony, at the juxtaposition: a bedroom of mirrors; a cold, unloving wife.

She had collected them on her trips abroad, her firm voice haggling with traders in oriental marketplaces and on the cobbled streets of old European cities. He'd been with her when she bought the first one, a tiny mirror set into a lump of crystal. The street trader's dark eyes had lit with pleasure when she haggled with him over the price he demanded for it.

'The mirror of the soul,' she'd said when she showed it to Peter. 'Such a small lost soul.'

CHAPTER TWENTY-ONE

The news that Marjory was spending Christmas in Kieran Grant's handsome brownstone house was an enormous relief to Beth. Marjory, who had always spent Christmas in Havenstone, had vowed never to darken Peter's door again. To invite her to Estuary View Heights would have meant uninviting Connie, who always spent Christmas Day with them. The thought of the two women meeting face to face was as unthinkable now as it had been all those painful years ago.

'I don't know how I'm going to get through Christmas without my darling child,' Marjory had said when she'd phoned. 'Albert is taking care of everything. Where would I be without him these days?'

Her thin, quavering voice had been like a nail on Beth's skin. 'Will you come and stay with us in the new year?' she'd asked. A token gesture. She already knew the answer.

Kieran Grant was a successful stockbroker. A Wall Street dandy with spotted bow ties and finely plucked eyebrows, he would treat Marjory with kindly condescension and she, impressed by his wealth, would find solace in his attention. Every Christmas, he sent Beth a personalised greeting card, a photograph of his family smiling their wide, white American smiles, accompanied by a computerised letter outlining their many achievements throughout the year. But the letter he wrote after Sara's death was for her eyes only. It rambled nostalgically through the past. Sunshine days in Anaskeagh and endless games of tennis in the back garden of Cherry Vale. So be it. Everyone was entitled to their own reality.

———

Christmas morning in Estuary View Heights was filled with en-
forced gaiety, endured for the children's sake, especially Gail's,
whose belief in Santa was ferociously indulged by everyone.
Preparing dinner was Stewart's prerogative, a tradition that had
started the first year they were married. His family arrived at
noon, bringing the excitement to a higher pitch as hugs were
exchanged and parcels unwrapped.

Marina McKeever, in her full-length faux fur coat and jun-
gle-print tights, was as exuberant as ever.

'Help has arrived, big brother,' she announced, invading the
kitchen where Stewart was basting the turkey. She cast a wary
eye over the preparations and edged towards the door.

'I'll be out to do my shift as soon as I sink my first gin and
tonic. Call me when you need me. Cheers, darlings.'

'Thank God for the gin bottle.' Stewart grinned at Beth. 'At
least it will keep her out of my hair for the rest of the day.'

Peter was equally loud and jovial when he called. Everyone
seemed determined to defeat the atmosphere with noise. He
dispensed his presents: gift vouchers for the children, boxes of
chocolates for Connie and Marina. Beth received perfume, gift-
wrapped, expensive, impersonal. It was obvious he'd been drinking. His cheek was swollen in a purple bruise that bagged the
skin under his right eye and emphasised his pallor. Gail cried
out in terror when he lifted her high in the air, bewildered by his
exuberance. He shook his head when Beth repeated her invitation to dine with them.

'Oh, please do, Peter. You can't be alone on a day like today.'
Marina linked his arm and fluttered her long eyelashes. 'Pretty
please?'

'I'd be a killjoy,' he said. 'Maybe you'll all come over for a
meal after Christmas. I'll give you a ring and arrange it early

next week.' He looked across at Beth. They both knew it was an empty promise.

She wanted to strike him and retreated to the end of the room, shaking with the force of her anger. His grief was so tarnished, tardy and self-pitying, his handsome face raddled under its force.

'I can't believe you drove over here in this condition,' she said when he followed her, an empty glass in hand.

He stared beyond her, as if trying to position himself into some time frame or location. She drew back, repelled when he lurched forward and kissed her cheek. 'My sweet, sensible Beth. My sister-in-law of mercy.' Every few minutes he stared at his watch, holding his arm stiffly in front of him to inspect its face. He began to hum, a hoarse off-key chorus. 'Goodbye lady, goodbye love. Goodbye lady. We hate to see you go.'

'Stop it, Peter.' She stayed calm, unable to bear the thought of a scene.

'Sorry… Sorry,' he muttered. 'It was a long night. Give me a drink – whiskey will do.' He placed the glass on the bookcase table and took her hand. 'I need a drink, Beth, not a lecture.'

She laced the whiskey heavily with water. 'Why are you doing this to yourself? You must know Sara wouldn't want to see you drinking so much.'

'Don't use platitudes on me, Beth. None of us ever had the slightest idea what Sara wanted.' His voice was barely audible as he drained the glass.

She picked up her car keys, ignoring his protests. 'I'm driving you home. You can come back here tomorrow to collect your car.'

The state of Havenstone depressed her. The drawing room, always the most elegant room and Sara's favourite, was overlaid with dust. The large mirror above the fireplace, with its carved gilt frame, was cracked, a jagged line angling across the glass. Old newspapers were scattered on the floor, along with empty bottles and unwashed dishes. She lit a fire and prepared food, an omelette with mushrooms. She buttered some stale brown bread she found at the back of the fridge. Not exactly a feast but starvation on Christmas Day went against the dictates of tradition.

'Beth, the dynamic homemaker,' he muttered when she placed the dishes on an occasional table and ordered him to eat. 'When did you first begin to disappear?'

'Take a look in the mirror, Peter, and try answering that question yourself.' She stood beside him and gazed at his distorted reflection. His eyes met hers in the glass but made no connection.

'Can you hear it?' he asked.

'What?'

'Her laughter. I hear it sometimes at night.' He winced. 'I can't sleep, Beth. I'm going crazy from lack of sleep.'

'See a doctor. A counsellor, if need be. Do something about it, Peter.'

'Is that the best you can suggest? You were never inclined to clichés, Beth. Don't start now.' He touched the bruise on his cheek and peered deeper into the mirror. 'I fell coming down the stairs last week. I'd been in the storage room looking at the Cat paintings. Remember them?'

She was surprised. 'I thought you'd burned them years ago. That's what you were going to do.'

'But I didn't. I took your advice and kept them for posterity.' He laughed harshly. 'Can you enlighten me as to what the hell I was doing?'

'You were good, Peter.'

'Sara could show more emotion in one photograph than I brought to that whole collection of pretentious shit.' He held her gaze in the glass, his eyes suddenly alert, searching. 'I married the wrong sister, you know that… Don't you?'

'That was your choice, Peter.'

'You allowed me to make it. Why didn't you tell me the truth?'

'What truth?' She was alert now, and guarded, her fingers clenching in an involuntary reaction against his question.

'She told me about Lindsey... The last night we were together. Was she lying, Beth?' His voice strengthened, as if his words had briefly sobered him. 'Was she the reason you left Oldport so suddenly?'

'You were in love with my sister. Was that not reason enough to leave?'

'I loved you, too–'

'Don't try and romanticise our relationship, Peter. We had a passing fling–'

'You're wrong. We were in love and I squandered it shamefully.'

He was struggling between drunkenness and cold recollection. The same familiar memory welled up inside her. Sometimes it came in a flash, vivid in all its detail, and, on other occasions it was a pale canvas, as if that time when they'd loved each other with abandon belonged to the memory of someone else, a stranger Beth had difficulty recognising.

Della had been dead by then and Peter – who'd returned from Italy after Beth rang to tell him his mother had suffered a fatal stroke – was running the factory. Ostensibly, he was the managing director, but it was Beth who'd guided him through those early months. Their roles had reversed in a subtle but unmistakable way. The young girl who'd first come to his studio, awed by her surroundings and infatuated with him, had become a self-assured career woman while he, no longer needing to rebel against his mother's iron will, had realised his talent was a mediocre thing, lacking passion and pain.

Together, they planned to change the staid image of Della Designs and create a new brand. Allure was aimed at attracting trendy, young customers and would be launched with an advertising campaign. Beth had placed a glossy fashion brochure in front of him and said, 'Recognise anyone?'

'My God… Marina McKeever.' He gasped and laughed. 'She actually made it.'

She'd smiled, flicking pages. 'We should ask her to model the collection. I'll contact Sara, my sister. She's also based in London and she's an excellent photographer.'

Shortly afterwards, their first order had come from the Fashion Lynx chain store. They'd celebrated in Havenstone with Louise Clifford, the Allure designer, and Stewart, toasting the future with champagne and an Indian takeaway. Beth had sat on the floor, her back resting against Peter's knees. Smoke had spiralled lazily through his fingers as he and Louise had passed a joint back and forth between them. Smoking hash belonged to his student days, lazy sessions in his studio, the Cat pictures. It had seemed so long ago, daft afternoons. He'd inhaled deeply before bending down and offering it to Beth.

'Relax and live,' he'd murmured. 'Life is not a sweatshop, no matter how much you insist on making it one. This is our golden time, Beth. We've earned it.'

He'd placed the joint between her fingers, moist where his lips had touched it. Flickering pain in her stomach, swooping on the verge of pleasure. Stewart had been watching, his expression grim, and it had annoyed her, this sense that he was waiting and hoping, always hoping. She'd relaxed, expanding outwards instead of inwards, the air around her sweet, languorous, heavy. Peter's hand had reached under her hair and stroked her neck. A light pressure that had begged her to stay when it was time for the others to leave.

Stewart had been reluctant to go. His hurt eyes pleaded with her until Louise propelled him firmly towards her car.

'He's one jealous man.' Peter had stood beside her at the drawing-room window. 'We're breaking his heart.'

She hadn't wanted to talk about Stewart. She hadn't wanted to do anything except watch the stars shimmering, orbs of milky light stretching into infinity, while she'd waited for Peter to make the next move.

'Look at you, trembling like a leaf and I haven't even kissed you yet.' With his fingers he'd traced her lips, a crushed flower opening. She'd stood perfectly still while he stroked the warmth within her. This time there'd been no monster in the wardrobe, no whimpering of newborn pups, and when Beth floated, falling far far down beneath him, her body feather light, she'd known there was nothing to stop the moment.

'Open your eyes and look at me, Beth,' he'd whispered.

No reason for shame, for false modesty. This was pleasure of the mind, of the body. Her eyes drowning in pleasure. Lost. Stoned on pot. Stoned on love.

Now they were older, middle-aged and immune to spent passions, or so she told herself as she stepped away from him and his dangerous memories.

'If I had wounds they healed a long time ago,' she said.

'You're wrong,' he replied. 'Sometimes it's impossible to avoid opening old wounds. You know what Sara told me, don't you?'

'No… And I don't want to know. Do you understand me, Peter? This conversation has to stop right now.'

'She said Lindsey is my daughter.' He ignored her cry of protest. 'If I thought for one minute that that was true—'

'It's a lie, Peter. I've no idea why Sara should tell such a cruel lie. I never want you to mention it again.'

She spun on her heel and walked away from him. When she tried to leave the room he stood in front of her and gripped her arms. She thought he was going to shake her. The belief was so strong that her head lolled forward as if the strength had gone from her spine.

'Please, Beth, listen!' he cried. 'I need you to listen to me.'

'No! You listen to *me*. Lindsey is Stewart's daughter. He's the most precious part of my life… and Lindsey's. I'd savage anyone who tries to hurt him or her. We've nothing more to say on this subject.' She struck his chest with her fist and he stumbled backwards from her fury.

'She deliberately set out to split us up.' His words were beginning to slur again. 'She was laughing when she told me–'

'And she succeeded because you wanted her to succeed,' she interrupted him harshly. 'Don't blame Sara for decisions you made yourself. Whatever torments she had, let them rest in peace with her.'

'How can I let her rest in peace when she's tearing my mind to shreds. Sixteen years of marriage! She owed me an explanation.'

'What explanation could she give? And would it really have made any difference?'

'She didn't have to die to escape from me.'

'You had nothing to do with it, Peter. Sara died to escape from herself.'

He stood at the door of Havenstone and watched her drive away. Tall trees lined the driveway. Bare and knuckled with the rigours of winter, they leaned their ancient boughs over her: oak and elm, chestnut and sycamore, ancient roots enduring while love and passion had withered and died.

Stewart had taken the turkey from the oven when she returned. She always found it difficult to tell when he was angry, to notice the little signs – his mouth tightening, a grimace, almost imagined. On this occasion his annoyance was immediately apparent.

'Dinner's been ready for ages,' he said.

'I haven't been gone that long, Stewart.' She kept her tone light as she shrugged out of her coat. This was not the time or the occasion to dwell on the hurts of the past. 'I'm quite sure the turkey hasn't been complaining.'

'What were you doing?'

'I cooked him something. You saw what he was like.'

'You're not his nursemaid, Beth. I could have driven him home if you'd asked.'

'It's Christmas, Stewart. It's bound to be difficult for him.'

'It's difficult for you too. Has he given a thought to how you're feeling? Of course not. He's holed up in that mausoleum with his whiskey and his self-pity and he doesn't give a tinker's curse about anyone's problems but his own.'

'That's not fair—'

'Don't give me fair, Beth. No one ever said life was supposed to be fair. We do the best we can and get on with it.' He rested the platter on the palm of his hand, composed his face in a smile and made his grand entrance into the dining room.

Gail clapped her hands when she saw his high chef 's hat. Excitement shone from her eyes as he carved the turkey and ceremoniously served her first. Beth wondered what would be left of Christmas when their youngest child lost her belief in magic. No more wish lists winging their way to the North Pole, no more home-made Christmas cards, tinsel and sudden sightings of reindeer on rooftops.

Throughout her married life she had worked hard at creating enchantment for innocent minds to savour, building memories that would carry her children into the years ahead. No one ever suspected how much she hated this season with its synthesised carols and unrelenting commercialism. Or the relief she experienced the following morning when she woke and realised it was over for another twelve months.

After dinner, if the weather stayed dry, they would go for a walk along the estuary shore. The traditional Christmas walk. When the sky darkened they would return home to play Trivial Pursuit, eat chocolates and argue over poker hands. The younger children would dress up and perform their concert. Tradition: a demanding tyrant or a reassuring ritual threading the years together?

CHAPTER TWENTY-TWO

Tork Hansen was busking on Grafton Street. A group of mes-
merised children watched him, fascinated by the flames he blasted above his head. Lindsey imagined her name floating towards
her on a ball of flame and ducked behind a burly man with a
child on his shoulders. When he was not delivering flowers for
his mother in Woodstock, Tork was a fire-eater and, today, disguised as a dragon, he was promoting a newly opened Mexican
restaurant. A part-time busker with dreadlocks and tattoos, he
looked more like a stoner than any of her new friends, yet he
disapproved of the garage gang.

'You'll regret hanging around with that lot,' he'd warned her
the last time she was passing Woodstock. 'Kev Collins is trouble
and he'll take you down with him.'

Lindsey had laughed and demanded to know what kind of
weed he was growing in his mother's shop. Tork was not amused;
nor was she. The garage gang was an exclusive secret club, or so
she had believed, and it worried her that he knew about it.

She moved deeper into the crowd of pedestrians and hurried
up Grafton Street to St Stephen's Green. The ducks were nose-
diving into the pond when Kev sat beside her. The garage gang
would have to do without him on Friday night. He was going
to be a DJ in Ibiza when he got the right break but, for the moment, he was content to work in Dublin and he'd been offered
his first proper, fully paid-up gig. He slipped a sealed plastic
bag into Lindsey's palm, casually holding her hand for a while
longer in case anyone was watching.

She was conscious of the packet in the zipped pocket of her jacket as she left the park. Afraid of meeting Tork Hansen again she turned in the opposite direction and walked down Kildare Street. Dáil Éireann was lit up like a palace. A group of protesters waved banners outside the gates. Last night she had seen her great-uncle being interviewed on television.

'Standing on the plinth, as usual,' her father had said and her mother, entering the room, had switched off the television. Lindsey tried to remember what he'd been discussing but she was unable to remember anything he said. She knew that politicians were crooks, corrupt and full of crap, so it was kind of weird to be related to one.

As if her thoughts had conjured him from the ether, her great-uncle appeared, striding with his briefcase through the gates of Leinster House. He wore black leather gloves and had pulled his coat collar up around his ears. The protestors waved their banners and shouted at him but Lindsey sensed he wasn't the politician they wanted to lynch. He strode purposefully past them and was beside her so quickly she had no time to avoid him. For an instant he looked puzzled then he slapped his thigh and boomed, 'Little Lindsey McKeever. How are you, my dear child?'

He shook her hand and said it was wonderful to see her again. 'And your family?' he asked. 'All in good form I hope?'

'Very well, thank you,' she muttered. How was she supposed to talk to a politician? The protestors certainly knew what they wanted to say. They began to shout about cutbacks at another politician, whose car was trying to ease out through the gates. They surged back so suddenly that Lindsey was almost knocked off balance.

'This could turn nasty.' Her great-uncle grabbed her arm to steady her. 'Let's get out of here before they trample you.'

He guided her across the road, his grip light but firm on her elbow. The noise fell away when they entered a hotel.

'We'll have coffee,' he said. 'The protest will be over shortly.'

The thought of drinking coffee with a politician was horrifying. What would he do if he knew she was carrying illegal drugs? She repeated the words to herself. They had a terrifying force that excited her. Imagine the scandal – 'Politician in Drug Exposé'. It was hard to remember a time when her heart was not doing little skips of anxiety. The sense of panic, of being on the verge of discovery, was such a high, an overdose of adrenaline.

'This is nice,' he said when the coffee arrived. 'I have so little free time when I'm in Dublin. It's a crowded city but it can be the loneliest place in the world when you don't belong in it.'

The hotel had swanky armchairs and was called Buswells. He said it was where politicians came when they were plotting how to knife each other in the back. He chuckled when she glanced nervously around. Not that she would recognise another politician if she saw one, though some of the older people sitting nearby recognised her great-uncle and stared quite rudely.

He told her about his home in Anaskeagh, how much he missed it when he was in Dublin on Dáil business. He enjoyed deep-sea fishing with his friends and climbing to the top of Anaskeagh Head where the view was magnificent. He made it sound like the centre of the world.

'My mother hated Anaskeagh.' Lindsey gulped the coffee, scalding her mouth. 'She said it was hell on earth.'

He stroked his chin, as if he was remembering way back. 'Perhaps it was to a child such as Beth. She took after her father, who had itchy feet. The faraway hills were always greener and Anaskeagh was a quiet place in those days. Not any more though. My son's children are around your age and have no desire to leave home.'

'How many grandchildren do you have?'

'Six.' He looked proud, counting out their names on his fingers. 'Kieran's three live in New York so I only see them occasionally. But I'm blessed with Conor's family. They live in my old house. It's too big and empty since my dear wife passed on, God rest her soul.'

His deep rolling voice grew pensive when Lindsey asked if he had any idea why Sara wanted to die.

'No one knows what goes on in another person's mind,' he said. 'We only think we know but that knowledge is based on the depth of our own feelings. The kindest thing we can do is to let her soul rest in peace.'

It sounded profound, the sort of thing a politician would say. It did nothing to help Lindsey understand. He was cute in a 'has-been generation' sort of way, calling her 'my dear child', but not in a patronising way, and able to listen without letting on he knew best. She told him about her paintings. He said a creative talent should be carefully nurtured and asked what inspired her. His questions challenged her, exciting her because her parents were never interested in discussing her art.

'I'd be very interested to see your portfolio.' He kissed her cheek as she was leaving and said it had been a pleasure to entertain such an intelligent, creative young woman.

'Why don't you come to our house for dinner some evening?' she asked impulsively. 'My mother would love to see you.'

A shadow crossed his face. 'Your dear mother and I didn't always agree on certain things when she was younger. We'd best leave well enough alone.'

He said time had wings when he was in such good company. 'I hope we have the pleasure of meeting again, Lindsey. You must come to tea some evening in my apartment. Or are you too busy to spend time with a lonely old man?' His smile was a question fixed strangely on his face, and he seemed pleased when she said she loved older people, especially Granny Mac.

'Young people are always in such a rush these days,' he said. 'They never have time for those who've lived a little while longer. That's all that separates the generations, my dear. A few short years.'

She thought this was quaint and sentimental, even ludicrous. Old age was a yawning gap. Lindsey could never imagine falling into it.

'Why don't you invite your uncle to visit us?' she asked her mother when they were having dinner that evening. 'He spends lots of time alone in Dublin and he gets awfully lonely.'

Beth sat perfectly still. Then her fists clenched on the table as if she were preparing to lift herself into the air.

'When did you meet that man?' she demanded.

'When I was in town today. What's the big deal? It's my half-day from school.'

'Albert Grant is not welcome in this house.' She spoke slowly, as if Lindsey were incapable of understanding her. 'You are not to have anything to do with him.'

'Why? He's really nice. I asked him to dinner but he said you wouldn't make him welcome. It's obvious he was spot on.'

'Do you hear what I'm saying?'

'Yes. But you're not giving me a reason.'

'I don't have to give a reason.' She stared at Lindsey as if she were a stranger with a bad smell who had wandered into her house. 'As long as you live here you obey the rules.'

'What rules? Thou shalt not talk to lonely old men. Which section of the rule book will I find that in?'

'Lindsey! That's enough,' her father snapped. 'If your mother tells you to do something she obviously has a very good reason for doing so.'

This only spurred her on. 'That's what I want. Just a reason. And what do I get? Behave yourself, Lindsey! Do as you're told! Don't ask questions! Obey the rules or we'll kick you out!'

She was unable to stop, even when Beth rose to her feet and left the room. Lindsey realised she was shivering and it was only later in her bedroom with the music filling her head that she allowed herself to wonder at the inexplicable hurt in her mother's eyes.

She was sitting cross-legged on the floor with her sketchpad when Beth entered her bedroom. She pulled the plug on the stereo, creating an instant ear-popping silence, and hunkered down beside Lindsey.

'Those mugs would crawl across the floor if they had the space to do so.' She pointed at the three mould-encrusted mugs beside Lindsey's bed but she no longer sounded angry.

'I'll bring them down later.'

'Do that.' Beth pointed to the sketchpad. 'Can I see your drawings?'

'No. I'm just messing.' Lindsey bent protectively over the page.

'Shouldn't you be studying instead of messing? I told you what your teachers said at the parent–teacher meeting last week.'

'Six times you did. But who's counting?'

'Your grades have dropped, Lindsey. They've more than dropped – they've plummeted. I know how much you miss Sara, but you have to pull yourself together. Is there anything I need to know? Anything you're not telling me?'

Lindsey sat perfectly still without replying.

'Trust me, Lindsey. I won't be angry if you tell me the truth.'

'Why do you never talk about your life in Anaskeagh? It's part of me too, you know. I've never met any of my relatives except for Marjory. You've never even taken us to Anaskeagh on holiday.'

'I had a difficult childhood, Lindsey. It's not something I wish to discuss.'

'Sara said you were always causing trouble, fighting and breaking things and giving cheek. You ran away without saying a word to her, not even a note. But I guess when it came to leaving notes she got even in the end, huh?'

'Why are you being so cruel, Lindsey?'

'Cruel? It was cruel to try and drown Sara's dog.' Lindsey closed her sketchpad and shoved it back into her portfolio case. 'What made you do such a horrible thing?'

She had not intended to ask the question. It just blurted out of her mouth, and her mother gasped as if Lindsey had punched her in the stomach.

'What did Sara tell you?' She sighed as if she was very tired.

'Just that. Was she telling me the truth?'

'Yes, she was. I did a very cruel thing. I'm ashamed that you should know about it.' Her voice was so low Lindsey could hardly hear her.

'But why try and drown a little dog? There must have been a reason?'

'He kept licking my hands and clawing at me. He slept between us. I couldn't stand it any more.' She looked down at her hands and shivered. 'I really don't want to remember that time, Lindsey. Let's just change the subject, shall we?'

For an instant, Lindsey thought her mother was going to cry. She wanted her to cry so badly. She hadn't seen her shed a tear since Sara had died. Not once. Lindsey wanted those tears to overflow like a waterfall and then she could lean into her mother's chest and cry her own tears, tell her secrets, spill them into their sorrow. She wanted to tell her about the row in Havenstone, the shouting voices that were growing louder in her head. The words that jumbled together like a crossword puzzle, a cryptic clue that would not go away. And how Friday night in the garage was becoming so important that she longed for it all through the week.

CHAPTER TWENTY-THREE

Connie McKeever had been Peter's surrogate mother. She had given him the love his own mother never had time to bestow. Did her son lift Peter's child with the same tenderness and cradle her? Surely he would know his own daughter? His blood would rush with recognition if she appeared before him. His heart would bond with hers the instant they met. Lindsey had been six years old when her parents returned from England. Stewart's child. He had never doubted it for an instant until that night when Sara, pale and remaining chillingly distant from the impact of her words, said, 'Lindsey is your daughter. Isn't it time you opened your eyes and saw the truth, you blind fool?'

Her mockery had been a dark pain. Peter understood that now, and only an echo remained of the rage that had driven him from Havenstone on that last, lost weekend.

Christmas Day was a blur but he remembered Beth's adamant denials. A tigress defending her young. His rights did not matter to her. If there was a truth to be prised loose, he would have to seek it elsewhere.

Marina McKeever was waiting for him when he arrived at the restaurant. She smiled across the wine glasses at him, a languid temptress remembering old times as only Marina remembered them.

'What else brings you to London, apart from an uncontrollable urge to look up an old flame?' she asked.

'A meeting with Sara's publisher,' he replied.

'Oh, my darling. How wretchedly sad for you.' Botox had immobilised Marina's features against sympathy but she gave his hand a comforting squeeze before accepting the menu from the waiter.

The meeting with Sara's publisher had been as emotional as Peter had expected. *Silent Songs from an African Village* was almost ready for publication. Jess had written the text that would accompany Sara's photographs and the book, sponsored by Della Designs, would be a fund-raiser for the health centre the nun ran.

Throughout the meal, Marina talked about her new boyfriend. He sounded indistinguishable from the other men who had moved in and out of her life. No doubt this one would also break her heart. The heat in the restaurant was overpowering. The food arrived, tiny portions arranged with artistic flair on their plates.

'Where on earth did you discover this place?' Peter asked. 'It must have been designed by a demented plumber.'

She glanced approvingly at the glittering chrome and glass décor, the utilitarian network of pipes across the ceiling, and assured him it was the latest *in* place. The place to be noticed. He believed her.

He cut across her description of a holiday in her boyfriend's villa in Provence and asked, 'How was Beth when she stayed with you in London?'

A short silence followed this abrupt change of subject. 'Beth always stays with me when she's in London…'

'I'm talking about the time she left Della Designs?'

'Oh… She was fine. Why do you ask?'

'Fine?'

'Yes, *fine*. Apart from the fact that you dumped her without warning–'

'It wasn't like that.'

'Yes it was, Peter. Dumping girlfriends was your area of expertise.' She placed her cutlery across her plate and rested her elbows on the table. 'Is that why you asked me out?'

'Of course not. I wanted to see you but—'

'But you thought we'd take a little trip down memory lane, is that it?'

'I'm not trying to upset you.' He touched her arm, running his fingers along her tanned skin. She drew away from him, deliberately allowing his fingers to rest on the tablecloth.

'From where I'm sitting, there's only one person at this table who's upset – and it's not me.'

'I'm simply trying to find out the truth about that time.'

'What exactly do you want to know?'

'Was she pregnant?'

She gazed impassively back at him and shook her head.

'Marina, please… I *need* to know. Sara said something… It's tormenting me.'

'Sara always tormented you, Peter. Whatever she said, you must let it go. Lindsey is Stewart's daughter. He knew Beth married him on the rebound but they've made a success of their marriage. The last thing they need is you stirring up the past, especially as it has nothing to do with you.' She gazed coldly across the table at him and signalled to the waiter to bring the bill. 'I hope you don't mind if we call it a night? I've an early start in the morning.'

She glanced down at the bill and removed a credit card from her handbag. 'I'm paying for this.' She refused to listen when he protested. Her voice grew louder, attracting the attention of nearby diners as she pushed her credit card towards the waiter. Peter fell silent, knowing her ability to create a scene and wallow in the attention she would receive.

He followed her outside. 'At least let me call a taxi for you,' he said.

She shrugged and stayed silent when a London cab pulled into the side of the road. Peter gave her address and thrust a twenty-pound note into the driver's hand.

'Thanks, mate.' The driver sounded surprised and appreciative. The journey to Marina's apartment was short. Peter knew it well. He made no effort to follow her into the back seat and she, turning her face to the window, gazed steadfastly into the night.

The factory was in turmoil when he returned from London. A rumour had started among the workers that production was being moved to the Far East. An immediate strike had been called and the machines silenced. Jon Davern informed Peter that he was resigning and the shareholders would make no further investment in Della Designs. He paused to allow Peter to realise the seriousness of the situation, then announced that the bank was calling in his loan.

Albert Grant was unavailable when Peter rang his clinic. His constituency secretary promised to pass on his message. Mr Grant was a busy man, she warned. She could not guarantee when he would return the call. Conor Grant was equally vague. His father had made a decision based on sound financial advice. An ungrateful workforce had left him no choice, and he was unwilling to risk any further losses.

It had been twenty years since Peter had taken over the reins of Della Designs. Twenty years blurring, undistinguished, wasted.

CHAPTER TWENTY-FOUR

Her great-uncle paused over each page in her portfolio. Each drawing received his full attention. Lindsey was nervous, unsure why she had accepted his invitation to have afternoon tea with him. It sounded so old-fashioned. She had imagined cucumber sandwiches in triangles and tiny cakes on a tiered stand but there had been no sign of food when she'd arrived with her portfolio case.

Answering his emails had been easy, especially when he had asked so many questions about her art, but here, in his apartment, with the sounds of the city too far below, she found it difficult to think of things to say to him.

'Why didn't you submit your portfolio to the art colleges?' he asked when he'd finished examining her work.

'I changed my mind,' she said. 'I'm much more interested in studying computer science.'

He looked unconvinced and, for an instant, she was tempted to tell him about that last weekend with Sara. The thought went just as quickly.

'You've a natural talent,' he said. 'You obviously take after your father.'

Lindsey disagreed but remained silent. Her father never claimed to be an artist. His drawings were precise, mechanical, unimaginative.

Her great-uncle ground beans and made coffee from a machine. No jars of instant in his kitchen press. He liked things exactly right, he said. That's why he was such a successful politi-

cian. He told Lindsey about his constituency clinic, so crowded
with people who believed he could move mountains on their
behalf. It was hard not to feel flattered that someone so important was interested in her work, even if she no longer cared
about art or college or anything to do with the future. He lived
in his apartment when he was in Dáil Éireann but he longed
for the weekends when he could return to Anaskeagh to see his
grandchildren. Framed photographs hung on the walls. Lindsey
saw her mother's cousins for the first time. Conor and Kieran
with their wives and children, so many relatives, and they were
all strangers to her. An older photograph hung among the newer ones. Carnival time in Anaskeagh. Swingboats in the background and the big wheel flashing lights. Sara was young then,
early teens, Lindsey guessed, and she carried a white bear she'd
won on the Wheel of Fortune. His arm was around her shoulders. His hair was dark then and shorter. His wife stood on the
other side of him, a small fat woman in ruffles. Lindsey leaned
closer. The charm bracelet she had taken from Sara's jewellery
box was on her aunt's arm. Sara must have inherited it when she
died. Marjory was there too, smiling into the camera, looking
so unlike the cranky old woman with the pursed-up mouth that
Lindsey knew.

He carried the coffee to a wrought-iron table on the bal-
cony. Lindsey sat on one of the two chairs and gulped great
mouthfuls of air as it rushed in from the coast. Dún Laoghaire
Harbour was visible, the sea glistening with sun-swept ripples.
The ferries sailing across Dublin Bay reminded her of lumber-
ing whales, thrusting their white snouts towards the horizon.
Had her mother travelled on a ferry when she left Oldport for
London? Weeks later, had her father followed her on the same
one? They were married in London. Their wedding photo hung
in the sitting room and Stewart, standing with his arm around
her, looked so puffed up with happiness it made Lindsey smile

every time she saw it. Until Sara had told her story – and then it just looked like a sham.

The coffee was too strong for her taste, but she drank it, unwilling to offend her great-uncle. He offered her biscuits curled like fine wood shavings and held one carefully between his thumb and forefinger. When she called him 'Great-uncle Albert' he said that made him sound like someone in a Dickens novel.

'Uncle Albi will do fine,' he said. 'That's what Sara and your mother used to call me when they were young.' The biscuit he was holding snapped and scattered crumbs on his trousers.

She was shocked when he asked if she was 'doing a line'. What did he think she was? A coke head?

'A pretty girl like you must have a boyfriend,' he said and they laughed together because language changed all the time. He used terms like 'courting' and 'dating', but she resisted telling him about Tork Hansen. How she used to walk past Woodstock, hoping he would notice her, but now she no longer cared if she never saw him again.

'How's Stewart?' he asked. 'He must be worried about his future, now that the factory has closed down.'

'He's upset in case he has to work abroad.'

'I'm sure that's not going to happen.' Her great-uncle sounded so definite.

'How can you be sure?'

'That's my little secret.' He tapped the side of his nose. 'Better say nothing to your mother though. She'll think I'm interfering in her business.'

'Why does she...' Lindsey searched for a diplomatic word but 'hate' was the only one that came to mind.

'Why does she hate me? Is that what you wanted to ask, Lindsey?'

She nodded. No sense pretending. He was a politician and used to being insulted.

'I'm afraid I made an enemy of her when her father became ill. Maybe I was wrong but I brought Barry Tyrell home to die among those who loved him.'

'Granny Mac loved him too.' It was weird to think that both her grandmothers had lived with the same man. But Granny Mac was the only one who loved him. His photograph was in a silver frame on a little table in her parlour. His eyes twinkled out at Lindsey. She could just imagine him being a charmer. A magical musician.

'Mrs McKeever was not family,' her great-uncle said. 'You must understand, Lindsey. Family means everything to me. That's why I'm heartbroken over Sara.' He pressed his fist to his mouth. She wanted to run from his grief. It opened something raw and wild inside her.

'Thanks for asking to see my work.' She picked up her port-folio case. 'I'd better go. Mum will be wondering–'

'What would she say if she knew you were here?'

'I'm not going to tell her.'

'Is that because she's refused to allow you to see me?'

'Yes.'

He sighed. 'We've all been through a terrible time. It's sad that such sorrow has not united your mother and I. But Beth could never let bygones be bygones. She broke Marjory's heart when she ran away and Sara's too. However, that's water under the bridge now. I've always had a soft spot for her, despite her wildness. Don't you worry about your father. I always look after my own. You'll see.'

Before she left, he cupped her chin in his big hand and said, 'You're a talented lass, and you'll make your mark on the artistic world, I've no doubt about it. I knew from the moment you were born that you'd make your parents proud. You were such a bonnie, bouncing baby.'

'Not me,' she laughed. 'You're mixing me up with Robert. I was the titch in the family.'

'Oh?'

'Premature,' she explained. 'I scared the life out of my parents.'

'Is that a fact?' He looked confused. 'Oh, dear, my memory is playing tricks again, but blood will out, I always say. You'll come and see me again, I hope.'

As she hurried towards the train station, she wondered what he meant by 'blood will out'. Such a strange thing to say. Unsettling too, because it forced her to remember that last weekend with Sara. It made no difference – no matter how hard she tried to banish it, the question was poised, ready to spring at her whenever she relaxed her guard.

CHAPTER TWENTY-FIVE

Connie, although she was retired, had wept when she'd heard that the gates of Della Designs were locked forever. Since then, Beth had hardly seen Stewart. He was busy working with Peter, negotiating redundancy settlements with the union and disposing of the machinery. The staff were being retrained to work in the pharmaceutical sector and the old building would be knocked down. A new factory would rise in its stead. Beth noticed an unfamiliar hardness in her husband's expression when she asked what he intended to do in the future.

'I'm not interested in repeating the mistakes of the past,' he replied. 'We need to get away from here.'

He talked about moving from Oldport and setting up his own manufacturing plant. In the past he had often mentioned this possibility, short-lived schemes that inevitably fizzled out. This time he was determined. The big fashion chains still needed small manufacturers on their doorstep who could respond to immediate trends. Fashion Lynx would back him with a major contract. He wanted Beth to work with him as an equal partner.

'Remember how you turned Della Designs around when Peter was incapable of thinking straight after his mother died?' he said. 'Imagine what we could do together, the ideas you'd bring to the business.'

'You're living in the past, Stewart. I was a different person then.'

Her life then and now. She was unable to make any connection between them. The excitement of showing a new range, of travelling to New York, London, Paris. Bargaining with hawk-eyed buyers in black suits and flashing jewellery. Boundless energy, her mind closed to everything but her career and her future with Peter.

'That's not true.' Stewart shook his head emphatically. 'Your life has changed since then but you haven't changed. Excellent grants are available if we move outside Dublin.'

'I'd no idea you wanted to move. You never said anything about it.'

'I've spoken about it many times, Beth. But I never thought you were listening.'

'I'm listening now,' she retorted. 'This is a big decision, Stewart. Lifestyle stuff, our future, the children. What if it doesn't work? What security have we to fall back on?'

'Trust me, Beth. It's a wonderful opportunity for both of us.' He reached across the table and clasped her hands, pulling her towards a new beginning they could share.

'Has it been difficult working with Peter?' she asked. 'I know how much you love Lindsey – what she means to you.'

He sat very still, measuring the words he needed to say in his deliberate way. 'Lindsey is an extension of my love for you and that has never had any boundaries. It's as simple and as complicated as that. As far as Peter's concerned, he was simply my employer. I had a family to support and, once we decided to come home, I refused to let personal feelings get in the way.'

'You never wanted to come back from London.'

'But you did. Even then, you were worried about Sara.'

'He believed I could talk to her, help her…' Her voice broke. 'It seemed possible at the time.'

'Stop tormenting yourself, Beth. No one could have done more to help Sara. She had everything going for her, *everything*. I can't understand. I simply can't get my head round it.'

She sensed his frustration, his anger over the hurt that had been inflicted on his family by Sara's suicide. Now he wanted a fresh start, but she was unable to feel anything other than weariness at the thought of another new beginning.

In the early, uncertain weeks of her pregnancy, Peter, unaware of what they had created together, had asked for forgiveness. She despised his platitudes, his appeals for understanding. As if the love he felt for Sara was beyond his control. He stood abjectly before her, and she knew then that there was only one thing to do. A debt had been paid in full and the guilt that had haunted her since that night on Anaskeagh Head fell from her shoulders. She loved Peter Wallace. She carried his child. Stewart carried her. She'd opened the door of Marina's flat soon after her arrival in London and found him standing outside.

Lindsey had been two weeks overdue, normal enough for a first baby, the gynaecologist had reassured them. She'd come into the world with a lusty cry and a strong confident kick.

'My daughter,' Stewart had said, staring in wonder when her tiny fingers gripped his thumb and held on tightly.

Watching them, Beth had vowed that this was the reality they would create together. Their own reality. She'd contacted Peter and Sara soon afterwards. A premature baby, she'd told them, growing stronger but still in an incubator. 'Lindsey will soon be discharged from hospital,' she'd said. 'Stewart is living for the moment when we can hold our daughter in our arms.'

How had Sara discovered the truth? Beth imagined her shock and anguish. Was that what she had intended to discuss when she'd called so unexpectedly to Beth's house? No. Sara had been carrying old secrets, not new ones. Beth would have known the difference. Something had happened between then and the night she'd flung that hard truth at Peter.

In bed, drifting into a dream, she was a young girl again, running up the driveway towards Havenstone. Snow fell around her. An avalanche burying her until she called Peter's name. He lifted her free, the heat of his hands melting the ice, the same heat radiating between them. Intense sexual heat that caused her body to throb with desire as she curled against Stewart. Her hand reached down, stirring him, and he, drowsily emerging from sleep, pulled her close, aroused as always by her touch. Aware of his heavy breathing as he entered her, the familiar contours of his body, and the hazy sensuous images from the dream, her excitement spiralled into an almost painful orgasm. She whispered Peter's name, unaware that she had uttered it aloud until Stewart froze. He pulled away from her and switched on the bedside lamp. The pain in his eyes shamed her.

'Look at me, Beth.' He angled the light towards her. 'This is my face – my body. If you're still confused then this marriage has been a travesty. I never believed that was possible until recently.'

She tried to hold him, knowing it would be useless to defend herself. Stewart seldom lost his temper. When it did happen it was a quiet fury that nothing could quell save his own decision to put whatever had triggered his anger behind him. He rose and left her, sleeping downstairs on the sofa, where Lindsey discovered him the following morning.

Across the breakfast table she fixed angry, accusing eyes on her mother. Stewart left for a business meeting without saying goodbye. Words were inadequate to ease his hurt. When he returned that evening he silenced Beth's stammered apologies, reluctant to discuss the matter any further. He moved back into their bedroom but they lay apart from each other, the space between them growing wider as the days passed.

In the heat of passion she had betrayed him. Infidelity of the mind, Beth realised, was just as unforgivable. A name spoken aloud and the years closed in around them. Old passions resurrecting. He was tired of playing second fiddle to a lost love.

CHAPTER TWENTY-SIX

Peter made her nervous, trying to be so friendly all the time. Lindsey preferred it when she'd been an invisible blot on his horizon. She was glad he was selling Havenstone. A photograph hung in the window of Carrie Davern's estate agency. Lindsey felt sad and nostalgic yet relieved, because if new people moved in they would change everything. They could knock it down and build a new house, maybe a ranch or a villa, and she would no longer have to think about Sara every time she passed it.

That last weekend should have been special. A memory Lindsey could cherish but, instead, she remembered Sara's expression when she'd arrived with her backpack and portfolio case. Surprised but also displeased, as if she'd forgotten they had made the arrangement before she went to Africa. She'd told Lindsey to bring her portfolio so that she could advise her on how to present her work to the art college of her choice. Even when Sara had smiled and slapped the side of her head, as if placing the memory back into position, Lindsey had still felt unwelcome. The feeling had lasted throughout the evening. Her uncle had been the only one who was interested in looking at her work. Hard to believe he had been an artist before he became a suit. He'd explained how he'd once tried to capture the energy of destruction and passion in his own paintings – using her own mother's eyes for inspiration. It sounded weird – almost as weird as imagining her mother having inspirational eyes.

'Just as well you weren't inspired by Van Gogh,' she'd said. 'Or you'd have been obsessing about her ears.'

He'd laughed, throwing back his head as if she'd said something hilarious. Sara hadn't been amused. She'd closed Lindsey's portfolio before she got to the last page and said her paintings were 'cute'. She'd tightened her mouth and, just for an instant, she reminded Lindsey of Marjory when she'd said something spiteful. Why had Sara used that word? 'Cute' was a code for everything that was mediocre and pathetic and naff. Since then, Lindsey had been unable to stop thinking about little things Sara used to say. And she figured they were not so little, not really.

Later, when she was in bed, she'd heard her aunt and uncle arguing in Sara's studio. Their anger had jerked her upright. It was awful, being alone in the dark listening to the ugly words they shouted at each other. To make out what they were saying was difficult but that didn't matter. The sound was everything and in its incoherent fury Lindsey had heard her name. Her scalp had tingled with embarrassment when it was repeated again. She was the reason for the row. Her uncle must resent her hanging around his house all the time. Why else would he shout her name as if he hated her? A door had banged and Sara had crossed the landing, fleeing from his anger to her bedroom. Then, later, Lindsey had heard his heavy tread, like he had rocks on his shoulders. Even when everything had gone quiet, she felt their anger seeping through the walls on either side of her.

The following morning his car had been missing from the driveway. Sara had been in the garden cutting roses when Lindsey had come down for breakfast. A straw hat with a drooping brim shaded her eyes. It had been impossible to tell if she'd been crying. In the kitchen she'd thrown her hat on the counter and begun to arrange the roses. She'd looked so young and pretty in her dark blue sweater and faded jeans, her hair tied in a ponytail. No shadows under her eyes, no tears ravaging her face. She certainly hadn't looked like a woman with an angry husband and Lindsey wondered if she'd dreamed the whole crazy scene.

Often on Saturday mornings they would go shopping in the city. Sara had an unerring instinct when it came to style, especially when it came to choosing clothes for Lindsey. But all Sara had wanted to do that morning was work in her studio. She'd made it clear she didn't want to be disturbed until lunch.

'I'm way behind schedule,' she'd said, as if Lindsey's presence was an extra hassle she had to endure.

The morning had passed slowly. Lindsey had been bored and resentful of her aunt's indifference. Melanie had told her about the garage gang. How they liked to hang around the city on a Saturday afternoon. It sounded way more interesting than emptying the dishwasher and tidying her aunt's kitchen. At lunchtime she'd made soup and sandwiches, and carried the tray upstairs to the studio. Sara had laid out her African photographs on the floor. Lindsey had stared at the images of children tumbling in the dust, laughing out at her with toothy grins, and the women with their dark, fathomless eyes, had been smiling, proud to be photographed with their babies. There had been other photographs of people in fields, carrying parcels on their heads, working on looms, baking bread, happy faces, sad faces, and the hard sun-baked face of her mother's best friend, Jess O'Donovan.

Sara had blinked when she noticed Lindsey, as if forcing herself from some imaginary landscape. Her eyes swept over the tray and away again.

'You shouldn't have bothered,' she'd said. Her impatience had been obvious. 'I'm not hungry.'

'You have to eat something.'

'Please, Lindsey…' She'd pressed her fingers to her forehead. 'Can't you see I'm working to a deadline? I'm very busy right now.'

'I'm sorry. I just wanted—'

'I'll make dinner when I come down. We'll talk then, but for the time being I can do without any interruptions.'

Lindsey had wanted to ask about the row. She wanted to know why her name had been shouted with such rage but the tension she sensed in Sara kept her silent.

Later, Sara chopped mushrooms, onions and tomatoes, simmered pasta and filled the kitchen with her laughter. She'd kissed Lindsey and apologised for being so offhand in the studio. She'd explained about the pressure of deadlines. Everything had seemed perfect again and Lindsey couldn't imagine ever wanting to be anywhere else.

A place had been set at the table for Peter but he never showed. They'd laughed, imagining him sulking somewhere, probably in the Oldport Grand, afraid to come home and face the music. After the meal they'd sat in the drawing room with the curtains open and the village lights winking back at them. Sara had poured brandy into a goblet and swirled it around, staring into the liquid as it swished from one side of the glass to the other. She'd spoken about her days as a professional photographer when she lived in London and how her uncle had given her the money to mount her first exhibition. The subject had been Irish emigrants, homeless people sick with the need to return to their families. The exhibition had been well reviewed but most Irish people hated it because it was so grim, all those sleazy rooms and weary, lined faces. They'd only wanted to know about the successful emigrants like her cousin, Kieran, who was hell-bent on becoming a rich stockbroker in New York.

One day, when she had still been living in London, Beth phoned her. She'd paid little attention to Sara since she'd run away from Anaskeagh, but then, out of the blue, she commissioned Sara to do a photo shoot.

Beth was always laughing, Sara had said, her voice so low she could have been talking to herself. Lindsey had imagined her mother looking glamorous and confident as she'd flicked back her long black hair, teasing Peter with her cats' eyes, tormenting Stewart, giving orders, ignoring Sara, who was just the hired photographer, nothing more. Why had Beth always been laughing? A sick fluttery feeling had started in Lindsey's chest. She hadn't wanted to hear about her mother and Peter being in love. To think of them in each other's arms was sickening – but Sara had kept going on and on about those days and Lindsey hadn't known how to stop her.

Then Peter had begun to stare at Sara instead. He'd found it difficult to breathe when she stood too close. Beth hadn't had a clue about what was going on right under her nose. Sara had swirled the brandy faster before drinking it down in one swallow then made a face. Her laughter had made Lindsey uncomfortable. She was unable to see the joke. She'd sensed an echo in her aunt's words, as if she'd wanted to harm Beth. It had seemed wrong to talk about her mother in this intimate way, as if these disclosures stripped away her privacy, laid bare her painful love.

Sara had pulled out a fashion brochure from a drawer and handed it to Lindsey. The photographs were brilliant. Lindsey had recognised Pier's Point, the high tide lapping the jetty. The models had looked as if they were suspended on sun beams, as vaporous as spray. Her crazy aunt Marina had been the main model, her face white as a vampire bride, skinny as a stick.

Sara had married Peter soon afterwards because, Sara said, when a force wind blows you either get out of the way or you blow with it. Beth had gone to London and Sara had come to Oldport – two sisters moving past each other in opposite directions. Lindsey had suddenly grown angry with her aunt when she'd thought of Beth in those days, living with crazy Marina, so miserable and sad, while Sara had stolen Peter away with her charms and settled into Havenstone. Queen of the palace.

How edgy Sara had looked when she'd finished her story. She'd crossed to the drinks cabinet and poured another brandy, her movements too fast, and when she replaced the bottle Lindsey thought it would break with the force she'd used. She touched Lindsey's hair, ruffling it, and smiling in a dreamy, off-focus way.

'I'm tired,' she'd said. 'I'm going to lie down. I'll see you in the morning.'

And away she went to her white bedroom, walking airy light, like egg shells would crack under her feet.

Lindsey had switched on the television, flicking channels, unable to relax. The story Sara had told her felt as cloying as a cobweb against her skin. She'd realised that she always saw her mother in a lesser way after being with her aunt. Remarks Sara made, nothing unkind or horrible, just remarks that made the feeling grow until Lindsey wanted to belong only to her. Then everything would be perfect, so effortless and elegant.

She would go home, she'd decided. That was where she belonged, not in this cold, cheerless house where she was obviously unwelcome. Sara had been sitting in front of her dressing table when Lindsey entered her bedroom. She'd twisted her hair into a tight knot at the top of her head, clamping it into place with a clip comb. It had shown off her long neck, so taut, as if the skin was stretched too tight. There had been lines on her cheeks, still faint, but Lindsey had seen them clearly, and known how her aunt would look in years to come.

She hadn't seemed to notice Lindsey standing behind her, even though their eyes had locked in the mirror. Her cheeks had been marked by angry red welts, as if she had slapped or scratched her pale skin. Her fingers trembled as she touched the marks, her eyelids flickering when she realised Lindsey was standing behind her.

'Oh, *Christ*... You even look like him,' she'd whispered and covered her eyes, as if unable to endure the sight of Lindsey. 'How dare you enter my room without my permission?'

'I'm sorry... Sorry–'

'Get out... *Get* out of my sight and don't ever come back here again,' Sara had shrieked and, in that instant, Lindsey understood that she'd been looking at a stranger – and that she had become a stranger to Sara. As she turned away, she'd seen her aunt's reflection fragmented on the mirrored walls, her neck bowed, her slender frame shattered.

Downstairs, she'd slumped on the sofa, weeping. Sara should have locked her door if she hadn't wanted to be interrupted. That was what she'd always done when she was in one of her moods, staying there for days or working in her studio all through the nights.

Yes, Lindsey had understood about those 'reflective moods'. That was what Sara had called them. Peter phoned her mother at such times and asked her to come to Havenstone. Beth usually returned home exhausted, pretending nothing was wrong, but talking low to Stewart and falling silent when Lindsey entered the room. She'd overheard them one night discussing depression and mood swings. She had wanted to tell her mother she was wrong, so very wrong, because when Lindsey was in Havenstone, it was impossible to believe such words could ever be applied to anyone as wonderful as Sara.

When Sara had come downstairs she'd been wearing make-up to cover the welts on her face.

'I'm *so* sorry, my darling.' She'd taken Lindsey in her arms and dried her tears. 'Forgive me. I drank too much brandy. A bad mistake. Say you forgive me, please.'

Lindsey had made excuses and left. She couldn't remember if they'd said goodbye. No matter how she racked her brains, she was unable to recall the last words she'd spoken to her aunt. All she knew was that she'd hated Sara and never wanted to return to Havenstone again. Such a horrible feeling and it lasted until her mother had taken her in her arms two days later and broken the terrifying news to her.

CHAPTER TWENTY-SEVEN

Bombshells, Beth thought, should be carefully introduced into conversations. Yet by their nature, bombshells, no matter how carefully they were handled, exploded lives that, moments before, had been seamlessly held together by habit and routine.

Stewart had been away for two nights. Business matters, he'd said. An opportunity he needed to investigate. She sensed his excitement when he returned home but he waited until the children were in bed before breaking the news.

She glanced down at the brochure he handed her, daunted by statistical information she would once have absorbed at a glance. 'Action on Creative Indigenous Industry' was embossed on the front cover. He pointed to a photograph of a small factory in a semicircle of eight similar buildings – a modern, compact industrial estate. His briefcase looked bulky and incongruous in the middle of the dining-room table. Like a fat squatting toad, she thought, its bottom lip hanging down, disgorging information she did not want to hear.

'This is a strong possibility,' he said, tracing the route on the map, his finger moving westwards towards a brown headland dominating a small town. 'There's a small clothing factory available here. The previous owner moved her production base to Morocco and we can set up immediately. There's a skilled workforce ready and willing to begin working for me.'

'But that's Anaskeagh,' Beth whispered. 'Are you crazy?'

'It's outside the town. Your uncle used to have his furniture factory there. Some years ago it was turned into an industrial estate by the ACII. They give excellent grants to first-time business ventures so it's ideal for our needs.' He stopped short when he saw her expression. 'Don't block me at the first fence, Beth. This could be the perfect solution.'

She was aware that her responses were too slow, the conversation running ahead of her. 'Has Albert Grant got anything to do with this?' she demanded.

'He contacted me after the factory closed and offered to help. At first I wasn't sure but he persuaded me to go down and look at what was available.' His voice quickened, as if he already sensed her resistance. 'He's got clout with the ACII and has offered to cut through a lot of red tape. The town is thriving, well worth thinking about as a place to live. I wanted to see it for myself before I told you. Honestly, Beth, he really has been invaluable with advice and support.'

'How could you even talk to him? I can't believe what I'm hearing!'

'He's only trying to help us. I'd never have considered Anaskeagh. But now that I've seen the centre, I believe it's perfect for our needs.'

'So you're handing me a fait accompli, is that it? Why didn't you discuss this with me at the early stages?'

'I didn't want your emotional responses stopping me before I'd fully investigated the possibilities.'

'There are no possibilities, Stewart.' Her disbelief gave way to fury. 'I've no intention of moving to Anaskeagh. Not now, not in a million years. Never! *Never!* Do you understand? I won't be involved in this – I'm not even prepared to discuss it.'

'Why? What's so dreadful about the town? I've never understood why you hate it so much.'

'I don't hate the town. I hate *him.*'

'You've a hard memory, Beth. Sometimes it's wiser to move on instead of living in the past.'

'Is that what you think I'm doing?'

'To tell the truth, I don't know what you're doing any more. I've no liking for him either. But maybe it's time to bury the hatchet. Life's short, Beth, too short to carry hatred.'

'How can you forget the way he behaved when my father was dying? How much he hurt Connie?'

'That was a long time ago. Why don't you tell me what's really bothering you?'

'Talking about Sara won't bring her back.'

'But it will help you to come to terms with it. And it will help us—'

'Us?'

'Yes, us. Your family. You know what I'm saying. This wall…' He sighed, a quiet man who usually relied on Beth to instigate conversations. 'You've been erecting this wall around yourself, pretending everything is normal, but you're not seeing us. You're not with us at all, Beth, and it's seriously beginning to bother me. I can't stand pretence. I'm trying to make important decisions, and I need to know you hear me when I talk to you.'

'I hear you. Of course I hear you. Are you saying I'm not allowed to grieve in my own way because it upsets you and the children?'

'That's not what I said.' He sounded weary. 'I do appreciate what you're going through. All I want to do is make a new beginning with you.'

'A new beginning? I spent my childhood taking charity from my uncle and now you want me to do the same again.'

'Charity! This has nothing to do with charity.' She had never seen him so angry. 'You've no idea of the work I've put into this project. Anaskeagh needs employment and I can provide it. Steve Maguire needs a supplier for Fashion Lynx and I can give him what he wants. I'm willing to beg and borrow and work all the hours God sends to support my family – and you have the gall to call that charity!'

'I won't return to Anaskeagh, Stewart. Don't make me.'

'I've never made you do anything you didn't want to do. But this is important to me. To *us*. I want to know the real reason why you're not interested. You still love him, don't you?' He held her face between his hands and forced her to look at him. 'I know the signs. I had a long apprenticeship on the sidelines, remember?'

She pushed him aside and ran upstairs. She locked the bedroom door and flung herself onto the bed, aching with the need for tears and release, aware of Stewart at the door, pleading with her to let him in.

All she could see was a slumbering country road. An old pub with a half door and milk churns in the yard. She remembered her father's strong arms when he'd lifted her up on the counter one warm autumn afternoon, and how he'd played his accordion until it was time to collect the furniture that stood in the building with the corrugated iron roof.

She'd heard the men sawing and hammering and the sawdust swirling like a snowstorm, making her sneeze and catch her breath when she tried to speak.

'Gold dust,' her uncle had said, laughing as he tossed the sawdust in the air.

Outside, her father had leaned against the van, smoking a cigarette and chatting to the woman who did the wages.

It had been musty in the big storeroom where chairs and tables waited to be delivered. She'd been ten years old, hiding. He'd found her though, as he always did. And afterwards there had been new furniture in her mother's kitchen, a table with a leg that was too short and had to be evened up with a folded cigarette box.

'Are you sick, Mammy?' Gail's sleepy voice sounded from the landing. The child clutched her teddy bear under her arm and held the end of her nightdress in her other hand. Her blonde hair was tousled and the sleepy expression on her heart-shaped face was an aching reminder of the young Sara. Beth hugged her daughter and carried her safely back to bed.

She was calm when she returned to the living-room. 'Go if you must, Stewart,' she said. 'The decision is yours. But I'm staying here.'

She no longer swam in the mornings and awoke heavy-headed, longing to sink back into the pillows and stay there for the rest of the day. She stared at her reflection and saw a faded woman with lacklustre eyes gazing back at her. She dreamt about Fatima Parade. A child's memory shaped into an adult nightmare. The faded cabbage-rose wallpaper, the lights from passing cars throwing shapes across the bedroom ceiling. The creak of a wardrobe door. A red dress swaying from a coat hanger. Her heart thumped as she curled into the empty space where Stewart's body had once warmed her. She turned restlessly and awoke. Was he also lying awake thinking about her, unable to understand why, so suddenly and so determinedly, she had turned from him?

He was staying in the O'Donovan farmhouse. On Friday evenings when he returned home he brought news from Anaskeagh, titbits to try and arouse Beth's interest. Sheila O'Donovan – who was once Sheila O'Neill, smuggler of forbidden baby photographs into school – had offered to mind their two younger children if Beth decided to move. Her sister, Nuala O'Neill, had returned from London and was running an arts and crafts gallery in the town. Nuala's baby, whom Beth remembered in white ribbons and lace, was now an architect, speaking fluent Japanese and stamping his signature on skyscrapers. Hatty Beckett sent her love. The corner building that had once housed her famous chip shop had become a shopping mall and she was running the café in Nuala's gallery.

He asked her opinion on machinery, fabrics, deals he was negotiating with Fashion Lynx. The factory would be called TrendLines. What did Beth think of the name? A bungalow near O'Donovan's farm was for sale. It had a view of the sea, wonderful cliff walks, a fifteen-minute drive from the town, no traffic jams. They could move in immediately.

Marjory had closed down her boutique and was drifting aimlessly through each day. Stewart had invited her out for a meal but his efforts to make peace were curtly rejected. What did he expect? Forgiveness for being a McKeever?

CHAPTER TWENTY-EIGHT

If anyone had asked Lindsey to describe her parents' marriage she would have said 'boringly contented'. As far as she was concerned, the two emotions were compatible. 'Boring' summed up the reality of two people living together and doing the same things year after year. Yet her parents seemed to accept this low-level existence with a certain degree of contentment. Or so she'd thought until the tension between them hit the high wires and everything changed.

Her mother kept denying there'd been a split. Her false smiles and denials were not reassuring, especially when her father was no longer living at home. Before he left, he took his motorbike from the shed where Granny Mac had kept it safe all those years her parents had been in London. He used to take Lindsey to the rallies with all the other bikers when they'd first moved to Oldport. She wore leather and rode pillion as he raced through the Sally Gap or Glendalough. When they returned home, covered in mud and unable to stop laughing over all their adventures, her mother would shake her head at the state of their clothes.

'You crazy pair of Hell's Angels,' she would say, pretending to be cross because she had to wash everything.

No pretence now. Her anger was for real, even though she pretended not to care that he had taken his Harley to Anaskeagh. It was gleaming in Reception, along with the hanging plants and posh receptionist.

He wanted them to move – her mother wanted to stay. Now they had reached a compromise. It made neither of them happy but compromise seldom did, which was why marriage was the pits. Sara had never compromised. She did what she wanted to do and when she'd had enough of doing that she'd bowed out. No note, no nothing, not even a grave with flowers, only her laughter rising, mocking Lindsey. Just thinking about it made Lindsey shake with anger.

If her mother finally decided to move to Anaskeagh, Lindsey would remain in Oldport and live with her grandmother. Granny Mac had hugged her tight and said she would love the company. Her uncle had had other ideas. There would be a room waiting for Lindsey in his new house, he'd said. She would be a free spirit, able to come and go as she pleased. He'd frowned when she'd informed him that she intended to move in with her grandmother.

'Connie is an elderly lady,' he'd said. 'She'll find it tiring having a young person around her house all the time.'

He made Connie sound like Methuselah's granny.

'Granny Mac has never found me tiring,' Lindsey had replied. 'Why should she start now?'

Robert thought moving to Anaskeagh was a brilliant idea. He planned on becoming a traditional musician like their grandfather. Granny Mac had given Robert the accordion that Barry used to play and the wailing sound coming from his bedroom was doing Lindsey's head in. When she tried to make him see that there was trouble on the domestic front he told her she was mental. Their mother just needed time to make up her mind. Lindsey's problem was an overactive imagination, brought about by an overindulgence of E at weekends.

'You're dead for real if the folks find out.' He knew what was going on from the school grapevine.

'Everyone's doing it,' she replied.

'I'm not.' He could look really smug at times. 'You shouldn't mess around with that stuff. It does funny things to your brain.'

She trusted him not to tell her parents about Friday nights. They shared too many secrets to break rank. Not that anyone would have cared. She remembered the fuss her mother used to make about her social activities, always checking out the scene before she gave permission for Lindsey to go out with her friends in the evening.

She saw Sara's ghost again. This time, the manifestation appeared outside Carrie Davern's estate agency. The ghost was not carrying her baby in a sling, which was just as well, because she walked straight into Lindsey and almost knocked her to the ground.

'I'm so sorry. Are you all right?' She grabbed Lindsey's arm, steadying her, a strong ghost with a solid grip. She looked thin and tense but the same wide smile lit her face.

'You remind me very much of someone,' Lindsey said as they waited for the traffic to stop before crossing the road.

'I hope she's a nice person.' The woman stepped off the pavement before the lights changed and staggered back when a driver blasted his horn at her.

'She was lovely,' Lindsey replied.

Tork was on the pavement stacking potted plants on stands when he saw them. For once, he ignored Lindsey, and smiled at Sara's ghost.

'How are you, Eva?' he said, but it didn't sound like an ordinary greeting. His mother joined him outside Woodstock and held out her arms.

'Eva! I'm so glad to see you,' she said. 'Come in and have some tea.'

She sounded motherly and concerned but the woman called Eva said she had to fly and drove away in a small white van.

Lindsey felt as if she knew her from a long way back. Not just because she reminded her of Sara – that was only superficial – but through something stronger than time or memory. Sara would have understood what she meant. She would have called it 'a meeting of dreams'.

CHAPTER TWENTY-NINE

Jess O'Donovan came back to Ireland for the launch of *Silent Songs from an African Village*. Little remained of the young girl who had left for her novitiate at the age of eighteen, her suitcase packed with black dresses and voluminous knickers; her child's face, puppy soft and innocent. Now her skin was leathery – too much sun, too little care. Her steadfast brown eyes were the only youthful thing about her. It saddened Beth, seeing this premature ageing, but she knew that Jess would dismiss her concerns as too frivolous to even warrant discussion. In famine camps in Ethiopia and Sudan she'd served out her mission. She now lived a quieter life in Malawi, working in the health centre she'd helped to establish. The years had taken their toll on her health and she'd returned to Ireland for a short break.

'Burnout,' she told Beth, who picked her up at the airport. 'It hit like a hammer blow. Serves me right for believing I was indispensable.'

She would stay with Beth in Estuary View Heights for a week before visiting her family in Anaskeagh. Their life paths had moved in different directions, but the friendship they had shared as children was still unchanged.

The hotel venue where the book was to be launched was packed. No one spoke or laughed too loudly, as befitting a launch that posthumously honoured the photographer. The arrival of Albert Grant, accompanied by two of his staff and a television crew, broke the sombre mood. He kissed Beth on the cheek before she had time to turn away.

'Poor Marjory is too broken-hearted to attend,' he said.

'I know. We spoke on the phone.'

'Why haven't you been to see her?'

'That's none of your business.' She kept her voice low. 'But Lindsey *is* my business—'

'Dear Beth, you made your views perfectly clear when you rang me.' He drew back, as if her fury had pressed against his chest. 'She's a charming young girl but why you should make such a fuss about a chance encounter outside the Dáil is beyond me. I never understood your hostility when you were a child and it's even more baffling now.'

'Is it? Perhaps you'd like me to analyse the reasons in more detail?'

'Be careful.' His fingers bit into her arm. 'Marjory is in enough distress over Sara's passing without you adding to her misery. She needs you now more than ever. Are you going to let her pine away from a broken heart?'

'She has four grandchildren here and an open invitation to visit us as often as she likes. She chooses to do otherwise, and I never intend setting foot in Anaskeagh again for reasons only you understand.'

He glanced across the room towards Stewart, who had driven from Anaskeagh for the launch. 'What about your husband? A man needs his wife by his side when he's trying to establish a new business. It would be a shame if he failed because of some misguided notions you have about Anaskeagh.'

'Are you threatening me?'

'Perish the thought. Family means everything to me. I'd never do anything to hurt or harm you. Whatever imagined ideas you have about the past need to be curtailed. You always were a troubled child and troublesome too. Now it's time to support your husband, as he has always supported you.' His fluid sincerity set her teeth on edge. He smiled over her shoulder as Greg Enright from *Elucidate* approached with a cameraman. Unable to listen to him being interviewed, she joined Stewart on the other side of the room.

Sara's photographs flashed on a loop behind Peter as he launched the book. Jess spoke movingly about her life in the village and the time Sara had spent there. Afterwards, Beth was unable to remember anything they had said. Her uncle's presence dominated the room. She bought a copy of the book from a young woman who was selling them and turned the pages, moved as always by Sara's stark, powerful images.

Stewart went to bed early when they got home from the launch, knowing the two friends would talk until the small hours. Jess opened the book and named her friends from the village, their children and the staff who worked with her in the medical centre. Beth pictured Sara's unobtrusive figure blending into the dusty landscape, knowing the precise second to capture a moment: a gesture, an unforgettable image.

Jess closed the book and stared for a moment at the photograph of Sara on the back cover. She began to talk, hesitantly at first, about Sara's trip to her village. How, at the end of the visit, she'd sat on the veranda of the mission house with Jess and wept as if she was releasing a terrible, wrenching sorrow. She had travelled through time and across continents for this moment of confession and, in the shade of an African night, she had opened her seal on the past.

'She told me everything.' Jess reached out to Beth when she saw her friend's stricken expression. 'She told me about the headland and how you helped her give birth to her child. Such a heart-breaking story, and you, my closest friend… All those years of silence. How you both must have suffered. I never thought she could have been the mother. Never. Sara had always seemed so… So unsullied by life.'

'Unsullied.' Beth repeated the word then nodded slowly. Jess was right. Unsullied children, sullied forever by shame and fear.

'She spent her life yearning for a child whom she believed she had no right to seek or to love,' Jess said. 'She was never able to move on from the terror that gripped her when she was pregnant and then overwhelmed her on that dreadful night. How could she love what she had been determined to destroy? How could she recover from such an experience when there was no one to understand or help her to understand?'

'I tried…' Beth's voice broke but she forced herself to continue. 'I wrote letters but she never replied. She was attending boarding school for six months before I even found out she'd left Anaskeagh. And when she went to London I only traced her when Marina told me Sara had had a photographic exhibition. When we did meet again it was as if nothing had happened. Whenever I tried to bring it up she froze me out – you've no idea how powerful her silence could be. She swore me to secrecy that night, but how could such a devastating thing happen and never be discussed? I kept that vow until now. Not even Stewart knows… Or Peter?'

'She told me about the oath you took,' Jess said. 'She was going to talk to you when she got home. And Peter too. She wanted to make a fresh start with him.' She lifted a glass of wine from the small table beside her then laid it back untouched. 'I guess the struggle was too great for her in the end.'

'Oh, Jess, she came to me… But I was too busy to listen.' The tears came at last, a river in spate as they stung her cheeks and left her gasping against her friend's strong shoulders. Jess held her until she could cry no longer.

'Who fathered the child?' Jess finally asked the question she had been dreading. 'Sara told me he was dead. Was she telling the truth? There was so much gossip at the time about my own brothers. That's why Jim went to Australia. Sheila even broke off her engagement with Bernard for a while because a rumour started that he was the father. It was a difficult time, so much media attention, and the guards asking questions. Do you know his name?'

Beth wanted to shout it out. To fling it into the light. But even as her mind rushed towards this release, she imagined Marjory's shock, her uncle's denials – his powerful control reducing her once again to the quaking, frightened child he had once terrorised.

'She never told me. It happened so quickly I never had time to ask.' She was speaking the truth, even though it felt like a lie. Sara never did utter his name aloud. Monster… Monster… They had both grasped that image and clung to it, as if their fantasies could detach him from the reality of his deeds.

'Do you know who adopted her baby?' she asked.

Jess nodded. 'I do, but I'm bound by confidentiality. I can't discuss this, even with you.'

'Just let me know if she had a happy upbringing?'

'She had a wonderful upbringing. You need have no worries on that score.'

'I'm glad… so glad. Does she know about her past? That she was the Anaskeagh Baby?'

Jess shook her head. 'Her family protected her from that information. She's never asked to meet her natural parents but lately…' She hesitated, then shook her head. 'She believes her birth parents were too young to look after her. She calls them "the puppy lovers".'

'Did you tell Sara?'

'I needed permission to tell her.' Jess's voice was laden with regret. 'I believed there was time… That this was the start of her healing. I left it too late, Beth. I'll always regret that I didn't seize the moment and tell her everything.'

Too late. How final it is when time runs out, Beth thought. A moment shapes itself and is seized or lost forever. She remembered that moment on Anaskeagh Head when she had hesitated at a fork in the path and decided to make the journey to the farmhouse, knowing instinctively, even in the midst of her terror, that she could trust the O'Donovan family. Now, so many years later, it seemed right that the young nun should have played such an important role in the life of the child who'd been thrust so arbitrarily on her doorstep.

'Will you talk to Peter?' Jess asked.

'He was unhinged by Sara's death,' Beth replied. 'He's finally beginning to pull himself together. I don't know what this will do to him.'

'It will help him to understand the cross she carried.'

'I don't think I can bear it.' Beth rocked forward and wrapped her arms around her stomach. 'I can't go on remembering. You've no idea how much Sara hated me.'

'Not hated – envied,' Jess replied. 'She envied the safe place you found for yourself. No matter where you went you made your life secure, but she remained the child who could do no wrong. Sainthood is not an easy occupation, especially when you hate yourself.'

'I'm inside her head. I don't want to be there, but I can't escape.'

'My poor Beth.' The nun sighed. 'I wish I could find the right words to comfort you.'

'There was a time you would have told me to put my faith in God.'

'Faith.' Jess savoured the word, then dismissed it. 'It's a long time since I afforded myself such a luxury.'

'No more voices?'

'No more voices.' Jess replied. 'I don't need them now.'

Tomorrow she had been invited to address students in Trinity College. They would ask her questions about her work in

Malawi. Some would accuse her of white imperialism, imposing Western solutions on African culture, proselytising, patronising. She was used to such accusations, immune to the views of radicals and reactionaries alike. She had exchanged the rugged hills of an Irish farm for the baked dust of an African village and was only resting briefly on this green shore before returning to her real world.

CHAPTER THIRTY

Everything was clear to him now. A mystery solved when it was too late for understanding. In the garden Sara once loved to tend, Beth told him about the headland and the leaning rocks that had briefly cradled his wife's child. Grief and fury strained against his chest as he listened to her unfolding story.

'Who was the father?' he asked when she fell silent.

'Sara never spoke his name,' she replied. 'There's so much I didn't know… Didn't want to know.' She shivered, her breath heavy and fast, as if she were reliving every moment she had spent with Sara on Anaskeagh Head.

He wanted to comfort her but his own memories stormed inside him. 'But you must have some idea–'

'How can I name someone when I've no proof?'

'She never hinted–'

'She told Jess he was dead. But their daughter lives and thrives. That's the one good thing to come out of that terrible night.'

Aislin's Roof, he recognised the birthing place from Beth's description – the last photographs Sara took. He had moved them to the attic without even pausing to wonder at their meaning. She must have gone to Anaskeagh after she'd returned from Malawi. What had happened to her during the time she spent there? What ghosts had she confronted? Was that where she'd learned the truth about Lindsey? So many questions that would never be answered. He ached with the need to see her again. To talk as they had never talked when she was alive. Analysing, understanding, forgiving each other. She had lost a daughter, just as he had lost Lindsey. But, unlike him, she had carried the knowledge inside her while he, unaware, uncaring, came to the knowledge too late.

'I've lost everything I've ever wanted,' he cried. 'My life is over.'

'No,' Beth replied. 'It's moving on. That's all we can do, Peter. We have to find a way to move on from this heartache.'

Time had not moved on for Sara. It had etched her future in a dark cavity between the rocks and an unyielding earth – and when she could no longer endure, she willed her ashes to merge with the cold tide lapping the pilings on Pier's Point.

'I need to make peace with Sara's demons,' Beth said when she was leaving.

'Is that possible?' he asked.

'In Anaskeagh it will be.' Her arms tightened around him then fell away again, her face taut with knowledge she was not prepared to share with him.

Della Designs was razed to the ground. A swing from the arm of a crane. A blow in its solar plexus from a swaying demolition ball. An instant of indecision, as if brick and mortar could withstand the forces ranged against it. Then the old factory buckled, bowed almost gracefully, before collapsing with a dull whoosh, a mushroom cloud of dust and debris rising in its wake.

Peter felt no emotion, no quiver of nostalgia to mark its passing. When the dust cleared, a new vista opened before him. Rows of houses, swatches of green, the distant estuary flowing under the arches. A heap of stone to mark the passing of Della Designs. His legacy, now dead.

He walked back to Havenstone. Estuary Road was desolate. He ignored the warning signs forbidding entry. Children were fishing off Pier's Point, just as he had fished with Stewart when they were young, searching for crabs among the rocks, building dams and channels in the soft mud. The new motorway would destroy old ways. As the suburbs edged closer to the city, Old-port was becoming another satellite town, but the pursuits of children would always remain the same.

CHAPTER THIRTY-ONE

Noise, light, energy. Lindsey could never remember feeling so happy. She was a kaleidoscope, high and spinning through the colours. Water flowed down her throat. It ran through her hair, cold on her skin, drowning her. She rose above the torrent, flailing towards freedom where there was space to dance into infinity. The floor juddered under her feet. The garage walls opened outwards. She reached towards Melanie and Karen, her friends. One mind, one sensation, one body. Not like Uncle Albi... She could never call him that ridiculous name. He was on the radio all the time – at least that was how it seemed – but Lindsey figured she just hadn't noticed him in the past. His voice was full of authority, boasting about all the things he did for the black spots of unemployment in rural Ireland. She supposed that was what being a politician was all about. The movers and shakers of the world. His emails had been wise and funny. He valued her opinions. He needed to understand the young voice if he was to appeal to the new generations. They held the future in their hands, he said. Young people like Lindsey with her artistic mind, which was capable of seeing beyond the obvious.

'A chip off the old block,' he'd said and touched her arm. Gentle kitten strokes, smiling, as if he'd known that sooner or later she would come back to his fancy apartment. The question had refused to go away. Even in the garage with the music mix thudding inside her head, it had been there, demanding an answer.

'Why did you say I was a bonnie baby?' Asking the question meant that nothing would ever be the same again but leaving it unanswered was no longer an option.

'That's how I always imagined you,' he'd replied. 'A strong, healthy child – not a little titch.'

'Not premature, you mean?' Lindsey had been unable to continue.

'What are you asking me?' He had leaned towards her and stared deep into her eyes.

'I want to know about my mother. Before I was born… and my father.' She'd stopped talking when he'd clasped her fingers between his warm, comforting hands.

'But you know the truth already, don't you, my poor, hurting child?' He'd spoken gently when the tears rushed into her eyes and had drawn her nearer. 'Lindsey, I know how painful the truth can be. But not knowing ourselves is the greatest pain of all. Your mother was a foolish woman in love with the wrong man. Don't punish her for a mistake that turned into such joy.' His eyes had glittered with knowledge. 'Cherish what you have, my dear. Stewart gave you as much love as any father could bestow on his natural child.'

Lindsey had felt no surprise, just an overwhelming tiredness, as if she'd come to the end of long journey that had begun in Havenstone on the night she listened to the bitter words Sara flung at her husband… at Lindsey's father.

Albert had stroked her hair. His fingers had nestled in the nape of her neck, moving in a slow, circular movement as his voice comforted her. She hadn't wanted him touching her hair. He had been drinking when she'd arrived and in his eyes she'd seen something unsettling, a flicker, a gleam of satisfaction. He had wanted her to ask the question. Sara had been right about secrets. There was a time when silence was more important than honesty. He had released her secret and she hated him for it.

'Let me go.' She'd struggled from his embrace.

He'd held her for an instant longer, his grip hard as steel.

'Can't you see his face when you look in the mirror? The sins of the mother visited on the child. The truth is everything but she refused to listen… Wicked girl…' His voice had broken as if glass had caught in his throat.

She'd walked towards the door, terrified he would try to touch her again. His words had followed her. She hadn't wanted to hear. He'd stood in his doorway, watching as she'd run down the long corridor towards the elevator. When it glided to a halt and the doors slid noiselessly across, he'd still been standing staring until she was safe in the mirrored space, gliding downwards towards freedom.

She'd walked for a long time. The lights of the city had melted into shimmering walls. The sound of traffic had been loud in her ears. People had moved too fast, jostling against her. Everything had looked the same as before – yet nothing would ever be the same again.

In the garage she could dance into the past. She tapped Peter's name on her mobile phone, the photograph of his face beside the number. He answered immediately. She was laughing fit to cry and he kept calling her name… Lindsey… Lindsey… But she shouted him down, her voice breaking on the word 'father', unable to say it aloud as all the dazzling lights spun her towards the ceiling. She was outside her body, her feet skimming the earth until darkness came like a plunging star and carried her away.

CHAPTER THIRTY-TWO

Beth eased herself out of bed and entered the children's bedrooms. Each room was a silent oasis of darkness and quiet breathing. She did not enter the attic bedroom. Tonight, Lindsey was staying at Melanie's house, celebrating her friend's seventeenth birthday. The Leaving was beginning soon and the strain was showing on her face: she was tense, distracted, turning resolutely away from Beth whenever she asked questions.

She returned to bed and listened to the night sounds: the creaks and sighs of seasoned wood, a distant house alarm activated, a sudden blast of music and laughter, probably a party somewhere nearby. Familiar comforting sounds which she gathered around her as she drifted back to sleep.

The telephone rang at two in the morning. Peter made no sense. How could Lindsey be unconscious and in an ambulance when she was staying overnight with Melanie? He was on his way to the hospital and would meet Beth there. Unconscious. Beth kept whispering the word as she pulled on a pair of trousers, fumbled in the wardrobe for a jacket. She woke Robert and told him to look after the younger children. In the midst of her terror, she realised that although he was shocked he was not surprised.

'What do you know about this?' She shook him fiercely and he sobbed, terrified by the dread on her face.

'She messed around with some stuff – nothing heavy. Some E.'

'E! You mean ecstasy? Jesus Christ! Why didn't you tell me?'

'I didn't want to upset you. You were so worried about everything. Dad and all.'

'She's unconscious, Robert. She could die. How am I going to feel then? When it's too late to be upset?'

'I'm going to ring Dad,' he shouted. He ran to the phone, his back turned to her as he rang Stewart's mobile. 'I want him here. You should never have sent him away.'

She needed him too. His calm solid presence, comforting her.

'I'll do it,' she said. 'I'll ring him as soon as I reach the hospital.' She hugged her son, inhaling the musky sleep smell on his skin. 'Don't worry. She's going to be all right. I know she is.'

Peter was sitting grimly in the waiting room between Lindsey's two friends when Beth arrived. From his expression it was obvious that words had been exchanged. The Gardaí had already been called and names taken. Melanie was crying into a tissue, her shoulders heaving. The second girl stared blankly at the opposite wall.

He rose and came quickly towards Beth.

'It's all my fault if anything happens,' she sobbed. 'I believed she was staying in Melanie's house. Why didn't I check? I always used to check…'

The young doctor who spoke to Beth looked exhausted – gritty eyes, his white coat as rumpled as his hair. Lindsey had become dehydrated and collapsed at a rave. Her body had been wrapped in a 'space wrap', a tinfoil blanket, he explained, seeing Beth's terrified expression, to prevent further dehydration. As her friends were unsure if she'd taken any substances other than E, Lindsey's stomach had been pumped with charcoal fluid and blood samples taken. Her heart was being monitored until the results of the blood tests came back and her medical team could determine if any of her vital organs had been damaged. Beth shied away from the information so casually offered. Her legs trembled as she followed the doctor towards a curtained cubicle.

'Can I see her?' Peter joined them as they were about to enter.

'Are you her father?' the doctor asked.

Beth did not turn her head when he replied, 'I'm her uncle.'

They stared down at their daughter as Lindsey drifted in and out of sleep. Her face was stripped of personality, energy, expression. Only the vital elements showed. In her wide firm mouth and long chin they recognised Della Wallace.

'Lindsey, what are you trying to do to us?' Peter whispered.

Her eyes flickered, staring at him without comprehension. She tried to speak.

'Can you remember anything?' Beth asked, moving to the other side of the bed. They leaned closer to hear her rasping reply. A rave in the disused garage on Estuary Road. The music mix, the lights circling too fast and a pain, as if her heart was forcing its way from her chest. Then nothing, no warning – she stared at the ceiling lights and at the screens surrounding the bed.

'Please God make me die,' she sobbed. Her stomach cramped. Waves of blackness came and went but she was unable to throw up.

'When will Dad be here?' she muttered. 'I want him with me.'

'He'll be here soon,' Beth promised, her eyes locked on her child, both of them excluding Peter.

A nurse entered the cubicle. 'Your husband is on the phone, Mrs McKeever.' She glanced at Peter. 'I'm afraid I'll have to ask you to leave, sir. Only immediate family members are allowed.'

Peter hesitated. When he touched Lindsey's hair she pulled the sheet over her eyes.

'I want him to go.' She sobbed louder. 'Make him go away, nurse. He has no right to be here.'

Without another word he left.

Lindsey slept and woke again. She shook her head from side to side then lifted her hands, staring at her long tapering fingers, as if she was seeing them for the first time. 'I want Dad here. Will he be here soon?'

'As soon as he can,' Beth promised.

'He'll kill me.' Her mouth trembled.

The doctor re-entered the cubicle. 'Why should your father do that when you can do the job just as easily yourself?' He stood at the foot of her bed and checked her chart. 'Feeling better?' he asked. He did not sound sympathetic or even interested in her reply. He shone a torch into her eyes and felt her pulse. 'Do you often make such serious attempts to kill yourself?'

'It wasn't like that…' She sunk her chin into the sheet, too embarrassed to continue, and touched her flushed throat, raw where the tube had rubbed against it. 'I took some stuff, tabs. I didn't care.' She spoke so softly that Beth had to bend forward to hear. 'I went to his apartment and asked him…' Tears trickled from under her closed eyelids.

'Whose apartment?'

'Your uncle told me the truth.'

Beth tried to speak but her lips seemed frozen, her mouth so dry she was unable to swallow.

'Albert?' She forced herself to utter his name. 'Are you talking about him?'

'I thought he was lonely. He told me about Anaskeagh and about Sara when she was a little girl, and all the relatives I've never met. He seemed so kind. But the last time, it seemed as if he hated me for something. He said—' She stopped suddenly and lay silent, her eyes fixed on the ceiling.

'What happened? Tell me, Lindsey. You have to tell me everything. Did he harm you in any way?'

'He told me about my father. My real father.'

Beth saw a tremor pass over her child's face and accepted that the moment she had dreaded but anticipated since Lindsey's birth had arrived. She had rehearsed what she would say many times, but explanations seemed futile, so hollow when measured against the loss she saw in her daughter's eyes.

'Why wasn't I told?' Lindsey cried. 'Didn't I have a right to know?'

'To know what, Lindsey?' She gripped her hands, relieved when her daughter did not pull away. 'To know that you wouldn't have had a loving father if it wasn't for Stewart? He was with me when you were born. Such happiness in his eyes when he held you, his daughter, his beloved child – our beloved child.' She sighed. 'I can't turn back the clock, my darling. No one can. You were always surrounded by love. You've no idea the difference that makes.'

Lindsey leaned over the side of the bed, retching violently. Beth grabbed a sick tray and held it under her chin, wiping her face with a damp towel. She tried to make her understand: old secrets, bare bones, breaking hearts. How could she explain dead passion to a young woman who faced the truth of her existence and found it wanting?

Beth gently laid her daughter's arms under the sheet and sat by her bed, watching over her. Raucous voices carried from the accident and emergency ward. Screams, arguments and tears, they were quiet noises compared to the clamour in her head. She had spent her life running from a monster, never realising he was always two steps ahead of her. He had dominated her sister's will and sought to do the same to her. He was her monster and now he had entered the nightmares of her child.

Stewart would arrive soon. He would demand to know everything. His fury would make any contact with the politician impossible, his fledgling company destroyed by the truth.

As if sensing her thoughts, Lindsey stirred and grasped Beth's hand. 'Is Dad here yet?' she murmured.

'Not yet… but soon. He's going to be very angry, Lindsey. He trusted Albert Grant… just like you did.'

Lindsey's mouth quivered as if she could no longer bear the enormity of her thoughts.

'Make everything all right again, Mum.' It was a childish whisper, repeated once more before her eyelashes closed over her bruised cheeks.

'Don't worry, I'll protect you all.' Beth held her daughter's hand as Lindsey sank back to sleep.

'I will destroy you, Albert Grant.' She whispered the words fiercely to herself, as she had never whispered them when her sister was alive. 'I will destroy you utterly.'

An insect, crushed under her feet. The sole of her shoe stamping him into a smear of blood that would be washed away forever in the rain.

Stewart rang again. 'I'll be with you soon,' he said. 'I'm driving as fast as I can.'

'We're waiting for you, my love,' she replied. 'Hurry.'

PART THREE

CHAPTER THIRTY-THREE

Everyone's story has a beginning. An instant when the earth moves. When ovum and sperm collide, collude, create. Biological facts are difficult to dispute. But afterwards, after the downward swim into light, what then? As Eva clawed the air, as she uttered her first mucousy cry, was she held briefly in a stranger's arms? Or did she lie abandoned, welcomed into the world with a stone?

On her forehead there was a dent, so slight it was difficult to see, covered by purple skin, almost transparent. A shiny purple coin. A fairy kiss that was, according to her father, bestowed on her the instant she was born. When she was older, she demanded a more rational explanation and sensible Liz provided it. A fall from the high steps at the back of the house when she was waltzing around in her baby walker. Her hair was heavy, a curly weight over her forehead. A birthmark was easy to ignore. She never paid attention to it until the night her grandmother confided harsh secrets into her ear and Eva finally understood.

She'd been six months old when she first came to Ashton, a soft blanket replacing sackcloth and the unyielding earth.

'A cocoon of love,' said Liz.

'A fairy princess,' said Steve. They had been trying for a long time to conceive a child, vigorously at first, then with grim and timely discipline. Month had followed disappointing month, and the arrival of this frail miracle child into their lives was a cause for rowdy celebration. Her parents had deep roots in Ashton and their families, the Frawleys and the Loughreys, arrived in droves to raise their glasses and welcome Eva into their lives.

Steve sang 'When I'm Sixty-Four' and Liz's sister, Annie Loughrey, played her fiddle until Liz, mindful of early-morning feeds and mysterious milk formulas, swept the revellers from her doorstep in the small hours.

Ashton was a small Wicklow backwater, and those who lived in its shade of spruce and beech prayed it would remain so. Steve's garden centre was a familiar landmark with a reputation that brought customers from the hinterland and beyond. Next door, Liz ran the guest house, Wind Fall, catering to commercial travellers and hillwalkers. While the garden centre budded and blossomed with the demands of the seasons, the ordered serenity of Wind Fall never varied.

Eva woke each morning to the sound of her mother's footsteps passing her bedroom door as Liz went downstairs to prepare breakfast for the overnight guests. She made no secret of her daughter's adoption, fearing traumatic disclosures in school playgrounds or in the hothouse environment of family parties if elderly relatives drank too much gin. At night, Steve sat by her bed and uttered the magical words that began her story.

'Eva's Journey to Happiness' was a fairy story of thwarted puppy love and family feuding: a vicious vendetta that forced a young girl and boy to give their love child to a convent of kindly nuns, who passed her on as a gift to her parents. Eva imagined herself as a parcel, wrapped in birthday paper and streamers. Her body tingled with sympathy for the puppy lovers and their desperate attempts to be together. But she remained untouched by any emotional reality, settling down to sleep afterwards with the same sense of exhausted contentment she experienced after the telling of 'Rapunzel' or 'The Sleeping Beauty'. Maria, her cousin, suffered regular crises of identity and confessed to Eva that she harboured deep suspicions that she too was adopted. It would explain everything. A swan in a nest of ugly ducklings. But that was during her teenage years, the war years when all

Maria wanted from life was to muck out stables and vow eternal devotion to horses.

For Eva, horses served only one function: bearers of dung for her father's precious plants. Maria hated the smell of roses and walked unheedingly over seedling beds until Steve barred her from entering the garden centre. Eva and her cousin were the same age – best friends, incompatible and inseparable.

When Maria grew tired of feeding sugar lumps to her favourite horses and mucking out stables at the Ashton Equestrian Centre, and Eva was not needed in the garden centre, they played in the long meadow grass or swam on summer evenings in Murtagh's River, soft sloshing mud between their toes, snapping rushes on their bare skin, the flow of water, boggy and brown, rippling over their shoulders. Sensations that belonged to a small space in summer yet, later, looking back to those days, they seemed to span the whole of Eva's childhood.

One evening, they saw Maria's older sister, Lorrie, walking hand in hand with Brendan Fitzsimon through the long grass in Murtagh's Meadow. They sank down in a hollow by the riverbank and failed to notice the girls hiding behind the bushes. A spasm of shock swooped through Eva as Lorrie lifted her slender knees and Brendan lay between them. Eva flattened her body deeper into the earth. When she looked across at her cousin, the glazed brightness of Maria's eyes and the flushed bloom on her cheeks reflected her own feelings. They began to giggle convulsively, hands clasping mouths, as they crawled away, terrified a snapped twig or the waving ferns would betray their presence.

Out of earshot they flung themselves on the ground, rolling wildly over the grass. 'Disgusting, oh my God, it's so disgusting.' They gasped, breathless and giggling, vowing they would never ever allow any man to do such awful things to them. As their blood cooled they became thoughtful. Maria wondered if her parents did it.

'You bet your life they do,' Eva replied. Maria's brother was six months old so it seemed a safe enough assumption to make, even if it was impossible to imagine her fragile Aunt Claire squashed beneath Uncle Jack, who auctioned cattle and had a voice as loud as a drum being played too fast. Her parents did not need to do it because they had adopted her. She felt proud of Liz and Steve. It set them apart from everyone else, gave them a dignity that removed them from damp riverbanks, trampled grass and noises that still sang inside her head.

Soon afterwards, she asked her mother how long she had stayed with the puppy lovers before she was sent to the convent. She wanted Liz's practical answers rather than the gentle rambling stories Steve would offer.

'Six months,' Liz said. 'You were a delicate child.' Suddenly, her words had a hollow ring, an echo Eva could not penetrate. For the first time the full significance of 'Eva's Journey to Happiness' dawned on her, and she understood how she, and not the rebellious Maria, became the swan in the nest of the clamorous Frawley and Loughrey clans. But this realisation did not fill her with curiosity about her past. She loved her parents and questions as to why, when, where and how she came to share their lives were irrelevant.

CHAPTER THIRTY-FOUR

When Eva completed her Leaving Certificate examination she decided to study horticulture. Steve was suspicious of his daughter's need for diplomas and degrees.

'Haven't I taught you everything you need to know?' he demanded, shaking his head when Eva outlined her plans for the future. 'You don't need a fancy piece of parchment to tend a sick rose. A diploma won't heal an ailing hydrangea if you can't give it the loving touch.'

Her father's ability to personalise his plants and shrubs was an endearing trait, but on the subject of parchment Eva was adamant. She wanted to become a garden designer and host her own television series. Frawleys of Ashton would be the perfect backdrop, she said.

Steve shuddered away from such ambitions, imagining bossy television producers ordering him around his beloved rose arbour and cameramen trampling his geraniums. He was a simple son of the soil, content to live his life selling his bedding plants, fruit orchards and weeping willows.

When Eva emerged from horticultural college, waving her fancy piece of parchment, she decided the time had come to modernise and expand his business. A new, state-of-the-art computer was installed. It reduced Steve to palpitations every time he laid his hands on the keyboard. She drew up a three-year marketing programme, forcing him to watch graphics and spreadsheets flicking across the screen. She submitted a proposal to RTÉ for her television series and waited in vain for a reply.

When she suggested buying the field next to the centre and turning it into a landscaped show garden with her design service and a coffee shop attached, he shook his head firmly.

'People want to dig their own gardens,' he argued. 'It's therapy, fresh air, good exercise.' His voice held more than a hint of suspicion that Eva was undermining his authority.

She told him about the time pressure young couples were under, how they were too busy to feel the soil under their fingernails. They had parking bays and gravel lawns and terracotta pots on patios. Those with gardens wanted water features and Zen layouts and lakes of exotic fish swimming under delicate water lilies.

'Not my customers.' He shook his head decisively. 'They want to pot and plant, to see the familiar flowers unfold with the seasons. It's the best therapy they can get.'

Her grandmother advised her to strike out on her own. As the owner of the Biddy's Bits 'n' Pieces chain of souvenir shops, Brigid Loughrey was a shrewd businesswoman who had made a fortune selling garish tri-colour mugs, shamrocks and shillelaghs. She had no problem tackling the intricacies of the World Wide Web and blocked her ears when anyone dared mention retirement.

'You'll never be able to move your father,' she told Eva. 'Steve runs his garden centre the way he wants it and forcing his arm will do neither of you any good. There's no sense burying your ambitions in Ashton, especially when you've so many excellent ideas.'

'What good are my ideas when I've no money to put them into practice?' Eva asked.

'Then borrow,' replied Brigid. 'How do you think I started my first shop? By emptying my piggy bank?'

Eva was still contemplating her future when Frank O'Donovan, a distant relation to her father, died. Eva had never heard of him until Steve read the death notice in the *Irish Independent* and decided to attend his funeral. Her parents left Ashton the following morning and Eva, busy throughout the day in the garden centre, was shocked when a phone call from Anaskeagh Regional Hospital informed her that her parents had been injured in a car accident. The nurse quickly reassured her there was no need to worry. It was a minor accident; Liz would be discharged in the morning and Steve transferred to a Dublin hospital within the next few days. Eva left immediately, driving westwards, obsessively repeating the nurse's words but unable to find a crumb of comfort in her crisp, clinical reassurances.

On the approach road to Anaskeagh, a tractor in front of Steve had suddenly stalled. Although her father had managed to brake in time, the driver following behind had skidded on the wet surface and ploughed into the back of his car.

It was late when Eva reached the small country town. Liz was sitting by Steve's bed. His arm was broken and X-rays had revealed a number of cracked ribs. Eva stared at the intravenous drip feeding into his arm and the closed screens surrounding his bed.

'I was so scared. Don't you dare do anything like that to me ever again,' she scolded him, then started weeping fiercely. Steve winced from her embrace, his body still in shock from the impact of the collision.

'It's not the end of the world, pet. I'll be right as rain in a day or so.' He offered her a tissue with his free hand and stroked her head. 'Sure, isn't it hard to kill a bad thing?'

Eva was blowing her nose when she became aware that another person had entered the ward and was standing at the foot of the bed. She noticed his eyes first, a penetrating blue stare that had an unsettling familiarity, yet she couldn't think where they might have met.

'Good heavens, Greg! It's so late.' Liz rose to her feet and warmly greeted the stranger. 'I didn't expect to see you back here again.'

'I wanted to make sure everything was okay before I returned to the hotel.' His eyes swept over Eva and he gave an apologetic nod when Liz introduced him as the driver who had been behind them when the crash occurred. He had been discharged earlier and, apart from a bandage around his left hand, he seemed unscathed.

'It's been a most unfortunate day for all of us,' sighed Liz. 'But Greg's done everything he can to help us through it.'

'If there's anything else I can do—' He glanced enquiringly at Steve, who shook his head, his body in spasm when he tried to cough.

'For starters, you could try practising the rules of the road,' Eva snapped, hearing the painful rasp of her father's breath. Recalling her terror on the long drive to Anaskeagh, her voice shook with anger. 'I hope you're satisfied with your day's work. You could have killed my parents with your careless driving.'

'I've already made my apologies to them and I'm glad to have an opportunity to apologise to you in person.' He made no effort to defend himself. 'I'm sorry you had to hear such frightening news over the phone. I can only imagine the shock you got—'

'You're right – it was a shock,' she interrupted, suspecting that such an abject apology was simply a ruse to diffuse her anger. 'Hopefully you'll remember that the next time you drive too close to the car in front.'

'There's no need to be so upset, Eva.' Liz's grave voice calmed her down. 'Greg has accepted full responsibility for the accident and we've sorted everything out between us. All that matters is that we're alive to tell the tale.'

'If there's any way I can make amends…' His voice trailed away as he shoved his hands into his pockets, the shock of the accident visible for an instant on his face. After he said goodbye to her parents she rose and followed him outside to the corridor.

'Thank you for stopping by to see them,' she said quietly. 'I'm sorry for sounding off in there. I'm not usually so rude when I meet people for the first time.'

'Then, perhaps, when all this is over, you'll have a chance to prove it.' When he smiled he no longer seemed so intimidating, just intriguingly familiar with his long, intense face and finely boned cheeks.

'Have we met before? You look familiar but I can't remember where or when…'

He shook his head emphatically. 'We've never met before. If we had, I'd remember you.' He made no effort to hide his meaning and Eva, responding, boldly returned his gaze.

'Then why do I feel as if I know you?' she asked.

'You've probably seen me on television.' He sounded embarrassed by this admission of celebrity, self-consciously pushing his fingers through his thick brown hair. 'I work on a current-affairs programme.'

'Of course – *Elucidate*. You're Greg Enright! I can't believe I didn't recognise you.'

'It happens all the time.' He laughed ruefully. 'I'm not instantly recognisable, just vaguely familiar. People usually suspect I'm their child's teacher or their window cleaner. It's not good for the ego but I'm used to it.'

'I suspect very few politicians would agree with you.' She smiled for the first time since receiving the call from the hospital. 'No wonder Liz forgave you so readily. *Elucidate* is her favourite programme. She enjoys seeing politicians shrunk to size and drenched in acid. Do you live here?'

'No. I'm from Dublin. I'm doing a feature on a day in the life of a rural politician. It's boring but occasionally necessary if we're to avoid accusations of only concentrating our reports on the capital city.' He shook her hand, grinning as a nurse passed and ordered him out of the hospital. Visiting hours had ended an hour ago. 'Is there any chance you might recognise me the next time we meet?' he asked when the nurse had returned to her station. He still held Eva's hand, the signals passing between them unmistakable. 'I'll recognise you, Eva Frawley. But not vaguely, believe me – not vaguely.'

The following morning Liz insisted she was well enough to attend the funeral. Frank O'Donovan was a local farmer and the church in the centre of Anaskeagh was crowded. The O'Donovan family filled the top pews, a large clan gathered to unite in mourning. Towards the end of the service, one of the O'Donovan daughters stood on the altar to give the eulogy. She wore a navy dress with a plain navy cardigan and her voice was filled with emotion as she spoke about her father. A nun, murmured Liz, working in a health centre in Malawi and home for the funeral. Another sister had returned from London and a brother had made the journey from Australia for the first time in twenty-four years. They reminded Eva of her own relatives, an Irish diaspora scattering and uniting to grieve or to celebrate as the occasion demanded.

Frank O'Donovan was buried in a country graveyard at the foot of a high headland. The lush slopes gradually rose upwards into a formidable rocky outcrop that loomed above the small town. The peaks were clearly visible on this fresh windy day, but Eva could imagine it cloudy and shrouded in mist, a hovering presence dominating the lives of the population.

Later, in a local hotel, the mourners gathered to shake off the chill of the graveyard, enjoying sandwiches and steaming whiskey toddies. Catherine O'Donovan, the recently widowed wife, sat in her family circle, flanked by the nun and a middle-aged man. The prodigal son from Australia, Eva guessed.

'Would you like to meet the O'Donovans?' Liz asked. She seemed subdued, uneasy in the presence of so many strangers and anxious to be back with Steve in the hospital. When Eva shook her head, reluctant to partake in the ritual of condolence when she didn't know the family, Liz made no effort to dissuade her. 'Then I'll say goodbye to Catherine and we'll be on our way.'

The arrival of the *Elucidate* television crew created a sudden silence in the bar. Unperturbed, Greg Enright led the way to the cordoned-off area that had been reserved for the funeral group. He shook hands with an elderly man whose thick mane of white hair gleamed under the lights. Obviously the local politician, Eva thought. She had noticed him shaking hands at the graveside, his expression concerned as he placed his arm around Catherine O'Donovan and escorted her back to the limousine. He was equally at ease in front of the camera, joking with the camera-woman, ordering her to focus only on his good side. Greg was in deep conversation with him as she passed and didn't notice her. Judge Dredd in action – the erring politician's nightmare.

The following Saturday, in the rose arbour uprooting bushes, Eva heard footsteps and knew, without turning, that Greg Enright was behind her. When she faced him, aware that she was flushed, her hair wind-blown, he exaggeratedly raised his eyebrows – his trademark gesture, which signified sardonic disbelief when seen on television – and stretched out his hand. 'Recognise me, Ms Frawley?' he asked.

'Vaguely,' she replied. 'What took you so long, Mr Enright?'

'I left Anaskeagh four hours ago,' he admitted. 'The journey usually takes five.'

'Still driving too fast, Mr Enright?'

'Not any more, Ms Frawley,' he replied. 'I've arrived at my destination.'

That night they dined in Ashton's only restaurant. He talked about his career, his future plans, his reputation. His admirers called him righteous and rigorous, a committed journalist who stopped at nothing to expose the truth. Those who disliked him claimed he was an opinionated, self-serving muckraker. He was twenty-eight years old and his only responsibilities were to his fish aquarium, which he managed with meticulous devotion, and to his mother, an independent widow who tolerated his fortnightly visits as long as they did not clash with her bridge evenings or the *Late Late Show*. He lived alone in a small apartment in The Liberties, with Christ Church Cathedral behind him and the downward sweep to the Liffey in front. He had his music, his books, his workstation, a futon and a streamlined kitchen in which he loved to cook. His future with *Elucidate* was clearly traced on an upwardly mobile graph.

Eva teased him, calling him a bloodhound who sniffed in the footprints of other people's sins. They laughed together, at ease in each other's company.

'Tell me how it feels to have the power to destroy people?' she asked.

'People can only be destroyed if they have something to hide.' Greg was suddenly serious. If that was wielding power, then so be it. He accepted it without being moved, intimidated or suppressed by its responsibility. 'That's why I always tell the truth,' he said. 'And why you must believe me when I tell you I've fallen in love for the first time in my life.'

How easily the words settled between them. How easily they were reciprocated. She watched him watching her and felt the same anticipation reaching her in waves, as if being close to each other released something unguarded, dangerous, thrilling.

They returned to Wind Fall where Liz, protective of her only daughter, subjected him to the same grilling he gave his *Elucidate* interviewees.

He commented on the resemblance between them. 'You'll never be able to disown each other,' he said.

'We'd never want to disown each other,' Eva replied. She placed her arms around her mother, demanding that Liz share her happiness. She felt as if she was falling from a safe ledge. This urge to fly was the most exhilarating emotion she'd ever experienced.

Afterwards, she told Greg that she was adopted. 'People are always commenting on the resemblance between us. Some tell me I'm the image of my aunts, that I'm a real Loughrey.'

'Then they must be the most beautiful women in the world,' he replied.

The Loughrey sisters were indeed a handsome trio. Annie, Liz's younger sister, was a musician, a fiddle player, never at home. Claire lived close to Wind Fall and managed Biddy's Bits 'n' Pieces with her mother. When people told Eva she was made in their image she had every reason to feel proud. Except that she didn't resemble them. An expression, imitative gestures, a head of shaggy blonde hair that broke combs and drew tears from her eyes when she tried to separate the strands. Superficial resemblances, but they satisfied her in those sparkling early days when nothing mattered except being with Greg and the slow, tender happiness building between them.

When Maria heard that her cousin was making wedding plans, she demanded to know if Eva was crazy or pregnant. Otherwise, why marry a guy who was probably a member of the Inquisition in a former life? She called into the garden centre one lunch hour to remonstrate.

'What's this nonsense about you and Judge Dredd getting hitched?' she demanded, perching on an upturned terracotta pot. She clicked her fingers in Eva's face and ordered her to get a grip. So what if he had a terrific dick, she demanded. Terrific dicks were ten a penny if one looked in the right places. It was a dismal excuse for marriage. Eva was rapidly regretting the indiscreet secrets she had confided in her friend's willing ear.

'Greg Enright is not the marrying kind,' Maria stated. This was a loaded comment, backed by insider information. Eva concentrated on the clematis plants she was staking and ordered her to dish the dirt. Maria prevaricated for a while before throwing the name Carol Wynne at her. Eva tossed it back, growing angry. But being angry with Maria was a lost cause. She simply ignored it, waiting until the emotion was exhausted before returning to her original point.

Eva knew about Carol Wynne. She had seen her for the first time in Anaskeagh, a camerawoman with cropped black hair and razor-sharp eyes, nifty on her feet when she filmed doorstep interviews, sharing Greg's excitement, the thrill of the chase. Her relationship with Greg never had a shape, easy to take up and put down again. No demands.

'She's dead wood,' said Eva.

Maria groaned, demanding to be spared the horticultural metaphors. Her childhood devotion to horses had never wavered and she now ran the Ashton Equestrian Centre. Carol Wynne was one of her pupils. If Eva was going to be metaphorical then she should know that the lady in question had a tight grip once she had a horse between her knees.

Eva hauled her to her feet and ordered her off the premises. Maria would be her bridesmaid. A vision in lilac.

Shortly before the wedding Annie Loughrey returned to Ireland after a European tour and called to see them. Eva adored her aunt, who was incapable of sitting still for longer than ten minutes without exhorting everyone around her to sing and dance. Yet she always had time to listen to her nieces and nephews, who inevitably confided their problems and secrets to her whenever she came to Ashton.

'So a marriage made in heaven,' she said when Eva asked her to play at the wedding. 'No rows? No dramatic break-ups and passionate make-ups?'

'None.' Eva shook her head, laughing. Then, without realising the thought had even existed, she said, 'I wonder if my birth mother senses what's about to happen in my life?'

'This is the first time I've heard you mention her.' Annie looked surprised. 'Have you discussed this with Liz?'

'No. And I don't want to. It's not important,' Eva retorted, and brought the conversation back to the wedding, allowing the sudden unexpected yearning to fade away.

Annie Loughrey played the fiddle as Eva walked up the aisle on the arm of her father. Steve grew quite emotional when he handed her over to her future husband. Although Eva had objections to this age-old ritual of being passed from one male to another, she loved Steve too much to deprive him of the pleasure of giving her away. At least on this occasion she had some control over who played pass the parcel. She suspected he was secretly relieved she would no longer be around the garden centre to bully him, but his eyes were touchingly moist when they danced together to the strains of 'Daddy's Little Girl'.

She and Greg honeymooned in Italy, an idyllic time that was marred only when they came home and discovered that Brigid Loughrey, Eva's beloved grandmother, had been admitted to hospital for tests. The prognosis was bad – cancer of the bowel, which had already metastasised to her liver. She was home again, Liz explained, and refusing to embark on a programme of chemotherapy.

'None of your nonsense now,' said Brigid when Eva called to see her. She was still working in her tourist shop, juicing and taking a concoction of herbs, and smoking weed. No hope of a cure, she admitted, but they were better than suffering the side effects of chemo, which would make no difference in the end. 'We've talked enough about me.' She cut across Eva's concerns and pinched her cheek affectionately. 'What are your plans for the future? I want to know what you'll be doing with your life when I'm no longer part of it.'

CHAPTER THIRTY-FIVE

Eva intended establishing her own garden centre. While she searched for a suitable site, she worked with Planting Thoughts. The company was owned by a friend from her college days, Gina Davies, who ran a garden-design service as well as supplying unusual and flamboyant floral arrangements for special events. Her business was expanding and she asked Eva if she'd be interested in managing the floral contracts. Eva agreed and was soon roaming the city in a Planting Thoughts van, decorating hotels and exhibition centres with exotic orchids and plants, turning dull rooms into vibrant jungles and tiger-lily sanctuaries.

Eva's possessions took over Greg's apartment. His sense of order, his meticulous need to have a place for everything, was impossible to maintain. She seemed incapable of moving without jogging her elbows off his stereo or tripping over the low sprawling armchairs. In the kitchen she eyed his presses of exotic cooking oils and spices with trepidation, unable to imagine herself feeling comfortable in a place where a stray orange peel on the counter or scattered breadcrumbs marred the perfect symmetry. Only in the bedroom did she feel at ease. At night, in the shadowed slant of light through the blinds, they made love on the tumbled futon. In such moments, when the terse control he exercised over his life was abandoned, she believed nothing could ever invade their happiness.

They invited his friends from *Elucidate* to dinner. Eva served lamb with a rosemary crust but they were mainly vegetarians and concentrated on the salads. They filled the apartment with smoke and hot air. Carol Wynne touched the furniture with familiar hands.

'I believe you arrange flowers,' she said. 'Such an interesting hobby.' A remark not exactly designed to inspire love. She asked Eva's advice about her yucca plant in case she felt excluded from the conversations about political manoeuvrings and who was sleeping with whom on the coalition benches.

The conversation turned to Michael Hannon, the leader of Democracy in Action. As the leader of a small right-wing party, his profile had risen considerably in recent months. He projected a moderate image, unlike the more reactionary members of his party, and spoke in measured tones about the rights of the unborn, about women dispossessed by divorce, and the assault by the media on the traditional values of family life. He believed it was only a matter of time before his party, small yet with a powerful voice, could enter a coalition arrangement after the next election. But a rumour, too vague to be taken seriously yet floating among journalists for years, hinted that after the cut and thrust of politics, his frustration needed an outlet. When Rachel Hannon appeared by her husband's side, her social smile never wavered. If she was a battered wife she wasn't the type to seek restraining orders or display her bruises as evidence to sympathetic judges. Those bruises, if they existed, were hidden behind designer suits and flawless handbags. Nothing had ever been proven. Journalists who dabbled with the story found themselves facing a wall of denial from anyone they contacted. Editors, imagining libel suits and early retirement without pensions, refused to touch it. Even the producer of *Elucidate* was adamant. If Greg presented her with broken bones she would give them full disclosure. Anything less, forget it. *Elucidate* sailed close to the wind but wasn't in the business of self-destruction. Michael Hannon remained beyond his grasp and Greg, patient and ruthless, was willing to wait.

Eva thought of wolves circling, her husband heading the pack. She listened to them talking, sharing in-jokes as they cheerfully dismantled the lives of the pompous and the powerful. She wanted them out of their apartment but it wasn't really their apartment. It belonged to Greg, whose ordered existence had ended as soon as she'd stepped into his life.

Shortly afterwards, Eva saw a site with land and a derelict cottage advertised in the window of an estate agency in Oldport.

'Where's Grahamstown?' she asked Judith Hansen, a florist who regularly supplied Planting Thoughts with dramatically sculpted reed and wild-grass arrangements. 'Is it worth checking out as a location for a garden centre?'

'Could be,' Judith replied, helping to carry her floral arrangements to the van. 'It's set for development now that work on the motorway has started. Talk to Carrie Davern. She's the estate agent looking after the site.'

Carrie Davern was a shrill-voiced, persuasive woman with a firm handshake and, Eva suspected, the jargon to make a cat's basket sound like luxurious accommodation. She showed Eva the development plans for Grahamstown and gave her directions to the site. It sounded exactly right. The following afternoon she drove with Greg northwards from the city, over the Liffey and past the Four Courts, through Drumcondra, Swords, Oldport and on to Grahamstown. February was a mild month with the promise of spring in the air. Early daffodils splashed gold along the central verge of the carriageway and the bare hedgerows tossed in a warm southerly breeze.

When the road narrowed, Greg viewed the fields and solitary roadside pubs with increasing nervousness. He stared in amazement when she braked outside a small cottage set behind a rusting gate. A corrugated iron roof was almost hidden beneath tufts of grass and ivy. The windows had fallen in. The door had also disappeared and there was ample evidence that cattle regularly sought shelter within its crumbling walls. But Carrie Davern had made Eva see beyond the obvious and she had no problem with vision and ambition, standing positive in front of her husband, who clung to the gate for support. It squeaked as he pushed it open and entered an overgrown, dilapidated wilderness.

He demanded to know if this was a joke, hoping against hope that she would laugh and say, 'Fooled you, didn't I?'

She did laugh. His expression demanded some response. She took his arm and led him forward, striding purposefully towards thick hedging. Eva had a fine stride, long and decisive, shoulders back. The ankles of a colt, said Maria, which may have lacked refinement as a compliment but her friend was precise in her observations and Eva's legs were her finest asset. They walked through a field at the back of the cottage.

'This is what it's all about, Greg.' She pointed to the knee-high grass and nettles where plastic rubbish bags had been dumped and torn apart by dogs. She saw her cottage rising from the rubble, restored, the roof thatched, secure. There would be a front garden with cottage flowers spilling perfume into the air. Her office would have long windows with a back view over her garden centre as it sloped towards a small lake where, even as she watched, two swans emerged from the rushes and glided through the water.

She wanted him to share her excitement. He was thinking about leaving *Elucidate* and writing a book about global politics, how it impacted smaller countries like Ireland. Eva saw this as the ideal opportunity to move from the city. Technology knew no boundaries. Corruption could just as effectively be exposed in the company of swans and hanging baskets of begonias.

'Can you think of anywhere nicer to live?' she asked.

'Yes, I could,' he said. 'How about hell – for starters?'

She pressed her fingers to his lips. Grahamstown would eventually have direct access to the planned motorway. She told him about the new housing estates that were being built, a new population seeking their dream gardens. The estate agent had recommended a builder, who was an artist when it came to re-storing old cottages. The more Eva enthused the more Greg's eyes glazed. He said it was too far out from work. He waved his hands towards the ruins, as if a frantic gesture would make them disappear. If she wanted to live in the company of swans why had she left Ashton? Why had she married him? In years to come maybe, when they had time to consider a family, perhaps then – but not now. Not when his career was carefully mapped within earshot of city bells.

Occasionally since their wedding she had sensed a slight air of pomposity about this man she had chosen to love; a self-righteous, hectoring note in his voice when she didn't agree with his opinions. Now, as they stood angrily apart, she realised that they each had completely different visions of their future life together.

'I'm suffocating in the city,' she cried. 'This place is perfect for my needs.'

They waded through dead ragwort, arguing bitterly. Their anger frightened them. The realisation that this was their first serious row silenced them and added to their tension as they tried to find their way forward. Below them, the swans streaked across the lake in a flapping rush of wings, then rose with un-gainly energy into the air. When Greg reached towards her, she walked without hesitation into his arms and the man she loved, the man who loved her with a raw and sensuous passion, swept her into the shelter of the ruined cottage.

'We'll work it out,' he said, kissing her urgently. They made love against the rough stone wall, finding an illicit pleasure in the discomfort of their surroundings. Beneath layers of heavy clothing they sought each other, laughing at the horror of being discovered even as they moaned with passion and came together, breathless.

When they left this hidden place the swans had disappeared. Perhaps there was a nest in the rushes. When they came back again there would be cygnets trailing in their wake. Eva believed it was only a matter of time before her husband believed in her dream as fervently as she did.

They conceived a child beside the lake. Having a child wasn't part of their plan, rather a decision they would make in time when they had the space to consider another person in their lives. Weeks passed and she was unaware of tiny cells relentlessly multiplying. Every time she mentioned the cottage Greg looked blank, suddenly busy on the phone or rushing to keep an important appointment, dodging and feinting. Her dreams were overwhelming him, demanding time and energy he was unable or unwilling to give. Not that it mattered. She needed money but her ambitious plans did not impress the financial establishment. An interesting project but high risk, she was told time and again by bank managers. Every week she rang the estate agent to see if the site had sold. Luck stayed on her side. No one else sensed the potential in the land and it remained fallow.

The city air choked her lungs. When she grew pale and wilted with tiredness she suspected it was due to the pressure of traffic and working indoors. As she stabbed flowers into an oasis one morning and nausea rose in her throat she was forced to a standstill, calculating backwards.

Greg's dismay was palpable when she told him. Too soon, he said. How could she be pregnant when they practised safe sex? She reminded him about a lake of swans and an exploding, lustful few moments against the back wall of her dream cottage.

He grappled with this truth, suddenly terrified at the thought of another intrusion into his busy, ordered life.

'It's the last thing we need at the moment,' he said. 'I can't believe this has happened to us.'

She saw his face and was unable to believe she had ever loved this man. She felt something else, vibrations of fear as this new life clung grimly to the walls of its dark protective cavity. She began to weep. He knelt before her and pressed his head against her stomach. He apologised for his unthinking words. That night when he held her, their passion was tender, a quiet loving shared with this new life they had created so unheedingly.

Their daughter was born on a silver morning in October. Greg was beside Eva throughout. She was swept high on a wave of pain, the mask flung aside because she wanted to know… to feel this moment. No epidural. The nurse told her to inhale deeply; she felt light-headed relief, voices floating above her. Fingers invading, another needle jab, pethidine. Her gynaecologist was on his way. She began to pray even though she hadn't prayed since she was fifteen, meeting Maria and the boys by Murtagh's River instead of going to evening Mass… Hail Mary full of grace… Blessed is the fruit of thy womb… Sweet fruit, my apple, my love.

The gynaecologist told her to push. She was hurting, tearing, bearing her body downwards as Greg called out, such joy in his voice as their daughter was placed on her stomach. Tiny fingers pressed against Eva's flesh. A closed, wrinkled old woman's face at the end of a long journey. Faye, a fairy child. So beautiful. So ephemeral.

CHAPTER THIRTY-SIX

Faye was three months old when the information about Michael Hannon finally landed on Greg's desk. The anonymous note contained a date and an address. In a plush hotel on the crest of a Portuguese mountain, Michael Hannon – whose maxim was 'God Save Our Glorious Family' – planned to engage in a discreet indiscretion with a female companion of long standing.

Greg was confident he knew the identity of the sender. Political destruction as compensation for domestic brutality. If the politician could not be nailed on a wife-beating accusation this would be just as effective. He showed the letter to Sue Lovett, his producer, who looked at it for only a moment before ordering him to pack his sunscreen – she was booking him on a flight to Portugal. Carol Wynne would accompany him.

'Don't worry, you can't not go,' said Eva, assuring him they would be fine on their own. Apart from the necessity of following the Hannon story to its conclusion, she suspected Greg would be relieved to escape for a short while from the domestic reality of a small baby. Night feeds, nappy changes, colic, windy smiles. Enchantment, chaos.

'Marital bliss,' murmured Carol Wynne when she joined them at the airport. 'Who would be without it? Just wait till you're a daddy of ten.' She hitched her camera over her shoulder and they marched side by side through the departure gate.

Breakfast, Greg would later tell Eva, had been decided as the appropriate time for a doorstep exposure. Who could dispute the evidence of a pot of marmalade on the table?

In a quiet hotel on the summit of the Serra do Caramulo, Michael Hannon and his companion dined on chilled fruit and cheeses, cold meats and crusty bread rolls. Below them, emerging from the morning mist, a grove of lemon trees edged the terraced fields like black serrated knives. The woman was the first to notice Greg. She stretched out a hand to warn the politician but it hung motionless between them.

'Is this your definition of family values, Mr Hannon?' Greg, like the politician, had been known to milk a platitude or two when under duress. Lime-flavoured marmalade, he noted, as he thrust his microphone forward to catch a muffled curse, the crash of an overturned chair. It was over in minutes.

As he drove down the winding mountain roads and the countryside fell away into forests of olive trees and eucalyptus, he wondered if his heart was large enough to entertain pity for the shattered ambitions of Michael Hannon. He wanted to believe it was, yet he knew it was not. His mobile phone rang as he checked into Porto airport. Eva's voice, calm with the numbness of grief, called him home.

Faye's death was an inexplicable mystery. Three months old, her downy skin frozen when Eva leaned over the cot to lift her for her morning feed.

She touched her baby's hands before they took her away, stroked the delicate skin between her fingers. She studied the veins on her eyelids, her spiky black eyelashes, the sweet curve of her mouth.

Greg wept bitter tears at the graveside. He begged Eva's forgiveness, crying into her shoulder as they lay sleepless in bed. She said there was nothing to forgive. It wasn't his fault. Or hers. No one was to blame. A cot death was an act of God. They still had each other, a future. Her words trailed into silence as they stared at each other across their daughter's empty space.

For a fortnight after the funeral they stayed at Wind Fall. Greg brought Faye's possessions to his wife. She gave them to the crèche in Ashton, keeping just a few mementoes that she wrapped in tissue paper. Days passed but she had no idea where time went. Liz made futile conversation, insisting that time would heal, insisting on understanding her pain.

'How can you understand?' Eva asked, refusing to allow her mother to condense such grief into a platitude. 'You can't compare a failed IVF procedure with my dead baby.' She was amazed at her cruelty. Liz hated her in that instant. She saw it reflected in Eva's eyes and, as her mother struggled to forgive, Eva loved her more intensely than ever. But she was caught in a bleak place and forgiveness could only come when she allowed herself to be absolved. She knew she would always remain her own judge and jury, condemned.

If only she had woken on time to feed her child. But she was tired. She slept on. If only the traffic had not been so heavy when the ambulance drove through the bottlenecks, its siren scattering cars too late. Her thoughts moved in a tight, unforgiving circle. It could have been different. It should have been different.

The tests came back from the hospital. All negative. A cot death was a riddle, the everlasting question. If only... If only... If only...

The paediatrician was willing to give them time. He seemed to believe they would draw comfort from knowledge. But what knowledge could be drawn from a mystery? Greg asked intelligent questions, as he always did in an interview situation. She could sense the paediatrician's surprise and growing admiration. No doubt he was used to parents collapsing in a muddle of grief and incomprehension.

When they were leaving, he told Greg how much he admired him on *Elucidate*. How important it was to have people of his fine calibre who were courageous enough to expose the ugly underbelly of life. Eva imagined rotting vegetation being raked over, translucent maggots scrabbling for cover before her husband pinned them to the ground with his piercing questions. Her head was full of hideous images. The paediatrician said it was a natural reaction and would fade away when her hormone balance settled back to normal. She asked him to define 'normal'. Greg frowned and held her arm as they walked away.

Liz, gazing at the bereft faces of her daughter and son-in-law, suggested they take a short holiday.

'You need time to find each other again,' she said as she waved them off. She was right. They had many things to discuss.

Greg's big opportunity had arrived. Since the Michael Hannon exposé his star had risen. Politicians, it seemed, erred everywhere, especially in New York, and the producer of *Stateside Review*, a prestigious US current-affairs programme, was headhunting him. A two-year contract was offered, linked to a salary that drew a whistle of astonishment from him.

He tried to discuss this new opportunity with Eva. It was a chance to begin their marriage anew in a ghost-free environment. But she found it impossible to visualise a future when the past held her captive and the present was a time that had to be endured.

CHAPTER THIRTY-SEVEN

They drove to Kerry on a rainy afternoon. Annie Loughrey had offered them her cottage while she was touring with her band. Loughrey's Crew was a seasoned group of musicians who lived in Dingle but was equally at home in the clubs and Irish pubs of New York.

The Dingle peninsula was quiet. The hedgerows, usually bowed with the weight of wild fuchsia, had not yet begun to green. They walked by the harbour and drove through the Connor Pass. They ate in candlelit restaurants and drank Guinness in pubs where a few locals gave them cursory glances before ignoring them. At night they made love with a rough, unthinking haste, as if the anonymity of a strange cottage gave them a freedom they no longer possessed in places where Faye had once rested her head.

Loughrey's Crew arrived back at the end of the week. The band was playing in one of the local pubs and Annie persuaded them to come along. Her fiddle trilled in welcome when they entered. As giddy as a poodle on speed, that was how Liz described her youngest sister: single, carefree, in love with the music and the young men who played it with her. After she finished her set she came down and embraced them.

'Stay on,' she urged. 'We're having a session after hours. That's when the fun really begins.'

Greg listened to the musicians, his face growing more clenched as the night wore on. Usually he was a cautious drinker, too self-contained to enter the realms of the indiscreet, and Eva grew nervous as he continued to drink with grim concentration.

When the session was over they left the pub and walked along the harbour. In the grey Atlantic swell a friendly dolphin rested his bones, waiting for summer when he would begin his high-diving performances, pursued by sonar boats and screaming children.

Greg's voice was slurred when he pressed his face into her neck. He sobbed and asked her to forgive him.

'You heard the doctor. There was nothing either of us could have done.' Eva stroked his face. His skin was cold, his high cheekbones raw and red from the wind. 'You have to stop tormenting yourself.'

'I could have phoned you – if I'd rung you'd have woken up and realised something was wrong with Faye. It might not have been too late – but I couldn't ring you... Not then...'

For the first time since their child's death she heard a deeper resonance in the words he uttered. His repentance was not just the grief of a stricken father. It demanded a greater absolution.

'What stopped you ringing me?' she asked.

'Guilt...' Guilt was tearing at the heart of his marriage. The truth shivered and broke between them. Many miles away on a mountain in Portugal, a world apart from her grief, her husband had triumphantly brought a politician to his knees – and then betrayed her.

Aerobics on a mattress. That was his description. Unexpected yet inevitable from the moment Carol came into his room with a bottle of vodka and they began to talk about old times. Nights when they had bunkered down on the edge of breaking a story, the intimacy of sharing anonymous hotel rooms in cities where they were strangers, walking free. Laden memories, stirring an unexpected, responsive desire as he'd pulled her close, her mouth opening, seeking him, their excitement heightened by the knowledge that Michael Hannon was enjoying the same swamping passion on the floor above them, unaware that retribution would come with the dawn.

Why do men insist on confession? Later, in the numbed aftermath of everything, Eva would ask herself this question. She had no desire to be the wife who was the last to know. She didn't want to know at all. Indiscretions could be absolved by time and silence. Guilt, on the other hand, was a heavier burden. Those who weren't strong in their resolve to keep their secrets had a need to share this guilt, to cast it off through the seeking of absolution. In a previous era Greg would have breathed his sins into the ear of a weary priest. He would have received a rosary as penance, recited slowly and with feeling. Eva would have received flowers and attention, perhaps even a fur coat, depending on the nature of the indiscretion, and worn it proudly because in the good old days it was not considered necessary to empathise with the suffering of skinned animals. Instead, she – wife, priest, psychologist, deceived – she got the truth.

CHAPTER THIRTY-EIGHT

When a problem was insurmountable, Brigid Loughrey never wasted energy trying to solve it. She was a shadow of her former self when she was admitted to the hospice to live out her final weeks.

'Morphine… So much more effective than weed,' she murmured, a smile playing around her dry lips when Eva visited the small, private ward. Her gaunt features looked peaceful as she drifted in and out of sleep. The previous night she and Liz had looked over old photographs and the box holding them was on her bedside locker. She gestured towards them. 'So many sweet memories,' she said. 'You were such a precious gift.'

'That's how I used to imagine myself,' Eva said. 'Wrapped in fancy paper and delivered to the door. What *really* happened to me, Gran?' This moment wasn't planned and Eva didn't realise that the subconscious is a treacherous force, at its most subversive when it appears to be quiescent.

'You were the Anaskeagh Baby,' Brigid whispered.

'Anaskeagh?' Eva remembered the town, the wide main street with its old-fashioned shops alongside the brash modern chains and new town houses, all overshadowed by the headland. 'Is that where I was born?'

'You were born on Anaskeagh Head but you belong to us.' Her voice, hoarse and shaky, was barely audible. Her breathing deepened and her eyes closed as she drifted away from Eva's questions. She awoke a short while later and sucked weakly on the moist lollipop sponge Eva held to her lips.

'Was I born on a farm, Gran? Why was I called the Anaskeagh Baby? Do you know my mother's name?' It seemed cruel to demand the truth from a dying woman, but Eva wanted a beginning to her story and Brigid Loughrey, high on morphine and the adrenaline of approaching death, replied, 'No one knows her name, Eva. She gave birth to you all alone in that lonely place, God help her. No more questions, now. I'm so tired. All that's left for me to do is follow the fairy child.'

'When you meet her, tell her I love her more than my own life.' Eva's tears soaked her cheeks. She allowed them to fall unchecked. She didn't feel courageous. She didn't feel angry. Twenty-six was too old to have an identity crisis. She kissed her grandmother's withered lips and sat silently beside her until the elderly woman drifted back to sleep and Annie arrived to take over the next shift.

Brigid died two days later. She had cast a faint but troubling light on a dark journey that had begun on a rock-strewn headland and, on the morning after her funeral, Eva strode through the black wrought-iron gates of the National Library. In the hushed hall, where fat-bellied angels on the ceiling stared impassively down on the rows of silent people scanning microfilm and old books, she sought her roots.

She steadied the viewfinder and focused on headlines. Her past did not take long to swim into view. '*Gardaí Plea to Mother of Anaskeagh Baby*.' '*Anaskeagh Baby off Critical List*.' '*Anaskeagh Baby in Care*.' '*Still No Sign of Mother of Anaskeagh Baby*.'

The young man seated at the reading table had brown hair tied in a ponytail. Eva thought he was a woman until she noticed his chin. Long and narrow, with a ridged bone jutting it forward, dark stubble. He reminded her of Greg. When he glanced over, her expression terrified him back into the fixed study of some ancient volume. An older women sat next to him, writing feverishly with a silver pen. Porters in uniforms loitered by the main information desk, chatting quietly. How many people had sat in this building, outwardly calm, while their past was enlarged on microfilm before their eyes? Did they, like her, want to scatter headlines in front of the hushed readers. To shout, 'Look – look – that's me!' To breathe slowly until the trembling ceased.

Was it Andy Warhol who said that everyone has fifteen minutes of fame? she wondered. Eva had had more than her average, being two weeks old before she was out of the public gaze. Journalists had had a field day, accusing the Irish nation of collective guilt. Old chestnuts pulled from the fire, still roasting. The irresponsibility of men who shagged and shied away from the consequences. Even the clergy were in on the act, writing about the need for charity, for soft hearts and open minds. Adopted women spoke about their mother searches and psychologists shaped the mind frame of Eva's birth mother, writing knowledgeably about her desperation, her pain.

The inhabitants of Anaskeagh bolted their doors. They drew up the drawbridge, refusing to comment on the reasons why their lack of charity and understanding had resulted in such a heinous act taking place on their doorstep. As Anaskeagh Head was an isolated headland, jutting into a raucous Atlantic, it seemed an unfair accusation, but then the whole country seemed convulsed by her mother's anguish. It was left to a county councillor to speak for the local population. They were heartbroken, said Albert Grant, by the plight of this unfortunate woman. Eva recognised him from the interview he'd given after Frank O'Donovan's funeral. He was older now, silver-haired and elegantly dressed. In those days he had a more belligerent image, his hair shorter, darker, his full-lipped mouth clenched, as if he was tired of answering questions. Had his people known this unfortunate woman's identity she would have received their full support, he said. They were a caring community and were being unjustly held responsible for a tragedy outside their control. Somehow Eva was lost in this forest of comment and opinion. She was simply 'The Anaskeagh Baby'. The catalyst. Then it all stopped. No more intriguing glimpses into her life. No sudden mother–daughter reunion.

Eva sat back and flexed her shoulders. She switched off the machine and left that monument to tall tales and forgotten history. Did she hate this faceless woman who had given birth to her? If she did, it was a hatred without passion. Did she understand her desperation as she struggled to hide her shame from a righteous society waiting to condemn? Could she forgive her for wrapping her newborn daughter in a sack and leaving her on the doorstep of a hill farmer? Eva didn't understand such actions. But neither did she hate or pity or condemn. She felt nothing but a growing awareness, questions answered, many questions still to be asked.

CHAPTER THIRTY-NINE

When Eva's grandmother's will was read it turned out that she had more than bits and pieces. With the stocks and shares, the properties and insurance policies, it came to a mighty sum, even when divided amongst her loved ones. Eva no longer needed to grovel to bank managers who waved her from their offices with regretful smiles. Thanks to Brigid's inheritance she had become a woman of means.

The Grahamstown site was still on the estate agent's books. She drove to Oldport and met Carrie Davern, who still spoke enthusiastically about the site's potential. Carrie would enthuse over an empty snail shell, Eva thought, as she left the office. In her haste, she almost knocked over a young girl who was passing, then narrowly escaped being run over. Shaken, she refused Judith Hansen's invitation into Woodstock and drove away, her decision made.

That evening she informed Greg she wouldn't be accompanying him to New York.

At first, he refused to believe her. 'This is your way of punishing me,' he said. 'How can I make amends? Tell me and I'll do it – and do it again and again.'

Eva imagined him and Carol Wynne lying together in the white dawn of the Serra do Caramulo and felt nothing. It was unnatural. Even though she didn't want to experience again the scalding hurt that had followed his confession, some emotion was essential.

'My decision has nothing to do with your infidelities,' she said. 'You made a decision to offload your guilt. You've no right to blame me for refusing to accept it.'

'Eva, you're breaking my heart. We can't destroy our marriage over one mistake.' His voice came to her from a great distance. Nothing could be resolved by running away, she told him. There was no ghost-free environment. The past was always present.

Two years of marriage. Such a short time, said Liz, awash with tears when they told her. It was too soon to give up. They mustn't make decisions when grief and guilt and loss were confused in their minds. Love, Liz believed, was elastic, expanding to the demands that were placed upon it. Eva reminded her that elastic also contracted. It shrivelled, sagged and no longer bound securely.

Eva drove him to the airport. The early-morning traffic moved forward in a monotonous crawl. The departure hall was crowded with early-morning commuters on tight schedules. The holidaymakers in their colourful parkas moved at a more leisurely pace. Eva saw everything and absorbed nothing. Beside her, not touching, not speaking, Greg loaded his luggage onto a trolley and they headed towards the check-in desk.

At the departure gate they faced each other. He pushed her hair back from her forehead, as if he needed to see her face unadorned before he said goodbye. He promised to ring when he arrived in New York. She wondered if he remembered Faye's grip on his finger the last time they'd stood together in the same place, a family huddle, embracing. Was he picturing her startled eyes, her tiny mouth puckered as the sudden announcement of an impending flight boomed around them? Eva shuddered away from the memory and from his tense embrace.

'I'll always love you.' His voice was bleak. 'No matter what we decide to do, that will never change.'

'I love you too,' she replied. Her voice trembled. 'What a pity it isn't enough.'

In the crush of passengers passing through the departure gate, he turned to stare back at her, unable to believe there were no words they could utter, no gesture that would bring them back together. In that waiting instant it would have been so easy to wish time away, to forfeit even the brief, unforgettable joy Faye had brought into their lives, so they could dally in the past. Her nose began to sting, a certain prelude to tears. She blinked them firmly away. Decisions had been made and enough tears had been shed in their making. She accepted that her feelings were not dead. They had simply been replaced by more demanding preoccupations. She would reserve her grief for Faye and build a new life on her own.

'Why won't you let us take care of you?' Liz demanded when Eva announced that Greg's apartment had been rented out for a year and she was moving to Grahamstown. She would live on site in a caravan while work on the garden centre and the cottage was underway. The caravan in the garden of Wind Fall was used occasionally by her parents when the guest house overflowed. Liz was horrified. It was too dangerous for Eva to live alone at the side of a remote country road. What protection would she have if she was attacked?

'Stay with us while the work is underway,' she pleaded, inventing horror scenarios of murder and mayhem.

'I can't.' Eva was adamant. 'I have so much to do and I don't want to waste time travelling.'

Steve helped her move the caravan on site, his disapproval obvious by his silence, but he hugged Eva tightly before he left and said she was to ring him at any time of the day or night if she had a problem.

Greg rang regularly from New York. He sounded purposeful and excited. He had moved into an apartment in Greenwich Village. A ghost-free zone. He told her he missed her. His voice stammered, as if he was ashamed that his emotions could only be expressed through such inane words. She wondered how he had time for such lost emotions. He was part of the new Irish wave of immigrants who drank in trendy bars and attended po-etry readings. On *Stateside Review* he had a certain novelty ap-peal. Viewers were impressed by his opinions. A new slant, an objective eye. He was a thorn in the side of right-wing Repub-licans. A fly in the ointment of liberalism. How happy he must be, Eva thought, pleasing no one.

She wondered how he would react if she told him the real story was here. The big exclusive, insider knowledge. She imag-ined him in action, lifting stones, letting the worms free. He would take her story from her and give it back to the world. Twenty-six years on, the Anaskeagh Baby searches for her roots.

Her real roots had been set deep in Ashton, a gentle place that nurtured her childhood, as if making recompense for the hard, unyielding landscape into which she had been cast. But now Ashton seemed caught in the time frame of a nostalgic postcard and those roots were loosening, their tentacles twining in new directions, linking her to a family of strangers: bound to them by blood and tears, by an ancestral history, and a se-cret that belonged to the foreboding headland she had last seen looming over the small town of Anaskeagh.

PART FOUR

CHAPTER FORTY

Beth made her way down the rocks to the small cove where she swam every morning. The sky, already streaked with crimson, promised a glorious day. Occasionally, she met Conor Grant jogging along the cliff path but this morning he'd climbed over the rocks and was watching her when she emerged from the water.

'Morning, Beth.' He touched his forehead in a mock salute. 'It's fit and well you're looking these days.' The sweat band across his forehead emphasised his large face and dark moustache. She'd heard he was a formidable solicitor and had no reason to doubt it. 'I presume you've heard the good news.'

'Yes,' she replied, towelling her hair in fast, furious strokes. 'A seat at the Cabinet table. Albert must be very pleased with himself.'

'Humbled, Beth. And honoured. Keep Saturday night free. We're organising a party in Cherry Vale to celebrate.'

'We're not free—'

'No excuses.' He wagged his finger warningly at her. 'We've seen little enough of you and your family since you arrived. Everyone who's anyone is Anaskeagh will be there. How would it look if those closest to my father stayed away.' His heavy thighs juddered as he prepared to finish his run. 'It's going to be a great night, Beth. We'll expect you and Stewart at eight.'

The Cabinet reshuffle had been the subject of speculation for weeks but the media clamoured with disappointment when the news broke. Apart from Albert Grant's appointment to a newly established ministry, it was the same old faces, same old rhetoric, same old promises.

Shortly after her arrival in Anaskeagh Beth had called to see him. His old furniture showrooms in the centre of town had been unrecognisable. Conor's law firm was located on the ground floor and the spacious upper storey where bedroom furniture was once displayed had been converted into his apartment and constituency clinic. The showrooms had seemed so large when Beth was a child. Fancy glass doors, the smell of leather and wood, the hum of fluorescent lights beating mercilessly down on the cheap furniture her aunt sold on credit to the women of Anaskeagh.

She'd tried to compose herself as the elevator moved smoothly upwards but once she'd stepped into the corridor she'd been swamped by long-forgotten sensations. The squeak of bedsprings, his hoarse, whispering threats, the dead weight of his mouth silencing her. She'd turned, ready to run, as she had never been able to run during those dark times. But now she had a family to protect and a debt to settle.

Her uncle had risen from behind his desk when she'd entered his office.

'Beth, my dear girl.' He'd moved towards her, his hand outstretched. 'Home to your own at last.'

'Yes, Albert, back at last – for better or worse.'

'A wise move, my dear. Your husband was a lost man without you. A stressful time starting up a new company but when domestic problems are added it makes everything so much more difficult. Don't you agree?'

'I do indeed.' Beth had ignored his hand and he, seemingly oblivious to her revulsion, had waved her into a chair. 'However it was necessary to be sure that this was the right move for my family to make.'

He'd sat down and smiled at her over his glasses. 'I'm glad you're settling into your new home. If you've any difficulties with schools please don't hesitate—'

'Everything is under control, thank you,' she'd interjected smoothly. 'Lindsey is staying with her grandmother in Oldport but she'll visit us on a regular basis.'

'The dear child. How is she? Recovered, I hope?'

'I think it's important that we understand each other.' She'd held his gaze, forcing him to glance down at his hands. 'Lindsey has told me everything. I repeat – everything. I've come here for only one reason. If you go within breathing distance of any of my children I'll have no hesitation in destroying you. Do I need to elaborate any further?'

'Dear Beth, you never change,' he'd said. 'Always the cruel word. I'll never understand how your mind works.' His arrogance, his instant control of the situation had been as forceful as ever. He remained immune from threats, holding power through indebtedness, and she'd been acutely aware that he'd smoothed the way for Stewart. Red tape cut, strings pulled, the first tranche of funding already spent, the second tranche delayed.

'Your daughter is a talented young lady but a mite unstable, wouldn't you agree?' He'd removed his glasses and dangled them from his index finger. 'It seems highly irresponsible to leave her in the care of that old woman instead of overseeing a proper drug-rehabilitation programme for her. I'm aware that the Gardaí took a lenient view of that whole sorry affair. Just as well we have an understanding police force. A criminal record at her age would be most unfortunate.'

She'd risen to her feet, relieved to find the floor still steady beneath her. 'I've nothing further to say to you, except to repeat my warning. You've a lot to lose, Albert. And I won't hesitate to take you down.'

He'd called her name as she reached the door. When she turned he'd been behind her, his fury forcing her backwards against the wood. She'd resisted the urge to strike him. What a relief that would be, letting go and clawing out his eyes, ripping the skin from his face. But that would mean touching him and the memories had started to overwhelm her, to force her further against the wall, to break the courage that had brought her here.

'Where is your gratitude, Beth? After all the help I've given your husband–'

'Why should I thank you?' she'd interrupted him curtly. 'Everything Stewart achieved was done under his own steam.'

'Then tell him not to be so impatient. He's making a nuisance of himself, phoning the ACII and accusing them of delaying his grants package. The staff have more to do than listen to a constant flow of unwarranted complaints.' His breath had blown faintly cold on her cheeks. He'd lowered his voice until the sound became an intimate whisper. 'But we're family, after all, Beth. Why do you think I invested in Della Designs–'

'What are you talking about?'

'How else do you think Peter expanded his factory and offered you and Stewart the chance to come home again?'

'I don't believe you.'

'I did it for Sara's sake. I loved her dearly but she was so fragile. Such a tenuous grip on reality. She needed security to pursue her own career and I wasn't going to see her wonderful talent wasted. Family, Beth, flesh and blood can't be denied. I'll do anything to protect my own.' She'd heard him swallow. His mouth must have been dry, parched from lies. 'Tell Stewart not to worry. The right word in the right ear is a marvellous lubricant when it comes to oiling the wheels of bureaucracy.'

He'd moved away from her. For such a heavily built man he was light on his feet. A dignified walk back to his desk, his

features arranged in his poster smile, ready to greet his next constituent.

Moving back to Anaskeagh had been as tough as she'd expected, yet, under the revulsion she felt at living in such close
proximity to her uncle, she was invigorated by the challenge of
working with Stewart. Sometimes it seemed as if the intervening
years had never happened and she was a young woman again,
decisive, determined. At home and in the factory she was busier
than ever, constantly on call to solve one problem after another.
She had no title, insisting she didn't want to be burdened with
one. All aspects of TrendLines interested her. She needed to be
accessible to everyone. It was an extension of motherhood, she
thought on more than one occasion, laughing out loud at the
absurdity and the truth of it.

Gail and Paul were up and dressed when she returned from
the cove. No problem getting them out in the mornings. Sheila
O'Donovan's bungalow was close to the old farmhouse, where
Catherine now lived alone, and the farm still held the same at-
tractions that had once enchanted Beth. Robert moaned when
she called him but he too came to the breakfast table on time,
ready to begin his summer job at TrendLines.

Stewart was shaving when she entered their bedroom en
suite.

'I met Conor in the cove,' she said. 'He's invited us to a party
on Saturday. Big celebration.'

'Do we have to go?' Stewart finished shaving and slapped
cologne on his cheeks.

'Yes,' she replied. 'This is a small town. People will notice if
we're missing. The powers-that-be from the ACII will be there.
Perhaps you can bang a few heads together and get some action
on your funding.'

She leaned into his back to hug him before slipping off her
tracksuit and turning on the shower. Sea salt had dried on her

skin. She needed scalding water to cleanse her, yet, even if she scrubbed and scrubbed, she would never be able to wash him away. But she would endure, as Sara had been unable to do.

His sister had returned to Anaskeagh Head for the last time. Catherine O'Donovan had seen her standing outside the farmhouse. Her camera hung from her neck. She'd worn a long navy jumper, trousers and walking boots. But when Catherine had gone out to invite her into the house, Sara had disappeared.

'Perhaps she was a ghost,' Catherine had said. 'She looked so insubstantial standing under the trees.'

No ghost. Beth believed it had been a time of confrontation. Perhaps, also, Sara had sought healing in the shadow of Aislin's Roof. Whatever she sought she hadn't found and Beth was here in this place of restitution, ready to avenge her memory.

CHAPTER FORTY-ONE

Eva watched from the window of Mrs Casey's guest house as the early morning mist cleared from the headland. As birth locations went Anaskeagh Head looked starkly picturesque. But as a secure cradle for a newborn baby it could only have been advantageous if she'd been a mountain goat or one of those statuesque sheep with their long black faces.

'Fair weather, that's for sure once that mist blows away,' predicted Mrs Casey, whose guest house lay at the foot of the headland. 'We're in for a hot summer by all accounts.'

When Eva had arrived the previous night they'd talked about Wind Fall, exchanging horror stories about guests who refused to leave by the allotted hour and stole the towels.

'You'll have a right hunger on you when you reach the top of Anaskeagh Head.' She handed Eva a packed lunch as she was leaving. Eva had a sudden desire to ask if she remembered the Anaskeagh Baby but the urge died as quickly as it had arrived.

As she approached the headland the road divided into a V. She drove towards a group of houses screened by long driveways of maple trees, cherry blossom and pampas grass. This was a narrow road with an insular sense of its own importance. Notices on the gates warned of dangerous dogs and retribution if anyone dared trespass upon the spacious gardens. The road was obviously only used for residential purposes and ended in a barrier of holly and ash lashed with ivy, too thick to penetrate. She returned to her car, reversing with difficulty, and headed back to the junction, following the sign for *trá*.

Ice-cream kiosks on the approach to the beach were opening for business. The sand was white and gritty, crunching underfoot, and the rock face of the headland protruded outwards over the strand. Further along the beach she found the path she needed. It zigzagged easily across the headland, offering safe footholds and regular plateaux for climbers to pull themselves upwards.

A shaft of sunshine struck the red roofs of barns on the foothills and a herd of cattle moved ponderously down a narrow lane to the side of the O'Donovan farmhouse. An elderly woman followed, accompanied by a dog. Eva recognised Catherine O'Donovan. The widow had been mourning her husband when Eva had seen her at Frank's funeral, but today, dressed in jeans and a blue sweatshirt, she looked curiously at Eva and asked if she was lost.

'I'm hillwalking,' Eva replied.

Catherine advised her to be careful. The mist could fall unexpectedly over the headland and confuse a stranger who wasn't used to the lie of the land. Eva thanked her and hesitated, undecided as to whether or not she should introduce herself. Better not. One step at a time into the past.

A car approached, the wheels easing into the edge of the hedgerow to allow the cattle to pass. The driver, a younger woman, turned to speak to two children in the back seat. When the cattle had moved ahead, the children leaped from the car and attached themselves to Catherine. She handed a switch to the little girl, who waved it bravely at the rumps of the cattle but made no attempt to hit them.

Eva nodded goodbye and walked on. She had reached the end of the lane when the car stopped and the driver leaned out the window to offer her a lift.

'My car is parked in the beach car park,' Eva said, hesitating. 'I was going to cut across the headland and climb down to the strand.'

'That'll take forever. I'm heading into town. I'll drop you off on the way.'

'Thank you.' Eva fastened the seat belt and tried to relax. This woman could be her mother. On the streets of Anaskeagh she had stared, sifting them into age groups. Young, she must have been young. A teenage mother, terrified. This woman, who introduced herself as Sheila O'Donovan, had pale blue eyes and a darting gaze. She talked about her family and her job as a childminder to the two children she had left with Catherine.

Her tone sharpened when Eva mentioned the Anaskeagh Baby.

'It's research,' Eva said. 'I'm doing a thesis on babies who were abandoned at birth. The Anaskeagh Baby was an important story at the time.'

'I wouldn't talk too loudly about abandoned babies in Anaskeagh.' Sheila brushed her fringe from her eyes, mousy-brown hair too limp to have ever held a curl. 'People still have hard memories about the lies that were written in the papers. Blamed it all on us. Even though no one had a blessed clue who the mother was.' She tried to stay silent on the subject but her resentment spilled over, the suspicions of that time, the interrogation her fiancé had been subjected to by the Gardaí. 'Mud sticks,' she muttered. She'd broken off her engagement for a while. But common sense had prevailed and in the end Sheila had accepted his innocence. 'Bernard is a good man,' she said. 'Why should he and his brother have been singled out because the baby was left on their doorstep? Jim headed for Australia because he couldn't cope with the suspicion.'

The hedgerows blurred as she picked up speed. Eva clasped the seat belt and closed her eyes. The same feeling she'd experienced in the National Library swept over her. The urge to shout the truth at this woman who obviously wasn't her mother and resented the trouble Eva's birth had caused. Did everyone live their lives in tandem with hidden desires? she wondered. Safely compartmentalised, safely controlled, while a tempest raged inside them.

'Does anyone know who the mother was?' Eva had no idea why she should sound so cool.

'Plenty of names were bandied about, including my own, but no one really knew,' Sheila replied. 'Now no one wants to know.'

In the late afternoon Eva strolled around the town. She entered a gallery where tapestries, stained-glass lampshades and pottery were displayed. A far cry from Biddy's Bits 'n' Pieces, she thought, checking the expensive price tags. She followed the smell of freshly baked cakes wafting from the café attached to the gallery. Women relaxed after shopping, drinking coffee and buttering scones. Some looked curiously at her, nodding politely as they summed her up, a stranger in town. One elderly woman with stooped shoulders met her eyes in a startled, devouring gaze before glancing fiercely down at the table.

Paintings hung on the walls of the café. These ones had an amateurish touch, the price tags cheaper than those in the main gallery. Eva moved closer to look at them. A pier with moored boats and the headland in the background. She stopped before another painting carrying the same initials. This was a town scene, the clock tower on River Mall, its face lit by moonlight. These paintings didn't interest Eva. She suspected they had been painted by a young hand; they lacked dangerous memories.

The elderly woman rose from her chair and joined her.

'A strange class of a painting, wouldn't you agree?' she said, nodding at the moonlight scene.

Eva muttered something inconsequential, wondering if she was a proud relation or a sales agent, but the woman volunteered no further information. She moved closer, a clinging whiff of expensive perfume and smoke on her skin. She asked

Eva's opinion of Anaskeagh. Eva told her what she wanted to hear. Yes, it was indeed a pretty town.

'Can I buy you a coffee before you leave?' The jacket of the woman's crumpled trouser suit was stained. Her heavily made-up face had the same slack appearance and her scalp was visible through dyed blonde hair. The image was too hard for a woman of her years, keeping time at bay with too many rings and pearls the size of small eggs around her neck. Her old hands remained by her sides, hanging listlessly. There was something so pathetic about those loose limp hands with their garish rings, too heavy for frail fingers, that Eva nodded. The woman clicked her fingers imperiously in the direction of the counter.

'Another coffee and scone, Hatty,' she said. 'Put it on my bill – and make sure the coffee is hot this time.'

A small woman with a mop of startling red hair emerged from behind the coffee urn to glower across at them.

'Keep your castanets to yourself, madam,' she snapped. 'You'll be served when I'm good and ready.'

'Staff nowadays – impossible.' Eva's companion sighed.

She made small talk until the coffee was served, shaking her head in disapproval when she heard that Eva had moved from Wicklow to Dublin.

'An atrocious accent,' she said. 'I'm glad to hear you haven't acquired it. My grandchildren could be talking a different language for all the sense I get out of them.' She dismissed her grandchildren with a snap of her hard mouth.

Eva thought of Brigid Loughrey, who had listened when her grandchildren spoke, hearing their words, not their accents. This elderly woman didn't have the attributes of a true grandmother. No soft flesh or hidden treats in large handbags. She ignored her coffee, the butter melting into the scone as she talked about a boutique she'd once owned, designer brands only. She listed designer names, looking at Eva for reaction, her sharp eyes summing up her jacket and trousers; cheap labels that would never have hung on her rails. She had sold her boutique – too many chain stores and shopping centres to compete against. Too many housewives in tracksuits, no style these days. She cast a reproachful glance towards a woman in a shapeless jumper and baggy trousers. Eva discreetly checked her watch, regretting her impulse to linger.

'Do you have relatives in Anaskeagh?' the woman asked.

'No.' Eva didn't know if she'd lied.

'Are you a photographer?' She glanced at the camera lying on the table.

'Purely amateur. I wanted to take some shots of the head-land.'

As the evening light flooded through the window, the woman's frailness was thrown into sharp relief. She remained silent when Eva rose to her feet. They shook hands. Eva turned back at the door but the woman was staring into space and didn't glance in her direction.

She drove past the brightly lit shopping centre with its arches and multi-storey car park. The flags of many nationalities fluttered from the courtyard of The Anaskeagh Arms. She crossed the bridge, where spotlights reflected on the river and the tall clock face marked time.

CHAPTER FORTY-TWO

Cherry Vale was decorated with congratulatory banners and balloons printed with the words *Albert Grant. Minister for Indigenous Enterprise*. Once Beth had danced in this room, her steps faltering, chasing the notes her father had played. The room had sparkled with Christmas lights and festive baubles. Outside, newborn pups had whimpered… She allowed her breathing to slow down. This was a game of control and there could only be one victor.

Marjory slumped in an armchair, a gin and tonic untouched beside her. Since she'd sold her boutique she drifted aimlessly through each day. She was usually in her dressing gown when Beth called, the air in the kitchen musty and stale, spilled milk and too many cigarettes.

After a few minutes of strained conversation with her mother, she wandered outside, searching for a familiar face. Stewart was talking intently to a man from the ACII and her uncle was surrounded by his supporters. Fleshy men who dined well and had a keen awareness of fine wines. Silver lights twinkled from trees and candles fluttered among the flower beds. The tennis court was still in place but the shed, where Sadie had once rested with her newborn pups, had become a high-domed glass conservatory. Tonight it had been converted into a bar yet still… Beth pressed her lips together and headed purposefully towards a statuesque woman in a backless dress, a dramatic silver choker around her neck.

'Your uncle's looking mighty pleased with himself tonight.' Nuala O'Neill kept her voice low as she tilted her glass in his direction. 'Lining your pockets at the nation's expense is a really good apprenticeship if you want to be a minister.'

'Some say he's done an excellent job up to now.' Beth too spoke softly.

'Who says?'

'Those in the know.'

'The Anaskeagh Mafia you mean.' They laughed quietly together, relaxed in each other's company.

A spontaneous friendship had developed between them when they'd met in Nuala's gallery shortly after Beth's arrival in Anaskeagh. They shared the common bond of outsiders who were part of the community by birth but separated by experiences and finding it difficult to reclaim their space.

They watched the minister as he moved effortlessly through the crowd, shaking hands, kissing cheeks.

'Have you spoken to Derry Mulhall yet?' Nuala leaned close to Beth.

'I called twice,' Beth replied. 'He never answers.'

'Keep trying. You'll be interested in what he has to say.'

'Does he ever ask about his son?'

'He would – if I gave him the opportunity.' Nuala smiled grimly. 'I don't.' She raised her voice as the minister moved from his circle of supporters and strode towards them. 'If you're talking to Lindsey tell her to call and see me when she's in town again. I've sold another one of her paintings.'

'Lindsey is a most talented young lady.' Albert moved smoothly between them. 'I've seen her work displayed in your wonderful gallery, Nuala. Mark my words, she'll make a name for herself one of these days.' He smiled steadily at Beth. 'That's if she manages to keep a sensible head on her shoulders.' He moved on, his hand outstretched towards his next constituent.

Lindsey was repeating her Leaving. If she achieved the necessary points next year she would study computer science. Painting was a hobby, a convenient way to earn extra money in Nuala's gallery. 'Painting by numbers,' she called her landscapes, deriding the pretty views she painted yet spending all her spare time working on them. Genetic roots sprouting.

Jean Grant appeared at the patio door to announce that food was being served. In the main drawing room Conor exploded bottles of champagne and proposed a toast to his father. As the glasses were raised Marjory rose unsteadily from the armchair and clapped her hands.

'For he's a jolly good fellow, for he's a jolly good fellow.' Her reedy voice trembled off-key. The guests, embarrassed, began to sing along with her. When the song ended she clawed the air in confusion before she sank back down again, breathing heavily.

'Poor Marjory. The medication she's on doesn't mix with alcohol but she never listens,' Jean said quietly to Beth. 'She's an incredibly lonely woman. We hoped when your family moved here she would begin to relax but she's as wound up as ever.' She paused diplomatically. 'Do you think you could persuade her to leave now, for her own sake?'

'Of course.' Beth crossed the room and took her mother's hand, suddenly moved by the desolate expression on her face. 'Marjory, if you're feeling tired I can drive you home.'

'Why are you always trying to ruin things?' Marjory sat ramrod straight on her chair. 'I'm enjoying myself. Leave me alone.'

'It's no trouble—' Beth stopped abruptly when the politician's arm encircled her waist.

'I'll drive her home when she's ready to go,' he murmured in her ear. 'I've always taken care of my own and I'm not going to stop now.'

Beth had fantasised about his death. A sharp knife between his shoulder blades. A pillow pressed hard against his face while he slept. She had the strength and the will to do such things then kneel at peace beside his coffin. But they would bury him with full honours, read tributes over his grave, write obituaries in newspapers. She wanted him to die slowly, loudly, aggressively. She wanted him to be the headline story and the inside page. She wanted journalists jogging his elbows, rooting in company records, researching, snooping, demanding answers. She wanted flashbulbs chasing his car and cameras on the plinth of Dáil Éireann. She wanted a modern-day execution. Death by a thousand media knives.

She parked her car close to the hedgerow surrounding Derry Mulhall's cottage. Generations of his family had once owned the land upon which the Anaskeagh industrial park now stood. Apart from a spiral of smoke drifting listlessly from the chimney, there was little sign of life within the flaking, mud-spattered walls. As before, the front door was closed, the curtains drawn.

Occasionally, Derry left his cottage and headed to the Anaskeagh Arms. On such occasions he talked too much. He'd been beaten up one night and left unconscious in an alley. He'd survived but not to tell the tale. After that, he drank more quietly, mainly in his stale kitchen in the company of his dog.

After knocking four times and receiving no reply apart from a dog barking, Beth was about to walk away when he opened the door.

'You're wasting your time if you're trying to sell me something, missus.' He held the dog by the collar but Beth suspected his grip would loosen at the slightest provocation.

'I only want a few minutes of your time, Mr Mulhall,' she replied. 'I work in the Anaskeagh industrial park.'

His eyes glittered. 'That shower of fucking parasites. Get back where you came from. Fucking blow-ins!'

'I'm originally from Anaskeagh,' she said. 'You used to know my father, Barry Tyrell.'

'By God, I did.' For an instant his face softened then settled back into belligerent lines. 'And your mother too, a rare bitch of a woman. Still is, from all accounts. You're Albert Grant's niece then?'

'We can't choose our relatives, Mr Mulhall, although we can choose to disown them. You look like your son. Nuala O'Neill showed me his photograph. It was taken in Tokyo.'

He moved from the shelter of his doorway and pushed his face forward. 'He's not my fucking son and it's none of your fucking business anyway. Don't you dare come here making accusations or I'll set this beast on you.'

'I'm not making accusations. I'm here to talk about the sale of your land.'

He pointed towards the gate, furrows of anger deepening in his cheeks. 'The gate's that direction, missus. Make sure you close it on your way out.'

'Who can you talk to any more, Mr Mulhall?' She stood firmly before him. 'From what I hear you've been well and truly muffled.'

'No one muffles Derry Mulhall. May their balls roast in hell for trying.'

'I heard you were badly beaten up.'

'Broken bones mend.'

'What a pity you didn't realise your land would be rezoned from agricultural to commercial use so soon after you sold it. Imagine the profit you'd have made if you'd known the ACII were interested in building on it.'

'What's your game, missus?' he demanded. 'If you're here to stir up trouble I've already told you where to find the gate.'

'You were robbed, Mr Mulhall,' she said. 'Everyone knows that for a fact but no one is saying it out loud. I came here this evening to see if there was some way of exposing the truth. But if you're not prepared to talk I won't take up any more of your time.'

He threw back his strong red neck and laughed. 'Jesus, missus, but you're soft in the head if that's the way you're thinking. There's stories I could tell that would make your hair stand up straight but what's the sense in being dead? I'll be there soon enough and I'd prefer to do it with the help of the bottle rather than them shaggers in the Anaskeagh Mafia. What did you say your name is?'

'I didn't, but it's Beth McKeever.'

'A quare sort of a niece you are – out here trying to make trouble for your uncle. You'd better come in seeing as how you've nosed your way into my business. But I'm not promising anything mind.'

The smoky kitchen caught against her breath. The dog, once released, cowered under a chair, obviously well used to dodging this surly man's boot. A bowl of eggs and a half empty bottle of whiskey sat on the table. He offered her tea and a boiled egg. She accepted. The egg tasted like rubber. He poured whiskey and watched while she drank it neat.

'What the fuck is Nuala's lad doing in Tokyo?' he asked.

'Designing skyscrapers,' Beth replied and put a newspaper cutting featuring his son's achievements on the table. Derry pretended not to notice.

As she suspected, her uncle had never received planning permission for his furniture factory. Different times, said Derry. A few pounds in the hand and no questions asked.

'I know your land was eventually sold on to the ACII but who bought it from you?' she asked.

'Talk to Kitty Grimes if you want your answer to that,' he replied. 'A more God-fearing woman never walked the streets of Anaskeagh and she knows what she heard from the mouth of that crook. Check out Hatty Beckett as well. She won't need much prompting to talk about Albert Grant. A few rum and cokes should do the trick there. Good luck, missus. I don't envy you your job.'

Beth left the newspaper clipping on the table. He shoved it out of sight behind a clock. She did not ask for it back; he didn't offer it.

Kitty Grimes had been Conor Grant's office cleaner but now she cleaned for TrendLines. A quiet, nervous woman, she'd arrived early for work one evening and overheard an argument between father and son taking place behind closed doors. The politician had been shouting about delays in a land transaction and she'd known immediately that they'd been talking about Derry's land. Liam, her husband, had worked in Albert's furniture factory until its closure. Not a word to the workers, no warning, no redundancy payments, nothing. Liam had died soon afterwards. Her mouth trembled when she mentioned his name. His life snuffed out with the stress of it all, and who cared at the end of the day? Certainly not Albert Grant and, knowing this, she did something she would never have considered doing under normal circumstances. Not in her wildest dreams, she added, her hands trembling when she showed Beth the document she had photocopied when she was alone in the office. She had also shown it to the farmer. Soon afterwards, Derry had been beaten up for talking too loudly about corruption in high places. Kitty had remained tight-lipped ever since.

Hatty, her tongue as sharp as ever, sat high on a bar stool in The Anaskeagh Arms and ordered a rum and coke.

'Transparency!' she snarled at Beth. 'Now that's a fine new word altogether. For what it's worth, your uncle is about as transparent as the arse on an elephant.' She took a powder compact from her bag, inspected her face and applied a streak of vermillion lipstick. It matched her hair perfectly. Hatty Beckett was determined not to grow old graciously.

A modern shopping centre stood in place of her once-famous chip shop on the corner of River Mall. Hatty had been the stumbling block in its development, the only tenant who refused to move from the building. Her lease still had eight years to run and she'd refused her landlord's offer to buy it back. Visits from a health inspector began soon afterwards. Rats were discovered in the storeroom and her chip shop was closed down overnight.

'I know Albert Grant was behind it,' she said. 'He was in cahoots with Ben Layden, the developer. That pair are as close as the hairs on a dog's coat.'

Little stories oozing quietly from the mouths of little people. Until Beth arrived in Anaskeagh no one was listening.

Justin Boyd, the reporter from *Elucidate*, was waiting when Beth parked her car at the foot of Anaskeagh Head. Sheep grazed nearby and a flock of crows wheeled over the empty fields. They picked their way through the long grass, heading towards the ruins of an old cattle shed. She disliked his lips, the pompous mouth that tightened angrily each time his fine woollen trousers snagged on briars. In the shelter of the walls she began to talk. Justin made no effort to hide his impatience.

'Let me get a grip on this,' he said, interrupting her to check over his notes. 'Your sources are an alcoholic farmer and a chip-shop owner whose business was forced to close because she broke hygiene regulations. The office cleaner who claims to have incriminating evidence could work if she's willing to go public–'

'She's very nervous,' warned Beth. 'You must appreciate that around here you don't make accusations about Albert Grant too loudly. He can be a powerful enemy. But I guarantee that once you scratch below the surface you'll be surprised at what people know and are prepared to reveal.'

'I can't help wondering why you're so interested in destroying his reputation?' He regarded her suspiciously.

'He's a sleaze merchant, always has been, and he controls most of the board of the ACII. The industrial estate was supposed to be located in Clasheen, which has a far superior infrastructure. Instead – overnight – the location was changed. We've constant problems with entry and exit, not to mention potholes. The communications system and our water distribution is not fit for purpose yet no one complains in case their funding is delayed. And that's never paid on time. I could go on…' Her carefully prepared scenario was falling apart. She sounded too anxious, a vindictive woman with an axe to grind.

'Please don't.' He flicked his note book closed. '*Elucidate* is inundated with stories and each one is carefully vetted before we make a decision. What I've got from you so far is mostly anecdotal. It's not enough, Mrs McKeever. Now, if you'll excuse me, I've a long drive back to Dublin.'

'Will you talk to those people?'

'I'll see them before I leave and talk to if it's worth pursuing. I'll let you know when I've made my decision.'

A week later Justin Boyd finally returned her calls. Derry Mulhall had been belligerent and drunk. A wild dog had shredded the leg of his trousers and the farmer had refused to call it to heel. Hatty Beckett had ordered four rum and cokes on his tab and told him a concocted story about two-legged rats with vendettas. Kitty Grimes had been incoherent with nerves and refused to show him her so-called evidence. The journalist's voice shook with anger. The file on Albert Grant was whiter than white. There was no story.

'The only problem I have with your uncle is that he's a puffed-up ball of self-importance,' he said. 'But if that was a crime they could move Dáil Éireann to Mountjoy Prison.'

'What about the Michael Hannon story?' Beth asked. 'How did that start? I can hardly imagine that information was presented to you in its entirety.'

'The Michael Hannon exposé had nothing to do with me,' Justin Boyd replied. 'And the journalist responsible is now living in New York. Believe me, Mrs McKeever, there's nothing to investigate.'

CHAPTER FORTY-THREE

New York was like a fist opening. Its noise overpowered Greg. He welcomed the obscene heights of buildings, the anonymous crowds, the ceaseless roar of traffic. His tears or his laughter would fall unnoticed amongst the clamorous mass of creeds, cultures and colours jostling past him. How could anything he had done have significance in such surroundings? A fist had opened, and he was free. But freedom came with a price tag. Loneliness that, at times, felt unbearable. He could have alleviated it. On *Stateside Review* there were beautiful women with anorexic shoulders and smiles that promised much. He resisted them, filled with a need to atone. Once a Catholic always a Catholic – punishment awaited those who sinned in the flesh. And when the punishment came it was a splinter, festering.

Ellen Lloyd, a Limerick woman who worked as *Stateside Review*'s chief advertising executive and had a soft spot for homesick emigrants, befriended him. Twenty years in New York had robbed Ellen of the insatiable Irish lust for personal information. She asked no questions about his past. He didn't mention Eva, and when he breathed Faye's name it was at night when he was alone and aching with regret.

Ellen called him into her office when he was passing by one morning. 'Watch out for leprechauns,' she said. 'There's an Irish trade delegation in New York, headed by Albert Grant. He's a new minister for something or other.'

Greg nodded. He kept up to date with news from home and the appointment of the politician had surprised him. Albert

Grant was a chameleon who blended into any environment, comfortable with his parochial roots, yet projecting an urbane image that embraced the problems of the nation. In the past, Greg had tried to penetrate the avuncular mask he wore and failed. Rumours occasionally surfaced about him. Questions about land deals had been asked but there had never been any evidence to carry a story.

The minister rose to his feet when Greg entered *Stateside Review*'s hospitality room and grasped his hand.

'Welcome to New York, Minister,' said Greg. 'Congratulations on your appointment.'

'My dear boy. What a pleasure it is to see a familiar face. I can relax now that I'm in the hands of a true professional.'

Kieran Grant, a small, colourless man with a startling dicky bow, had accompanied him. His handshake was lacklustre, as if the ebullience of his father had drained him of any desire to compete.

The politician was relaxed in front of the camera. He spoke movingly about the curse of emigration and how Mother America had taken the Irish diaspora into her welcoming arms. But a new day was dawning. He had a vision that would stem the haemorrhage of young blood from his native land. In forgotten corners of Ireland he was involved in establishing creative centres of opportunity and employment. Greg admired his ability to flog the same hobby horse and make it sound different each time.

'I must say that went extremely well.' At the end of the interview Albert rubbed his hands together.

'As always, Minister.' Greg unclipped their microphones and escorted him back to the hospitality room where his son was waiting.

'It was a pleasure meeting you, Greg,' Kieran said as they were leaving. 'I hope you'll come to dinner soon. I'll be in touch shortly to arrange it.'

Greg was unaware that clips from the interview had been shown on the evening news on Irish TV. Shortly afterwards, he received a call from a viewer in connection with his interview. Beth McKeever claimed to have incriminating evidence about the minister. Was his move to New York permanent? she asked.

'I'm here for the foreseeable future,' he said. 'So I'm afraid I can't be of any assistance.'

Albert Grant and his misdeeds were no longer his concern, yet he was unable to forget her call. Out of curiosity he phoned the *Elucidate* office. Justin Boyd insisted that the story had no legs. Beth McKeever had a grudge against the politician because an ACII grant due to her husband had been delayed. She obviously expected preferential treatment because Albert Grant was her uncle and unable to pull a stroke on her behalf.

Bad blood, Greg thought, the worst kind. The thrill of the chase – but he had to let this one go.

In his high-rise apartment he watched the lights of New York scar the skyline. Between the towering skyscrapers he could breathe again. The radio played classic hits. Freddie Mercury singing about champions with no time for losing. You lost out on that one, Freddie, he thought. But what a voice to leave behind. Such power. That was what it was all about. To leave something fine behind – music, words, a painting, a child... Something to mark the fact that he had lingered for a short while on the cusp of time.

CHAPTER FORTY-FOUR

By the magic of moonlight Eva's cottage looked beautiful, but she woke every morning in her caravan to a heap of stones, protected by tarpaulin covers. The site had become a blight on her horizon. She wondered if she was mad, chasing a dream amidst the clamour and humped earth with only Matt Morgan and his crew of head-wreckers, who called themselves brick layers, carpenters, plumbers and plasterers. Tractors and diggers added to the din. Even the swans were hiding in the rushes, furious over the drilling and hammering. If only this hullabaloo made a difference. It should be possible to bury her thoughts in the thump of a kango hammer or the crash of falling masonry, but sometimes there were phantom yearnings when she imagined the cry of a baby and her breasts tingled, as if milk was still flowing. The summer nights were mild. A full moon shone on the lake. The reeds stood tall and straight. The swans were sleeping, indifferent to her problems.

Her father arrived one afternoon and bullied her into coming back to Ashton for a week. Liz fussed and complained that she was too thin, malnourished and obsessed with murdering Matt Morgan. Eva obediently swallowed multivitamins and ate three solid meals a day, fretting and contacting Matt continuously on her mobile.

The early-morning routine in Wind Fall hadn't changed. Guests rising for breakfast, the slamming of car doors as they departed. Eva seldom entered the breakfast room, preferring the intimacy of the kitchen, where she helped Liz prepare a full Irish breakfast and slice freshly baked brown bread.

One morning, on her way to the river, she passed the wide window of the breakfast room. It was empty except for one guest who was speaking to her mother. The slope of Liz's shoulders and the man's serious expression as he turned to gaze at a christening photograph on the wall alerted her. They were talking about Faye. For an instant, Eva felt exposed, gossip fodder for a stranger. Her apprehension quickly died away. Liz was not a gossip. Her relationship with her guests was friendly but confined to light conversation about the weather and places of interest they should visit.

She saw him again by the river. At first she thought he was an angler and, having registered his presence, forgot about him. She was startled some time later when he spoke, apologising for disturbing her. He was staying at Wind Fall and wondered if she was Mrs Frawley's daughter?

Eva nodded, angry at having to make conversation, then angrier still when he sat on the grass beside her. He laid a sketchpad between them. A briar had torn the pocket of his jacket and rust-coloured threads hung loose from it.

'This is such a peaceful place.' He gazed towards the river. 'It must have looked exactly the same a hundred years ago.'

His voice had a hesitancy that irritated her, as if he was judging each word before he uttered it. Yet it was a strong voice, too loud in her head, too intrusive. He wondered if it was possible to paint such stillness. She glanced at his sketchpad. Scribbles, slashes. She didn't want him drawing her river. She didn't want him sitting beside her, disturbing her solitude. His beard gave him a wild look, as if he should be climbing mountains or hacking forgotten trails in some far-off outback. When she asked him to leave her alone he rose to his feet immediately. He was composed as he gathered his pad and pencils.

'Mrs Frawley told me about your child,' he said, his voice dropping low. 'I wish I could find words to comfort you.'

She flinched from his well-meaning sympathy and made no reply.

He acknowledged her desire to be left alone and said good-bye. His car was missing from the driveway when she returned to Wind Fall.

Eva had her first garden-design contract if she wanted to accept it. It could be a lucrative contract, Judith Hansen said when he rang. The florist had purchased the building next door to Woodstock and was expanding into organic fruit and vegetables. Tork was setting up a market garden to supply most of the produce.

'He's gone into partnership with a local man, who's renting land to him and helping him financially,' Judith said. 'But the land needs to be cultivated and landscaped. The owner wants to meet you. Are you interested?'

'Yes, I'm interested,' Eva replied. It sounded like a lucrative contract and she desperately needed money. A bad drainage problem and subsidence in her cottage foundations had taken their toll on her grandmother's legacy. Her bank manager displayed little sympathy when Eva mentioned cash-flow problems. The future was uncertain. In truth, when she had the courage to think about it, her future was a mess.

With advance warning, Eva had time to tidy the caravan and tie up her hair before her potential client arrived. She changed her jeans and took off her wellingtons. She applied perfume and eyeliner. Word of mouth was the best advertisement and first impressions were important.

She recognised him immediately. His beard still needed trimming. He had a firm, dry handshake and held her hand for a moment longer than she thought was necessary. The same jacket, crumpled rust-coloured linen with a torn pocket. Judith said he was a widower, awkward without a woman to sew him into shape. Eva wondered what he had been doing in Ashton. Painting, probably.

Aware that she'd recognised him, he apologised for intruding on her privacy when she'd sat alone by the river. He understood grief. He knew what it could do. The personal nature of his conversation surprised her. Business deals weren't usually done in an atmosphere of yearning memories. Nor were they done in the middle of a bomb site.

She invited him into the caravan, thankful she'd taken the precaution of tidying it. She was startled how at home he looked relaxing against the cushions and discussing money in the matter-of-fact manner of an experienced businessman.

'When will it be convenient to visit Havenstone?' he asked.

'Havenstone?' She glanced enquiringly at him.

'My house. I want you to see the grounds first. Then we can discuss the possibilities.'

She was suddenly nervous at the thought of her first major contract without her father's knowledgeable hand on her elbow. He saw her hesitation and misunderstood it, offering immediately to pay for the consultation.

'It's not that. I haven't worked since before…' She paused, unable to continue.

He spoke gently for her. 'Since Faye died.'

The name of her child on this stranger's lips seemed natural. She took a deep breath and nodded rigidly. Only afterwards did she wonder about the emotion in his voice.

'Monday,' he said. 'Come and see me on Monday.'

Judith rang the following day. 'Well, what do you think?'

'I have to see the grounds first.'

'You don't sound too sure. Did you have a problem with him? He can be rather aloof, but he's fine when you get to know him. He's been through a hard time since his wife died.'

'When did she die?'

'Last year – a sad affair.'

'She must have been quite young?'

'Too young to die,' Judith agreed. 'Afterwards, he was going to sell his house but he changed his mind and now Tork has persuaded him to lease his land.'

The decision to withdraw his house came without warning, Judith added. Carrie Davern was furious. She had potential bidders lined up and was counting on her commission. Tough. Eva disliked the estate agent with her cold, speculative eyes and the ability to sell a nightmare under the guise of a dream.

Peter Wallace had intrigued her. Before he'd left her caravan he'd glanced out the window and asked how she was managing to stay sane with the wrecking crew in action. He knew Matt Morgan by reputation.

'A temperamental man,' he'd said. 'Have you noticed?'

Eva nodded. The floodgates had opened. She'd found herself telling this stranger about the rows and the delays and the hearing problems Matt suffered if she pointed out a flaw in his work. How she was afraid to bully him in case he downed tools and headed off to another job.

He'd asked to see the architectural plans. After studying them intently he'd gone outside to look around. He'd talked to Matt, pointing to the walls and the bricks stacked on one side of the cottage. He'd tapped the plans, forcing the builder to look closely at them. His manner had been high-handed, a born autocrat. She'd waited for Matt to stride off the site in a temper tantrum but, before she could intervene, he'd nodded sheepishly. She'd almost expected him to touch his forelock. Peter Wallace had returned to the caravan, ducking his head as he entered. He'd offered his opinion: Matt had experienced some problems but he would soon have everything sorted out. She need have no further worries.

'I'm perfectly capable of looking after my own business affairs,' she'd said, angry that she had inadvertently revealed so much to a stranger.

'I wouldn't dream of suggesting otherwise.' He'd stared evenly back at her. 'But the bricks Matt intended using looked different to the ones specified on the plans. An understandable mistake and easily rectified.'

The thought of someone looking out for her interests had made her legs tremble. She'd sat down, suddenly realising she was exhausted. After he'd driven away she'd marched over to Matt.

'If you ever try to pull one over on me again you'll be off this job so fast you'll think there's a rocket up your arse,' she'd shouted.

'Mother of God!' Matt had been shocked. 'That's no way for a lady to talk. Your mother should wash your mouth out with soap.'

'I'm not joking, Matt. Don't you dare cut corners with inferior materials when you're working for me. I want the exact materials that are in the architect's plans. Understand? And I want this job finished on time. If you skive off and do any more nixers you can sing falsetto for your money.'

He'd turned nasty, gesturing towards the mud heaps. 'If you insist on using threats instead of acting in a civilised manner we might as well call a halt to things right now. But I'll drag you through the courts for every penny you owe me.'

'What about the Revenue Commissioners?' she'd demanded, enjoying his startled expression. 'How much do you owe them?'

'Don't bluff with me, lady.' He'd been rising on his toes, ready to walk. 'Everything I do is straight up.'

'I'm not a lady, Mr Morgan. On more than one occasion I've been called a thundering bitch – and everything you do is not straight up. I have the evidence to prove it. I followed you last week and two days the week before when you were supposed to be working here. Mobile phones are so handy these days. Those little videos I made should make interesting viewing. But that's between you and your friendly tax inspector. As long as you understand that you're working to a contracted time frame and doing the job to the exact specifications in my plans, we should be able to get out of each other's hair as soon as possible.'

'It was never going to be otherwise, lady.' He'd sounded grimly resigned. 'If you'll allow me to resume my work, I have a contract to honour.'

Back in the caravan Eva hadn't known whether to laugh or cry. He'd bought her bluff. For the first time since Faye's death she'd felt elated, without guilt, without kitten claws tearing her chest apart.

In the garden of Havenstone, the roots of old trees splayed like magnificent tendons across the grass. Roses climbed the walls, an abundance of white blossom forming an arch above the entrance to the house.

'Why do you want to change such a beautiful garden?' Eva asked. She was uneasy in this peaceful space, strangely reluctant to see it torn apart by diggers and landscaped to a new plan. Bees droned and hovered over lush borders of summer flowers; spires of colour spilling their delicate fragrance into the air.

'That was never my intention,' Peter Wallace replied. 'The project I have in mind is at the back of the house.' She followed him around the side entrance into a terraced garden. White camellias blossomed in terracotta pots but the garden furniture looked neglected. Steps led down to a second level where an ornate fountain had become a repository for bird droppings and dead leaves. They reached a copse of slender trees that eventually led into a claustrophobic wilderness of briars, hawthorn and a shrivelled crab-apple orchard. Rusting remains of metal frames and an old wall were almost obscured by thick layers of ivy.

An evening mist was falling. Midges swarmed around them, swirling on the smell of dead vegetation. When Eva slipped on rotting leaves he reached out to steady her, his gaze inscrutable in the flickering shadows.

'My father used to grow vines here,' he said. 'Some notion he had about making his own wine. This is the area Tork Hansen wants to cultivate.'

They returned to a house filled with antique furniture sitting in dusty, airless rooms. The walls were bare. Lighter patches showed where paintings or photographs once hung. Eva wanted to fling open windows, fill the rooms with flowers, drown the fusty atmosphere with loud music. Marching bands might do the trick.

She promised to draw up plans, do her costings. Heavy machinery would be involved in the early stages and she would need to check access. For the first time since entering Havenstone, she felt motivated. In her mind she saw how it would look. Greenhouses and a walled kitchen garden. Trees heavy with fruit, vegetables all in a row, tubs of marjoram, rosemary, sage, dill, a bay tree, vines clinging and climbing.

When he wasn't attending horticultural college, Tork Hansen worked by her side. The florist's son was a melancholic youth, a busker who performed a dramatic flame-swallowing routine in his spare time. Occasionally, his girlfriend arrived with sandwiches and flasks of the vilest, strongest coffee Eva had ever tasted. Her fine dark eyebrows were decorated with precisely carved studs that reminded Eva of bullets. A ring glistened on her tongue when she opened her mouth and her clothes – an oversized military jacket, khaki trousers and aggressive combat boots – looked as if they'd been scavenged from the body of a dead soldier. She never stayed for long. If Peter appeared she took off with speed, as if her appearance in the garden would anger him. She offered to design a publicity leaflet for Eva's garden centre and brought samples of her work to the caravan one night. She suggested the name Eva's Cottage Garden. It sounded exactly right.

'We met before you started working in Havenstone,' she said when she and Tork were leaving. She had a penetrating stare that verged on rudeness. 'In the village. I thought you were a ghost – not that I believe in ghosts or anything crazy like that. But it's kind of weird. Every time I see you I think of Sara.'

Eva had no recollection of their meeting. 'Sara?' she asked, puzzled.

'She was married to my uncle. She's dead…' Her voice trailed away. She climbed into the Woodstock van and Tork accelerated away.

Eva drove to Oldport on the finished section of the motorway – a long grey slash with flashing signs, bypassing narrow main streets that had been crumbling under the force of juggernauts and traffic jams. Peter Wallace expressed surprise that the work had progressed so fast. He complimented Eva on what had been achieved, examining the walls she'd uncovered, and listened intently when she discussed her plans with him. She was conscious of his scrutiny, a subtle, brooding awareness, difficult to pin down. Not a look that said he desired her. Her instinct was never wrong in that department. No, it was something else, something too private for her to fathom, but she sensed it and it made her nervous.

One evening, when Eva was leaving the garden, he stretched out his hand as if he wanted to remove something from her hair. For an instant, his hand remained in a reaching position before falling to his side. A sharp, almost painful sensation flickered in her stomach as she imagined his fingers touching her. She flinched, moving quickly aside, shocked at her reaction. Later, alone in the caravan, she found twigs and leaves tangled in her curls. She brushed them furiously to the floor.

The heavy work on her cottage was finished and the landscaping was now underway. Soon the greenhouses would be assembled, ventilated and electrified, their wooden frames blending easily into their natural surroundings. Slowly, Eva was bringing order to this wild place and her relief in the mornings when she left her caravan to drive to Havenstone was palpable.

She tried to sense his dead wife's presence in the old house. There were no photographs, no clothes, no odds and ends to suggest she'd ever existed. Eva imagined her shadow wandering lost in those empty rooms where all that remained were the colours and textures Sara Wallace had created around her.

CHAPTER FORTY-FIVE

October was a month of mist and light rain. Red-gold leaves on the trees, not yet ready to fall. Faye's birth month. A month that should have had a cake with one candle and balloons on the door. Eva stood in a cemetery of angels, teddy bears and toy windmills blowing silently in the breeze. She laid flowers by Faye's tiny headstone. In the afternoon she spoke to Greg on the phone. He hung up when their silence grew too deep to break.

Peter Wallace had mentioned that he would be away for the day and she worked in his garden without resting. Tork, sensing her mood, kept his distance. Before leaving for Grahamstown she stopped off at the local supermarket to buy bread and milk. A baby lay in the cradle of a shopping trolley, pink and calm in a quilted sleeping bag. She raised her tiny fingers in a fist and let them fall again.

Eva stopped, unable to move past her. She wanted to lift her in her arms and run to a silent place. She wanted her nipples to pucker under the suck of tiny gums. The back of her neck was cold with sweat as she moved away. Was this what she was destined to become? A demented baby thief, ripping babies from their prams and from the arms of their mothers?

She walked quickly from the supermarket and climbed into her van. Her legs trembled so much she was afraid to drive far. It was dark when she reached Havenstone. Peter had given her a key to the front door when she'd first accepted the contract. She entered the empty house, sat by the long kitchen table and stared at the surface, her eyes following the curving grain until it blurred. Then she placed her head against the wood and began to weep.

She didn't hear him enter. Her first awareness of his presence was the feel of his hands on her shoulders, a steady, comforting touch. She raised her head and covered her cheeks, appalled that he should discover her in such distress. Unable to speak, she ran from the kitchen, through the hall and down the front steps. She heard his footsteps behind her, his voice urgent, concerned. He caught her on the bottom step and forced her to a standstill. She did not resist when he led her back into the house.

In the drawing room he poured her a brandy and stood over her while she drank it.

'Please don't apologise.' Her silenced her attempts to explain her presence there. 'I know today is your child's birthday.'

'How do you know?' She was startled by his knowledge and when he mentioned Wind Fall she remembered the first time she'd seen him in the breakfast room with Liz.

Heat returned to her cheeks. Her breath steadied. She told him about the supermarket and about the National Library – where her past was a headline on microfilm – and how she was unable to stop crying because she'd climbed the headland and believed she was on the other side.

Once again she was confiding in this stranger. He listened intently and did not make futile, sympathetic remarks. Nor did he hold her hand or stroke her hair, even though he was so close she only had to stretch out to touch him. When she was composed again he ignored her protests and drove her to Grahamstown in her van.

The site looked desolate. The caravan was cold. He looked around the cluttered, untidy space then stared through the window at the darkness outside. He asked how work was progressing on her garden centre. Some planting for spring had been done but the cottage – she shrugged, too weary to talk about debts and her bank manager, who refused overdrafts because it was a high-risk project. She saw him frown, tension gathering between his dark eyebrows, as if her problems were also pressing down on him. She ordered a taxi for him on her mobile and they drank coffee while he waited. Once again she apologised for intruding into Havenstone.

'I'm glad I came home and found you,' he said.

For an instant she thought he was going to take her in his arms. She stepped backwards, relieved when the lights of the approaching taxi swept over them. He signalled to the taxi driver to wait and turned back to her.

'If you're free some night I'd like to take you out for a meal.' He spoke carefully. 'I want to discuss something with you. Strictly business,' he added hastily, seeing her startled expression.

She agreed, too weary to think of an excuse. Later, when the day with all its grief had faded, she would cancel. If he needed to discuss business, the garden in Havenstone was the appropriate place.

It rained that night. The wind grew in strength. The plastic coverings on plants fluttered, loud as the wings of angry swans. In the small hours she rose from the bed and phoned Greg. She wanted to talk to him about loneliness and empty nights. When an automated voice told her he was unavailable on his mobile, she rang his landline. A woman answered. Her assertive drawl grew impatient at Eva's silence. In the background she heard music playing on a stereo. She hung up without speaking and tossed sleeplessly for the rest of the night.

When Peter Wallace informed Eva that he'd made a reservation in Goodlarches she did not demur. She would wear black, a sleek dress with shoestring straps, and sheer black stockings to tease and tantalise. They would dine by candlelight and drink a toast to the future. The evening could take care of itself.

Goodlarches was silent with the weight of money and diners in their twilight years. Elderly wives in floral silk dresses flanked by serious husbands, silver-haired devils behaving themselves for a change. No prices on the menu. Greg would immediately have demanded to know why. He would probably have done an *Elucidate* special on the scam of the celebrity chef.

Peter Wallace had shaved off his beard. He looked younger without it, more exposed: firm full lips, a strong chin. He ordered their meal with authority, chose the wine after a brief glance at the menu. A sophisticated man, used to dining out in restaurants without prices. They were tense throughout the meal, unsure of the roles they should play. Their voices sounded too loud when they spoke.

As soon as the meal ended he flashed his credit card and they left the restaurant. He suggested a nightcap in Havenstone. Eva accepted. He poured brandy into goblets, handed one to her and proposed a toast to the success of her garden centre. She raised her own glass and they drank together. He seemed calm, but she sensed his uneasiness – shared it – and when he leaned towards her, she thought he was going to kiss her.

She tensed her knees, acutely conscious that she'd sunk deeply into soft cushions and her black dress was sliding up her thighs. The thoughts she'd harboured of making love to this middle-aged man mortified her. She wanted to pull her dress over her knees, but that would have made her embarrassment obvious. The room seemed hot suddenly, or perhaps that was the scorch of embarrassment on her cheeks. She heard a clock ticking somewhere nearby and wondered again about the woman who had once shared this house with him.

'Are you having financial problems with your garden centre?' He asked the direct question without preamble. She agreed. No sense denying it any longer. He had paid for her work in Havenstone, and the money had sank without a ripple. He didn't seem surprised when she outlined the problems she'd encountered. He believed her idea for situating a garden centre in Grahamstown was excellent. But she was under-capitalised. He wanted to invest money in it.

The suddenness of his offer took her breath away. He spoke carefully, as if he understood the thoughts going through her mind. There would be no strings, emotional or financial.

'Why?' Her question was blunt and he answered calmly.

His offer had certain stipulations. He wanted a share in her company. It would be a silent partnership, and she would be completely free to make her own decisions.

'I have the money,' he stated. 'You have the expertise. When your garden centre is established I expect to make a return on my investment.'

'Why should it matter to you whether or not my business succeeds?' she repeated her question, keeping her tone as businesslike as his.

He hesitated before replying, as if he too sensed the tension in the room. 'When Sara died...' He stumbled over his wife's name, as if the sound was strange to his lips. 'When she died I went to pieces. I drank too much and made stupid business decisions I now regret.'

'You must have loved her very much.' It seemed the right thing to say, but she knew it was an empty comment.

Love. He shrugged the word aside. He'd wanted to destroy everything in this house that reminded him of their life together. What he hadn't realised was that in destroying her memory he had almost destroyed himself.

He stood up and walked to the window, pulling the curtains closed on the night. He had money to invest. Tork Hansen had been his first investment. He was prepared to offer Eva the same opportunity.

Who was this man who was willing to invest a small fortune to help her business stay afloat – or, to be more precise, rooted to the earth? Either way, Eva was in the black again.

The night was over. They shook hands. He stood at the entrance to Havenstone, watching her until the taxi rounded the bend in the driveway and turned towards Grahamstown.

The leaves were falling, rustling dry at the edge of the lake when the thatcher finished her roof. A roof put a stamp of permanence on a home. It was an undeniable fact, a shelter from the world. Her cottage walls stood sturdy and strong, a sun splash of yellow on the front door. Matt Morgan declared a ceasefire. He collected mushrooms in a nearby field and brought them to the caravan. Eva fried them in butter and garlic then called him in to share them. They talked about joists and thatch and the number of angels that could dance on the head of a nail.

Eva's Cottage Garden was officially opened. With her new partner's investment securely lodged in her bank account, she was able to hire an assistant to help her in the centre. Muriel Wilson belonged to the Grahamstown Horticultural Society. Her delphiniums had won first prize at the annual Festival of Flowers. She would bring business to Eva's Cottage Garden, spreading the word where it mattered.

Sometimes, when she was on her knees, her hands deep in the soil, Eva forgot about Faye for a short while. There were terrifying moments when her child's face wasn't so clear in her mind.

Then she took out her photographs, devouring them. Her father was right. Gardening was therapeutic – thoughts sinking into the earth and finding rest. This, she believed, was what healing meant. Short bursts of amnesia. Time was a thief that eventually took everything, even memories.

CHAPTER FORTY-SIX

At the end of November a new producer was appointed to *State-side Review*. Falling ratings – the cardinal sin. Desks were emptied. Greg was appalled by the ruthlessness of it all. He waited for the axe to fall – last in first out – but, to his surprise, he remained in his usual position by the window. It offered him a view of trains running across the skyline and ant-like figures hurrying beneath grey spires.

Stateside Review was going for a softer touch, dumbing down and focusing on the human side of the political image.

'I'm becoming a purveyor of pap,' he said to Ellen after interviewing a congressman – who supported the death penalty – about the welfare of domestic pets in New York apartments.

Ellen briskly ordered him from her office. She had a new sales target to reach.

'From now on, Enright, you can forget about slush funds and misappropriated documents,' she warned. 'If you want to save the world, join Greenpeace. If you want to hold this job, keep your head down and your chin in. Viewers have complained about its aggressive slant.'

He returned to his apartment where a voracious shoal of piranha, left there by the previous tenant, was prepared to offer him more sympathy. They, at least, would eat the hand that fed them – an acknowledgement of sorts that he still existed.

Eva was constantly in his thoughts. He was aroused by the sound of her voice when she rang, picturing her tall, rangy body and tumbled hair lying beside him, the soft contours of her breasts, the muscular strength of her arms. She was such a contradiction, blowing hot and cold, yielding in love yet unbending when it came to forgiveness. And reticent when it came to talking about the man who had become a partner in her company.

'He's an entrepreneur,' she said. 'Elderly.'

If this was meant to reassure Greg it failed.

'Stop behaving like a ridiculous fool,' she snapped when he demanded more details of their financial transaction. 'I need the money and I accepted. It's strictly business.'

'There's nothing left for me to say then.'

'What makes you think you have the right to say anything?'

'I'm still your husband.'

'That wasn't the impression I got the last time I rang your apartment.'

'I can't remember the last time you rang. I'm always the one who rings you—'

'On the night of Faye's birthday… what should have been her birthday. I rang and had the pleasure of hanging up on your girlfriend.'

'I don't know what you're talking about.'

'Forget it then.'

'Eva, wait,' he shouted, sensing she was about to end the call. 'For God's sake, let me explain.'

Ellen Lloyd was hard-edged and tough but on the night of Faye's birthday she had arrived at his apartment with two king-sized steaks and her vinyl collection of Janis Joplin originals.

'No sense suffering in silence, Enright,' she'd said. 'It's time to tell me why your heart is breaking.'

It had seemed strange to breathe private confessions into the ear of a woman he hardly knew. But she had listened and hadn't passed judgement. Instead she'd spoken of lost loves and lost op-portunities. After divorcing two husbands, she'd settled on cats as the only tolerable live-in companions. The phone had rung when he was in the kitchen turning steaks.

'Must be the office,' he'd shouted. 'Take a message and tell them I'll ring back.'

'No one spoke.' Ellen had lowered the music when he'd returned. 'But I could hear someone breathing.' She'd figured it had been a crank call. One of the many crazies who haunted the Big Apple.

'Eva, listen to me… You're talking about Ellen Lloyd. She's a good friend, and quite ancient.'

'Ancient?' Eva laughed, unamused. 'Then she must be the same age as my business partner. It's such a relief that neither of us has anything to worry about.'

'I miss you, Eva.' He was weary of these brittle exchanges. 'There's no one else in my life. No one but you.'

Her voice was softer when she spoke again. 'When you come home for Christmas we'll talk.'

'Can I stay with you in the cottage?' he asked.

'I'd like that.'

'Eva… do you still love me?'

'I'm confused and I'm angry. But love doesn't die easily.' Her words were hesitant but he sensed their truth. Soon they would be together. In the spirit of Christmas they would find a new path.

The season of goodwill was a short break in the Big Apple where the population faltered briefly in its pursuit of the big buck. Unlike in Ireland, where the population glutted on pleasure and sloth for a week. Who was right? Who was wrong? What did it matter? Greg was not coming home for Christmas.

Stateside Review had planned a festive special that he would present. In the hostels of the greatest democracy in the world he would walk among the homeless who had found shelter at the inn. Cameras would be aimed at their grateful faces. There would be many politicians present.

He reminded his producer that a flight home at Christmas had been built into his contract.

'What d'ya expect us to do? Line up the bums a week beforehand and feed them turkey so you can have a holiday?' His new producer was a man who did not mince his words. 'Get fucking real, Enright.'

'I can fight this on a point of principle.' He tried to make Eva understand. 'But they'll find an excuse to shaft me when I get back. Things are uncertain at the moment. Falling ratings. I can't take the chance. Why don't you fly out here?'

'I won't close until late on Christmas Eve. You know it's impossible.'

'Nothing's impossible, if you make the effort.'

'You make the effort then.'

'I told you! I'm filming on Christmas Day.'

'Then we're hardly going to have time to pull the turkey wishbone together, are we?'

'I suppose you'll do that with your *business* partner,' he snapped back.

She hung up on him. How quickly arguments flared between them. So silly to believe a marriage could be saved in a festive atmosphere of holly and mistletoe.

Stateside Review filmed the unwashed, the unloved, the forgotten. Smooth-faced congressmen shook Greg by the hand and offered their tanned profiles to the camera. He returned to his apartment to shower away the smell of overcooked vegetables and took a cab to Kieran Grant's house.

Albert Grant was present at the Christmas feast, his complexion gleaming with good cheer and fine malt. His sister sank deep into the cushions of an armchair and sipped sherry. Marjory Tyrell had the vague look of someone who would forget names as soon as the introductions were made. A cigarette dangled dangerously from her fingers. The hostess cast desperate looks in her direction and nudged ashtrays under her hands. The guests recreated an Irish Christmas, becoming noisily jolly and singing nostalgic ballads. They argued about politics and religion. Albert made a rousing speech about Ireland's finest asset. He raised his glass in Greg's direction and inclined his head graciously towards Ireland's youth – her diaspora, long may they spawn the world. Greg felt a hundred years old. He wondered how soon it would be appropriate to leave.

His wife was sleeping alone that festive night. Last Christmas, in her parents' house when everyone was in bed, and Faye was contentedly sleeping close by them, they had made love in front of the fire. The room had flickered with flame and passion. Such pleasure, deep yet soaring, lifting them, sinking them into each other's being. How could it fade so quickly?

He saw her image that night in Kieran's house, a photograph on top of a display cabinet. A young woman, laughing, blonde hair falling over her eyes.

Marjory Tyrell followed his gaze. 'My child,' she sighed. 'My poor lamb.'

CHAPTER FORTY-SEVEN

Christmas week was hectic. Most of the time Eva was out on the road making deliveries while Muriel shifted poinsettia and chrysanthemums, holly wreaths and Christmas cherries. When the last customer left on Christmas Eve, they locked the gates of the centre and drank a toast. They were exhausted and giddy, unable to wind down now that the rush was over. The centre resembled a scene from the Blitz but the cash register had keyed in profits. Her business partner would be pleased. Earlier, he had stopped by to say goodbye; he was driving to the country to stay with relatives.

'I wanted you to have this.' He'd handed her a parcel wrapped in gold foil paper. When she'd opened it she found a painting of Murtagh's River. A strange abstract image, as if the river flowed through a shrouded landscape where nothing had a recognisable shape, sound and movement suspended. Their first meeting place.

'It's beautiful.' She'd been immediately embarrassed at not having a gift to give him in return.

He'd brushed aside her apology. 'It's the first thing I've painted in years that gave me pleasure. I wanted to share it with you.'

She'd walked with him towards his car.

'I'll see you in the New Year,' he'd said and leaned forward to kiss her cheek. The sudden image of their mouths opening in a deep, searing kiss had shocked her equally as much as the jolting excitement that shivered through her. He too had seemed infused with the same desire and when she'd pulled away she'd been aware of an almost physical wrench separating them. Inside the car she'd seen the glowering face of Lindsey McKeever and an elderly woman who'd smiled back at Eva as he'd driven them away to celebrate a family Christmas.

It was late on Christmas Eve when she reached her parents' house. At midnight Mass she dozed off, unmoved by the singing and the wafting clouds of incense drifting over the congregation. Yet when she went to bed, she was unable to sleep. Peter Wallace intruded on her thoughts too often. His direct gaze, always watching her. When he'd first come to her caravan and by the river, even when she'd sat mourning Faye, he had watched her. She remembered the close, almost claustrophobic feeling when they'd walked through the copse at the back of Havenstone, his strong grasp on her waist when she'd slipped. What was happening to her? Was it a reaction to Greg's decision to remain in New York? He made excuses, repeated apologies. His words had a hollow echo and the imagined face of Ellen Lloyd was vibrant, young – as sensuous as the dawn on a Portuguese mountain.

Her relations came to Wind Fall on Christmas morning, the Frawleys and the Loughreys, hearty voices noisily greeting each other, hugging Eva too tightly. Maria arrived, radiant, accompanied by the first two-legged love of her life. Desmond Thorpe was a rugged man with good shoulders and a strong pair of hands for handling high-spirited fillies.

'Magnificent in jodhpurs,' Maria confided to her cousin, her eyes glowing joyously.

'Spare me the lurid details,' Eva warned. 'And run as fast as you can in the opposite direction.'

Her friend placed two fingers in her ears and said, 'I'm joyously deaf. Shut up.' She skirted around the subject of Greg's absence before asking outright if their marriage was over.

'Was it ever on?' Eva replied. 'We had nothing in common. Nothing. When it came to making choices between his career and his marriage there was no competition. Do we have to talk about him today? I'd much rather hear about Desmond. Tell me everything. I mean everything.'

Maria moaned happily. 'Where do I begin?'

Dinner was boisterous. They wore party hats and read silly riddles from Christmas crackers. It was their first Christmas without Brigid Loughrey and everyone was determined to be merry. This time last year Faye had been a bundle of love passed from one set of arms to the next. They toasted absent friends and Liz cried quietly into a paper tissue printed with holly.

Greg rang from New York. He was sharing a meal with some Irish friends. When his call ended Eva told her mother she was returning to the cottage.

Liz protested, shocked at her decision. 'I have to go.' Eva had no excuse to offer her. The words became a mantra. 'I have to go.'

Liz followed her to the bedroom. 'What about your marriage?' she demanded. 'You hit the first wall and that's it, is it? Is that all your husband means to you?' She fired questions, her face flushed, sternly challenging. Did Eva think her marriage to Steve was easy in those early years? Their dreams falling apart month after month. 'It's not that easy to cope with a failed IVF procedure, no matter what you might think,' she cried.

Eva winced back from her anger. She sank to the edge of the bed and placed her hands over her face, shamed. 'I'll never forgive myself for that remark, Liz. All I can do is ask you to forgive me.'

Her mother's shoulders slumped, weary suddenly from the intensity of emotion in the room. 'Go if you must,' she said. 'But remember this, Eva – grief is a lonely journey if you insist on walking it alone.'

CHAPTER FORTY-EIGHT

This was Connie's first visit to Anaskeagh. Until then, she had resisted all of Beth's invitations. Anaskeagh was Barry's life before they'd met and she had always displayed a quiet deference towards his wife's wish that their paths never cross. She only agreed to come when she heard that Marjory was once again spending Christmas in New York.

Peter escorted her into the house, carrying her suitcase and leaving Lindsey to trail behind. Trouble was brewing, Beth observed; it was obvious from his grim silence and Lindsey's sullen glare, which changed to a delighted shriek when she greeted Stewart. Soon afterwards they left together for a long walk, something they always did whenever Lindsey visited Anaskeagh. Beth had no idea what they spoke about during their time together, and they didn't confide in her. She felt no resentment at being on the sidelines of the close-knit relationship they had always shared. It would be Stewart, not she or Peter, who would bring their child through this crisis.

'She was arguing with Peter the whole way down,' said Connie when Beth showed her into the spare bedroom. 'She's a bold brat when she makes up her mind to torment a body.' She gazed out the window over the darkening headland. 'Barry talked so much about Anaskeagh. I'm glad I've had a chance to see it at last.' She smiled and hugged her daughter-in-law. 'You're looking well, pet. Don't worry about Lindsey. She's a prickly little madam but her heart's in the right place. I'd be lost without her these days.'

The spirit of Christmas did not improve Lindsey's mood. She deliberately stepped out of Peter's way every time he walked past. His gift to her remained unopened under the tree. He had chosen his gifts with care this year: a book on traditional music for Robert, a magician's set for Paul, and Gail's present – a toy dolphin that could swim and leap in the bath – created such excitement that she insisted on Peter filling the kitchen sink and showing her how it worked.

He pretended not to notice Lindsey's unopened present. Nor did he react when she refused to sit near him during Christmas dinner. He even remained calm when she contradicted him every time he spoke. Connie ordered her to behave, using a tone of voice that would have invoked instant rebellion if Beth had tried it. Lindsey subsided for a short while but her resentment cast a pall over the festivities. Stewart was the lash she used. Never had her love for him been displayed so openly, and she seemed elated by the tension she created.

'Have you any idea how much you're upsetting everyone, especially your father?' Beth asked when she found her wrapped in her anorak in the back garden, swaying listlessly on Gail's swing.

'Which one are you talking about?' Lindsey snapped back. 'The one with my heart or my DNA? What did you ever see in him? You must have been stoned out of your mind.'

From the mouths of aggressive teenagers, thought Beth as she retreated indoors, a truth could sometimes shine.

Nuala O'Neill drove to the bungalow the following afternoon and announced that she had sold three of Lindsey's paintings before Christmas. This innocent remark proved to be the spark that struck the tinderbox. Afterwards, Beth could only wonder how the row hadn't erupted sooner.

'I'd love to see your work, Lindsey.' Peter was unable to hide his pleasure as Nuala discussed the sold paintings. Beth watched the storm clouds gather as he asked Lindsey about her techniques and the materials she used.

Lindsey, tired of her monosyllabic replies, jumped to her feet. 'Mind your own business and stop poking your nose into mine,' she yelled. 'This has nothing to do with you and never will – understand?' She turned to Stewart and smiled brilliantly. 'I need fresh air, Dad. How about a walk? I'll get my jacket.' She stalked from the room, leaving a stunned silence behind.

Nuala looked bewildered. 'Was it something I said? I've never seen Lindsey behave that way before.'

'Count yourself lucky,' sighed Stewart, rising to accompany his wayward child on a walk over the blustery headland.

Nuala left shortly afterwards. Connie retired for a nap. She was pale, her eyes red-rimmed, looking old and vulnerable in a way that worried Beth. But Connie insisted she was simply tired – too much rich food. She closed her eyes and waved Beth from the bedroom. Robert went off to join his friends on Turnabout Bridge, a meeting place for teenagers. He was creating a new musical wave, he told Peter. Celtic rock rage was a protest against manufactured boy bands and would soon take the country by storm.

'Sounds like Horslips on speed.' Peter laughed. 'How do you intend promoting this new wave?'

'I've formed a band,' replied Robert. 'We're called Hot Vomit. Packs a punch, don't you think?'

'Right in the gut,' agreed his uncle. 'I'd love to hear you sometime. Perhaps when I'm senile and totally deaf.'

Peter left soon afterwards. 'I'm sorry to have been the cause of so much upset,' he told Beth. 'Coming here wasn't a good idea.'

'Lindsey's rudeness is unforgivable,' Beth replied. 'I don't know what to say…' She faltered before his penetrating gaze. 'She's stressed over repeating her Leaving—'

'Beth, stop pretending. We can't keep up this charade any longer. You must tell me the truth about Lindsey. Sara knew. I convinced myself she was lying. That she'd found another way to torment me but, deep down, I realised it was true. I've lived with the knowledge since then but I need to hear you say it out loud.'

She bowed her head, weary of lies and prevarication. 'Lindsey is your child. But she's Stewart's daughter. She loves Stewart too much to let go of any part of their relationship. You'll lose her if you attempt to take that from her.'

'What can I do?' he asked bleakly. 'How can I reach her, knowing she hates me so much?'

'Stop trying so hard. Nothing about Lindsey is easy but if you give her the space she needs then maybe you'll both be able to form a different bond in the future. For the moment the only room she needs is in here.' She touched her head with her index finger.

He offered to come back at the end of the week to collect Connie. Beth told him she had an important meeting in Dublin early in the new year and would drive Connie home then. On his way out, they passed the open door of their daughter's bedroom. Paint tubs and brushes were heaped untidily on the floor. His eyes rested hungrily on an easel holding a half-finished canvas. What would their lives have been like if they'd stayed together? Beth wondered. Reared their child and the others who followed? Useless speculations, filled with the reverberations of old passions. An abstract thought, fleeting. Once it had filled her world.

He was gone when Lindsey returned. She pretended not to notice.

CHAPTER FORTY-NINE

Eva spent time preparing an evening meal – fresh herbs and an expensive white wine poured generously into a sauce that bubbled gently when she added chicken and sun-dried tomatoes. She placed it on the coffee table and watched it congeal.

It was cold in her bedroom. She stood in front of the long cheval mirror and pulled a nightdress over her head, a sleek ivory robe she'd bought for her honeymoon. On those nights with Greg, it had enhanced her complexion. Now all it did was emphasise her pallor. She touched her face, cupped it with both hands, and stared into the mirror. Grief, like love, needed a companion.

She returned to the living room where the fire still burned brightly and the aroma of her untouched meal made her realise how little she'd eaten that day. She was about to pick up the phone to ring Greg when she heard the doorbell. Her body quivered with shock, her need for him so immediate that she believed he was standing outside. The thought died just as quickly and when the bell rang again, a prolonged, impetuous summons, she figured it was a motorist lost in the labyrinth of narrow country roads surrounding her cottage. She draped a jacket over her shoulders and opened the door.

Peter Wallace had started to walk away. He apologised for intruding so unexpectedly. He'd noticed the light when he was driving past. She could have reminded him that Grahamstown was now bypassed by a motorway but that would have added a personal element into their conversation.

He followed her into the living room and sat down beside the coffee table. She whisked the dishes past his troubled gaze and out to the kitchen. He too had found the spirit of Christmas too tedious to endure and had headed back early. He refused her offer of a drink and they sat in uneasy silence before the fire. Sparks spluttered when she added a log, conscious that he was watching her every movement. He looked out of place in her small room, his long legs stretched too close to the flames, his shoulders too broad for chintzy armchairs. Impossible to imagine him in a factory or an office. Her mind was set with him beside a riverbank. She would hang his painting on the wall when he left. It would always remind her of Faye.

'You should be with your husband tonight.' His words startled her. 'You should be in his arms, talking of love. Why are you sitting here alone? I want to understand… How can he love you and let you go?'

'What do you know about love?' she demanded. His questions were so attuned to her own thoughts that she wanted to lash out at him. 'How can you talk to me about my marriage when you banish mementoes of your wife from the rooms you once shared?' She rose to her feet. 'I think you'd better leave now before we say things we'll regret later.'

He too stood up, facing her, standing too close. 'I came here to talk to you – to tell you things you need to know.' He paused, his gaze sinking into hers, as they held each other captive in a tense, unwavering stare.

'Why do you keep staring at me?' she cried. 'You watch me constantly… I feel your eyes on me all the time.'

'All the time.' He echoed her words. 'Always…'

In that instant there was a shift in desire, so sudden that when she swayed towards him she knew before she reached him how it was going to end. She didn't resist when he kissed her, their lips pulsing as she drew him in deeper, the tingling shock of their tongues touching, probing, their mouths crushed in that first, wounding kiss. The jacket slipped from her shoulders and she heard him moan as he pulled away, almost forcing her from him, and when she gasped, shocked by his abrupt withdrawal, she saw such passion in his gaze that she closed her eyes and cried out his name, her arms urgently pulling him close again. Her hands were on him and his on her, touching her breasts, sliding the nightdress upwards, the fine silk shimmering as he slid it smoothly over her hips, his fingers on her bare flesh, opening her to his touch as she too sought and held him, unable to believe she was seeking such relief; sunk in shame and pleasure and escape.

He loosened her hair from its clasp until it hung to her shoulders, showering over them. The savage intensity of their passion amazed her – so demanding, infinite, free. She didn't want to move from this place, or to slow the intensity of their lovemaking, knowing that anything else, a movement towards her bedroom, delicate foreplay, teasing words of anticipation, would bring her back to her senses. She was lifted in his arms. Her legs encircled him. The power of his desire moulded her into him. She felt the thrusting strength of him entering her, heard their breath shuddering as they moved together.

She didn't reason why she was in his arms. She only knew that her body had taken control, battering her through the numbness that had overwhelmed her for so long, and when they came together, it was an aching release, as if they'd spent a lifetime knowing each other's desire. She cried into his shoulder, clinging to the pleasure of the moment, wanting to surge forever on its crest, his voice calling her name – Eva… Eva… Eva…

It was over as suddenly as it had started. His arms supported her when she collapsed against his chest. He sank back onto the sofa, pulling her with him, breathing fast, their clothes still tangled around them, half on, half off, and they huddled together, unable to talk, to understand, to make sense of the wildness that had consumed them.

For a while she slept. He was watching her when she awoke. This time their lovemaking was slower, more deliberate. She stared down into his eyes as she sank into him, their bodies unable to rest until they had driven each other to the edge of oblivion – and even then, she suspected, they would never be satisfied.

He left in the morning. She ached with exhaustion, still feeling his touch on her skin, suffused with the heat he'd left behind. In the shower she switched on the cold water and gasped as it spilled over her breasts. He had touched them with reverence, his lips gently arousing the area where Faye has once suckled so voraciously, as if he was trying to imprint another memory on them. Gradually, she calmed down but she was unable to think beyond him.

She opened the garden centre, relieved that her sales assistant was still on her Christmas break. Business was brisk: last-minute gifts, bouquets and plants purchased on the way to parties and festive dinners. She had little memory of the day, the customers, the mundane chores that killed time until the night.

They hadn't planned a further meeting and she decided to go to bed early. He phoned as she was about to lie down. He said he was sorry. He had abused her trust. He never intended it to happen. She clamped her lips together and held tightly to the phone.

'I love you desperately,' he said. 'But we can't see each other again, not like that… not like that.' His voice shook, a raw gasp, as if he too was remembering the sounds of their passion.

'Stop it!' She groped blindly for the duvet and pulled it over her. 'How can you patronise me after what we've just experienced?'

'No, no! Listen to me, Eva. I don't want to hurt you. But I know I will.'

She hung up on him and his faltering excuses. She tried to sleep. She heard his car outside. His footsteps on the gravel. She went to the door. Wordlessly, he took her in his arms and carried her to her bedroom. Sated with pleasure, they finally slept.

Eva was caught in the waiting stillness, wondering. How did it happen? What chemistry merged and melted them? She tried to understand this passion, to seek some relief from it. She drove too fast, turned corners too sharply. Once, when her van rocked on a bend, she pulled into the side of the road and tried to compose herself. Was this a nervous breakdown? Was she exhibiting symptoms of exhilaration? Did she love him? The answer no longer mattered. She loved Greg and he'd betrayed her. She loved Faye and she had died. Love had no substance. No root.

CHAPTER FIFTY

The producer from *Elucidate* flew to New York to attend a conference on racism within the media.

'A tricky subject at the best of times,' said Sue Lovett when the speeches were over and she was relaxing with Greg in her hotel foyer. She informed him that his destiny in life was to be a big fish in a small pond. In New York he was a flounder, floundering out of his depth.

'Come home,' she said.

'What's at home?' he asked.

Ireland was a time bomb, ticking with the excesses of the past. Politicians trying to shake off the touch of golden handshakes. Bankers thumping their breasts and shouting 'Sorry… *Sorry*…' for bringing the country to its knees. Developers scrutinising their tax returns and discreet off-shore accounts. Brutal, sacred secrets finally spoken aloud through the media confessional. Albert Grant's name was mentioned, the hint of a land scandal. It came to nothing in the end, as all enquiries did when they concerned him.

'Our source is his niece,' said Sue. 'Her name is Beth McKeever.'

Greg reminded her that Justin Boyd had dropped the story. No proof.

'She went over Justin's head and contacted me directly.' Sue smiled, a hint of approval. 'She's a determined woman.'

'Bad blood between them, obviously.'

Sue nodded. 'Sounds like it. Her story could be worth a second look. Are you interested?'

'Not particularly. In case you've forgotten, I have a job here.'

'I've watched *Stateside Review*,' Sue said. 'Interesting stuff. Why aren't you surrounded by dancers with sequins in their belly buttons?'

'It's not that bad.'

'Yes, Greg, it is that bad. What's happened to you?'

'Nothing. Apart from clearing out the "we-make-a differ-ence" crap from my head. What difference did I ever make? Mi-chael Hannon? His party forgave him as soon as he prayed for forgiveness. His wife is still holding his hand and his girlfriend has her own reality show.'

'While your marriage has broken up – and your child is dead. Is that what you're thinking?'

'I'm not thinking at all, Sue. I'm surviving. That's what you do in this city.'

'Or disappear into a programme called *Stateside Review*.'

'My friend Ellen calls it candyfloss. Her advertising revenue has never been higher.'

'I believe you.' Sue stood up and shook his hand. She'd ar-ranged to have dinner with some friends and he was due back at the office. 'You have a job waiting if you decide to come home.'

'I thought Justin Boyd was more than adequately filling my shoes.'

'Justin's a boy scout, not a muckraker.' She frowned. 'I need you on the programme, Greg. But I've no intention of begging. Albert Grant's niece said the story would never have died if you'd been handling it. Do you want her number?'

'For what purpose?'

'Oh, you know.' She shrugged and opened her briefcase, briskly handing him a business card. 'Just in case your producer decides to bring on the belly dancers.'

In his office he thought about Albert Grant and how, on Christmas night, he'd drunk malt whiskey and delivered a lusty rendering of 'A Nation Once Again'. A true-blue armchair patriot who would take credit for the building of a dog kennel.

Justin had dismissed the woman's evidence. Stories, rumours, pub gossip. Yet each had its own momentum. Greg had seen the rumour mill in action, the media frenzy once the hint of a scandal was floated and discovered to have substance. The hidden voices coming out of the woodwork when they knew there was someone who would listen. He felt an almost forgotten clench of excitement as he lifted his phone, tapped a number and asked to speak to Beth McKeever.

Greg had forgotten the moist wind, the hint of rain, the buffeting, restless clouds. He had forgotten the patchwork green that rose to meet him as the plane flew low over the Irish coast. But when he walked into the arrivals hall of Dublin Airport and saw Eva waiting, he felt as if the fist was closing around him once again. He looked into her eyes and knew that nothing had changed.

Back in the fold of *Elucidate* he found it difficult to believe he had ever been away. The sounds were the same: hothouse gossip, speculation, the excited buzz of facts confirmed and packaged for an evening's viewing. He took back his apartment, which had been rented to a friend, a forty-year-old engineer with the hygiene habits of a student on the razz. By the time Greg finished sponging, mopping and bleaching, it was as organised as it had ever been in his pre-Eva days. The household plants gleamed. The exotic fish still swam with stately grace in their aquarium, friendly and darting – unlike the sullen killer shoal he had left behind in New York. He sat watching them at play, wondering if they had noticed his departure or grieved for his friendly hand to feed them. He knew the answer to that one. Why clutter your mind with incidental emotions when you only have to concentrate on swimming in a straight line? Sometimes even fish could be a source of envy.

CHAPTER FIFTY-ONE

In the flesh Greg Enright was less intimidating than on television, with kinder eyes and an attentive manner that immediately reassured Beth.

'I can't be associated with this story,' she warned him when they met in a small hotel on the outskirts of Dublin. 'My husband's future is tied up with the Anaskeagh industrial park. I'll help behind the scenes in every way I can but I need to know I can rely utterly on your discretion.'

He listened carefully to everything she had to say. Under his careful questioning Derry Mulhall's rambling story began to take shape. She told him about Kitty Grimes and her fear of exposure.

'Don't worry, I'll handle her gently,' he said and smiled wryly when she advised him that a rum and coke would be appreciated by Hatty Beckett. His gut instinct was to start the investigation with the industrial park. He would focus on its development and start digging the dirt from there.

'I've checked the ACII records,' he told her. 'You're right about Clasheen being the original location. That makes sense. Trucks would have had direct access to the main Dublin Road, unlike in Anaskeagh.'

Beth nodded. 'I've spoken to a builder who was promised work on the Clasheen site. I think he'll talk but you need to appreciate that these people are afraid. You'll have to gain their confidence first.'

'Why aren't you afraid?' he asked. 'Your uncle is a very powerful man. Why are you so determined to bring him down?'

'I want justice–'

'Justice? Or revenge?' Greg Enright had a narrow, watchful face. A gaze that sharpened, searching, Beth suspected, for a story behind the one she'd handed him.

'My uncle controls Anaskeagh,' she said. 'He sees it as his own personal fiefdom. He's your story. Mine is my own business. If we're to work together you have to respect my right to privacy. You also have to trust me.'

'Trust must be mutual,' he said. 'If I feel that you have an ulterior motive then the story is dead.'

They shook hands before they parted. Beth thought it was a pity he didn't smile more often.

Before returning to Anaskeagh she drove to Havenstone. Swans would never again swim on Estuary Road. The narrow potholed lane had disappeared, replaced by a slip road banked by flyovers and roundabouts. Peter looked younger, as if years had fallen away from him. His skin was fresh, no angry blotches, his eyes alive. She recognised the old restlessness from his student days, the same contagious energy. She walked with him to the back of the Havenstone and entered the garden, standing still for an instant to absorb the transformation. Within this walled enclosure, onions burgeoned like fists from the soil and the ridged rows of vegetables captured the spirit of the market garden that was still an important feature of the old village.

Later, when she called to Connie's house and met Lindsey, she understood the reason for Peter's enthusiasm.

'Her name is Eva,' Lindsey announced. 'And he's absolutely crazy about her. Imagine falling in love at his age?'

'He's not due for the old folks' home yet.' Beth laughed. 'Falling in love isn't solely the prerogative of the young, you know. Is the feeling reciprocated?'

'I'm not sure.' Lindsey shook her head, as if puzzled by the complexities of human emotions. 'She spends a lot of time at

Havenstone and he cooks her fabulous meals, so she's either in love with him or she's a compulsive overeater.'

'What's she like?' Beth asked.

Lindsey frowned, a puzzled expression on her face.

'I like Eva a lot – but I don't know if it's because she reminds me of Sara.'

'Sara?'

'It's kind of weird. Sometimes I think it's my imagination and then she moves her head a certain way or smiles and it's as if I'm looking at Sara. I thought she was a ghost when I first saw her. I hope Peter's in love with her for the right reasons.'

Beth was startled by her daughter's comment but before she could reply Connie arrived home from the village. She was carrying grocery bags and seemed frailer than she'd been at Christmas but cheerful as she fussed over Beth and enquired about her grandchildren.

'You have to visit us again,' Beth said. 'No more excuses.'

'Maybe I'll come for Easter,' said Connie when Beth was leaving. 'If you're sure it won't be upsetting for your mother.'

'Don't worry about Marjory.' Beth was unable to keep her bitterness at bay. 'She hasn't visited us once since we moved. I call to see her every few days and do her shopping. It makes no difference. She can't forgive me for marrying Stewart.' She hugged her mother-in-law. 'Your grandchildren miss you. And so do I. That's all that matters.'

Twilight was settling on Anaskeagh Head when Beth reached the town. She parked her car on the old pier and walked along the stony, uneven surface. The tide was in, lapping dark against the wall. A white cruiser came to a stop some distance from the shore. She watched a group of men on board busily anchoring and securing the vessel. Seagulls screeched and swirled above them, anxious to partake in the results of a successful fishing trip. Four men climbed down the ladder and into a small dinghy. It cut swiftly through the waves and, as they mounted the stone steps at the side of the pier, she saw her uncle. Ruddy and relaxed from his day's fishing, he was flanked by two friends and his son.

'Well, if it isn't Beth McKeever.' Her uncle's handshake was hard and purposeful. She tried not to flinch. 'You remember my favourite niece.' She recognised his two companions, Ben Layden and Harry Moore. They nodded politely, anxious to be on their way.

When their cars disappeared from view she returned to her own car and watched the sun sink beyond the headland. Greg Enright's hair was dark with a smattering of grey. Too young to be going grey but there was nothing youthful about him. He would take her uncle apart and Beth would finally breathe freely again.

CHAPTER FIFTY-TWO

Spring brought the garden centre to life. In the mornings it was mostly older men and women who wandered among the plants and shrubs. At weekends young couples arrived, baby slings and strollers, planning gardens, buying trees and shrubs that would grow with their children. In the evenings, while she waited for her lover to arrive, Eva walked by the lake, where bluebells, cowslips and forget-me-nots fluttered in green shady hollows.

Her husband was back in the interrogator's chair. A class act to watch, and Eva did watch him. She was still fascinated by this unflinching man who had wept with joy when their child was born and wept so bitterly into her shoulder when her brief life had ended.

In his apartment they sat stiffly opposite each other. He spoke about their relationship. They were both ego-driven individuals who'd rushed into marriage without considering each other's needs. They had an unplanned baby. Faye broke their hearts. He'd been unfaithful to Eva, but that hurt could have been absolved if they'd stayed still in the welter of grief that had surrounded them and considered what they meant to each other. Instead, they'd run in different directions and now, quiet at last, they had a chance to salvage something from their experiences.

How she envied his ability to lay his thoughts out in such a logical order. Hers were incoherent. She wondered what he would say if she told him about Peter Wallace. Would he reason with such calm assurance if he knew about those nights, the lust and thrust of passion?

There was no going back, Eva told him. For an instant he was silent. Then he offered her something they both needed. Friendship in exchange for pain. No demands. No expectations. It would be a new experience for both of them. Could friendship rise from dead love? It was something they both wanted to believe.

She met Maria for a meal that night. They ordered wine and the early-bird option on the menu. Maria's engagement ring sparkled as she discussed her wedding plans. Eva would be her bridesmaid... Or would she be the matron of honour? In other words, Maria demanded, was her marriage on or off? Eva told her she and Greg were friends.

'No such thing!' Maria rolled her eyes. 'Never heard of it before.'

The restaurant filled, the noise level rose. This was passing time, a choreography of movement that would carry Eva nearer to real time and the wanton pleasure of Havenstone.

They made love in his bedroom. It reminded her of an old man's room: dark walls and walnut furniture, a solid bed with a carved wooden headboard. It had once belonged to his father, he told her. A silent man with fine silver hair who grew grapes in the garden she'd restored and collected religious icons. His mother had been a strong woman, dominant. He brought his parents alive with a few words but he would not talk about his wife. Eva shivered when she passed the locked room where Sara Wallace once slept. She didn't want to think about her but somehow, surreptitiously, she was becoming part of her thoughts. Why did she die? Had her husband's passion been repugnant to her? Was there ever any passion between them? What did she know about Peter Wallace: lonely only child, one-time factory owner, failed artist, childless widower?

CHAPTER FIFTY-THREE

Gossip in the pubs, in the shops and on the streets. Beth McK-
eever was right. They were coming out of the woodwork, rolling
back the years. Slights and oversights, grievances, humiliations.
Derry Mulhall had the bulbous nose of an alcoholic and a high,
whining voice that stumbled over facts until they sounded like
lies. Greg believed him when he claimed he'd been hoodwinked
by Conor Grant, who'd claimed he was buying the land for a
consortium of farmers. Anxious to make a quick sale, Derry
had been beaten down easily on the price he'd demanded. Soon
afterwards, the land had been rezoned from agricultural to industrial use and sold for a prime price to the ACII, who'd built
the Anaskeagh industrial park. Derry had no doubt as to the
true identity of the purchaser: Albert Grant, lining his pockets
as usual, the wily old fox. He glowered, unable to hide a skulk-
ing admiration for underhand dealings. His story was explosive,
but if Greg ever managed to get him in front of a television
camera, the sympathy vote would be lost as soon as he opened
his mouth.

Kitty Grimes shied away from his questions. She was a nervous, elderly woman who had never stepped out of line in her
life. Her thin face flushed anxiously when she told him she was
worried about her children. They had good jobs in Anaskeagh.
If she spoke out of turn it could damage them. Greg assured her
that no pressure would be put on her to go public with her story.
He soothed and charmed and listened. Eventually she allowed
him in.

The builder who had been promised work on the Clasheen site claimed he'd been forced to seek employment abroad since he'd complained aloud about the change of location. Like Derry, he'd discovered it was unwise to make such accusations out loud and now spent most of his time on building sites in Germany, separated from his family. He paused for breath and said, off the record, 'I know for a fact that the consortium was a cover for Albert Grant and every contractor who got work on the Anaskeagh industrial park paid a percentage to him.'

'Will any of them go on record and admit it?' Greg asked.

'They might.' The builder smiled grimly. 'But, then again, pigs might fly on a Sunday. If you want answers there's only one person who can provide them. But I wouldn't put money on your chances of getting an honest word out of his mouth.'

'Albert Grant has a finger in every dubious pie in this town,' said Hatty Beckett, a small, feisty redhead, who was prepared to speak publicly about the shopping mall. Greg believed her story, but she had no concrete evidence, only her unshakable conviction that Albert Grant was a rat.

Beth McKeever's most notable feature was her eyes. Vengeful. A bold, green stare that demanded attention. She could control her emotions in a deadpan recital of facts, but those eyes could not disguise her hatred. Greg sensed another story behind the trail she laid before him. It would come to the surface eventually and, when the time was right, it would settle firmly within his grasp.

He walked through the centre of Anaskeagh and stopped outside the politician's headquarters. Only one light shone from the upstairs window. The politician lived in a humble enough abode considering the amount of money he'd salted away over the years, probably offshore, coded, untraceable.

'Good evening, Greg.' He answered the door in person. 'I hope you've been receiving a true Anaskeagh welcome.'

'Thank you, Minister. I've no complaints so far.'

'How long will we have the pleasure of your company in our little town?'

'Until my story is fully investigated.'

'An investigation!' He raised his eyebrows and smiled. 'That sounds very serious. Are you suggesting we have secrets to hide in Anaskeagh?'

'Secrets?' Greg shrugged. 'How can we tell if there are secrets? Unless, of course, people are prepared to reveal them. I hope you'll do us the honour of being interviewed.'

'My pleasure, Greg. When are you thinking?'

'We'll be filming in the Anaskeagh industrial park. I believe you were actively involved in locating it in Anaskeagh. I thought it would provide an interesting location for your interview.'

'An excellent idea.' The politician clasped Greg's hand in farewell. 'I'm delighted to be of assistance. But please remember I've a busy schedule and need advance warning before any interview can take place.'

The Anaskeagh industrial park was a compact semicircle of white buildings that looked as if they'd been dropped into the green countryside from outer space. The meeting with the business people was held in Stewart McKeever's office. They were enthusiastic and excited, anxious to milk the publicity their companies would receive from the television exposure. Greg felt embarrassed, as he often did on such occasions, knowing that most of the filming would be edited out by the time the programme appeared. But when the shit hit the fan, as he hoped it would, the Anaskeagh industrial park would receive more nationwide publicity than any of the group of people facing him could possibly realise. Beth McKeever didn't attend the meeting. A busy woman, she had a factory to run.

CHAPTER FIFTY-FOUR

Marina McKeever arrived unexpectedly at Havenstone one evening. From the drawing room Eva heard her high-pitched laughter and Peter's surprised voice at the front door.

'I'd no idea you'd company.' She stopped abruptly when she entered, unable to hide her surprise. 'Introduce me please.' She held out a cool hand and tipped Eva's fingers before archly turning back to Peter. The sinuous ease with which she moved was in marked contrast to her shrill voice. 'Be a darling and pour me a gin and tonic. I've had a wretched day with my poor mother.'

'How is Connie?' he asked.

'Not good at all, I'm afraid.' Marina took off her jacket and sank gracefully into an armchair. 'She puts on a show for everyone, but I'm the one who has to deal with the reality. Who'd have believed I'd end up emulating Florence Nightingale?'

'I've told Connie I can hire a nurse—'

'She's stubborn,' Marina interrupted him. 'And having neglected her all my life, the least I can do is look after her when she's so ill. But I'm hoping you'll be able to help me in a small matter concerning my sanity. It's about Lindsey. I haven't room to breathe with her rubbish. And you know me – I need my space uncluttered. Why don't you offer her a room here?' She glanced at Eva and smiled. 'That's if you have the space. I wouldn't dream of cramping your style.'

'I've already asked her.' Peter's tone was curt. 'I won't repeat what she said. I'm sure you're aware that my relationship with Lindsey is far from cordial.'

'I can imagine. She's such a histrionic little bitch. How Connie copes with her is beyond me. But in the present situation it's impossible for her to stay with us. You're the obvious choice, Peter.' She tapped a long blue nail against her glass, watching him as he moved to the window, his face caught in a sudden spasm of grief.

'Whatever else I may be, I'm far from Lindsey's choice. I'll ask her again, if you wish. But I already know her answer.'

'I'm sure you'll be able to persuade her. You always had a way with words.' Marina smiled languidly at Eva. 'Oldport was a dump when I was growing up. A tomb – except for Peter, of course.' Her voice lilted suggestively over past indiscretions. 'He was the only asset, as far as the girls were concerned, weren't you, darling?' Her insistent voice forced him to turn around. 'Then Sara came along and the rest, as they say, is history... Or does history begin to repeat itself?' She held her empty glass towards him. 'One more for the road and I'll be on my way. I've intruded enough already.'

'You haven't intruded,' Eva said. 'I just called to discuss some unfinished work in the garden. I didn't intend staying so late.' Eva walked quickly towards the door, anxious to escape the woman's aimless chatter. Marina McKeever would always be a woman who challenged other women, forcing them to either compete or retreat before her coy domination.

Eva had met Connie McKeever one evening on Main Strand Street. Frail and old, trembling on her granddaughter's arm, the old woman had asked questions about the garden at Havenstone, remembering how it used to be – luscious vines and a spreading crab-apple orchard, white pear blossom in the spring and a plum tree that cast its summer fruit on the ground. When they were parting she'd called her 'Sara', lifting her hand to her mouth in apology when she'd realised her mistake.

Bit by bit the layers peeled away. One night Peter spoke about Lindsey McKeever. Afterwards, Eva was surprised she hadn't guessed. His broad forehead. His penetrating stare. On the rare occasions when Lindsey smiled, it was his smile Eva now saw. The same impulsive mouth and aggressive energy. He found it difficult to talk about Lindsey's mother. Beth McKeever had left for England and he – unaware and engrossed in his new love – had never paused to wonder why. But what of Sara? Eva asked. Had she known? He shook his head. Not then but later, many years later, she'd realised the truth and it had consumed her. He hesitated, unwilling or unable to continue. Eva probed deeper, shocked to discover that Sara Wallace had trampled on her sister's love and claimed it as her own. What kind of relationship had the two sisters had, Eva wondered, that one could wound the other so deeply?

Lindsey refused to acknowledge him. Peter had no rights. No rites of passage leading to fatherhood. We don't own our children, Eva thought. We don't own anyone but ourselves. She had never thought about her natural father. He remained an icon in a fairy story, a blond prince with a sturdy shield and bravery in his heart. She didn't stare into the faces of strange men, hoping for a sudden revelation. Instead, she became a watcher of women.

CHAPTER FIFTY-FIVE

Brushed up and made over, Derry Mulhall looked quite present-
able as he displayed the documents he'd signed on conclusion of
his land deal. Kitty Grimes was nervous but she told her story in
front of the camera in simple words and showed the document
she'd photocopied. The builder produced a letter he'd received
from the ACII, promising him work on the Clasheen site, but
Hatty Beckett sulked in the craft café because Greg had refused
to interview her. He claimed her analysis on human rats was
fascinating but lacked the clout of an incriminating document.

The Anaskeagh industrial park had been turned into a forest of cables and cameras. On the production floor of Trend-
Lines, the excitement heightened among the machinists as a
burly cameraman positioned his equipment. Computerised cutting machines sliced through layers of fabric. Sewing machines
clattered as the women, self-conscious in fresh hairstyles and
make-up, ran fabric through their fingers. Some, unable to resist, waved at the camera. Greg stood calmly amidst the clatter,
waiting for Albert Grant to arrive.

The machines were silenced when the minister, accompanied by his entourage, breezed onto the floor. On first-name
terms with the machine operators, he asked after the health of
their children, making jokes – familiar local banter. He chatted
knowledgeably to the *Elucidate* crew as he was wired for sound.
Noise and action surrounded him until the interview began.

Once again he outlined his unstinting efforts to create rural
employment – not just for his constituents but for small forgot-

ten parishes throughout the rural community. His own furniture factory had provided much-needed local employment in days gone by, but he'd been forced to close it down when cheap imports had flooded the market. He deftly evaded a question about lack of planning permission. Such a trivial consideration when he was putting bread on the tables of his workers. But these were modern times, a new era. The Anaskeagh industrial park was a shining example of his commitment to his constituents.

'Why was the location changed from Clasheen to Anaskeagh?' Greg asked. 'Surely Clasheen, with its superior road infrastructure, would have been much more suitable for an industrial estate?'

Albert Grant did not appear surprised at the sudden change of questioning. He smoothly offered statistics and solid reasons why Anaskeagh had been the better choice. 'It was an ACII board decision. Unanimous.' He stared steadfastly into the camera then turned and made a slight bow towards the staff. 'I'm sure any of these lovely ladies will be happy to explain why Anaskeagh is the perfect location. This is a small town, Greg. Employment opportunities mean the difference between emigration or building a prosperous future in one's own community.'

Beth McKeever stood in the background. Although Greg was unable to see her, he knew those arresting green eyes were boring into him as he asked the next question. 'Minister, can you explain why Mr Derry Mulhall's land was rezoned for industrial use so soon after it was purchased?'

'The decision to rezone was unanimously passed at county council level.' Once again, the minister appealed to the women, spreading his hands outwards, as if to indicate his bewilderment. 'I wasn't present when the decision was made so I'm afraid I can't assist you any further. In my role as a public representative I've staked my reputation…' He smiled into the camera. No tell-tale flush on his face. No flustered hand movements. An actor who never fluffed his lines. He shook his head gravely when Greg asked if he knew the identity of the consortium that had purchased the land from Derry Mulhall then sold it on to the ACII. His shoulders gave an involuntary jerk when one of the women muttered something, creating a low ripple of laughter among them.

Greg sensed something rising from them, a palpable wave of antipathy. Albert Grant knows he's in trouble, he thought, unsure if it was exhilaration or terror making his heart race as he ended the interview. The minister strode from the factory without shaking his hand.

Conor Grant's office was spacious, with wide-winged armchairs for his clients, fine art on the walls, and a large desk with a framed photograph of his wife and children. He had the same jovial smile as his father, the same firm handshake.

'Could we please get to the point of this meeting, Mr Enright? I've an extremely busy afternoon ahead of me and fail to see how I can assist you in the making of this documentary.'

'Four years ago you acted as solicitor for a consortium who purchased Derry Mulhall's land.' Greg sank deeply into a leather armchair and wondered how he would rise again with dignity. 'Obviously we're not suggesting any impropriety on their part but *Elucidate* needs confirmation of certain facts. I've compiled a list of questions and would appreciate you passing them on to your clients.'

The solicitor moved to the water cooler and poured a drink into a plastic container. He sipped thoughtfully. 'You must be aware that all business conducted on behalf of my clients is strictly confidential. If *Elucidate* is inferring that incorrect procedures were carried out, I must warn you that such accusations will be answered with the full rigour of slander laws. Do we understand each other?'

'Perfectly, Mr Grant. But as an investigative journalist I have a responsibility to explore any allegations connected to this story. Your father has gone on record and denied any connection with this consortium. Yet claims have been made that he was the sole purchaser of the land in question.'

The solicitor sat down behind his desk and surveyed Greg. 'I know you have a reputation as a serious journalist, Mr Enright. My father holds you in high esteem. If you want to keep your reputation intact I suggest you leave my office immediately.'

Greg placed a sheet of paper on the desk. 'I'll be in touch with you tomorrow. If you wish to make a statement on behalf of your client – or clients – *Elucidate* will be happy to accommodate you.'

The solicitor tore the sheet of paper in two. He folded his hands over the torn sheet and smiled. 'Allegations don't bother my father, Mr Enright. He has enemies who'll gladly try to damage his reputation if journalists are gullible enough to listen to them. If you will excuse me, sir' – he stood up and opened the office door – 'you've taken up enough of my time. Any further queries must be made through your company's legal representative.'

The builder from Clasheen was the first to ring Greg. He was taking a plane to Berlin where there was work waiting on a building site. He refused permission for his interview to be used on *Elucidate*. He gave no reasons and hung up on Greg's questions.

Derry Mulhall sounded drunk when he came on the line – belligerent, threatening, and shouting above the noise of a barking dog. He'd been conned into saying those things. If the interview wasn't pulled immediately he was going straight to his solicitor.

A gently apologetic Kitty Grimes rang soon afterwards. Her children were horrified that she'd allowed herself to be exploited by the media, who would use her and then desert her, leaving her to pick up the pieces.

His producer listened as Greg outlined his disintegrating story. 'The man is as guilty as sin, and I can't find a shred of evidence that'll stand up against him.' He clenched his jaw, frustrated yet not surprised. 'I'm not giving up. I'm onto something, Sue. I want to see it through.'

'You may not have the opportunity, Greg,' she replied. 'Conor Grant is threatening to apply for an injunction if you continue harassing his father.'

'Harassing? Don't make me laugh. That old fox doesn't know the meaning of the word and I can prove—'

'You've been ordered back to Dublin,' Sue interrupted his protestations. 'We've arranged a meeting with our legal team and we need you at it.'

'Abandoning the sinking ship?' Beth McKeever rang as he was packing to leave.

'I'm going back to Dublin for a meeting with my producer,' he snapped. 'There's no reason to stay here unless you have more trustworthy sources at your disposal.'

'You give up easily.'

'*Easily*? Conor Grant has documentation that proves beyond doubt that his father wasn't involved in the purchase of the farmer's land. Information from the Office of the Revenue Commissioners also shows that everything in your uncle's life is above board. His son is claiming that a systematic attempt by *Elucidate* to damage his father's reputation is underway and we haven't come up with a shred of evidence to refute this accusation – except from your friends, who are now falling over backwards to deny everything.'

'Which of us do you believe?'

'At this point it doesn't matter. I've no reliable sources willing to go on record.'

'What about the Anaskeagh Baby?'

'The what?'

'The baby who was found on Anaskeagh Head. I thought you would've researched the town's history more thoroughly.'

'What do you mean?'

'Do your research and ask the right questions.'

'Ask who?'

'You're the journalist, Greg. Investigate!' she said and ended the call.

'Damn you, Beth McKeever.' He stood for an instant with the phone to his ear, as if, in the silence she'd left behind, he expected to find answers to a story that had been hovering out of reach since the first time they'd met.

He switched on his laptop and Googled 'Anaskeagh Baby'.

He'd been six when her story had hit the headlines. Albert Grant had made a public appeal to the mother to come forward and be comforted by her own people. His photograph was large, his expression concerned.

CHAPTER FIFTY-SIX

Beth was about to knock on her uncle's office door when Conor emerged. His eyes narrowed suspiciously when he saw her.

'What are you doing here?' he asked.

'I want to talk to your father.'

'What about?'

'It's personal.'

'Personal? Is that a fact?'

'Yes.'

'Well, here's another fact. We're a small community here, suspicious of outsiders – especially those who try to stir up trouble. If I find out you have anything to do with these slanderous rumours about my father your days in Anaskeagh are numbered.'

'Don't threaten me.' She faced him squarely. 'If your father was able to truthfully answer the questions he was asked, there'd be no slanderous rumours.'

'How dare you presume to know anything–'

'It's okay, Conor. I'll take it from here.' Her uncle came between them and waved Beth into his office. 'I'll talk to you later.' He closed the door on his son's face and sat down behind his desk.

'What is it this time?' he demanded wearily. 'I've had an extremely busy day, and I hardly imagine you've come to enquire about my health.'

'It must make you proud to be so indispensable.'

He frowned and waved her to a seat. 'I do the job I've been elected to do.'

'You do it well.' She continued to stand. 'That was an impressive interview you gave at the factory. I was quite impressed by the way you stood up to Greg Enright's insinuations.'

He sighed. 'The media are part and parcel of a politician's life. We tolerate them, just as we tolerate earwigs or bad breath. But that doesn't mean we have to give them credence. I presume you know the story is dead.'

'I heard. It seems that mud doesn't stick after all.'

'There was no mud, Beth. You'd be a foolish woman to suggest otherwise.'

He sat back in his chair, legs crossed, his top leg casually swinging backward and forward. Sometimes, in his presence, she imagined a pool, opaque at first but gradually becoming clearer until she could see herself as a child spreadeagled, speared, submerged; a discarded scrap, filled with loathing and disgust. She struggled against these sensations, knowing the flashbacks would follow before she had time to brace herself. Now, in that sudden flash, she saw him sitting in the chair where her father used to sit, the same rhythmic leg movement, drinking tea and asking about school. Was she behaving herself or being a naughty girl again? She should kneel and ask God's forgiveness... Beth pressed her hands flat against his desk to stop them trembling and leaned towards him.

'Greg Enright is looking for background material on Anaskeagh. It seems he did some research about the baby. The one abandoned on the headland. I hope I wasn't acting out of turn by mentioning your name?'

His body stilled, the tilt of his head almost imperceptible. 'Why would you mention my name?'

'You were a county councillor at the time and in a position to talk knowledgeably about it.'

'And now I'm a minister. Time moves on, Beth, but I still look after my own. I've just interviewed a deserted young wife whose husband left her with four children under the age of six. I hope to move her into a council house on Fatima Estate next week. My clinic is filled with constituents with similar problems. That's the reality of the here and now, not some forgotten incident that no one wants—'

'An *incident*?'

'It's history. No one in this town has the slightest interest in revisiting that tragedy.'

'Perhaps not. All Greg Enright needs is background information. I'm sure you'll be able to help him. It's the least you can do, especially as you've effectively killed his investigation. I wanted you to know in advance so you have time to refresh your memory. Good evening, Uncle Albi.'

CHAPTER FIFTY-SEVEN

The group of men parked their cars on Anaskeagh Pier. They removed fishing tackle and chatted quietly as they pulled peaked hats over their heads and belted their life jackets. It was a balmy early-summer evening, the sea gently rocking the large white cruiser moored offshore. Albert Grant was late arriving. He strode towards the men and uttered a brief apology for keeping them waiting.

'This is it, Chas,' Greg said tersely to the cameraman. They emerged from behind the corner of the high pier wall. The *Elucidate* crew had returned to Dublin, leaving him and the cameraman, Chas Woods, to wrap up. Chas stepped backward as his camera swept over the group of men. Greg moved close to the politician and held the microphone towards him.

'Minister Grant, we're doing a story on the Anaskeagh baby. I have a primary source who maintains that you are familiar with the events leading up to the tragedy.'

The politician turned away from the camera, shouting. 'Jesus Christ! As well as harassing me you're breaking the law! Are you aware that there is an injunction about to be served on your programme?' He breathed heavily as he tried to move past Greg and reach the steps.

'The Anaskeagh tragedy is a different story.' Greg kept in step with him. 'It's a human-interest story. I repeat – we have a primary source who is willing to go on record to tell her story. As you were a county councillor at the time you were obviously involved in the investigation that followed and—'

'This is outrageous!' The politician lashed out at the microphone. 'That unfortunate tragedy had nothing to do with me. Like everyone else in Anaskeagh, my only interest was in helping the mother – but, as she never came forward, there was nothing more any of us could do.'

One of the men pushed against Greg. 'You're upsetting the minister,' he shouted and shoved him again. Greg staggered, almost losing his balance. Sweat trickled under his arms. He was too close to the edge of the pier. Another man tackled Chas, blocking the camera with his hand and attempting to push it to one side. The cameraman fell as he tried to keep his balance, hitting his head against the wall. His camera crashed down on the stony surface. Casually, as if he was kicking a fish back into the water, his attacker nudged it over the side then dragged Chas to the edge.

'Can you see it?' he roared. 'Do you want to go down and look for it?'

Chas's head was forced downwards. He made a choking sound, wheezing as the craggy surface of the pier pressed into his neck. Greg recognised the attacker as Ben Layden, the property developer who owned the shopping centre in Anaskeagh.

'Fucking media!' Another man jabbed him in the chest as he struggled to reach the cameraman. 'You think you've nothing better to do than come down here hassling people.'

'Gentlemen, please.' The politician's words immediately eased the threatening atmosphere. Ben Layden loosened his grip on Chas, who moaned loudly, too breathless to rise to his feet.

'My camera! He kicked my camera into the sea.' Chas was almost incoherent with rage as he struggled upright. He flung himself towards the burly man who'd attacked him but Greg held him back, frightened by the intimidating stance of the men. Pillars of Anaskeagh society, the politician's men, each with their own reasons for keeping their dealings with Albert Grant under wraps.

'A most unfortunate accident.' The politician stared down into the rippling water.

'Accident! You call that a fucking accident?' Chas roared.

'That's exactly what I call it, young man. And these four men are witnesses.' He faced Greg, unflustered. 'Just remember this, Mr Enright. You and your colleague have attempted to besmirch my reputation with innuendo and allegations. This incident has added to the seriousness of your situation. I suggest you leave here quietly and allow us to begin our fishing trip. I wish you a safe journey home. The next time we meet it will be in a court of law.'

Greg was checking out of The Anaskeagh Arms when his producer rang. She came straight to the point. 'They're screaming assault, intimidation and defamation of character.'

'That's rich coming from the Anaskeagh Mafia. You're lucky you're not bearing two drowned bodies back to Dublin.'

'It might be an easier option for us to handle,' Sue snapped back. 'I can't believe a journalist with your experience would undertake such an inept doorstep interview without the proper support systems in place. The end result was the destruction of a valuable camera, but that's another matter, which will be dealt with in the fullness of time.' Her voice carried to Chas who grimaced and formed a noose with his hands. '*Elucidate* is successful only because we've always based our investigative features on a solid bank of evidence. I want the two of you in my office as soon as you return to Dublin. And the sooner the better. The programme controller has raised serious questions about your futures with *Elucidate*.'

CHAPTER FIFTY-EIGHT

Marjory opened the door before Beth had time to ring the bell. Lipstick smudged her upper lip, a garish slash on her ashen face. She had rung when Beth was reading a bedtime story to Gail. At first, it had been difficult to make out what she was saying but one thing was clear: she wanted to see her daughter immediately.

She walked rapidly ahead of Beth into the dining room. The television was on with the volume lowered. She slumped into a chair and stared at the silent screen.

'What have you been saying to that television reporter fellow?' Her voice shook with anger. 'Ben Layden's wife told me he was down on the pier asking questions about that baby. What's that got to do with Albert? What's it got to do with any of us?'

'How should I know?'

'Oh, you know all right. Your conniving mind never changes. Always making trouble for your uncle.' She slipped lower in her chair. Her jutting bottom lip and hooded eyes reminded Beth of a lizard, wrinkled and burned out. 'Even when you were a little girl there was badness in you – and you're doing it again. You hate Albert so much you'd bring disgrace on this family to destroy him.'

'Why do I hate him?' Beth shouted so suddenly that her mother's thin frame jerked with shock.

'It's your father in you. He was always jealous because he had neither the brains nor the drive to be like my brother. All he ever did with his life was play music and run around with whores.'

Beth trembled, still raw from the shock of Connie's prognosis. Cancer, as Beth had feared. Terminal. 'This has nothing to do with Connie. Why do you always avoid my question? How much longer will you go on denying—'

'My tablets... My tablets... Where are they?' Marjory lifted her handbag and fumbled inside it. 'My doctor says I'm not to be getting upset about things. But how can I avoid it when you're spreading slander about your family?' She raised her thin shoulders so high her face seemed to shrink into them. 'Get me a glass of water. I need to take my heart tablets immediately.'

'What's wrong with your heart?'

'It's broken. That's what's wrong with it!' Marjory snatched the glass of water Beth brought her and swallowed two tablets. 'That journalist says he knows the identity of the baby's mother. How can he know that? How can he?' Her mouth quivered. 'No wonder May hated you. She never had a good word to say about you. She hated you until the day she died.'

'She had good reason to.'

'Not like Sara, my lamb. She loved Sara. Why did she say such a thing... Such a terrible thing to say to me. My Sara... How could she hurt me so?' Her hands fluttered upwards then fell limply to her lap.

Beth stared at her mother's bent head. 'Sara told you, didn't she? She came to Anaskeagh before she died to talk to you. But you refused to believe her... as he did—'

'You filled her head with your crazy nonsense–'

'You *cherished* her,' Beth cried. 'How could you deny her when she needed you so desperately?'

'She was sick, Beth. Don't you understand *anything*? She was having a nervous breakdown. Those antidepressants she used to take. My poor lamb, they made her delusional... saying those awful things to Albert. He was so good to her! Sending her to boarding school, the best education, always watching out for her. He would have done the same for you too. But oh no, you had to go your own road, always making trouble… accusations. And now you're here spreading those same filthy lies. Trying to bring shame on our family name.'

'As Sara failed to do. Is that what's frightening you, Marjory? That you denied the daughter you loved rather than accept her truth?'

The words thudded towards Marjory, who bent forward as if she'd been struck.

'Stop it… Stop it at once! You'll kill me with your lies. I don't want you coming near my house again with your charity.' She struggled to her feet, tears furrowing her cheeks. 'How dare you think you can make up for years of neglect by shoving a few tins into my presses. I managed well enough on my own until you came back and I'll manage when you're gone. And mark my words you'll be gone soon enough if there's one more word out of your mouth about that baby. It's got nothing to do with us. It never had and it *never* will.'

Beth imagined gripping the embittered old woman by her shoulders and shaking her until her head lolled to one side and she stopped breathing. Horrified by the thought, she grabbed her jacket from the back of the chair and left.

The engine cut out when she tried to start her car. She banged her fist off the steering wheel, hitting it repeatedly until pain shot through her arm and sobered her. Her sister had gone to Anaskeagh to confront her past and been denied twice by those who claimed to love her. But first, strengthened by Jess's comfort, she'd gone to Estuary View Heights seeking solace from Beth. The last time they'd been together. Beth could recall the day in all its petty demands. Safe in her cosy citadel where meals needed to be served on time and the dictates of family life dominated her days, she'd refused to listen to her sister. Thrice denied, Sara had gone to her death as alone then as she'd been on Anaskeagh Head when darkness had closed around her childhood.

CHAPTER FIFTY-NINE

On the outskirts of Anaskeagh Greg's mobile rang. The female voice on the other end of the line was elderly, quavering. He waved his hand towards Chas, ordering him to pull the car into the side of the road. At first he was unable to understand what the woman was saying. He would have ignored her, put it down to a crazed wrong call, except that the politician's name ran like a refrain through her stumbling words. She gave him directions to a small estate of town houses.

A stained-glass lantern lit the front porch. She opened the door and beckoned him inside.

'You – stay outside!' She gestured towards Chas, who retreated from her fierce expression with a muttered oath.

Mutton dressed as lamb, Greg thought. She had a leathery tanned complexion, gold neck chains, knuckleduster rings on her wrinkled fingers. When she drew deeply on a cigarette he remembered her. That last time they'd met she'd been slumped in an armchair in Kieran Grant's brownstone in the rarefied atmosphere of New York's Upper East Side.

He followed her into a small room with a velvet three-piece suite and a cabinet where dusty Waterford glasses were on display. Marjory Tyrell did not ask him to sit down. From a drawer at the base of the cabinet she lifted out a thick folder of documents.

'Land deals,' she said. 'My late sister-in-law May believed they could be useful one day. A silly woman who never understood the virtue of silence.'

Greg removed the documents from the folder and examined them. Albert Grant had trusted his wife in the days before his son had taken over his legal affairs.

'You do realise the implications of handing this information to me,' Greg warned her. 'They'll destroy your brother's political reputation. They could lead to his imprisonment.'

'Oh yes. I understand.' She pressed her hands against the folder. Her nails turned white from the pressure as she forced the file towards him. 'There will be a scandal. But the truth is important, don't you agree, Mr Enright?'

'You've had these documents in your possession for some time, Mrs Tyrell. Why have you decided to release them now?'

She stood up and waved her hand towards the door. 'My reasons are my own business. You have the story you came to investigate, Mr Enright. There's nothing more for you here. Now please leave my house. I seldom welcome visitors.'

Elucidate devoted its entire programme to Albert Grant. Kickbacks, insider information; the familiar tale of power and corruption. The story gathered momentum on the later news broadcasts. A close-up of his constituency clinic flashed onscreen. Journalists hovered outside, microphones poised, the scent of blood in their nostrils. A closed door opened to reveal the stocky figure of his son, who read a prepared statement. Conor Grant spoke slowly, with sincerity. Since his father had entered politics he had served his constituents unstintingly. Phone calls of support and endorsement had been flooding into his clinic ever since that inaccurate and derogatory programme had aired. Albert Grant would be happy to address these allegations frankly but he was unavailable for comment until he had completed a thorough investigation of his files and diaries. These allegations dealt with issues from the past, an era when his father had worked tirelessly at a local level to stem the tide of emigration. How could a man of his advanced years be expected to remember every meeting he'd attended, every decision that had been made in council chambers? He had nothing to hide.

Journalists jostled forward, barking questions. Past land deals were the tip of the iceberg. What about the recent allegations? The industrial estate, for instance? The farmer who was cheated on a land deal? Conflicts of interest were everywhere. Conor fled before the hail of questions.

Albert Grant resigned from the party and announced that he would run in the next election as an independent candidate. He was confident of being elected. His constituents were loyal and appreciative of the work he had done, and would continue to do, on their behalf. Yes, Greg thought, a few shady land deals – what of it? He would win the popular vote. He was, at heart, a parish-pump politician. It was always thus. And somehow, in the midst of the hype, Greg knew that the main story had slipped from his grasp.

CHAPTER SIXTY

Marina McKeever drove into Eva's Cottage Garden and pulled to a halt on the gravelled parking area. Eva, locking up at the end of the day, suggested they go into the cottage for coffee. Whatever reason Marina had for visiting, it wouldn't involve advice about flowers. Instead the older woman suggested a walk by the lake. She'd heard there were swans living in the reeds.

They sat on the garden bench and stared at the water. Marina's voice droned aimlessly as she described a brief affair with a rock star that had turned her into tabloid fodder for a while. Her career as a model had been short-lived and excessive. The fashion industry had changed, just like Oldport. A changed village, friends married and even those who were widowed had nothing to offer. Nowadays, she worked on a cosmetics counter in a department store, warring against free radicals and wrinkles. Efficient in a white coat, she used the language of science to sell the vision of youth. Eva wondered how long it would take before she got to the point of her visit.

'How is your mother?' she asked, trying to fill the sudden silence that fell. 'I met her recently in the village with Lindsey.'

'She told me. You remind her of Sara Wallace.'

Eva was shocked by the blunt admission. 'Do I look like her?'

'Superficially, yes. I knew her briefly when she lived in London. We were never friends – too much history. Her father and Connie lived together after he left his wife.' Her high energised voice faltered as she stared at the swans gliding by with the same lofty indifference she must once have displayed on the catwalk.

'My father's bones were hardly recovered from the sea before she took up with Barry Tyrell. I never forgave her. Even now I can't.'

Eva was surprised to discover that the frail old woman had such a past. Swallows dived and skimmed over the water. The wind suddenly picked up. Marina pulled her jacket tighter around her. 'You and Peter…' Her perfect face tautened. 'Spring and autumn lovers. Not always the wisest combination.'

'You disapprove?'

'What's disapproval got to do with anything? You're a big girl now.' She told Eva about his London trips, how he occasionally spent nights in her apartment. 'It didn't set the sky alight for either of us. He was sleeping between cold sheets by then, seeking comfort.'

'Weren't they happy together?'

'Happy? Who's happy, for Christ's sake?'

'They were married a long time. Surely that had to mean something.'

'What does it mean? You can be a long time on heroin but that doesn't mean you love your addiction. Does he ever speak about her?'

'Why should he? Their past has nothing to do with me.'

'He's not the right man for you, Eva.'

'And he is for you?'

The look Marina gave her was neither bitter or jealous. 'Not for me either. But for different reasons. He knows who I am. Does he know who you are?'

The question hung between them in the silent twilight, unanswered.

Sara Wallace, ghostly wife. Eva wanted to picture this woman who once knew Peter's body as intimately as she did. Was she jealous of a dead woman? She shied from the thought. The dead did not inspire jealousy – unless they consumed the living – and sometimes, when he loved her, Eva wondered whom he saw lying beneath him. Was she his fantasy, his undying love?

He was visiting Connie in hospital when she arrived at Havenstone. Apart from the anniversary of Faye's birthday, Eva had never entered the house when he wasn't there. She stood in the drawing room and looked down on the lights of Oldport. Had his wife stared at that same view before turning her back on it and slowly climbing the staircase to her bedroom? Did she know, as she closed the door behind her, that she would never open it again? Eva wanted to leave this house with its haunting past, yet she longed to know more about this mysterious woman. She climbed the stairs and hesitated outside Sara's bedroom door. The feeling that she was moving through an invisible barrier was so strong she had to force herself to turn the key and enter. Such a weird eerie space, white walls decorated with mirrors. So sterile and narcissistic, so devoid of warmth. Her reflection was replicated, scared and tentative, as she approached the bed and rested her hand upon it.

Later she asked him to tell her about Sara, to give her a shape. She wanted to see a photograph. He shook his head, refusing to listen.

'You must have something!' Eva cried. 'A lifetime together. Why did you hate her so much? Tell me about her.'

He groaned and pressed his lips across her mouth.

She forced him away. 'Marina told me I look like her. Do I? Answer me?'

'No! Don't listen to her, to anyone. The past no longer exists. The love we have, that's all that counts.' He touched her fingertips. 'Can't you feel it?' he demanded. 'Electricity. We charge each other.'

She told him she'd trespassed in his dead wife's room. Now she felt as if part of her had been left inside it. He rocked her in his arms, accusing her of crazy superstitions. She refused to be comforted.

'I want to make love in her room.' The words were out, a thought hardly realised. 'Did you hear what I said, Peter? I want to love you in her room – on her bed. She's haunting us – and I want to banish her.'

In her bedroom of mirrors they lay together. Eva heard him moan when he came, grasping her hair, his hands tangled so deep in the tresses her eyes stung with pain. He laid her back against the high white pillows. She gave herself up to his mouth, his hands, the rhythm of his body.

Later he opened the wardrobe and removed a dress, a delicate fabric with the gleam of dark wine. It fitted her, a second skin moulding her body. In the dining room candles burned on the polished table. He laid food before her. White roses sat in a silver dish. The curtains were open. The lights of Oldport wavered below, diamonds spilling into the black night. He lifted her in his arms. He bruised her throat with kisses. She rejoiced in his touch, in his drowning pleasure.

What was happening to her? How could she tell this to Maria… To Liz… To Annie? Impossible. This was dark, secret passion. She was a whore, a virgin, a bride. Without shame. She would do anything for him. He would do the same for her. They were reflections of each other's deepest desires. Reflections trapped in a white room. Their hearts beating time together, counting down the hours.

Peter rang to break the news of Connie McKeever's death. He'd spent the night in the hospice with her family and they were returning to Havenstone, where they would stay until after the funeral. Remembering the speculative gaze of Marina McKeever, Eva had no desire to meet his relatives or to be the subject of their curiosity, and was relieved when he didn't suggest seeing her during that time. The following day she drove to Woodstock with emergency flower supplies. Judith was busy with wreaths for the funeral. Connie McKeever was well respected in the village and beyond.

Annie Loughrey, Eva's aunt, stood among the mourners at the graveside. She rang Eva that evening, demanding freshly percolated coffee before heading off to a gig in the city. She arrived shortly afterwards, giddy from too much wine and memories, old friends from Celtic Reign reunited around the graveside.

'Of course I was just a tot in my Celtic Reign days, not an old crone like now,' she said.

She was accompanied by the singer from Loughrey's Crew, a young man with a shaved head, who protested vigorously over her use of the word 'crone' and was ordered off to look at the swans. Eva had stopped keeping track of her aunt's companions, who got younger as Annie grew older.

'Sexually, we're both in our prime,' Annie explained when Eva had once asked when she was going to stop behaving outrageously with schoolboys. A slight exaggeration. They'd usually received the key of the house when Annie invited them in.

Her good humour quickly disappeared as she surveyed her niece. 'How are you enjoying life since you decided to become a hermit?' she asked.

'Busy, busy,' Eva replied.

'Don't annoy me, Eva. I'm too long in the tooth to listen to balderdash.' Annie had a fine snap to her voice when she was irritated. 'You should never be too busy to visit your family. Liz said you look as skinny as a bag of bones and she's right. There's only one thing that makes a woman that way and it's not happiness.' Annie's eyes narrowed. 'So tell me. Is he also married?'

Eva shook her head. 'Annie, nothing you say will make any difference. I've got someone who loves me, who cares. You've no idea how much he cares.'

'And what about Greg? Have you thought about his feelings in all of this?'

'It's got nothing to do with him.'

Impatiently her aunt slapped her words aside. 'Fine sentiments. I hope they don't bite you back. Who is he?'

'No one you know.' Eva wondered if they'd rubbed shoulders at the funeral. Perhaps they'd spoken in the graveyard or in the Oldport Grand, where Annie had gathered old musicians around her to reminisce about times past and smoky ballad sessions in The Fiddler's Nest.

CHAPTER SIXTY-ONE

Loughrey's Crew were playing in Temple Bar. Annie saw Greg in the crowded pub and raised the bow of her fiddle in salute. He waited until the session ended and the musicians were packing up their equipment before approaching her.

'How serious is it?' He sat down on the stool next to her. 'She usually confides in you.'

'It's difficult to communicate with her these days,' Annie replied. 'As far as Eva's concerned, you betrayed her at the most vulnerable time in her life.' She ran her fingers over the strings of her fiddle, as if checking its perfect pitch. 'But I believe she still loves you, despite everything she says to the contrary.'

'Loved, you mean. We operate in the past tense, Annie. If what I hear in her voice is love, than I guess I've been listening to the wrong songs.'

'Eva's in the grip of a fever, Greg. You screwed up once but if you want to save your marriage don't do it a second time. Just be there when she falls – because that's exactly what's going to happen to her.'

'How can you be so sure?' he asked.

Annie smiled as she packed her fiddle in its case. 'I know a thing or two about love. If you weren't my niece's husband I'd show you my bruises.'

He saw Eva in the city one night. She passed by without noticing him and turned into a restaurant. He watched through the

window as a man stood to greet her. Older yet still disturb-
ingly handsome, he took her hand with the familiarity of a lover
and guided her into the seat opposite him. This, then, was Peter
Wallace. His name and face were familiar to Greg, though he
was unable to remember where they could have met. The shock
of having his suspicions confirmed sent blood rushing to his
head. He had offered friendship to his wife in the vain hope
that it could lead them back to love. But friendship, he realised,
was impossible. Did he want to hang around and pick up the
pieces? He'd become a journalist to find the beginning of a story,
but the story kept fragmenting. There was no logic to anything,
just random events that defined people for the rest of their lives,
leaving them with the eternal, unanswerable thought – if only…
If only…

CHAPTER SIXTY-TWO

Eva believed their passion was strong enough to vanquish Sara Wallace, but she still walked by their side, a ghost made stronger by her invisibility. The nights they had spent in her white bedroom had the substance of a dream, still vivid enough to shiver through her thoughts yet unreal, the actions of strangers. She would never again enter that space.

He moved into the studio his wife once occupied. She watched him painting. Sometimes she saw parts of herself, a curl of blonde hair in a green circle, her fingers reaching out from a flame or perhaps it was a sun blast, a nuclear explosion. Like the painting of Murtagh's River, nothing had a recognisable shape yet there was such vigour in the colours, in his bold sweeping strokes. She didn't understand what she saw but it moved her, this excitement he created. Her passion strayed far beyond the pleasure she'd shared with Greg and the other young men she'd known briefly and carelessly in her student days. It was madness, this desire. It had to burn out. But not yet… Not yet.

One evening she arrived early at Havenstone. After a day of rain, she'd closed Eva's Cottage Garden early and driven directly to him. A light shone from the studio. Loud music played, thunderous notes beating with life. She still had her own key to the house and he was unaware that she'd entered the studio. His expression when he noticed her was transfixed, as if he'd seen an apparition standing in the doorway. When his face lit with pleasure she wondered if she'd imagined that unnerving pause, an instant when it seemed she'd become insubstantial.

He would be finished in a moment, he told her. A casserole was already in the oven, the table laid for two.

She closed the door of the studio and walked across the landing, where a wrought-iron staircase twisted upwards towards a closed trapdoor. What possessed her to climb upwards? Was it the same compulsion that had drawn her into the mirrored room where his wife once slept alone? What was she expecting to find? His wife mad and raving in the shadows? Afterwards, Eva would ask herself these questions. She would remember the sense of detachment that came over her as she stood in the dim slanted attic where cobwebs hung thick in corners and the remnants of other times lay under a shroud of dust.

In a wooden chest with a curved lid she found books on wine, old yellowing recipes, histories of vineyards and a diary kept by Bradley Wallace on his winemaking successes and failures. She studied an old painting: a young woman, a teenager surely, her arms upraised and chained, fear shining from her startling green eyes. Eva winced and placed it back against the wall. Accordion files of business documents were stacked in plastic containers, with newspaper features on Della Wallace, who had been a role model for journalists in the early wave of the feminist movement. How dated it all seemed, Eva thought, reaching towards a thick leather-bound scrapbook.

The pages were filled with information about Sara Wallace. Over the years, Peter had collected everything, every column inch of newspaper space, reviews, features, photographs, catalogues from her exhibitions, a miscellaneous collection that charted the photographer's success. Eva found prints and transparencies, files of them stacked together, as if they'd been taken from the studio, dumped and then forgotten.

With her camera Sara Wallace had created another world. The boy sleeping in the shelter of a cardboard box could have been a dog or a heap of discarded rags. Fat women in miniskirts stood on street corners. Wasted young girls lingered on the canal banks. Neon glitter; the Liffey reflecting.

She was leaving when she noticed his sketchpad. She stiffened as she flicked through the pages. These were no abstract images swirling with life. One woman's face had been drawn in all of them – a tense, beautiful face. She stared at her own reflection, and yet she knew it wasn't her, the features too mature. Eva wasn't beautiful. Her mouth was wide, her forehead too high. She lacked the delicacy that Peter had drawn into this wounded face. Yet she saw herself, her expression framed in mirrors, angry, aroused, laughing, crying. She was able to trace the chronology of these drawings. Two faces battled for supremacy. In the final page Sara Wallace was a ghostly image, ephemeral, submissive. Eva was the stronger. The younger. The victor. Superimposed. A mirror framed in red stones held her face. The same mirror that had held her reflection on those searing nights when she'd stared from its depths. She felt as if she was choking, as if her soul had been taken without permission.

When she returned to his studio she demanded to know whom he had been drawing. He tried to calm her down, dismayed by her fury.

'It was an experiment that failed,' he explained. He wanted a theme of reflections and the mirrors in his wife's bedroom had inspired him. Listening to him Eva felt breathless, as if his hands were on her throat. Possessing her.

'Leave me alone,' she shouted. 'You're strangling me… it's too much… too much!' She ran to the white bedroom and tore the mirror from the wall, smashing it to pieces on the floor.

His hands shook as he picked up the shards. He promised to destroy them all. He gathered her close, not possessively, not even passionately. As if the words she'd screamed had sobered them for a short, resting time.

CHAPTER SIXTY-THREE

'The Anaskeagh Baby,' Greg Enright said when he met Beth for the last time in Dublin. 'Was she bait to keep me on the investigation or do you want to tell me a different story?'

Beth imagined the past uncoiling like an octopus, tentacles reaching around her children and husband, Marjory's shrunken face, gossip in the schoolyard and the town square. A media rampage, her face the headline on the evening news. The enormity of the truth overwhelmed her once again and she averted her eyes from the journalist's challenging stare.

'There's no story,' she said. 'I don't have any further information on the Anaskeagh Baby.'

Albert Grant had been brought down but not by her hand. Greg Enright would never betray his source but Beth knew her identity. Marjory hadn't left her house since her brother's resignation. She refused to speak to Beth or answer the door to her. When Catherine O'Donovan sent her an invitation to her seventieth birthday party it remained unanswered.

The O'Donovan family had gathered together for the occasion of their mother's birthday and, on the night of her party, the old farmhouse blazed with lights. Catherine greeted her guests warmly, flushed and happy to have the people she loved around her. She admired Gail's new party dress, applauded the funny poem Paul had written for her, insisted on hearing Robert playing his accordion and hugged Lindsey, who presented her with a painting of the hill field on a starry night.

Beth moved freely among the guests. She was at home here, able to relax with friends. The party was a welcome distraction from the shock of Connie's death. It had only been two months from her prognosis to her last battling breath. Serene until the end she had bid them goodbye and passed quietly away as a new dawn had brightened the sky. Since then Marina seemed adrift. She talked about returning to London yet made no effort to do so. Connie's cottage was up for sale and she was living there with Lindsey until a buyer was found.

The night passed swiftly. The younger children were carried into Catherine's bedroom when they fell asleep. Marina, who was visiting Anaskeagh, danced across the floor with Jim O'Donovan. The only unmarried brother, he'd made the trip from Australia once again to celebrate with his mother. He spun Marina around so fast that she lost her balance. The suddenness of her fall took everyone by surprise. Jim helped her into a chair and apologised for having two left feet.

'Nothing's hurt except my dignity,' Marina assured him. 'That can easily be restored with another gin and tonic.'

She gestured to Beth while he was refilling her glass. 'I've had too much to drink,' she whispered. 'Take my arm and help me out of here.'

She allowed Beth and Jess to link arms with her and lead her to a garden bench outside the farmhouse. The noise from the party faded into the background as they lifted their faces to the balmy night air. Marina talked about men, her words slurring as she grew more agitated.

'Unreliable swine,' she said. 'They make us invisible. Once we're past our prime they don't want to know us.' She grasped Jess's hand. 'You had the right idea, Jess. At least God doesn't pretend to be faithful to his brides. What's it like in his harem? Does it give you peace of mind?'

Jess laughed and freed her hand. 'Peace of mind is reserved for the hereafter, no matter what path you take. Why are you tarring all men with the same brush? I thought you were getting on very well with my brother.'

'I was, until I discovered he cohabits with kangaroos.' Marina laughed shrilly. 'I want to love the boy next door but he's gone for the younger model. Have you seen Peter's green-fingered girlfriend?'

'No,' Beth replied. 'Lindsey says she's lovely.'

'I call her Sara Mark Two. She's only half his age and he's acting like a Boy Scout who's discovered a good deed.'

'Don't call her Sara Mark Two,' Beth said. 'It's hurtful and unnecessary.'

'Sorry, Beth, sorry. I called to Havenstone one night and it was like I was looking at Sara again. Eva Frawley's planted deep roots in Havenstone and not only in the garden.'

'Eva?' Jess half rose from the bench, then sat down again when Marina began to cry.

'Oh Christ, I'm so fucked up since Connie died.' Mascara streaked her cheeks. 'I spent my life being angry with her. Such a waste. She was right to grab a bit of love and hang onto it. In the end that's all it's about. A bit of love to make it worth our while getting up in the morning.' She wept harder, maudlin tears that she wiped with the back of her hand. She nodded obediently when Beth suggested they leave now.

'Jess, will you say goodbye to Catherine for us?' Beth helped her to her feet.

Jess looked at the weeping Marina and sighed before rising to hug her. 'You'll never be invisible, Marina. Not to the people who count.'

'You wouldn't need a degree in maths to count those.' She sobbed and laughed and leaned on Beth as they walked to the car. She'd clung too long to a girlish dream, not realising that dreams needed to be shattered for the truth to become visible.

CHAPTER SIXTY-FOUR

The red light on the answering machine winked in Eva's Cottage Garden. Only one message had been left. A woman's voice, deep and assertive. Jess O'Donovan hoped Eva would agree to meet her soon. There was something she needed to discuss with her. A story she had to tell.

Jess O'Donovan spoke hesitantly, as if feeling her way through unfamiliar territory. She seemed nervous, yet Eva, looking into the resolute brown eyes, knew that this woman would not flinch from the truth. They drank tea together, polite strangers who should have been making polite conversation.

Eva had been right. A teenage mother, terrified. Her child's mind closed down to her baby's existence so that Eva became a growth without shape, without meaning. Something to be destroyed and left beneath a rock. Her sister had run through the night to the lights of a farmhouse and saved Eva's life. Jess O'Donovan did not use those words but Eva heard them nonetheless.

An aunt made the child mother strong again. She stopped the bleeding and gave her tablets to banish bad dreams. No one could know she was unclean. She was a shining star. A good girl. She was told to carry her shameful secret to her grave. Otherwise she would destroy the good name of her family forever. And so she remained a shining star. Twenty-six years later, in an African village, she'd confided her secret and returned home ready to confront the past. But fear had destroyed her and she'd chosen death instead. At first Eva didn't understand.

'Your mother is dead,' Jess said. 'Sara is at peace.' She made it sound like a prayer.

'Sara?'

'Her name was Sara Wallace.'

Eva wondered how she could breathe so calmly… How she could breathe at all. When she looked down at her hands, clasped tightly in the nun's strong grip, she realised they were shaking. Jess O'Donovan's words were far away, somewhere above her head, soaring away from her.

Tears glistened in the nun's eyes. 'I'm so sorry, my dear, so sorry. I realised Peter had contacted you when I spoke to Marina McKeever. She has no idea about your identity, but she suspects Peter's love for you is based on your resemblance to his wife. It's important that you know the truth before this relationship continues.'

Peter Wallace had traced her to Ashton. He knew – that day when she'd sat by the riverbank mourning Faye… He knew. When he'd held her, dominating her with his passion, he knew. When he'd spoken of love, searching her heart for the same passionate response, he knew.

Soon afterwards Jess O'Donovan left. She embraced Eva and said they must meet again. Eva sensed the nun's uneasiness, the worry that she'd made a wrong decision. She assured Jess she was fine. She needed to know. Why expend energy on a dead search?

The crunch of tyres outside startled Eva from her reverie. The garden centre was closed for the evening and when she looked out the cottage window she recognised Greg's car.

'What's happened to you, Eva?' He followed her inside. 'Why haven't you answered my calls? I've been ringing you for days.'

'I can't talk about it.' She walked ahead of him into the small living room.

'Is it that man? What's he done to you? Talk to me, Eva. Trust me.'

'Go away, Greg,' she cried. 'I have to work this out for myself.'

'Let me stay with you tonight?' he pleaded. 'Just for tonight. You need me here. We promised each other friendship. This is how it works.'

They slept fitfully together in her bed. Friends. It had been easy. Her grief separated them, killed any desire that might have flared when their bodies touched.

Peter Wallace came in the early morning. Greg opened the front door to him. She sensed their hostility flaring. To rattle antlers, to butt and charge and roar victorious would have been a simple way of dealing with a love triangle, if it existed. But nothing existed for Eva except the truth that Jess O'Donovan had seared into her.

'I've got to see her.' She heard his voice break, plead. 'Tell her I'm not leaving until she gives me a chance to explain.'

'If it's business it can wait for another day.' Her husband sounded loudly aggressive. 'If it's something else – it can wait forever.'

'For Christ's sake! What are you? Her bodyguard?' Peter demanded. 'This is between me and Eva. You may think you're helping her but you haven't a clue. It's essential that I talk to her – just once. Then I'll be out of your lives forever.'

'That's not long enough,' Greg replied but she came from behind him and said, 'He's right, Greg. We have to talk.'

She had refused to answer his letters, his phone calls, his emails. He had called in vain to the garden centre, to the cottage, but had been unable to bypass Muriel Wilson's determined stance. Now he was here early in the morning, his face ravaged with guilt, his passion undiminished as he forced her to listen, to understand what had happened between them.

They walked to the lake. His sister-in-law had told him about Sara's baby. An incomplete story without a father and no knowledge about the family who had adopted her. He had phoned Jess O'Donovan, pleaded with her to reveal Eva's name. The nun had refused to divulge it but she had mentioned a village set in a Wicklow valley and a garden centre where Eva had once worked. He'd searched and found Ashton.

In Wind Fall, he'd seen photographs on the wall of the breakfast room, school photographs, a graduation, a wedding, a young mother with a baby in her arms. Liz had been happy to talk about her daughter. Eva's life was secure and he'd had no desire to intrude any further. But something, a restlessness, a need to know more about her, had made him return. He'd found her sitting by the river. Her baby was dead, her marriage over. Her grief had been raw enough to touch, to understand.

'I wanted to help you,' he said. 'You have to believe me. That was all I wanted in the beginning. To play a small part in your life. I'd be giving something back to Sara, making some kind of restitution for the pain we'd caused each other throughout our marriage. But… I didn't realise I would fall in love with you.' His eyes darkened with yearning. 'I won't make excuses for what happened between us. You brought me back to life and I think… I know I did the same to you. It was incredible—'

'But did you once stop to think of the pain you'd cause if I found out?' she demanded. Passion had turned to ash. Only her anger burned, blistering him. 'Or was that part of the thrill? The ultimate hit. Who did you think I was? Your dead wife?'

The colour drained from his face. He moved closer to her. 'I won't let you distort our love. You can't destroy what we shared—'

'Shared! When have you ever shared anything?' Her hand flamed against his cheek. 'How dare you come here demanding my understanding – my forgiveness – when you've destroyed me with your obsession?'

He tried to hold her, to prevent her walking away. 'Do you want to cut into my flesh, Eva?' he asked, his lips almost touching hers. 'Will that help? Will it?'

'Nothing that gives you relief will help me.' To believe him would draw her back into his all-consuming love and she wasn't prepared to offer him mercy. 'You deceived me from the beginning, just as you deceived yourself. You were in love with a ghost… Or some ideal woman you created. But not with me… you were never in love with me!' She believed he understood, even when he shook his head in denial.

'I love you, Eva, only you. You have to believe me.'

The early-morning mist lifted above the water. Cobwebs, glistening in the rising sun, linked the dark reeds. Fragile chains that swayed and broke when the swans stirred in their nest.

'I never want to set eyes on you again.' She walked away from the jagged sound of his grief – and from a truth that no longer mattered.

Greg was gone when she returned to the cottage.

CHAPTER SIXTY-FIVE

Annie Loughrey had spoken of a fever. Greg understood what she'd meant when Eva had opened the door to him. He had been shocked by her appearance – her lank hair and bleak expression. When Peter Wallace arrived the following morning he bore little resemblance to the suave person Greg had seen rising to greet her in the restaurant. Nor did he look like a smooth financier who invested money in struggling garden centres. He was a man who couldn't sleep. A man whose eyes reflected the same anguish he had seen in his wife's tormented gaze.

He watched them walk towards the lake. They faced each other. Angry gesticulations. Greg wondered if she would raise her hand and strike him, willed her to lash out and, when she did so, he saw Peter Wallace flinch and grasp her shoulders. As her head moved back in submission, and it seemed inevitable that they would embrace, he knew he had to leave.

There was nothing left to hold him here. In this fertile garden, they had once loved against a crumbling stone wall and conceived their child, the swans raking the air with their wings. Unrecognisable now. Everything gone, everything… Yet it nagged him continually, this sense of recognition. The feeling that he and Peter Wallace had met on an occasion that had nothing to do with Eva. The memory was tantalisingly close yet still out of his grasp. And so it would have remained if he hadn't noticed the book on his shelf. *Silent Songs from an African Village*. A freebie, he remembered, offered to him at a book launch. A collaboration between a nun and a dead photographer. He suddenly realised why Peter Wallace had seemed so familiar the night he'd seen him with Eva in a Temple Bar restaurant. Greg recalled the speech he'd made at the launch, the emotion in his voice as he spoke about his deceased wife. Another memory clicked into place. He had interviewed Sara Wallace during the motorway protests and attended an exhibition of her photographs. Swans swimming down the centre of a road.

He replayed the interview in the *Elucidate* library. A tall blonde woman, cool and distant, her personality at odds with the energy of her photography. He freeze-framed her image. Her resemblance to his wife was striking. The same high cheekbones, her long, slim neck, and the full, sensuous lips that had instantly attracted him to Eva.

Muriel suggested he wait in the cottage. It wouldn't be long before Eva returned. She was designing a water feature for a client and had phoned to say she was on her way back to the garden centre.

'How is she?' Greg moved carefully between a stacked aisle of pansies.

'As busy as ever,' Muriel replied.

'That's not what I asked.'

'It's not my place to pass personal comments, Mr Enright.'

'I care about her, Muriel. I can't help worrying about her.'

'If you're that worried than stay with her and block your ears when she says she doesn't need you. You're not the only one who worries.'

He watched from the window as Eva parked her van and spoke briefly to Muriel.

'Why are you here, Greg?' she asked when she entered the cottage.

'We need to talk, Eva.'

'What about?'

'Us. Divorce. Marriage. Whatever.'

'If you want a divorce I won't stand in your way.' Her voice was as expressionless as her face.

'I'm not talking about me.' He wanted to shake some life into her, rouse her to anger, lift her from a sadness that seemed overwhelming. 'Do you want to be free to marry this man you love? If that's it then for Christ's sake say so.'

'He's moving to Italy. A one-way ticket.'

'Then go with him. I can't stand the way we're living any longer.'

'I don't love him.' She drummed her fists off her thighs, her hands moving fast over the rough denim.

'Then what is it? Tell me what's wrong.'

'You wouldn't understand. I can't understand it myself.'

'Let me in, Eva. Nothing can be so bad that it's beyond understanding. We'll make sense of it together. Can you hear what I'm saying to you?'

'I don't know who I am,' she whispered. 'I'm lost… I can't find my way back.'

He took the book from his briefcase and laid it on the table. She stared at the title and waited, puzzled, as he turned it over to reveal the author's photograph on the back cover.

'Is that the reason?' he asked. 'Did Peter Wallace try to make you his wife?'

She sat down on a chair and studied the photograph. Her stillness unnerved him. Then, just when it seemed he would be unable to endure another second of silence, she pushed the book away from her. A child's gesture of rejection, wincing when she heard the thud it made when it hit the floor.

'Tell me if I'm right.' He forced her to look at him, helplessly reaching towards the woman he had known and loved.

'My mother.' Her voice trembled on the edge of hysteria. For an instant he thought he had misheard. 'My murdering dead mother.'

She reached down and picked up the book, tore the dust jacket from it and crumpled it into a tight ball. 'It was my mother he loved all the time.' Still clutching it she began to sob. 'Can't you understand why I don't want to talk about it? Can't you… Can't you?'

But she did talk, faltering at times, stumbling under half-understood facts, and when she mentioned Beth McKeever's name he was convinced he'd misheard. She repeated the name and he could picture her then, her black hair flailing as she ran through the night with Eva in her arms.

'Your father?' he asked when Eva fell silent.

'I don't know if he's alive or dead. Jess was told he was dead but she thinks Sara was too frightened to reveal his name. The only thing that's certain is that I'll never meet my mother now.' She smoothed out the crumpled dust jacket and stared at the image of a woman whose existence she had never questioned throughout her tranquil childhood.

A more disturbing understanding dawned on Greg. The story that had evaded him since his first meeting with Beth McKeever at last began to make sense. Albert Grant… His breathing was laboured as he listened to Eva's hesitant revelations. Could there be a link? The idea was too preposterous to consider, yet the fragments of a story kept slotting together until all he could see was the glitter of revenge in her steadfast green gaze. She had been determined to destroy the politician with a lesser story – but when she'd failed it was Marjory Tyrell who had sacrificed her brother to protect the darker secrets of his past.

Greg had his big scoop. As an investigative journalist his job was to lift the stones and let the worms wriggle free. This would be the scandal of the century. A story that would keep growing as journalists vied with each other to see who could dig up the grimiest details and the public, addicted to political scandals, would hold out its arm for the mainline hit.

He gathered Eva to him, shocked at how thin she'd become. He thought of Albert Grant, his high forehead and fleshy neck, the arrogant sweep of silver hair, his appraising gaze – and tried to equate him to the woman he loved. He imagined her horror as she searched his face for similarities, haunted by the fear that she could have inherited his darkness, the evil within. Greg knew then, with a fixed certainty, that this was the one stone he would never lift. The one story he would never tell.

CHAPTER SIXTY-SIX

They climbed together towards the summit of Anaskeagh Head. Below them kittiwakes swooped and turned, skittish birds fanning out above the murmuring caves. Waves crashed upwards. Eva watched them break over the rocks until all that remained of the ferment was the sting of salt on her lips. They continued climbing, dipping and rising with the lie of the path.

She was tireless in her search. On the way down they found it. Aislin's Roof. The ground beneath the boulders was mossy and dank. She moved forward. Large putty-coloured fungi mulched beneath her feet. The rank smell of dead vegetation seeped upwards, a curiously private smell that belonged to private places. From her mother's womb she had been forced into this odorous, brooding landscape. She imagined a child staggering into the reaches of wild ferns, knowing she would never escape the clutches of that dark, dreadful night.

She fell to her knees, pulled at the grass with her fingers. The rough blades cut deep into her hands. She called her mother's name – Sara... Sara... Sara. She began to cry. It was Faye's cry that rose from her lips, a whimpering, bewildered, newborn cry that understood only the spill of light on bare flesh, the flow of wind through the trees, the crashing tide, the call of night creatures, the earth beneath. And pain. A splintering red light filling her head. The cry rose and fell and faded. She touched her forehead. Her hair was limp and damp. No blood. Rising to her feet, she moved away from the shade of Aislin's Roof. Birds sang and the sun shone above the headland, a molten pulse beating against the waves.

Her legs trembled as she was forced to a standstill at the edge of a steep rocky shelf. No safe footholds to steady her. Nothing but a sheer slice of granite between her and the drop below.

The decision came suddenly yet she knew it had been seeding in her mind ever since her meeting with Jess O'Donovan. Her father wasn't dead. If he was, her mother would still be alive. Somewhere, in the town she glimpsed in the distance, he walked free and unconcerned. A brute who'd forced a child to give birth to his daughter under Aislin's Roof. She would expose him and make him pay for his crime.

Greg shook his head when he heard what she intended to do.

'What if this man is repugnant to you?' His expression was grave, concerned. 'How will you cope then?'

She wondered at his hesitation. The fallout from an *Elucidate* exposé – a marriage break-up, a career destroyed, a nervous breakdown or a heart attack – had never been his concern in the past. Why now, when she needed him, was he so worried about the consequences of exposure?

'I have a mother and father who love me as much as I love them.' She cut across his arguments. 'This man, whoever he is, means nothing to me. He's a brute who murdered my mother.'

'Sara died by her own hand—'

'He murdered her through stealth and secrecy. I'm going to tell her story. Will you help me?'

He moved ahead, lowering his body until he was secure on the flat plateau of rock. 'Yes, I'll help you,' he said. 'But let me talk to someone first.' He held out a hand to Eva and held it tightly as he guided her downwards to safety.

A cormorant nosedived into the waves then swooped upwards, wings outstretched, its body etched like a cross against the firmament.

CHAPTER SIXTY-SEVEN

Greg Enright's hair had been cut since the last time Beth had seen him. It spiked aggressively in front and the glasses he wore added to the severity of his image. She had never imagined him outside the lens of a camera but now, as they spoke, she realised he was a husband, a troubled one, intent on protecting the woman he loved. They had met secretly in the discreet alcove of a pub in Clasheen where the roads were smooth and the half-finished foundations of an industrial estate scarred the countryside.

This was a time of revelation. A time of coincidence and discovery. He told her about Faye, nurtured, adored – safe yet gone. She told him about Eva, unwanted, wounded – unsafe yet alive. He took off his glasses and pressed his hand against the tears that sprang to his eyes. Eva, birth daughter of Sara and Albert Grant. Would this last truth wound his wife so deeply that she would never recover?

Beth, her heart in turmoil, couldn't answer him. They shook hands outside the pub then hugged spontaneously, still amazed by the twisted path that had brought them to this moment.

The bungalow was silent when she returned home. In the bedroom she studied the photographs of Anaskeagh that the young Sara had taken. She spread them fan-like on the bed and lay beside them. Beth had banished her childhood memories – those starry nights on the hill field, the steamy comfort of the O'Donovans' kitchen, the thrill of riding high on her father's shoulders, blood sisters with Jess, giggling with Sara in the dip of a horsehair mattress – the happy moments vanquished by the darker memories, which she'd been unable to share until now.

The sound of the front door opening roused her. Voices rose. Laughter, arguments; familiar sounds, safe.

She huddled into Stewart's arms and tore open the membrane of her childhood terrors. He listened without interrupting her, his incredulity turning to fury, grief and pity as he grasped the enormity of what she was telling him. Finally, she fell silent, hollowed out, knowing that his love, constant and true, would see her through this final stage.

Would the truth destroy his wife? Greg Enright had asked. She knew the answer now. Secrets and lies had destroyed Sara. The truth would heal her daughter.

A late-afternoon hush hung over Eva's Cottage Garden when Beth entered the domed interior. Wooden stands overflowed with bedding plants and heathers. A middle-aged woman directed her to the garden behind the main centre where the land was partitioned into avenues of shrubs and rose bushes, the ground sloping gradually towards a lake.

The young woman watering the roses was unaware of her presence. An outdoor face, tanned and lightly sprinkled with freckles, her hair, loosely tied in a ponytail, escaping in curly tendrils. She stopped the flow of water when she noticed Beth. Her forehead puckered, as if she had recognised someone familiar yet was unable to name her. Beth gazed into her niece's blue eyes, so achingly familiar – into the vibrant gaze of what might have been... What should have been. She raised her hand to her lips to stifle an involuntary cry, then allowed the memory of Sara to rest peacefully among the scented flowers.

'Do I know you?' Eva asked.

'We met once before,' Beth said softly, tremulously. 'You won't remember me, Eva... it was a long, long time ago.'

CHAPTER SIXTY-EIGHT

A sign on the door of the politician's waiting room told Eva to enter and take a seat. His reassuring face beamed down on her from an election campaign poster. An independent candidate, soliciting the population of Anaskeagh to cast their number-one vote in his direction. Her father. Albert Harrison-Grant. She had seen his birth certificate, read his life story in newspapers, heard it from the mouth of Beth McKeever. Not easily – nothing about this had been easy – but Eva had pleaded, demanded, insisted on the truth, and Beth had eventually breathed his name, nightmares in her eyes. Eva had seen them, attuned to every expression that flitted over her aunt's stricken face. But that was another story and, perhaps, Beth would tell it to her another time. Their relationship was still too tender to challenge new truths.

The queue in the waiting room moved swiftly. Albert Grant must be an efficient administrator, Eva thought. However long his constituents wanted to gripe about their social-welfare benefits, savage dogs or difficult neighbours, they were smoothly ushered in and out with the minimum of delay. She wished the queue would move more slowly… wouldn't move at all… she wanted to run from this most momentous of meetings, yet she stayed sitting between a skinny man who smelled of cigarettes and a woman whose baby clawed at Eva's hair with sticky fingers.

The thin man emerged from the clinic and held the door open for her. She entered a spacious room with a large desk, neatly organised with stacked trays of forms, a telephone and laptop, and, in front of him, a foolscap pad open on a fresh page. He filled his chair, a heavily built man who rose, his hand outstretched, to greet her. His broad smile faltered when he looked at her. Was he seeing a ghost? Eva wondered. A slender wraith who tormented his dreams?

'I don't think I've had the pleasure of making your acquaintance.' His smile was puzzled as he waved her into a seat in front of his desk. 'You must be a stranger in our little town.'

'My name is Eva Frawley,' she said. 'I'm here to film a documentary.'

'May I ask who will be the subject of this documentary?' No longer smiling, he stroked a finger across his chin and regarded her thoughtfully. 'If you've come to ask questions about those slanderous allegations that were made against me, I must remind you that the matter is now in the hands of my legal team. Any further attempt to accuse me—'

'The documentary is about me.' She cut across his bluster. 'I've come to Anaskeagh to search for my roots.'

'My apologies, Ms Frawley. Usually it's American tourists who are on that trail. If you give me the name of your family I'll do everything I can to assist you.'

'Thank you,' Eva said. 'My problem is that I don't have a name. I was the baby who was born on Anaskeagh Head, and my father has never come forward to claim me.'

She heard a clock ticking on the wall behind him, the door of the waiting room opening then closing, and his hard, explosive gasp as he pushed himself to his feet and walked to the window.

'I'm afraid no one in this town can help you,' he said eventually, his back to her. 'That tragedy happened so long ago and, although every effort was made to contact the unfortunate mother, we failed–'

'I've traced my mother,' Eva interrupted him. 'She'll be part of my documentary.'

'What are you saying?' He was unable to hide his shock when he faced her.

'My mother told me all about that terrible night.'

'That's not poss—' He cleared his throat, his Adam's apple jolting. 'Who is your mother?'

'I promised her confidentiality until the documentary is aired,' Eva replied. 'But we both hope you'll participate in the filming.'

'Why on earth should you think that?'

'You were the voice of the people at that time. I'm sure you must have some memories you'd like to share.'

'All I remember is the appalling publicity that was visited on our town in the aftermath of that tragedy. I've no intention of revisiting that time or participating in your documentary, Ms Frawley.' He sat down again, legs crossed, one swinging over the other. A nervous habit Eva recognised. This man was a biological detail in her life, but this fact would never bind or bond her to him. Blood was not thicker than water, she thought. Not in this case. She wondered if he was trembling inside, as she was, his monstrous past escaping from whatever murky hole it occupied in his memory.

'I'm afraid I can't assist you any further.' He stood, their meeting over. He did not offer her his hand. 'It was a pleasure meeting you. Now, if you'll excuse me, I've many constituents waiting to see me.'

She held his gaze until he looked down at his desk. His hands were trembling, she noticed. He folded his arms across his chest and waited for her to leave. In that instant, as Eva's biological father dismissed her, Steve, the father she adored, had never seemed so near, the image of him so vivid, so strengthening, that she was able to speak with chilling composure.

'Thank you for your time, Mr Grant. Tracing one's roots can be a joyful experience, but it can also be a horrendous ordeal if the person we long to meet fills us with revulsion. My mother's story is harrowing but she *will* tell the truth so that the man who raped her can be brought to justice. She was only a child, you see, innocent and terrified. Now she's ready to talk – and the world is ready to listen.'

CHAPTER SIXTY-NINE

Beth was at home when her uncle phoned. He wanted to see her in his clinic immediately. The waiting room was empty, magazines scattered, the faint whiff of perspiration still lingering in the air. When she entered he tried to lock the door. The key fell between them with a clang. He pushed Beth aside when she bent to pick it up.

'I can manage,' he said. 'I can manage.'

'Locking the door won't keep the past from being exposed,' she said when the lock clicked. 'I wondered how long it would take you to contact me.'

'I want to know what game you're playing,' he said.

'Wrong question, Albert. I don't play games.'

'That young woman… It's all your doing. You're determined to destroy me. It won't work. You're a vicious liar, but you won't get away with it. Just you listen to me for a change–'

'No, Albert, *you* listen to me. I came here tonight to talk to you about my childhood. I believed I was a victim but I'm not. I'm a survivor who stayed silent for too long. Not any more. I want you to know how it was… Your touch always on my skin, your shadow walking behind me. And how, when I was no longer around to abuse, you took my sister's innocence – Sara's sweet, lovely innocence – and you destroyed her.'

She heard his deep intake of breath, saw the quick, uncontrollable flush on his cheeks. His fingers trembled as he lifted an envelope opener and turned the blade in his hand. When he looked up again his eyes reminded her of a dead fish. Frozen on a slab but still staring.

'She came here to confront you and you told her about Lindsey. How did you know? Even my secrets… *Nothing* was safe from you!'

'What did she expect, coming here with her ridiculous accusations? Did she honestly expect me to sit by and allow my reputation to be ruined by the ravings of a crazy woman?'

'And Lindsey? You built up her trust, knowing I'd never have allowed you within breathing distance of any of my children.'

He slapped his hand hard on the desk. 'Your daughter also wanted the truth. If you're trying to destroy me, you're playing a dangerous game. Stop and think before you say anything else.'

'I'm not going to destroy you, Albert. All I intend to do is tell the truth.'

'And what truth would that be, Beth?'

'The truth about the Anaskeagh Baby.'

'Bitch… I'm warning you for the last time. This farce has gone on long enough.' He moved swiftly towards her. For a moment she thought he was going to strike her. Close to him she could smell his fear – rank, like something exposed after a long burial. She winced when he gripped her wrists, his nails digging deep into her skin. His breathing was so laboured she thought he would keel over from a heart attack. Would that make her a murderer? It was a burden she would carry willingly.

'Let me remind you of the real truth, Beth.' His voice grew louder. He still held her in his grasp, even when she struggled to free her arms. 'I gave Stewart an opportunity to make something of himself. We're a small community, suspicious of outsiders. I smoothed the way, even persuaded Fashion Lynx to take him on – and now, just when he has it all together, you want to ruin him? What kind of vindictive wife are you? I could lift the phone to my contacts on the ACII board this instant and they'll pull the plug on your pathetic factory so fast you won't have time to blink. And that's exactly what I intend to do if you dare threaten me again with your foul insinuations. You are evil incarnate. You carried it within you even as a child… The soul of evil.'

'No, Albert. I carried innocence and you trampled it under your feet. And Sara too…' Her voice broke. 'She finally found the courage to confront you and you destroyed her again. May God forgive you. I know I never will.'

'What do you know about God?' he shouted. 'When did you ever raise your hands in prayer? Filth… Filth. How dare you tarnish your sister's memory with disgusting lies? She was a beautiful woman but weak. Delusional, hysterical… Claiming she was that mother–'

'Your daughter is in Anaskeagh, Albert.' Beth stared coldly at him. 'But you know that already. I'll be by her side when she leads the television crew to Anaskeagh Head. I'll take her to Aislin's Roof so that she can film our daughter's birthplace. That's where it happened, Albert. A hard cradle rocked our daughter into life. I'll show her the rocks that sheltered me and the path I walked on my way to O'Donovan's farm.'

'Jesus Christ, you're every bit as crazy as your sister!' His fury came towards her in waves. 'Are you trying to kill your mother? Have you any idea how ill she is? She could die any minute – too much stress and her heart will give out—'

'I *will* tell our story, Albert. Every single ugly word of it. I will name your crime and I will name you. And when you're in jail you'll find out how many supporters you have left.'

The strength left his body. He staggered back to the chair and stared at her, speechless. For the first time she saw him as a withered old man. Not elderly or stately but *old* with liver warts on his hands, his teeth bared in a grimace, too white and perfect for an old man's face. He rubbed his eyes, as if to banish her from sight. Or perhaps to stem tears of shame, of regret? She would never know. As she walked towards the door the words he spoke were barely audible. 'Liar… Bitch. You're not the mother.'

She turned to confront him for the last time. 'But I could have been, Albert,' she said. 'That's the one and only truth we both share.'

She unlocked the door and walked out of his life.

'Anaskeagh Baby Seeks her Roots' was shown after the evening news on *Elucidate*. Viewers watched as Eva climbed over the rugged terrain to the shelter of Aislin's Roof. She laid flowers under the slanting rock and spoke about Sara Wallace, the mother she would never know. Viewers followed Beth's journey to O'Donovan's farm and listened to Catherine's recollections of that night. Jess, interviewed in her medical centre, described her joy when Eva was adopted by Liz and Steve, who also appeared on the documentary. Ashton looked tranquil and green, in stark contrast to the bleak earth where Eva had first laid her head. One question overhung the documentary. Who was the father? Beth faced the camera and said he was a respected and admired member of the Anaskeagh community. She was unable to name him as his crime was under police investigation. DNA, she said, could never be denied and, in time, when charges were heard and judgements made, his name would be known to all.

Rumours were rife in Anaskeagh. In the pubs and restaurants, the shops, cafés and hairdressing salons, everyone asked the same question. How many men were respected and admired in their town? It had been twenty-seven years since the Anaskeagh Baby scandal. Were the names of men, now middle-aged, about to be pilloried once again? Then, like a cobra wriggling into a room, unnoticed until it rose and spat, a name was whispered.

A fearful whisper at first but gaining volume. Albert Grant had been brought down once. Could it happen again?

Word spread that he had disappeared. Journalists and television crews gathered outside Cherry Vale and the politician's apartment. Adding two and two and getting four, the media bayed loudly. Was Albert Grant the respected and admired member of the community mentioned on the documentary? Was that why he was in hiding? Conor read out a statement. His father had gone sailing – his favourite hobby – before the documentary had aired. How could it have anything to do with his departure? He was a seasoned sailor and he would set the record straight as soon as he returned to shore.

A search operation was organised. When his cruiser was located it was drifting, empty. Broadsheet headlines read 'Disgraced Politician Disappears' while the tabloids stated 'Sicko Sex Fiend on the Run.' Rumoured sightings were reported. He'd been seen drinking champagne on the deck of a luxury yacht in West Cork. He'd been spotted on a beach in Spain, drinking an espresso on a pavement café in Rome. These claims grew more ludicrous as the days passed, but Beth knew he was dead. She had killed him as surely as if she had placed her hand on his back and pushed him violently from the deck of his boat into the ocean.

Did he hesitate before taking those final steps? she wondered. He was a coward and it would take courage to drop into the deep. He was manipulative so he would have weighed up his options, considered calling her bluff. His word against hers. The accusations of corruption fading into insignificance against the weight of a far juicier media scandal. The shock and odium. Paedophilia – the most hated crime of all. How could he prove his innocence when he'd looked into her eyes and seen her hatred made visible? The determination etched on her lips. Was the sea calm or sun-speckled when he finally decided it was over? Did the waves heave with violence when they claimed him or sink him gently downwards? Was Anaskeagh Head the last place he saw before the darkness came?

He was buried quietly when his bloated remains were washed onto the rocks of a distant coastline. Suicide or accidental death by drowning? The media pondered this mystery but they were already moving on to the next scandal. Anaskeagh was at peace again. A small town minding its own business.

'The media hounded him to his grave,' said Marjory when Beth called to see her after his body had been formally identified. She had endured the wait for news of his whereabouts with an unnerving calm. 'My brother was a good man. He may have pulled a few strokes in his day but he never knowingly hurt anyone in his life–'

'*Stop.*' Beth pressed her hands to her ears. 'Why must you keep up this façade? Don't you owe it to Sara to accept the truth of what she told you?'

The two women stared at each other across the kitchen table. Marjory's mouth puckered and tightened, as if she was forcing back a torrent of words.

'I can't… I can't… endure it…' She swayed, defenceless against the sobs that racked her thin frame.

Beth held her hands. When Marjory tried to pull away, she clasped her firmly until the old woman became still. The moment passed. No words were spoken. The body of Albert Grant, washed from its watery grave, had ended their story. Perhaps it would begin another, where forgiveness was not demanded but gently passed from one to the other in silence.

In the distance, the headland loomed, a bloated shadow falling silently as a shroud over the secrets of Anaskeagh. Life's problems were not always resolved. Sometimes they were just contained until it was time to deliver them into the void.

EPILOGUE

Eva sinks a spade into the loamy soil and turns the first sod. She continues digging until the hole is deep enough to receive the roots of a slender magnolia tree. Beth places it carefully in position and Lindsey flattens the earth around it. Years will pass before it blooms but when it flowers its beauty will be unsurpassed. Beth kneels to hammer a small plaque with Sara's name emblazoned on it into the earth. She wills her sister to speak to her, to breathe gently through the green, fluttering leaves. This search for an ethereal presence never leaves her but Sara's spirit still eludes her.

Eva lays the spade aside and instinctively presses her hand against the small of her back. Rebuilding her marriage has been painful but now life grows within her, a fragile beginning but strongly rooted.

Lindsey stands above the plaque, her head bowed. Soon she will travel to Italy. Her tentative first step towards reconciliation with Peter. This is another beginning that may in time develop roots but she will only ever love one father.

In a small medieval hamlet in Tuscany, Peter gazes out over a valley where rows of vines are guarded by sturdy rose bushes and avenues of poplars tremble in the evening breeze. So much beauty laid before him but he turns to the white studio wall where Sara's photographs are displayed. He begins to paint. Familiar smells, the heartbeat of anticipation, the knowledge that it is pain, not pleasure, that will dominate this painting. He does not stop to eat or drink. When darkness falls he is still at work, stretching beyond hunger and loss until there is only the sense of movement fused on canvas. This painting is alive. Leaning rocks, mossy and dank, sentinels guarding an ancient site. The play of light and shadow on a jagged landscape. Dangerous clouds darkening the moon, haphazard and chaotic; a world ending and beginning. He continues to paint until the night closes in and he is able to lay his love to rest.

LETTER FROM LAURA ELLIOT

Dear Reader,

My books always begin with an idea, shadowy yet insistent. This is the one percent of inspiration described by Thomas A. Edison, who claimed that the other ninety-nine percent was due to perspiration. But that one percent is the catalyst that propels an idea from my imagination onto the page. The months that follow, as the story forms and reforms, allows plenty of time to mop my brow and wonder why, when the sun is shining and the world is at play, I'm creating an imaginary world with rules that only I understand. Finally, it's over – the redrafting, editing, proofing and angst are forgotten as my book travels outwards into that great space occupied by you, The Reader. I cannot watch you turn that final page, or lay down your reading device, yet I know you are out there – and your support is the motivation that inspires me to begin yet another book.

Sleep Sister was influenced by hidden stories that are locked away in the memories of women, their secrets carried to the grave. Some stories become public, either through whispered word of mouth or as a headline on a news bulletin. I remember a young woman from my childhood who gave birth secretly in her small bedsit. When her baby's body was found abandoned in a nearby doorway she was traced, arrested, charged with infanticide and confined to an asylum. Years later, I was shocked and appalled when a teenage mother died with her son after she'd given birth to him secretly beside a grotto. Even as recently as last year, a day-old baby was found abandoned by the roadside. The baby survived against great odds, so, although the dark days of a one-time closed, judgemental society have passed, these tragedies can still occur.

Sleep Sister is a fictitious story set in an imaginary landscape – but those are some of the stories that inspired me to explore the corrosive nature of shame and secrecy, the corruption of innocence and the brutality of power. If you enjoyed *Sleep Sister* (which is an extension of a novel I wrote some years ago called *When the Bough Breaks*) and would like to leave a review on Amazon or Kobo, I'd be most appreciative. Finally, if you'd like to **keep up-to-date with all my latest releases**, just sign up here:

www.bookouture.com/laura-elliot

Warmest regards,

Laura Elliot

@Elliot_Laura
lauraelliotauthor
www.lauraelliot.com

ACKNOWLEDGEMENTS

Writing a book can be a solitary occupation but that solitude is softened by the people surrounding me – and I'd like to take this opportunity to thank them. To my family, my husband Sean, my son Tony, my daughters Ciara and Michelle, and their spouses and partner, Roddy, Louise and Harry. To my extended family and to my friends, thank you for your support and wonderful encouragement over the years. I wish to acknowledge a special debt of gratitude to my mentor and writer, the late, great Sean McCann, who, sadly, passed away last year, but will never be forgotten.

To those of you I don't know but who have taken the time to read and review my books, I offer you my gratitude and thanks. Sometimes, it feels as if my book has entered a black hole – then a review appears, a letter or an email arrives, and I read them with pleasure.

Finally – thanks to my agent Faith O'Grady and to the Bookouture team – the intrepid Oliver Rhodes, the unflagging Kim Nash, Emma Graves for the incredible cover, the vigilant Laura Kincaid, to Natasha Hodgson for her cooperation and attention to detail – and to my editor Claire Bord, whose editorial insights I respect and admire.

Lightning Source UK Ltd.
Milton Keynes UK
UKHW05f1408270518
323209UK00010B/193/P

9 781910 751985